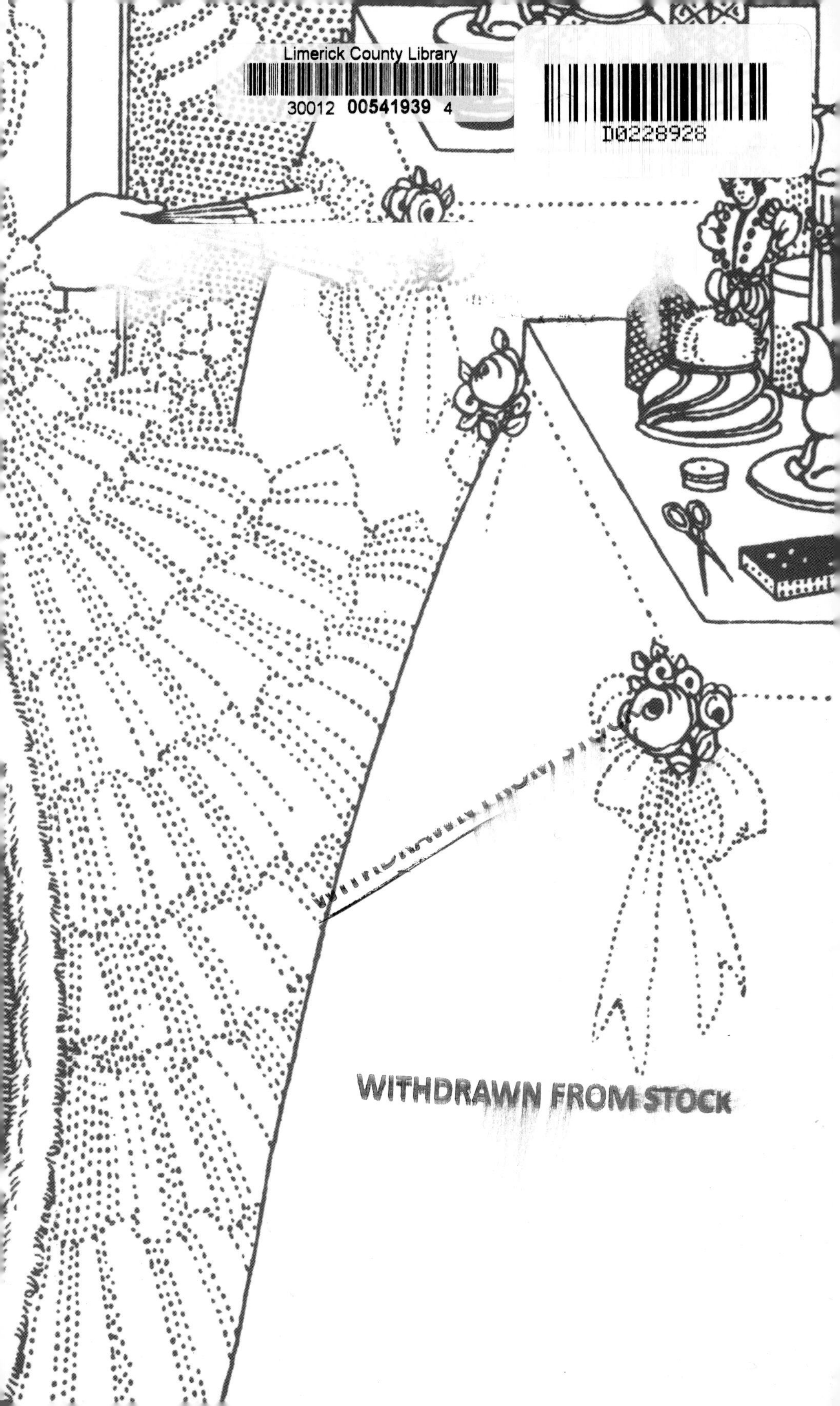

THE SCANDAL OF THE SEASON

The Scandal of the Season

Sophie Gee

Chatto & Windus
LONDON

Published by Chatto & Windus 2007

2 4 6 8 10 9 7 5 3 1

First published in Great Britain in 2007 by
Chatto & Windus
Random House, 20 Vauxhall Bridge Road,
London SW1V 2SA

www.randomhouse.co.uk

Addresses for companies within The Random House Group Limited can be found at: www.randomhouse.co.uk/offices.htm

The Random House Group Limited Reg. No. 954009

A CIP catalogue record for this book
is available from the British Library

ISBN 9780701181161

The Random House Group Limited makes every effort to ensure that the papers used in its books are made from trees that have been legally sourced from well-managed and credibly certified forests. Our paper procurement policy can be found at: www.randomhouse.co.uk/paper.htm

Typeset by SX Composing DTP, Rayleigh, Essex
Printed and bound in Great Britain by
Clays Ltd, St Ives plc

FOR MY FATHER, CHRISTOPHER GEE

1941–2003

WITH LOVE

Historical Note

In the sixteenth century, England changed from a Catholic to a Protestant country when Henry VIII dissolved the monasteries and stripped the Catholic Church of its wealth. But Catholicism was never quelled; even though the official religion in England was Protestantism, vast numbers of Englishmen remained true to the Catholic faith. The Catholics resented the Protestants for taking away their wealth and privilege, and the Protestants feared a Catholic uprising that would some day oust them from power. For the next two hundred years, England would be immersed in religious turmoil.

By 1711, England was finally starting to feel secure. Queen Anne—a Protestant, but descended from the Stuarts—was on the throne and for the first time in two centuries, the Protestants and the Catholics felt able to live in relative amity. The persecution of the Catholics declined. England was on the brink of unprecedented prosperity.

But one question remained. When the childless queen died, who would succeed her? A clandestine alliance had been formed among those who supported the return of a Stuart monarch. The allies called themselves Jacobites. Secretly, they conspired to bring back to England the Catholic King James III, presently exiled in France. So far, all attempted Jacobite plots had been discovered and prevented, but the Protestants in power could never be certain when the next rebellion was coming, or whether it might, after all, succeed.

What dire Offence from amorous causes springs,
What mighty Contests rise from trivial things.

Alexander Pope, *The Rape of the Lock*

Prologue

London, 1711

The noise could be heard streets away. There were bursts of music and drifts of laughter and talk, louder when the revellers spilled into the courtyard. Every few minutes new shrieks of merriment echoed on the night air. It was the French ambassador's masquerade ball.

The embassy on the Strand blazed with candlelight. Every window along the façade was bright, and the courtyard was lined with a hundred flaring torches. More lights burned a corridor down to the river, where boats pulled up at a landing stage to unload groups of guests. Everybody was in costume: carnival figures, Russian princes, Chinese merchants, butterflies and bears, fairies and goblins, piping shepherds. Cases of wine were opened, supper was carried out in silver dishes, and the maskers danced on. Scattered groups lingered in the courtyard talking to one another in English or French, often a mixture of the two. More laughing, yet more talk; an endless movement of carriages.

A little priest left the embassy and made his way towards a hackney cab waiting outside the gates. As he walked away, a pair of masked ladies turned to greet him.

"Good night, Father."

The priest bowed and stepped into his cab.

Across the courtyard, two figures called out to the driver, and then ran haphazardly towards the carriage, with much laughter and stumbling. They were dressed in the long silk gowns and black hoods of the domino costumes common among the masquerade guests; the robes almost entirely obscured the men's forms in dark folds. One man's hood began to slip as he ran, and he pulled it back up clumsily, calling to his friend to slow down.

"Leave your damned hood behind!" the friend called back, a

French accent inflecting his words. He ran up to the priest's carriage. "Father, will you be so kind . . ." he began, "my friend and I—"

Not waiting for a response, the Frenchman opened the door to step in, while the other fellow swept a low bow to a passing lady and gave a final pull to the costume. Then he too ran up to the carriage and scrambled inside as it drove away.

Behind them, the noise and light of the party continued unabated.

The priest smiled warily at the hooded men. He saw that they were both laughing, still out of breath. It had reassured him to hear one of them speaking in an accent—they were probably Catholics. The cab turned into the street and began to clatter across the cobbles.

After a moment's silence, he spoke. "Where are you travelling to, gentlemen?"

Neither of the men answered.

The carriage took a turn to the right. They were now on a road that was covered in straw to muffle the sound of horses' hooves, and the cab was suddenly much quieter. This street was empty and dark; the lamps had all guttered many hours before. He could hear the men's breathing, quick and rough, but he could not see their faces at all. They were no longer laughing. The darkness pressed on his eyes like a blindfold. He began to feel afraid. What if that Frenchman knew who he was?

He tried to stay calm, hearing his voice echoing in the intense blackness of the carriage as he repeated his question, "Where are you going to?"

Still there was no answer. His throat tightened. Perhaps they had not jumped into his carriage by chance. How easy it would have been for two figures in domino robes to stand unnoticed in the busy courtyard, waiting for him. He had taken little care tonight to be guarded about his visit.

"For God's sake, who are you?" he cried aloud. "What do you want?"

Neither sound nor movement from the two strangers. Suddenly the priest heard a rustle of fabric and a shuffle of feet. He shrank away, but felt the wall of the carriage against his back. He opened his mouth to call out, when a hand came out of the darkness to silence him.

He was struck violently on to the floor, and the back of his skull cracked against the seat. He felt a wave of dizziness; one of the men was upon him, pinning his body down. There was a rattling movement above as the other man closed the window shades. He knew that it was not necessary; nobody would see them on this deserted street. The gesture made him feel that a shade had fallen down upon his life.

He struggled free from the arm that stifled him. "You are too late," he cried. "Others already know." It was a gamble; the slimmest of chances.

There was a fraction of a pause.

"He lies," came a new voice at last. An English accent, well-bred.

Before the priest could say more, he felt the cold edge of a steel blade pressed hard against his throat.

He struggled to retain a sense of what was happening. Again he opened his mouth, but as he did so he felt a prick of the knife going in like a needle. His throat felt suddenly loose, though a moment before it had been taut with fear, and his blood poured out as warm and soft as silk. He felt his skin and clothes become hot and sticky as it soaked into the fabric. The men remained silent, waiting while his life ebbed away. He could struggle no more. Already he was weak, his limbs heavy; even now he could barely frame clear thoughts; his mind was dim. He tried to hold fast to life, but the blackness closed in. It was over.

Chapter One

"In tasks so bold, can little Men engage"

The worst of country life was that the houses were always cold. Alexander sat as close to the fire as he could manage without blocking his parents' access to its modest heat. He suspected that his mother, at least, was suffering, but that she stayed further back to allow him most of the warmth. Outside it was either snowing or raining; Alexander could not be sure which. It had been dark since three o'clock. They had dined at noon; tea had been brought in at four, and there were still another three hours before bed. His father had not allowed him to go to his chamber to write, because the fire had been overlooked during the afternoon and had burned out. He had not finished twenty lines of verse since Christmas, nearly a month ago.

The *Georgics* was open in his lap, and he had been reading the same poem for two hours. Virgil was all very well when Alexander was feeling that he, too, might write a poem as good as the *Aeneid*, but tonight Virgil's youthful verses reproached him. Will it always be like this if I obey my father? he asked himself. He heard his mother cough, and guessed that she was about to break in upon his thoughts.

"Sir Anthony Englefield asks you to pay him a visit," she said, holding out a letter. "He offers to send his carriage. I think that you should go, Alexander. Are not Teresa and Martha Blount presently at Whiteknights?"

He made no reply. But his heart leapt at the sound of Teresa's name, and he looked up, knowing that he was blushing. The Miss Blounts were both about Alexander's age. Their family seat, Mapledurham, was an estate on the other side of the Thames, but the girls visited their grandfather Sir Anthony Englefield at

Whiteknights several times each year. Like Alexander and his family, the Blounts were Roman Catholics.

"I do not attend to the details of the Miss Blounts' arrangements," he said, in as careless a tone as he could manage.

"But you have not seen Sir Anthony since the beginning of December, Alexander," his mother replied. "Your health is enough restored. And you must make yourself pleasing to women," she added.

If only she knew how much he wanted to please Teresa, Alexander thought. But he said instead, "I think that Sir Anthony might have written the letter to *me*."

Alexander's spirits rose excitedly, even as he began to feel nervous. It was always thus. Teresa loved to tease him, but she did so with a sly smile that made him like her even more. Not wanting to appear too eager to reply to Sir Anthony's invitation, however, Alexander turned to his father, who was reading a newspaper. "What news from town?" he asked.

"A priest has been murdered, and the body left in Shoreditch," came the reply.

Alexander felt a surge of alarm. Shoreditch! Poor Catholics still worshipped there secretly, in chapels above the taverns.

"Murdered?" Alexander echoed. "A priest?"

His father would never allow him back to town now. He had paid one short visit eighteen months previously, after his first poems had been published, and had longed to return ever since. But the capital would always be haunted by the persecutions his father had once seen. Alexander's parents had been driven out when the Ten-Mile Act had been passed forbidding papists to live within daily reach of the city. Years had gone by since then, and Catholics were returning to London, but Alexander's father was immovable. His son would not live in town. Alexander knew that the place had changed—for three glorious weeks he had seen it with his own eyes. But supposing he were to disobey his parents' strictures, only to find himself in danger?

He reached for the paper and began to read the story.

"This man was not a priest, sir!" he exclaimed. "Indeed he may not have been a Catholic at all. It says here that he was dressed in ecclesiastical costume to attend the French ambassador's masquerade. A ticket for the ball was found in his pocket." He looked up with a smile. "So you see," he finished, "the murderers made a mistake."

Alexander's father gave a mirthless laugh. "If the men thought the fellow was a Catholic priest, it hardly matters if he was not," he replied shortly. "The town is a dangerous place. I was sorry to see you so eager to visit last year."

Alexander felt the protest rise within him. "I was there but three weeks, sir," he burst out, "and staying in Westminster with my friend Charles Jervas!" His father knew perfectly well that Jervas was a Protestant, and that Alexander's contact with Catholics had been confined to the few wealthy families who kept houses in Westminster and St. James's. There had been no secret masses in alehouse garrets—indeed there had been no talk of religion at all. "Queen Anne is a Stuart! You have said yourself that we have nothing to fear while she is on the throne."

The older man's face remained grave. "I was not sanguine while you were there, Alexander," he said. "I should be disappointed to learn that you have thoughts of returning."

His parents rose for prayers, and Alexander was obliged to join them. His father darkened the room, old habit prompting him to make sure that they could not be seen. As he watched his father's bent head and the quiet movement of his lips, Alexander felt a pang of remorse. Had not his parents once been banished from their old home like vagrants, forced to leave the city where they had lived respectably? Now Alexander, scorning what his parents had suffered, was demanding to return to the place of so much misery. Ashamed, he bent his head, trying to feel the piety that he knew was proper.

After their worship was over, Alexander asked his father if he would leave the candles burning downstairs so that he could sit up by the fire to work.

"Late hours will make you ill," his father replied, and waited until Alexander had gathered his books, following him up the stairs to his bedroom.

Alexander said good-night and closed the door of his chamber, pushing a rug against the space at the bottom to mask the light of his candle. His father had been right—it was freezing cold, but he must finish ten lines before the end of the night. He pulled a blanket over his shoulders, spread another across his knees, and set to work. He wrote for an hour, ignoring the headache and sore throat that had begun to nag. It was not hard to do so. After so many years, the symptoms seemed like old, familiar foes, urging him to greater efforts, reminding him that his time was short.

He had been fourteen when he became ill. The sickness fell across his memory like a curtain, shrouding the weeks, and then months of pain that followed in suffocating darkness. At first the doctors had thought that he would not survive, but slowly he began to get better, the recovery more agonizing to him than the blank days and nights of feverish coma that preceded it. His clearest memory was of a morning when at last he had been able to stand up from his bed and walk to the window. Outside, the first marks of autumn were just beginning to rust the landscape, and he had been sad to find that he had missed a whole summer. His parents had come into the room, the physician following behind them. They had sat him down upon the bed and the doctor had told him the news. Though he had survived the illness, it would cripple his growth. His back would become hunched, until eventually he would be unable to move. The physician could not say when it would occur—perhaps by the time he was thirty, later if he was lucky.

And, as it turned out, he was lucky. At twenty-three, his back was bent, but if he stood up straight it was barely noticeable. He was not tall, but his face was handsome, he thought. And he was quick and funny. When he was in good health, he knew that he could be very charming.

An image of Teresa came to his mind, running across the lawn on a summer afternoon long ago. He had been completely well again after the sickness, restored to his old self, and she was fifteen or sixteen—it was before her father died. She had taken him by the hands, starting to tell a story about the convent school in Paris where she had been living. How lovely she had been then; how lovely she still was. As soon as his poems became famous, Alexander would claim her, and he believed that she would receive him once more with open arms. But he looked again at the pages on his desk. Still no closer to a finished poem. He needed a new subject, something that would give his talents their proper range. In his heart he knew that he would never find it in Binfield. Somehow, anyhow, he must get to London.

Two days later, Sir Anthony's carriage took him to Whiteknights. As he drew up outside the old house, Alexander saw that it was Martha Blount, and not Teresa, who had waited to greet him. He stepped down, and she came towards him, smiling and blushing.

"My dear Martha," he said, taking her by the hands. "You look very well."

"Alexander!" she exclaimed. "We knew that you were coming to see us today, but you are here so soon! My grandfather is abroad seeing to a tenant." She pushed aside a lock of hair that had fallen across her face, but it slipped again, and she pulled it up with a little laugh. It was a gesture that Alexander had seen her make since she was a young girl.

Martha led him through the great entrance hall into a morning room where she had been working. As he took a seat beside her, Alexander found himself almost glad that the elder sister was absent. Martha's morning gown was covered in little threads from her needlework, which she had not noticed. Teresa would have picked them off instantly. He was determined not to ask where Teresa was, and spoil this moment that he and Martha had together.

"A cold day for Sir Anthony to venture out," he observed. But he could not help himself, and after a little pause he asked, "Is your sister also out?"

Martha's face fell for an instant as she answered, "She is writing letters in her sitting-room, and probably does not know that you are arrived." Before he could speak again she composed herself, and smiled. "Shall we find her?" she asked, putting her sewing to one side.

When they entered the upstairs parlour, Teresa was reading a letter at her table by the window. The pale sunlight fell upon her face and on the delicate folds of her silk dress. On the desk was a little vase with a few snowdrops and narcissi, which Alexander guessed must have come from the hothouse. The curve of Teresa's arm rested beside the flowers, and the dark curls of her hair fell forward loosely as she bent over the pages.

"Teresa!" Martha exclaimed. "Alexander is come. Look—he is here to see us."

She did not turn around immediately, and her smile was far less forthcoming than Martha's. It was arch and teasing. But how pretty she was!

"Here already indeed," Teresa said in reply. "It is not done, Alexander, to visit a lady before eleven o'clock. If you are to be a man about town you will need to know such things."

The note of provocation thrilled him. "I cannot bear to be a short coach ride from the brightest eyes in England, and yet remain apart," he said, looking back at her with a playful smile.

Teresa raised an eyebrow. "Alexander is being very charming this morning, Patty," she answered, looking away from him and calling her sister familiarly by her pet name.

"My office is to charm those who charm the world," Alexander replied. He gave a bow, but as soon as he had done so he cursed himself. He was talking like a fool; the truth was that Teresa was making him awkward.

Martha watched closely as the exchange unfolded. She guessed that Teresa was nervous about seeing her old admirer again; she was always at her most contrary when she felt ill at ease. Martha blushed for her, and at the sight of Alexander's eager, anxious face. How little he understood her sister.

But Teresa and Alexander were sparring again.

"In speaking as gallantly as you do," Teresa said, "I fancy that you try to imitate your London friend, Charles Jervas, of whom you love to boast. You are always copying the manners of those around you."

Alexander knew better than to let this rattle him.

"Then I hope that I shall not omit to imitate yours," he replied. "Your wit has a sparkle that makes it as precious to me as gold."

Teresa looked away. "I fear that it shall likewise be as scarce," she said. "My sister and I go to London tomorrow."

He knew that his face betrayed the terrible sting of disappointment he felt. He had not expected this!

Martha rushed to join the conversation. "We were to tell you this morning, Alexander," she said. "We are to travel up to town for the season with our mother, and to take a house in King Street."

"Your grandfather is not afraid of your being in danger?" Alexander asked, turning to her with a look of appeal.

"Of course not," Teresa interjected. "What do you imagine will happen? Plague and fire! Nobody is afraid of London anymore, Alexander." Although it was the sort of impulsive naivety Teresa always showed, Alexander did not smile.

"Alexander is talking about the recent murder in Shoreditch," Martha said, cutting her sister off. "We did think of postponing our journey, but Shoreditch is a long way from St. James's. Though it was vicious, it can have nothing to do with our own circle."

Teresa tossed her head at the serious turn their conversation had taken, and began to gather up her letters, suggesting that they take a turn out-of-doors.

The day was cold, but they were well wrapped up in fur collars and muffs and shielded from the wind by the high yew hedges that grew up around the edges of the lawns. Alexander and Teresa walked on ahead. When they had been outside for a few minutes Alexander smiled and said, "Were I a handsome fellow, Teresa, I believe that I could do you a vast deal of good."

Teresa laughed, and Martha knew that she was in high spirits once again.

"Were you a handsome fellow," Teresa answered with a taunting smile, "I should devour you as I do my other admirers. You owe your preservation to that very oddity of person which you so lament. But as it is, you are safe, and I must look elsewhere for somebody to feed upon."

Martha wondered whether Alexander meant his reply to sound as serious as it did.

"Take care, madam," he said to Teresa. "The handsome fellow who adores you for a few months will neglect you for many years together. The fawning servant turns the haughty lord."

Teresa was silent a moment, contemplating, Martha suspected, the pleasures of being married to a lord, be he ever so haughty. But she replied instead, "I am rather glad, Alexander, that you will have to write to us while we are in town. You do have a way of expressing yourself that can be exceedingly diverting."

Before he replied, Alexander turned to Martha with a wry smile of apology for the excesses of his gallantry.

"In truth, Teresa," he said at last, "when I consider how often and openly I have declared love to you, I am a little affronted that you have not forbidden my correspondence altogether."

Everybody smiled at this observation, reflecting that it contained a good deal of truth.

When they came in from the garden, they found that Sir Anthony had returned from seeing his tenants. He greeted Alexander and led him into the library, leaving the girls together for the half-hour that remained before dinner.

"You were rather more severe upon Alexander than usual today, Teresa," Martha said as soon as they were alone.

"But I am always severe upon him," she replied. "He expects it, and would think it strange if I were otherwise." She looked away as she said this, pretending to adjust the sleeve on her gown so that she need not meet her sister's eyes.

"I always anticipate that Alexander will be rather afraid of you—yet your severity seems to make him more fond," Martha added.

"Most gentlemen are fond of the ladies whom they fear," Teresa replied evasively. "It is a paradox of the sex. In rebuffing him as I do, I am preparing for the gentlemen I shall meet in London."

Martha caught a note of uncertainty in her voice, and took her sister's hand. "Are you concerned for our arrival in the city?" she asked. "I thought that you were eager for it."

Teresa stepped forward quickly to open the door into the drawing-room, saying with a little laugh, "Well, I am eager and afraid of it at once—just as Alexander is of me."

The sun had gone from the room now, but the candles had not yet been lighted. Outside, the grounds were already in shadow, though it was only two o'clock. They sat down on the sofa where Martha had left her sewing, and Teresa leaned across to move it. Martha used the chance to take her sister's hand again, and this time she did not pull away. Martha hoped that she might get Teresa to talk more about Alexander.

But before she could frame a question, Teresa began to speak in a low, fretful tone. "Suppose that people should think me rusticated?" she asked. "I will be going about with Arabella's friends, who may find my appearance dowdy. Here everyone thinks that I am pretty—but I should be ashamed of seeming plain in town."

Martha looked at her sister's face, vulnerable in the melancholy half-light. So this was what preoccupied her! Not Alexander at all, but their cousin, Arabella Fermor.

"But people will find you more charming if you are natural," Martha replied.

"Not the people of whom I am speaking," Teresa insisted, her voice rising sharply. "When gentlemen go to town they wish to avoid nature, not to be charmed by it. Simplicity is regarded with the deepest suspicion, and sincerity with a kind of abhorrence."

Martha laughed at this formulation. No wonder Alexander liked her sister's quick wit; it was a side of her character that Martha did not often see.

"Oh, Teresa, you will have plenty of admirers," she replied. "Quite as many as Arabella, I am sure." Martha was surprised by Teresa's intimation that she and Arabella had been exchanging letters. When she had seen them together in the past, affection had not figured visibly in their interactions. They had seemed rather to be locked in an unspoken contest as to which of them possessed the greater share of wit and beauty—and if Arabella was now offering to take Teresa around town, she must be sure of a victory on both counts. They were interrupted by a maidservant coming in to light the candles. The crackling of the fire, which had seemed so desolate a few minutes before, began to sound cheerful again.

"So Bell has been writing to you?" Martha asked when the servant was gone.

"Not lately," Teresa replied after a short pause. "But I told her that we were coming, so I expect we shall spend a great deal of time together." Martha was silent, knowing how much Teresa longed for a fashionable companion. It would be cruel to dampen her sister's hopes by expressing her scepticism of the friendship with Arabella.

Teresa, too, fell silent, deep in thought. When Alexander had come into her room that morning, she had felt a thrill but she had recoiled, not wanting to show how pleased she was to see him. She wanted to think of Alexander merely as a friend from her past; to show him that things were different now. She was determined to make a splendid match in London. But how funny Alexander had seemed when they were younger! His jokes, his letters, his amusing gallantries—all so delightful to her. If only he were more successful, she reflected. He was a Catholic and a gentleman, and her grandfather, at least, believed that his talents as a poet were considerable. His suit might one day be worth a good deal. But she shrank from the thought. Such an odd man, subject to headache and ill-humour; writing his poems and talking about Virgil, with no fortune to speak of. So why did she feel such a lurch in her heart when she saw him?

The girls' thoughts were interrupted when they were called to dinner. As soon as they were seated, Sir Anthony proposed a toast to his young guest.

"My congratulations on the printing of your verses, Alexander," he said. "And to have been published by the great Jacob Tonson, too: the best in London."

Alexander bowed and thanked him. "Another of my poems is to be printed very soon," he said, "by an old schoolfriend of mine who has gone into the trade. I have called it *Essay on Criticism.*"

Sir Anthony paused, and looked at him. "Not by Tonson, then," he said.

"The poem is somewhat out of the ordinary," Alexander said hastily. "I feared that Tonson might not care for it."

His host frowned. "I wonder whether you have given careful thought to pursuing poetry as a profession," he said. "Most poets are poor, dreary fellows who hang about at the court in hope of a pension. I should not like to see you join them."

Alexander suspected that Sir Anthony had deliberately saved his remarks until Teresa was present, and he felt a blush of self-consciousness. She looked at him with a mocking smile. With an effort, he exerted himself to sound unconcerned.

"The main trouble with poets," he said, "is that so few of them ever write a poem worth reading. Men of perfectly sound mind in their letters, who express themselves in eloquent, red-blooded prose, become mincing fools when they turn to verse. Their poems either descant in purple epithets upon the joys of spring, or salivate over a glimpse of some lady's bosom in a tightly laced dress. Verse makes a eunuch or a whoremaster of them all."

"Are you talking about Thomas D'Urfey's success with his poem 'Paid for Peeping'?" Teresa asked lightly. "It was very shocking. But I haven't the slightest doubt that for all your railing against it, Alexander, your own copy is well worn along the edges."

Alexander brightened at Teresa's teasing.

"I would as soon read that man's verses as I would write like him," he answered. "D'Urfey's poems come out of him like a succession of noisy farts," Alexander continued. "Diverting, but exceedingly nasty."

Everybody laughed at this, and Alexander looked at Teresa with a self-deprecating air, pleased with the success of his joke. With renewed confidence, he said, "In any case, Jacob Tonson doesn't need my help to make his fortune. He has made thousands since he bought the copyright to *Paradise Lost.*"

"I'm bound to say that I've never got through that book myself," said Sir Anthony. "I know one shouldn't admit it," he added.

To Martha's delight, Alexander shot her a glance of companionship. They had often talked about *Paradise Lost* together—it was the poem that both of them most admired.

"I heartily assent to your estimation of Grub Street, sir," Alexander was saying to Sir Anthony, "but Tonson and his ilk are my own best hope for making a fortune."

"But surely you will inherit your parents' house at Binfield," he answered.

"Yes, of course," said Alexander quickly. His father had entailed the house on two Protestant cousins who would inherit it on Alexander's behalf. This must be what Sir Anthony was hoping to hear; he would know that he could inherit nothing directly.

At this moment Teresa stood up to leave. Martha therefore did the same, but she looked back regretfully as she quit the room; she had been a good deal interested in the men's conversation.

With a sigh of his own that the girls were gone, Alexander turned to Sir Anthony and said, "Your granddaughters' situations are little different from my own, after all. We are engaged in most risky speculations! The Miss Blounts wager that their beauty and good nature will find them rich husbands—and I am gambling my talents as a poet on an open market. No wonder we all long for London, where stock-jobbing is the rage."

Englefield seemed to deliberate before answering.

"I will bring you into my confidence, Alexander," he said. "The girls will soon find themselves in an awkward position. When their brother Michael inherited Mapledurham last year, it was encumbered by far greater debt than we had imagined. When Michael marries, I fear that he will no longer be able to support the girls and their mother. I have not told them, of course. They must not feel that they are being sent to London to be sold off."

At another moment Alexander might have observed that nothing would give more pleasure to the elder Miss Blount than knowing that she was to be sold to a rich husband. But he checked himself, considering more carefully the implications of this news. Sir Anthony must know that the girls' prospects would be doomed.

"Surely Blount will not leave the girls without dowries and their mother without a proper living," he said.

"The expense of maintaining Mapledurham is great," Sir Anthony replied. "We all pay double taxation still, you know. Mapledurham will require almost all of Michael's income."

Alexander felt anger rising within him. "But it is never beyond a man's power to do what is right," he insisted.

"In this case it may be," said Sir Anthony. "A Catholic who is forced to give up his land these days is in a pretty desperate predicament. No, the estate must be held at all costs."

"But the Miss Blounts have been brought up with expensive habits and extravagant expectations," Alexander protested. "They were educated in Paris; they have lived in the best society. They go to London confident of their success with the first men in the country. It is not fair to allow them into the world under such a misapprehension. Every sacrifice must be made—"

"That is precisely why I am hoping that they marry soon, Alexander. It is a wretched thing to say, and there is hardly another person with whom I would share this confidence. But I pray they will become attached to persons of fortune before their full circumstances are known. I speak to you as a man of the world."

Alexander's reply to Sir Anthony was cool. "As a man of the

world, sir," he answered, "I know that there is not a baron alive who will marry a girl without a dowry, be he more in love with her than Romeo."

When Alexander bid them adieu at the end of the day, Martha turned to him with a hopeful look. "Perhaps you will come to town to see us, Alexander," she said.

Alexander felt a wave of sympathy and affection, but he replied with an attempt at reserve, aware of Teresa's scrutiny. "I hardly think that it will be possible," he said. "My obligations in the country—"

"What nonsense, Alexander," Teresa cut in. "One has no obligation to the country but to quit it as quickly as possible. You have told us that your friend John Caryll is always inviting you to ride in his coach. 'Tis but thirty miles."

Alexander wished that he was not so pleased by this careless encouragement, but he could not help himself. He bowed, hoping for more.

But Martha said instead, "I do think that Mr. Caryll is very civil to you, Alexander. And he has a great regard for your family. The esteem of such a man is worth a good deal." John Caryll was a Catholic landowner like Sir Anthony, whose estate, Ladyholt, was a short distance from Alexander's family home in Binfield. But Caryll's good opinion mattered very little to Alexander this afternoon.

He tried, however, to speak lightheartedly. "It is certain that the greatest magnifying glasses in the world are a man's own eyes, when they look upon his person," he said. "But even in those, I appear not the great Alexander Mr. Caryll is so civil to, but that little Alexander the women laugh at."

Martha gave Alexander's arm a squeeze as she kissed him goodbye. She wished that she could make him smile, and was sorry when it was Teresa who said, "You are in your sad dog pose today, I see, Alexander. Mind that you have cast it off before we see you again. I shall certainly not stand up to dance with a Great Dane caught in a fit of melancholy."

Alexander straightened his back and stepped into Sir Anthony's carriage.

As he drove home, he reflected upon the situation in which the girls would find themselves in town. For all Teresa's pretended sophistication and Martha's good sense, Alexander knew that they had never lived in the world. London society would not give two pennies for a pair of pretty, high-bred girls without expectations. The fashionable world was a precarious enough place for the daughters of the very wealthy, who were prey to the designs of heartless young adventurers. But for lovely young women without a fortune, mixing with men who were bred to think that they had a right to every imaginable gratification, the danger would be serious indeed.

Though he had dismissed his father's fears about London, Alexander shuddered at the thought of the guest at the ambassador's masquerade, arriving at the ball for an evening of lighthearted pleasure: murdered by men who thought that they were killing a priest. An innocent bystander; perhaps he had passed by his assailants all night, feeling no shadow of suspicion. Even as the knife sliced into his throat, had he realized what had happened? But was he really the chance victim of an anti-Catholic crime—or had he, in truth, been a man with a secret?

Chapter Two

"He saw, he wish'd, and to the prize aspir'd"

Alexander returned to find his house in darkness, save for a candle burning in the kitchen, where a meal of bread and cheese had been left out. He warmed himself by sitting close to the oven. The clock sounded eleven, and he listened as its strokes echoed hollow through the empty house. He had expected to find his mother waiting up for him, but it seemed that nobody was awake. His candle's uncertain flame made long shadows on the walls, looming up around him like the grotesque fingers of a hand. He was reminded of nights towards the end of his illness, when he had lain awake in the silent house, stranded between the worlds of the living and the dead.

But once he was inside his little bedroom the candle burned steadily, lighting the familiar forms of his bed and books and fireplace. He undressed and sat wrapped in his nightgown before the low fire. They had not forgotten him, then. After a short time he took his candle over to the desk and began to look at the lines of the poem he was writing. For a few minutes he sat and worried at a couplet, crossing out a word, changing a rhyme, and then changing it back. But he pushed the paper away.

He could not remain here. This house, and his parents' elderly habits, the suffocating routine of their religion, even the countryside itself, with its chill and damp seeping into his bones—slowly but steadily these things would kill him. During his weeks in London last year he had been filled with more energy than he had imagined his meagre frame could contain. But, home again, he was growing increasingly feeble as the months went by.

Though he had scarcely acknowledged it until now, it had been Whiteknights that had kept him here; his pleasure in seeing Teresa and his hope of recovering the old, happy intimacy of their childhood. But how long would pleasure persist in the face of her new resistance? And soon she would be gone, Martha with her. Martha: so patient, and with so keen an understanding. The picture of his parents came to him, setting aside their own comforts for his sake; year upon year of deferring to his delicate health. The thought moved him to tears, but he knew that they could do nothing more for him—and he believed even they had begun to see it.

No matter that he was a Catholic. No matter that he was a cripple. Fear and doubt must not stop him. He would go to London and seek his fortune.

He seized a clean sheet of paper and wrote to John Caryll, asking him for a ride to the city in his carriage. He sealed the letter and, taking up his pen once again, he began a second letter to Charles Jervas, asking if he might stay at his house in town. He told Jervas that the visit would be for about three weeks, but in his heart he knew that it would be much longer.

The next day he shrank from telling his parents what he had done, deciding instead to wait until the arrangements were certain.

He did not wait long. Caryll was delighted to get the letter, and wrote to say that they would be gone as soon as the roads were dry. And Jervas urged him to come as soon as he could and to stay for as long as he liked. At last, Alexander steeled himself to tell his father about the plan.

He was sitting in a chair by the fire when Alexander broke the news, and, to Alexander's astonishment, he was not angry. As he turned to his son, his face was crushed with sadness.

"My dear boy," he said, "how can I stop you? You are right; I know that you are right. You are the son of a tradesman, a Roman Catholic. Yet you are to stay in the city at the house of a man who is an artist and a Protestant. London must be a changed place indeed, and were I to see it again I fear that I would not know it. Yours is a world that I can never be a part of. Go to town with John Caryll. Write your poems. I know that you dream of fame, I pray that you will find it, and I pray that you will be safe."

His father's words affected Alexander far more than anger and resentment could have done. Deeply shaken, he thought for a moment to stay safe in Binfield with the people he loved so well, but he knew that he must go forward. For better or for worse, his future awaited him in London; it was there that he must put his talents to the test. He wanted the elation of success; it was time at last to confront the terrifying possibility of failure.

When Caryll arrived to collect him a few days later, Alexander was eager to be gone. Caryll shook his hand warmly, and put his arm about his shoulders in a hearty, paternal embrace.

"Good of you to let him go, ma'am; sir," he said with a confidential nod to Alexander's parents, and Alexander was reminded that Caryll must be about his father's age. "Though who would choose to be in London if he could be here, eh? You shall see him back again in no time." Alexander stepped away from Caryll's protective grip. Until now, he had thought very little about his patron except as the means by which he would get to London, and he was surprised to find that Caryll was a much more forceful personality than he had remembered. He knew that Caryll had a reputation for being adept politically; many years ago Caryll's uncle had been accused of Jacobite treason in a plot against the crown, and it had been he who had saved the family from losing everything.

"Did you read of the priest murdered in Shoreditch, Mr. Caryll?" Alexander's father asked him.

Caryll looked sombre. "The dangers of the city are not yet past, sir," he answered.

Alexander looked up sharply, the thought suddenly striking him that his patron knew something more about this murder than he had let on. But Caryll's face revealed nothing.

When at last the farewells had been made and they were driving away, Alexander was overcome by a surge of exhilaration. The countryside was brightly iced in the rising sun: white frost and purple shadows were tucked into the snow, which lay in little hollows like fleece. The spell of dry weather had made the road hard and smooth. A vapour of dew rose from the ground with the warmth of the morning, and gathered about the feet of the cold sheep turned mournfully towards the pale sun. They passed a covert of oak trees at a merry clip, and the sound of the wheels startled a pair of deer who broke away across the open grass, their warm hooves stirring up a silver trail in the frost. Far, far in the distance Alexander glimpsed the spires of London, glinting as the first sun caught their sides.

"Well, how are you then, Alexander?" Caryll asked. "Keen enough to be in town, I'll wager. 'Tis a good while since your last visit. No need to hurry home. Your parents will do well enough without you." He gave Alexander a playful shake, more like a friend than a father.

Alexander wondered why Caryll had spoken so differently to his parents about this sojourn in London. It was difficult to tell when Mr. Caryll was really being sincere. But he was eager to remain in Caryll's favour, so he said, "My father was apprehensive of this visit, but you calmed his fears adeptly."

Caryll's reply was cold, however. "Do not forget, Alexander, the things your father and I saw in London," he said. "Your generation did not witness the executions after Sir Edmund Berry Godfrey's murder. Men I had grown up with were torn into four in front of my eyes, while they still had breath in their bodies. The Protestants did not scruple to send fifty men to the gallows, merely for saying that the King's first-born son had claim to the throne."

Alexander blushed. "I fear that you found me impertinent, Sir. I did see a pope-burning once, and I will never forget it. I am sorry for your rebuke."

The scene, long pushed to the back of his memory, returned to him. It was just before his family had fled London. He had gone with his father to the docklands to see some newly imported linens that he wanted to buy for the shop. As they turned towards home they came upon a street entirely blocked by a crowd of men and women, pushing and jostling one another. One moment Alexander and his father were outside the crowd, and at the next they were in the middle of it, swept along in the raucous tide of movement, its force too great to be resisted by his father's light frame.

His father had snatched his little son to his shoulders, and as he did so, Alexander saw a strange, costumed group at the front of the pack, which he thought at first was a party of friars and monks and priests, familiar to him from pictures in books from his own religion. But then he saw that they were holding tankards of ale, gripping each other in lewd embraces, laughing and shouting cruelly. Alexander's father struggled to get free from the mob. But he stumbled, and gave in to the surge of the crowd, which pushed them towards a village green where people were singing and dancing around a bonfire, bright with lashing flames. A band of musicians played jigs; dancers were writhing in a wild, drunken passion.

Then Alexander saw the most astonishing sight. In front of him was the Pope.

The man was seated in a chair, wearing a scarlet cassock and a triple crown, just as in the pictures. Beside him stood a figure whom Alexander did not recognize, but he thought it must be a king, and wondered if it were the King of England or of France. A third man climbed on to the stage, dressed in black, with two horns and a long black tail that hung from his waist. Alexander gasped. It was the Devil. The crowd cheered in excitement.

Alexander sat motionless, captivated by the wild light of the fire and the gleeful faces of the people. Suddenly two men pushed their way to the stage, carrying sacks that jumped about as they walked. The crowd screamed and shouted in delight—"Puss, puss," they called—and Alexander realized that the bags were full of live cats. The men tore open the chests of the Pope and the King to shove the animals inside—the figures had been made from cloth. Alexander turned away in horror. Were the cats to be burned? Murdered, in cold blood. Unable to stop himself he looked back, and saw the Devil pushing the writhing mannequins on to the flames.

"No popery in England!" the Devil shouted, and the crowd gave another cheer. The light papers and clothing of the Pope and King caught fire, and Alexander heard the sound of high, anguished screams, which seemed to come from the very mouths of the two cloth men as the cats felt the blasting heat of the flames around them.

"No Catholics," the crowd kept on shouting. "Bring in the Ten-Mile Act!" Alexander's father staggered back, pulling his son down from his shoulders and holding him tightly. His face was ashen.

"My God," he gasped, breaking free from the mob at last. "We are not safe. I believe that we shall never be safe again."

Afterwards, his father had not spoken of what they had seen. But a few weeks later Alexander had woken in the night to loud noises and the sound of his father's voice raised in anger. His mother had come to comfort him, telling him that thieves had tried to break into the shop, and that his father had driven them away.

But in the morning, Alexander's father had stared dumbly at the windowpanes broken in and the filthy muck thrown across the shop floor. Some words were written on the wall: "No popery," Alexander had read aloud. His parents had abandoned the house in which Alexander had spent his childhood, and his father had never returned to town.

It was hard to imagine what his life would have been like had his family not gone to the country. Had they not lived in Binfield, he would never have known Sir Anthony—and would never have met Teresa. Strange that they should both be going to London now, filled alike—alike, as always—with hope and ambition. Yet of such different kinds. He hoped for glory. She longed to be introduced into the fashionable circle of their cousin Arabella, who had been described as the greatest beauty of her age. An extravagant phrase, Alexander thought, unlikely to be true. But even so, he would be curious to see her.

He noticed that they had reached the outskirts of the city. They passed an abandoned market garden and then a slaughterhouse, where a group of boys were fossicking in the yard for bits of offal to throw at passers-by. The road was lined with deep ditches hiding unsavoury sights from view: highwaymen and vagrants—perhaps even corpses, Alexander speculated. A tavern came into view, where a large group of people was waiting in the cold to board a coach.

He exerted himself to speak again to Caryll. "How glad I am not to be standing among them," he said. "It is most kind of you, sir, to give me a seat in your carriage."

"You will always be welcome to it, Alexander," Caryll replied. "I am particularly glad that you do not board that coach, for you would soon find yourself very far from where you want to go. It is bound for Liverpool."

"Liverpool!" Alexander exclaimed in astonishment. "What a wretchedly long way to be going," he added. "They have days of travel ahead of them."

"And that will be only the beginning. Some of them will surely sail on to Africa and the New World."

"They say that vast fortunes are to be made from slaves, but I would not be part of it for anything," Alexander said. "Think of spending so many months on a tiny, cramped boat; constantly ill, and uncertain as to whether one will see home again. I don't know how a man can bring himself to it."

Caryll laughed. "And if it is so dreadful for the men, only think what it must be for the slaves! You are much better off in London, Alexander. I am glad to have brought you here."

Just as Caryll finished speaking, Alexander's attention was caught by two fellows standing together in the stable yard nearby. One of them was ill-kempt—he had a five days' growth on his cheeks and chin, and was wearing an old cape and muddied boots. But the other was a gentleman, tall beside his companion, and holding the reins of a chestnut horse. This horse, as handsome as its rider, looked up alertly as Alexander's carriage approached, flicking a hind foot in a quick, authoritative movement.

Alexander studied the gentleman's outfit with interest. His boots were highly polished, and cut in a style that he instinctively recognized as belonging to the first fashion: coming halfway up his calves, with a smartly turned down cuff in a fine leather. Alexander guessed that he had just ridden from London. He was too well dressed to have come from the country. The man's surtout was firmly cut to his figure, with a vent for his sword, and long, low pockets that reached nearly to the hem of the garment. He realized with a sinking feeling that his own coats and their pockets were cut in a style that was no longer fashionable.

He observed the gentleman until the pair disappeared from sight, hoping to remember all the details of his attire. The surtout had a collar made from a dense, luxuriant fur, and as Alexander watched the gentleman removed a glove, and raised a hand to smooth the pelt around his neck. It was a controlled gesture, but commanding—as though he were touching the skin of an animal that he wished to restrain. It made Alexander imagine him stroking the sleek neck of his horse, showing that the beast belonged to him and that he knew how to make it obey.

They drove on. Alexander decided that he had rather liked the way the man had been smoothing his collar. He imagined himself, rich and self-assured, doing the same thing in front of Teresa, though she would probably only laugh at him for it.

Caryll interrupted his thoughts. "I think we shall be another hour at the most."

"Where do you stay, sir?" Alexander asked, rousing himself.

"At my Lord Petre's house on Arlington Street," came the reply.

Lord Petre, Alexander repeated to himself. Baron Petre of Ingatestone. Heir to one of the greatest Catholic families in England. "I believe that you once were Lord Petre's guardian, sir," Alexander said.

"Until he came of age two years ago," Caryll replied.

Alexander had met Lord Petre at John Caryll's house at Ladyholt once, when he could not have been more than eighteen or nineteen. It was not easily forgotten. Petre had been on his way to London, and Alexander remembered him jumping down from his horse, throwing the reins carelessly to a groom, and walking with a long, confident stride to greet Caryll and his wife. He had been very tall. Alexander was standing shyly to one side when at last Petre caught sight of him. How vividly he recalled his expression. He had started with surprise, and stared, and then tried to cover over his discomfort in vigorous talk. Alexander had been trying to stand so that his stooped back could not be seen. But of course it was impossible to hide it. In the country, his figure had become familiar, but in town scenes such as this would begin again. Others would look at him as Petre had once done.

"Is His Lordship presently in town?" Alexander asked.

"He remains in the country for the sport," Caryll replied.

Alexander was glad that he would not have to meet the baron again. He wondered whether he had married—what a prize he would be considered. He tried to imagine the sort of woman Petre might fall in love with. A man who could have almost anyone. She would be remarkable indeed.

He was about to ask Caryll whether Lord Petre had a wife when the carriage gave a violent lurch and dropped on to the London streets. Its axles cracking as though they would break in half, they teetered and tumbled across the cobbles. The streets were filled with hackney carriages being driven in sudden stops and starts, loping from side to side on their loose springs, the passengers inside contorting themselves uncomfortably in an attempt to look dignified. Mud was splayed against the carriage sides and on the window. Alexander began to feel ill.

It was very kind of John Caryll to imperil his carriage by

bringing it into town, but Alexander found himself wishing that he was not always in the debt of one friend or another. He dreaded being the kind of man who needed favours; a person could only get so far by being an object of charity. Too much pity prevented a man from making enemies, and no one had ever become famous without also being pretty thoroughly envied and disliked.

When at last they drew up outside Jervas's townhouse, Jervas's butler Hill rushed to help Alexander down, and he was pleased at the prospect of the good fire and excellent dinner waiting inside. He suspected, indeed, that part of his host's delight in having guests was that it gave him an excuse always to be having another little something to eat and drink.

"Good afternoon, Hill," Alexander said, putting a piece of silver into the servant's hand as he took his arm. Caryll drove away immediately, and Alexander allowed Hill to help him into the hallway.

"Welcome back to town, sir," Hill said. "Mighty chilly today."

What a civilized place Charles Jervas's house was, Alexander thought as he walked inside: elegantly furnished, with a robust masculine taste; excellent paintings in the hall and the reception rooms; a good cook and fine servants; and a light studio at the top of the house where Jervas painted. It was exactly what a gentleman's establishment should be. As Charles walked down the handsome staircase to greet him, Alexander felt a pang of envy. Jervas, wearing a housecoat with velvet slippers and no wig, extended his hand to his friend with the kind of easy, unconscious confidence that was born of good breeding and a happy life.

"My dear Pope!" he exclaimed. "How was your journey? I've been marching about the house all morning, warming it until it feels like the Indies, imagining that you would scarcely be alive when you arrived."

"My health was never better, Jervas," Alexander replied, untruthfully. He felt that Jervas had a tendency to lay the hostly performance on a bit thick. He and his friends conducted themselves with a seductive charm, which had the effect of making their guests understand how very much less charming they were themselves.

"Come, you were a dead man not two weeks ago," Jervas insisted.

Alexander was about to reply scornfully that Jervas was exaggerating, but he checked himself. His host spoke with such a pleasant manner, and yet with the polish of a person unmistakably from town. It made Alexander determined to prove his own sophistication. "In that case, my dear Jervas, I must be the Messiah," he said. "For I am perfectly resurrected in body and spirit."

"I cannot believe you, Pope—but I will indulge you," Charles conceded at last, with a smile of goodwill towards his friend.

Alexander removed the silk cushion against which Charles had propped him on his little chaise.

"You keep a mighty fire, Jervas," he said.

"Well, why not, my dear Pope?" his friend replied, settling his own cushion more comfortably. "I am not bred for country pleasures. My idea of life is to have as much to do with English men, and as little to do with English weather, as the present age can afford. A fine table, capital wine, first-rate plays, and the best conversation: that is all I have to ask. Rusticity is the worst of affectations. If one can spend the week in silk stockings and dancing shoes, eating asparagus, who would ever wish for the foot of mud and frost that cakes our country in misery—or think of the wretched sods who tramp about in it?"

"Sitting as a guest in your house, Jervas, I should say that you have more sense than any man alive," Alexander answered.

Jervas noted Alexander's studied manner with a smile, realizing that his young friend must have been told that elegant phrasing was the fashion in London conversation. He decided not to tease Alexander about it, guessing that he would soon learn to modify his speech. "You flatter me, and you know it," Jervas said instead. "But you must admit, Pope, that modern luxury deserves its good reputation. I have, for example, recently acquired a tap. I now have running water inside the house, guaranteed except in the worst of frosts! What say you to that?"

"I say that your habits of luxury will be checked by the expense of a house guest who will never leave," Alexander replied with a smile.

"Come, you must have a glass of my wine," Jervas was saying. "I had my man bring it up especially for your arrival. Your being here has given me a chance to open it, but I will not drink alone."

Without waiting for his footman, Jervas picked two glasses up from the sideboard in one hand, and splashed the burgundy into each. The wine folded against the side of the crystal, catching the light from the fire as it was poured. Jervas handed one of the glasses to Alexander, and raised his own.

"To the pleasures of the season," he said, and they drank together.

Their dinner consisted of a fish, plenty of good beef, and an excellent cheese. Alexander asked Jervas if he would show him his paintings in the studio after they had dined.

The servants were preparing to take away the plates, and Jervas was rising to lead Alexander to the top of the house, when they heard a visitor in the hallway. Jervas rushed forward at the prospect of offering his services as host once again.

"Douglass!" he called to the handsome gentleman who now entered his dining-room. "What are you about? What excuse can you give for arriving too late for dinner and too early for tea?"

"A very simple one, Jervas," the friend replied. "I dined in Westminster at noon, and I am to take tea in Piccadilly. I could not pass by your house without visiting."

Jervas turned to Alexander, who had also risen from his seat at the table. "Allow me to present my young friend Alexander Pope, just arrived from Binfield," said Jervas. "Douglass is lately returned from abroad," he added.

Douglass looked startled at the sight of Alexander, but said quickly, "Binfield! You came by the Windsor road, I imagine."

Alexander nodded.

"Pope," Douglass repeated. "A good Romish name, sir."

Alexander's heart sank at the remark—the very first person he met in London had raised the matter of his religion. And yet something about Douglass's tone of voice made Alexander look at him more closely. Was it possible that this man could have another reason for asking about his name?

As though he sensed Alexander's curiosity, Douglass spoke again. "I come to issue an invitation to Tuesday evening's masquerade at the Spring Garden," he said with a smile. "I need not tell you, Jervas, what these nights are generally like, and I leave it up to Mr. Pope to envisage a gathering at which every man and woman imagines that they are disguised beyond the possibility of recognition."

Jervas laughed, and said that he was longing to attend.

Alexander murmured that he would do his utmost to construct the spectacle.

"He need hardly imagine it, Douglass, for he is soon to see it for himself," cried Jervas, covering over Alexander's diffidence. "But come! I am about to show Mr. Pope my new paintings. Will you come upstairs too?"

Douglass said that he would, and threw his gloves down on to a chair in the hall, where his greatcoat was already lying. As they walked up the stairs, Douglass turned to Alexander. "How did you find the road today?" he asked. "Very wet, I dare say, at this time of year."

"On the contrary," said Alexander, looking at him closely again. "It was dry, and not at all crowded. The hard frost has kept the roads in excellent repair, and the sportsmen in the country."

Jervas interrupted with delight, oblivious of Alexander's wary tone. "Speak not to Douglass of hard frosts and sportsmen," he said. "I do not believe this man has left town for the country since we were at school. Frosts and thaws are of no account to him, as I do not think he has chased after a deer or shot at a bird in his life."

"Charles is quite right," said Douglass, glancing into a room where a large looking-glass was hanging just inside the door. Alexander watched as he made an adjustment to his cuffs. Then, as though he could not help a small gesture of arrogance, he lifted a hand to his neck and smoothed his collar. Seeing it, Alexander drew in his breath sharply, and the men's eyes met in the glass of the mirror. At first Douglass's expression was blank, but, as Alexander stared at him, a shadow of comprehension crossed his features. He recovered quickly.

"Nothing would induce me to leave town at this time of year," Douglass said confidently. "I cannot bear the damp of an English country house. In my mind's eye the road to London is always wet in the winter, and since that is the only eye with which I shall ever see it, wet it remains."

With this they reached the door of the studio, and the sight of Jervas's pictures distracted Alexander from his fledgling thoughts about Douglass.

The room was just as he had remembered: a delightful miscellany of drawings and pictures brought back from the Continent, half-finished canvases, a pair of busts from Rome, and a figure that he had found in Greece. There was a considerably larger number of paintings by Jervas himself than there had been on his last visit, all of them of grand-looking people whom Alexander took to be Jervas's patrons. His friend must be doing well.

"These are not *likenesses,* Jervas!" Alexander exclaimed. "No woman made of flesh and blood resembles these divine creatures. Your patrons must be paying you very handsomely indeed!"

But Douglass cut in across him. "Here is a picture of my Lord Petre, and very like. Do you know that family much, Jervas?"

Alexander looked at the picture that Douglass had pointed out, and saw that it was indeed the boy who had paid a visit to Caryll several years earlier. But he was now unmistakably a man, with no lingering disparity between the freshness of his face and the commanding court dress that he wore for the portrait. It was a good painting. The expression on Lord Petre's face was what made it memorable, thought Alexander—detached from the setting in which Jervas had placed him, seemingly scornful of the rich brocade fabric that he wore. He looked out from the canvas with an assured, ironic gaze that Alexander couldn't help but admire.

Jervas answered Douglass's question. "I met His Lordship at St. James's, and he has bought a few paintings from me," he said. "But I do not find that workaday artists, however mighty their patrons might be, are much taken into the confidence of the first families in the land. Everything is very merry when I meet my Lord Petre, and he flatters me a good deal and charms me into believing that I am the cleverest artist in the world. But I cannot pretend to know the first thing about the man's private character. The Petre family has done well, of course. They have stayed papists, and kept their titles and their land. Few families can boast as much."

"They have kept all their property, have they?" Douglass asked sharply. "Lord Petre must have inherited a vast fortune."

"I believe that he has," Jervas replied. "And yet he is unattached—uncommonly selfish of him. Not a woman in London will spare the rest of us a glance until Lord Petre has been claimed."

So Petre was not married. But everybody was in love with him. Alexander frowned, thinking of Teresa.

Douglass announced that he was late for his appointment in Piccadilly, and Alexander stayed in the studio while Jervas went downstairs with his friend.

He stared abstractedly at a painting. Mr. Douglass's discomfort upon meeting had not, Alexander thought, been occasioned by his crippled frame but by his mention of travelling down by the Windsor road. At first, when they were in the dining-room, he had thought little of it. But as soon as he saw Douglass raise his hand to his collar, he began to doubt. When they entered the studio, Alexander had glanced back down the staircase to where Douglass's surtout was thrown down on a chair. A fur collar lay there, curled like a living thing under the folds of fabric.

But what to make of it? Douglass had told them quite plainly where he had been that morning, and had made it clear that he had not even the most perfunctory notion of what a country road would be like on a freezing January day. Alexander would seem like a madman if he were to tell Jervas that he thought he had seen him from the coach. And seen him doing what? Talking to another man. What business was it of Alexander's if a person he did not know should lie about where he had been?

Jervas returned to the room, full of enthusiasm for the ball on Tuesday night.

"I never enjoyed myself so much in my life as at the last masquerade," he said, sinking into an easy chair and gesturing to Alexander to do the same. "Music, dancing, wine—and women such as you have never seen," he chattered, waving an arm around at his paintings. "Ladies are a good deal more willing when they are disguised," he said with a smile.

"Tell me about these glorious creatures you keep gathered about you," Alexander said, abandoning his thoughts of Douglass and stepping up to one of the finished canvases. It was of a young woman, perhaps nineteen or twenty, and very pretty. But it was not the girl's beauty that made the portrait so striking. It was the freshness and vitality with which she carried herself, looking out at the world with brilliant eyes and a playful lift to her mouth.

"That is the Lady Mary Pierrepont," Jervas replied. "Daughter to the Earl of Kingston." A Protestant and a noblewoman, thought Alexander.

"She is to inherit a fortune," Jervas continued, "but people say that she runs very wild. She has too much spirit for her father, to be sure—he cannot get her to meet the men he wants her to marry." He shrugged, and added, "So he ordered the painting to show it to her suitors!"

Alexander smiled. He walked over to a picture on the easel that was finished but for some work on a draped plinth and pillar against which a young woman was, rather improbably, leaning. She was exceptionally beautiful; so beautiful that it was impossible not to stand and stare.

"Now *she* is one of the most ravishing girls I have ever painted," said Jervas, staring at the picture, too. "The popular press has named her as one of London's 'Reigning Beauties' for the last two years. Her name is Arabella Fermor."

"Oh!" said Alexander, stepping back and looking at him. "So *that* is the celebrated Miss Fermor. She is cousin to the Blount sisters who live at Mapledurham. They have mentioned Miss Fermor often, but I am astonished to see that her beauty has not been too warmly described."

"It seldom is," said Jervas, "when the description is given by a lady."

Chapter Three

"A Youth more glitt'ring than a Birth-night Beau"

Arabella Fermor was looking at herself in the glass, considering on which side of her cheek the morning's beauty patch should be placed. She stepped back so that Betty, her maid, could tighten the robings on her stays. Arabella's lapdog, Shock, got up from his basket, gave himself a rousing shake, and trotted around to the other side of her bed. When Betty had made the last adjustment to her gown, Arabella picked the dog up and carried him down the stairs, leaving the room in disarray behind her. A footman gave Arabella her hooded mantle in the hall, and she wordlessly handed him Shock in return. Immediately he passed the animal on to another servant, and went to help Miss Fermor into the carriage.

Arabella, known to her friends as Bell, was blessed with an almost perfect face and figure—and had been told as much from the earliest age. But in spite of this, Arabella had not allowed her loveliness to be the ruin of her character. She had long known that she was very pretty, but that knowledge had not distorted her powers of perception or understanding, with the result that at the age of twenty-two she combined beauty and cleverness in almost equal parts.

She was well educated, having been provided as a child with a governess, and afterwards with some expensive years at a convent school in Paris. And yet it was not formal education that made Arabella remarkable. She was distinguished rather by her capacity for observation and judgement, and for these she relied not on books and learning but upon life itself. Here again Arabella had been lucky. Her parents had taken up residence in a town house in the smart London parish of St. James's, and granted their eldest daughter as much access to life (at least as it was lived in this small corner of the world) as she ever could have wished for. Arabella had good manners, excellent conversation, and highly developed powers of social observation. She was, therefore, uniquely positioned to put her talents to the use for which they had been cultivated: the acquisition of a rich husband.

Arabella was in London when she received the letter from her cousin Teresa announcing that she and Martha were coming to town. Teresa and Arabella had been in Paris at the same time, and Teresa had greatly admired her cousin's worldliness and sophistication. Back in England, they had continued to meet periodically, tied by bonds of family and religion, but they had never been intimate friends. Teresa spent almost all of her time with her sister, Martha; Arabella was several years older than her own sisters, and saw very little of them. Neither did Arabella spend much time in her parents' company, busy as they were with social preoccupations of their own. She enjoyed being self-reliant, pursuing her life in London largely independently of her family and childhood friends. It had long been her intention to make a glittering match, to become the envy of the close-knit Catholic circles that she had always found so stultifying. But after two seasons in town she had met no one to inspire the kind of passion that she yearned to feel, and she had found herself withdrawing from romantic intimacies that she knew most girls would have been delighted to entertain. She had met rich men; she had met handsome men. But she had not fallen in love.

When Teresa's letter arrived Arabella at first thought little of it, but as the days passed she found herself looking forward to her cousin's arrival much more eagerly. In spite of her many diversions, in spite of her enviable independence, she had grown bored. Arabella did not imagine that Teresa herself would provide the variety and change that she sought, but it did occur to her that, in showing her cousin the town, she might encounter new scenes to refresh her world-weary gaze.

So it came about that on a Friday morning, when the Blount sisters had been in town for a few days, Arabella had dressed early and was stepping into her carriage, preparing to collect Teresa for a trip to the shops at the Royal Exchange.

The coach drew up outside the town house in King Street where the Blounts were staying, and after a minute or two Teresa came out of the house.

Arabella greeted her, kissing both cheeks.

"Hello Bell," Teresa replied. "How glad I am to see you." She looked at her cousin appraisingly. Arabella was just as handsome as ever, she was disgruntled to note.

Arabella saw the glint of envy in Teresa's eye, and wished that she did not feel so gratified by it. "Where is Martha?" she asked.

"Abroad with our aunt and mother," said Teresa. "They are gone to visit Mrs. Chesterton, exactly the sort of tiresome thing that Martha likes to do. Your gown is handsome, Bell," she said. "Is it the one you wore at Mapledurham when I saw you last year?"

Arabella had noticed before that her cousin became competitive whenever she felt ill at ease.

"I haven't had that gown for quite some time," she answered. "This is another in a newer style, without flounces." She straightened out the lace fringe of her sleeve. Better pay Teresa a compliment in return. "Your hair looks well, Teresa. I suppose that your aunt's maid helped you put it up."

"Not at all," said Teresa. "Martha and I brought our maid to town."

"Ah!" Arabella raised her chin in assent. That explained why her cousin's hair had been done in such an old-fashioned style. She wondered whether she ought to point it out to her, delicately of course.

But the carriage turned from Cheapside into Cornhill, and both girls were distracted by the sight of the Exchange. Teresa forgot her envy and unease, and gave a gasp of excitement. "What a magnificent building!" she exclaimed. "I had quite forgotten."

Their coach was dwarfed by the immense stone front of the façade, its high arcades and columns reaching skyward beside a great formal arch. The massive windows of the first floor stretched towards a noble balustrade, and high above the whole was the tiered clock tower, piercing the sky like the dome of a cathedral and chiming out the hour of noon across the City.

As Teresa swung the carriage door open, sound and smell assailed her forcefully. Here at last! In London, on a glorious morning, the whole visit stretching before her. She caught the jingle of the muffin man's bell as he pushed through the crowd with a tray of hot cakes. A heavy thump as bales of cloth were thrown down from a cart. The stamp of hooves on the muddy straw when the carriages stopped, steam hissing off the horses' backs. A constant shrill of whistles from messenger boys. She could smell chestnuts roasting and the acrid smoke of the braziers; the spice of warmed cider; the piercing stink of fresh dung. She stood on the step of the cab, her breath misting in the cold air as she took in the scene. Then she jumped down to the pavement, thrilled to be in town and determined to make the outing a success.

Arabella lingered in the coach, retying the hood of her mantle and arranging the folds of her cloak. A gentleman in military uniform bounded across to the carriage and offered her his hand, and she it took with a smile, stepping down onto the cobbles. The man bowed and hurried on his way.

"Who was that gentleman, Arabella?" Teresa asked as they walked under the arch and into the courtyard.

"I've no idea," she replied. "But he was rather handsome, did you not think?" Arabella now felt in much better spirits.

She took hold of Teresa's arm, and said, "The shops upstairs are always the best, but I think you will like the little stalls in the yard, too. Last time I was here I bought a yard of silk ribbon. I wonder if the woman will be there again."

The arcaded square of the Exchange opened up before them, filled with merchants and traders and hawkers of wares, mingling with people of all occupations and positions. The ladies and gentlemen were walking arm in arm with friends or meeting new acquaintances across the yard. A pair of men in beaver fur hats bowed as Arabella pointed and exclaimed, "Yes, look! There is the silk lady again."

Teresa turned to watch as a tiny old woman shook out a length of fabric that rippled open in the breeze like a fast stream. The winter sunlight, catching in its folds, made it shine.

"How pretty!" she murmured, enchanted by the sight, and she would have stopped, but Arabella was moving on through the yard. She hurried to join her.

"You have probably not heard that Maria Granville is to marry

Tommy Hawkins," Arabella said, and Teresa was reminded of how very little news reached her in the country.

"Maria Granville?" she echoed. "I have not heard of her since we were in Paris."

"She caused a great scandal last year—it was discovered that she and Edward Fairfax were in an intrigue."

"An intrigue?" Teresa repeated. "You mean that they were . . . bedfellows?"

Arabella nodded. "But Fairfax married Lord Chester's daughter, and Maria was left high and dry."

"So she is to marry Tommy Hawkins instead," said Teresa thoughtfully. "There can't be much of a thrill in capturing a quarry so thoroughly worked over by every other girl in London. He had a nibbled look about him even when I met him in the country two years ago—he will have been half eaten by the time Maria gets him to the church door."

Arabella smiled. "I am surprised that she managed to marry at all. Twenty other women might have told her that Fairfax was a scoundrel. But the girl thought that she had fallen in love!"

They stepped around a beggar who had lifted his crutch to block their way, and Arabella moved her skirts expertly to one side. "At one stage I heard talk that Tommy Hawkins was paying his respects to you, Teresa. You sent him on his way, of course . . ." Arabella had not meant to tease her cousin, but she found herself falling into the kind of talk that the fashionable set engaged in. To her surprise, Teresa caught the style quickly.

"Charles Stafford was overheard saying that he would shoot himself if you did not marry him, Bell," she said. "That is quite a feather in your cap. He is said to be worth five thousand a year."

"Then I am afraid that we must expect to hear at any moment the news of Charles Stafford's death." Both girls laughed. They were beginning to enjoy themselves.

"Oh!" Arabella cried. "That sweet pippin-monger is here. Shall we buy some of his liquorice?"

They looked over the bursting stall, with its boxes and baskets of Kentish pippins, pearmains, lemons, and pomegranates. They knew that they cut a fine sight, admiring the fruit and laughing at the little pleasantries of the pippin-monger. Arabella ordered a pennyworth of crystallized ginger that she would never eat, conscious that she looked very well searching about for a coin in her silk purse. She noted with pleasure that two smartly-dressed gentlemen were watching them from the cover of the arcade.

She was still searching for the penny when one of them walked over. He handed a coin to the stall keeper, took the paper of ginger, and gave it to Arabella. She looked up with surprise, noting that he wore expensive gloves and that his coat was adorned with a rich fur on the collar. When she thanked him, he cocked his head in response, but said nothing. More interested by them than she had expected to be, Arabella turned to look at his companion.

As their eyes met she shivered with an involuntary surge of excitement. She knew him! He was a tall man, with a high forehead and an even, well-bred nose and mouth. He wore no wig, and his dark curls were tied in a black ribbon at his neck. The expression on his face was calm and controlled—he was obviously a man much used to being looked at—but when he smiled at her it was with the open smile of a boy.

"Robert!" she exclaimed. "It is you, is it not?"

The gentleman started. But as he stepped forward into the yard, his eyes brightened with recognition. "How do you do, Miss Fermor?" he said. "You have become very beautiful."

"I forget that we are no longer to be known as Robert and Bell," she replied, composing herself. "How do you do, my lord?"

"A great deal better when you call me Robert," Lord Petre answered.

Arabella touched a hand to her neck. "We were in the nursery when we saw each other last," she said.

He took another step forward, saying, "The nursery—hardly! I was a great man of eighteen, returned from school in the certain knowledge that the world had nothing more to teach me. Do you not remember my swaggering about with my sword and snuffbox?"

Arabella looked at him teasingly. "Those items, at least, you appear to have retained," she said.

"Do not make me ashamed of what I have become," he protested, and Arabella thought how fine he looked, standing with his sword glinting in the winter sunlight. "When I knew you then, you were the brightest nymph upon the green, the object of every pining swain. And though you are now a great lady, I suspect that little else has altered from that time."

Arabella wrinkled her brow. "You are right—I am changed very little," she replied.

"I have been largely in the country since my father died," he said thoughtfully, as if considering why they had not met before now.

Teresa stood awkwardly aside as Lord Petre and Arabella spoke, pushed backward until she felt the pippin-monger's stall against the hoop of her gown. She felt foolish, wanting to be gone, and she tried to step around Arabella so that she might at least wait in company with Lord Petre's friend. But he had slipped away, and in his place there was a little Gypsy acrobat with a monkey on his shoulder, who watched over their party with a leering grin. Teresa jumped backward violently, knocking into the pippin-stall.

"Look out there!" the owner cried, and a dozen ladies and gentlemen turned towards Teresa. She went scarlet, and pointed speechlessly to the monkey. Lord Petre swatted the man away with a wave of his hand, the other resting on the hilt of his sword.

His face changed from playfulness to anger when he saw that his friend had gone. "Where is Douglass?" he demanded. Arabella saw that in the place of idle amusement was a look of awakened concentration. "We had not been together five minutes before I saw you," he added. He looked around, but his companion had disappeared.

"Did you see where my friend Douglass went, Miss Fermor?" he demanded again. Arabella shook her head coldly, put out by this change in Lord Petre's manner. He stood looking at the ground in silence, and then continued to look around, seeming for a moment as though he might walk away altogether.

Suddenly he collected himself. "There's nothing to be done; I suppose he must be meeting an acquaintance," he said, and made an effort to smile. But Arabella believed that he had not put Douglass out of his mind.

"Will you do me the honour of introducing your companion?"

Arabella was disappointed. Perhaps he had not singled her out after all. What if he were to smile at her cousin as he had smiled at her? In a constrained voice she said, "I present to you my cousin, Miss Teresa Blount of Mapledurham."

Lord Petre looked up with real interest, and exclaimed, "Mapledurham! A lovely spot, on the prettiest elbow of the river. I envy your growing up in such a place, madam."

Arabella frowned; she had forgotten Mapledurham. Of course Lord Petre would know of it. She found herself wanting to tell him that Mapledurham was Teresa's brother's—that her cousin had no money of her own—and was surprised by such immediate jealousy.

Teresa, for her own part, sensed that her moment had arrived at last.

She laughed brightly, but, because she had been silent beforehand, it sounded much louder than she had meant it to. "But you grew up at Ingatestone, my lord," she said, "a place of which the whole world has heard a great deal. What a beautiful park you have there."

Lord Petre nodded at her and said, "Your brother has visited my family there, has he not? Do I recall that he is a fine sportsman?"

"Oh, yes, he is!" she said. "A wonderful rider."

"You are a fond sister, I see," he answered kindly. "And you, do you like to ride?"

"I rode with Michael very often at Mapledurham."

"Teresa is being modest," said Arabella, interrupting their conversation. "She is an excellent horsewoman. I hope that we shall see you ride in town, Teresa."

The intervention had been well judged, since Arabella was well aware that Teresa did not have a horse in London.

"Do *you* ride, Miss Fermor?" Lord Petre asked her at last.

"I ride when I am in the country, but in town I sit only pillion," she said. "If a woman in London is mounted alone upon a horse, she declares to the world that she wants for either a carriage or a cavalier. But pillion is another thing altogether. How pleasant to ride in the green shade of the park at noon, sitting comfortably behind one's companion, just as though one were about to drink bohea on a sofa at home."

Petre nodded. "You paint an alluring scene, and one that tempts me to offer myself as your cavalier. But, since you would hardly admire a man who could fall into a trap that he had seen you set, I shall walk away, to leave it ready for another gentleman."

Arabella's spirits rose gloriously once again. "If the world should ever see you trapped, my lord, I, at least, will know that the device must have been very well concealed," she answered, biting her lip to suppress a smile.

"But I suspect that Teresa is in a hurry to be gone," she added, turning to her cousin. "We only came to buy gloves. Shall we go upstairs to Fowler's now, Teresa?"

"We need not linger at the Exchange at all," Teresa answered mischievously, resentful that Arabella had made her the foil in her flirtation with Lord Petre. "Why do not we go to that shop in Cheapside where my mother gets her gloves?"

But Arabella was more than a match for her cousin. "Oh, I much prefer Fowler's," she said. "The gloves are smarter, and they have newer stock. The other shop feels rather decrepit, don't you think?"

Lord Petre said that he would accompany them, and offered an arm to each of the girls, but he looked around distractedly as they climbed the stairs to the shops on the upper galleries.

"You are being maddeningly discreet, Teresa," Arabella said, looking across Lord Petre as she did so. "I am wild to know which young men in the town are presently your suitors. I think it only fair that you should warn me of those admirers whom you wish particularly to avoid."

Teresa answered her cousin crisply. "I wish to avoid them all, Arabella," she said.

"I celebrate your discretion," Arabella replied. "But remember that if a lady is *too* discreet, people begin to suspect that she has nothing to hide."

"There is one acquaintance of mine, lately arrived in town, for whom I shall likely make an exception," said Teresa, and Arabella saw that she glanced at Lord Petre to make sure that he was listening. "An old friend, and in a way to becoming famous. He is a poet." Teresa coloured as she spoke.

Arabella answered, "Ha! I was certain that you had a secret. A poet! Perhaps he will make you immortal."

"I believe that he does have every chance of success in his profession," Teresa continued. "Tonson has published him already, and a much longer poem of his is soon to be printed. The *Tatler* has called him the new Denham."

"What is this gentleman's name?" Arabella asked.

"Alexander Pope," said Teresa, gaining confidence.

"Pope?" said Arabella, amusement immediately entering her voice. "You mean that strange little man whom you know from the country?" Teresa gave a scowl. Of course Arabella would remember his crippled back.

"Yes . . . I suppose that must be he," Teresa replied.

"I thought you said he was sickly," said Arabella.

"Mr. Pope is not my suitor, Arabella. I mention him as an old friend of my family's."

"Mr. Alexander Pope is a young poet of some note," said Lord Petre.

But Arabella was not listening. "It would be great fun to be the heroine of a poem by someone very dashing," she said. "Suckling, or Lovelace—or Rochester, even though he was so wicked. 'Pope' has such a morbid ring to it."

"Do not listen to Miss Fermor," Lord Petre intervened. "She would do well to spare her censure of a man whose only fault lies in a misfortune he suffered as a child. Remember that excellent adage, Miss Fermor: Charms strike the sight, but merit wins the soul."

"That is one of those preposterous falsehoods that is put about from time to time, but which no one ever actually believes," Arabella replied. "What a prude it makes you sound! A man in *your* position, my lord, could hardly wish to discover that merit is the true source of human felicity."

Lord Petre looked as though he had a retort ready for this observation, but he was prevented from delivering it by their arrival at Fowler's glove shop. The two girls walked up to the counter, and the shop-wench, whose name was Molly, eyed them with a resentful air. Arabella noticed with interest that she gave a saucy sort of curtsy and a smile of half-familiarity to Lord Petre, who responded to neither overture, giving no sign that he had seen her. Instantly Arabella was curious. It was obvious that they knew each other, despite Lord Petre's affectations to the contrary.

Molly, for her part, had sighed when she saw Arabella enter. She was a keen observer of her customers, and she knew what girls such as this were like. She guessed that Arabella would walk around talking to her friend, taking down the leather gloves and dropping them carelessly upon the tables. She would have one box brought out and then another, would turn the goods over once, and ask coldly for another colour that they did not stock. She would pick up the most expensive fan and flounce it open and closed, knowing that Molly's wages would be docked if it were torn. And then she would leave, buying at most a sixpenny ribbon for a hood that she would never wear again.

But Arabella had no desire to linger in the shop today. Briskly she chose three pairs of kidskin gloves, ordered ostrich feathers for her spring muff, and then waited while Teresa bought two pairs of the same gloves for herself. As the girls walked away, Lord Petre turned back quietly to give Molly a shilling. But she took it with none of her usual fluttering and flattery, seeing that he was no more disposed for distraction than Arabella. Instead she bobbed her head neatly, and Lord Petre joined the others.

They stood in the gallery in an uncertain little group, looking away from one another and towards a stout lady who was holding up a sleeve of a delicate striped fabric.

"Garden silks, ladies, Italian silks, brocades, cloth of silver, cloth of gold, very fine Mantua silks, Geneva velvet, English velvet, velvets embossed . . ." she called out.

Arabella said irritably, "What a fearful noise that woman is making. The trouble with this place is that one cannot get out of it so easily as one can enter. I suppose one must grant that point, at least, to the divines who would liken London to the fires of Hell."

"Infernal as the Royal Exchange is, Miss Fermor," Lord Petre answered, "it has yet one advantage over Hell: one can make a quick escape by chair or car. May I hand you into a carriage?"

He led them out through the back of the building, where hackney cabs were to be found.

There was a crush of sweaty, smelly men out here: Frenchmen doing business with Jews; traders shouting at the Dutch merchants about their cargo from the Indies, whores eagerly pressing up to apply for the gentlemen's custom.

The ladies walked in front, Lord Petre bringing up the rear.

They were nearly in the street at last when they heard Lord Petre exclaim, "Douglass—you are here!"

Arabella turned around to see the man with the sable collar. He was smiling as he walked away from a fellow who called out a remark in colloquial French that Arabella did not catch. But as soon as Douglass saw Lord Petre and his companions his face assumed its habitual coolness, which, Arabella was forced to acknowledge, rendered his features all the more handsome. He walked quickly up to Lord Petre, and Arabella watched him press in closely, murmuring, "That was our man . . ."

But Lord Petre motioned towards the women. "Where have you been all this time, Douglass?" he demanded.

Douglass acknowledged Arabella and Teresa, and said, with a smile that announced his intention to provoke, "I got trapped in a crowd of bum-firking Italians! You were in the gallery of shopgirls above, no doubt. It is a merchant's seraglio up there. For five shillings every one of them is ready to obey the laws of nature. And even better, for a guinea she'll disobey them."

Arabella's lip twitched, but Teresa turned away.

Lord Petre looked irritated. As he pushed a lock of hair from his face, Arabella noticed how like a small boy's it looked alongside the other man's harder features.

Lord Petre changed the subject. "I am going to Pontack's," he said. "I have an appetite, and I am disposed to eat a goose or two for my dinner. Shall we make a party of it, Douglass, and order a calves' head hash and a ragout?"

"Are the ladies to join you, my lord?" Douglass asked.

To Arabella's surprise, Lord Petre did not turn to them with an immediate invitation, but hesitated before he said, "I hope that I may say yes to Douglass's question."

Arabella answered his look haughtily. "I never dine while it is still light outside," she said. "And I could not begin to think of eating again until after four in any case—I was drinking chocolate in my nightgown at eleven."

"Your hair in a nice disorder and your gown ruffled with great care, no doubt," said Douglass with a playful look. "Miss Fermor wishes us to know that she receives her admirers in her chamber, like all modern ladies of fashion. If the practice of seeing morning visitors in bed did not permit a woman to look so temptingly undressed, no one could bear the discomfort of sitting in unmade sheets until noon."

Lord Petre caught Arabella's eye and smiled an apology. "Happily for us both, the eye of the mind may visit Miss Fermor in her nightgown at any hour," he said. "For that is a luxury which must compensate for the total improbability of our ever seeing either of these ladies again in anything but their outdoor clothes, and then at a great distance. Even if Miss Fermor and Miss Blount were to fall in with the remarkable habit of receiving visitors in bed, they would admit only their most intimate acquaintance. After today, I am certain that neither lady will be 'in' to either one of us again."

Since a man of Lord Petre's experience could not be suspected of delivering a speech like this without full knowledge of its likely effect, Arabella reflected that the excursion to the Exchange had been a great success.

Having declined Lord Petre's invitation to dine, the girls were handed into a carriage back to St. James's. By now they were tired, and tired even more of one another, and they welcomed the distractions of the streets in the early afternoon, which saved them from having to talk.

A street crier stopped beside the open window of the carriage. "Twelve pence a peck oysters," he called, making Teresa jump.

"Buy my four ropes of hard onions!" shouted another, on Arabella's side of the coach.

"Just ignore them," she instructed Teresa, struggling to draw up the tackle of the window sash, and falling back clumsily on her seat when she could not move it. "Will we never be out of this crush?" she asked, grappling in vain once again with her window. She sat back into her corner, brooding over the meeting with Lord Petre. What could be his business with a person such as Douglass? How curious that he had asked him to dinner—it appeared that they were friends, yet Lord Petre was the infinitely superior man. She pondered the question for a moment longer. The explanation was probably that Lord Petre was bored with his old acquaintance—and bored with himself, just as she had been before Teresa's arrival. With a smile she recalled the long jackboots he had been wearing (how well his legs had looked in them) and the way he swung his sword when he became excited. She had been struck forcibly by the sense of a man in want of adventure.

Teresa interrupted her thoughts. "Lord Petre's hair is very fine, don't you think?" she asked.

Arabella longed to agree with her cousin, to laugh about how handsome he was, to confess how much she wanted to see him again. But she was proud. "He must arrange it each morning at his toilet mirror, like a lady," she said instead. "Rather vain, I think."

"But he is exceedingly handsome, Arabella—even you must have noticed that." Teresa, still smarting from Arabella's slighting her in front of Lord Petre, wanted at least to make her cousin admit that she admired him.

"Lord Petre makes sure that everyone notices that," Arabella replied coolly. "Strange that he should be so precious about his appearance, when every girl in London must hope to marry him anyway."

"*Every* girl?" Teresa echoed with a sharp look.

"Well, the 'every girl' of daily speech—which is to say every girl except oneself," Arabella answered, and they both fell silent.

When they arrived at the Blounts' house, Teresa hurried out of the coach. But she turned back, fearful that Arabella might exclude her from future expeditions. "Shall I see you at the midnight masque on Tuesday evening?" she asked.

Her cousin smiled. "You certainly will, for my disguise is thin. I shall be the only woman there not attired as a shepherdess."

"Oh, I daresay there will be enough milkmaids and serving wenches to keep people guessing," Teresa answered, encouraged to find that Arabella, too, seemed to want the friendship.

"How shall I know *you,* Teresa?" asked Arabella, placing one hand on the carriage door in preparation for closing it.

"I am going as Shakespeare's Viola, when she is disguised as Orsino's page," Teresa replied. "My sister is to be Orsino himself. We have borrowed some of Alexander's things for it." In spite of her best efforts to remain indifferent before her cousin, Teresa could not help but allow a little enthusiasm to break through on the subject of their dress. Arabella seemed unmoved by the news.

Chapter Four

"Mark'd by none but quick, poetic eyes"

Arabella was right, of course. Lord Petre had recognized Molly instantly. There had been a period of intimacy between them—two or three months at most, nearly a year ago—which he looked back upon fondly. In truth, Molly was a common enough wench, a shopgirl willing to lift her skirts for anybody who would pay her. But he had felt a powerful attraction nonetheless. She was handsome, with a strong square jaw and high cheeks that gave her a look of fierceness. And there had been something else—something about the way that she had looked at him when he had first asked her to step into his carriage. She would not be diminished by his rich clothes and grand manners. When he kissed her she had laughed at him, making him feel like a schoolboy making love to a duchess.

It was curious that he should have seen Molly again today of all days. He had not felt that surge of strong physical attraction for a long time. But he had felt it the moment Arabella Fermor appeared before him in the yard. When Douglass stepped over to hand Arabella the penny for her ginger, Lord Petre had wanted to shove him out of the way.

Relieved, he watched as the girls drove away. He had been so distracted by Douglass; he feared that Arabella would think him a fool. Frowning, he raised a hand to hail a waiting carriage.

"To Pontack's!" he directed, and stepped in. Douglass climbed in behind him, and shut the door with a click.

Douglass had said beforehand that they should take a cab ride after meeting; only in a carriage could they be sure that their conversation would not be overheard. Lord Petre turned to him, expecting to hear news. He tried to look sombre, but in truth it was excitement as much as idealism that coursed through him at this moment. He suspected that the feeling had something to do with seeing Arabella again, but he pushed the thought from his mind.

He opened his mouth to speak, when Douglass spoke across him. "Splendid-looking girl, Arabella Fermor," he said.

Petre was taken aback; this was not what he had expected. But of course he should have realized by now that Douglass took pleasure in being perverse. Petre recalled the night on which they had first met, only a few weeks ago, but already it seemed like many months. Petre had approached Douglass discreetly, expecting to be led away for a private meeting. Instead Douglass saluted him in the middle of the ballroom, bragging that he had just danced with a countess. It was at the French ambassador's masquerade—the night on which a guest was later murdered. Lord Petre felt a chill as he recalled it. He and Douglass were not the only people there with a secret. How macabre to think that the murderers had been lurking somewhere in the darkness, waiting to see the priest leaving the ball. The victim might have been any guest, anyone they had taken for a Papist.

That night Douglass had explained that they would meet regularly over the next weeks and months as he received details of the plan. His taunting manner today must mean that intelligence had not yet come. Douglass teased him because he liked to do so, in order to test his mettle.

He did not mind—on the subject of women Lord Petre felt quite sure of himself. "Miss Fermor is the handsomest girl I have yet seen in London," he answered. "We were companions in childhood—our families were often together—but I have not seen her since my father died."

"Lucky for you to have renewed the acquaintance, then," said Douglass, "for I fancy she's ready enough to be your playmate again. And who would not be willing to play any game Miss Fermor devised?" he added. "Only think of a visit to her chamber in the mornings: the nightgown scarcely upon her shoulder, a glimpse of her snowy breast . . . a hand upon her thigh . . ."

Lord Petre felt a surge of jealousy. "Enough, Douglass!" he intervened.

"You are coy, my lord!" Douglass exclaimed. "I should not have expected it. Nor, may I venture to add, would Arabella Fermor."

"On the latter point, Douglass, I think you could not be more mistaken. A woman such as Miss Fermor does not fall prey to gentlemen like me. She has lived long enough in town to know that reputation is the most volatile of stocks; incalculably high at one moment, worth nothing at all at the next. Miss Fermor will not float hers in so tempestuous a market."

"Spoken like a giddy young lover," Douglass replied. "I see that you are not likely to be carried away by strength of feeling."

"As the seventh Baron Petre, I am not rich enough to be carried away by my emotions," said Lord Petre gravely. He wondered what Arabella's dowry might actually be. Four or five thousand, he guessed, knowing that she had several younger sisters, all of whom would require marriage settlements. As the eldest, Arabella's would be the largest, but if he was right about the Fermor family's fortunes, his mother would never approve such a union.

Douglass had turned to look out the window, but at Lord Petre's remark he turned back sharply. "Not rich enough? What the devil do you mean?"

Lord Petre caught the note of alarm in Douglass's voice. So this idle banter had not been idle after all. Douglass was trying to determine how wealthy he really was. It was a salutary reminder that Douglass was just as much in want of Lord Petre and his money as he was in want of a role in Douglass's plan.

"When I marry, it must be to a woman whose dowry is enough to give importance even to our estates," he replied with aristocratic assurance. "It is my obligation to the title. I have lived three and twenty years in unstinting luxury—and they have made a slave of me."

Douglass shook his head with a smile. "Your situation is desperate, my lord. I am heartily sorry for you."

"I merely point out that I am at liberty only to fall in love with girls like Molly Walker, where there can be no expectation of marriage," Lord Petre replied. As soon as he spoke he reproached himself. Why had he brought up Molly? It was unchivalrous. He still had a good deal to learn about dealing with a man like Douglass.

"Molly at Fowler's glove shop, you mean?" Douglass retorted.

"There is not a gentleman in London who hasn't given his heart to Molly Walker. It is a wonder that there are hours enough in the day for her to accommodate so much heightened feeling. Though I suppose that since none of Molly's devoted sparks will ever try to make her their wife, she will always be at leisure to receive fresh declarations."

In spite of his awakened caution, Lord Petre could not help but be amused by Douglass's frank way of talking. "Very true," he answered with a smile. "Poor Molly is at the mercy of many a besotted young gentleman."

Douglass guffawed. "Would that Arabella Fermor could hear you talk now. I would give a great deal to tell her about this conversation, and bring a glow to that calm smile of hers. Still, it is as they say, my lord: cold smile, warm—"

Lord Petre laughed, and clapped his companion upon the shoulder. "Your company does me good, Douglass," he said as the horses rattled to a halt and they were flung forward in the carriage, each putting up a boot to stop himself from falling.

Before they got out of the cab Douglass turned to him, his expression earnest at last. "No news yet, my lord," he said. "But watch and wait."

"Watch and wait," echoed Lord Petre, and Douglass opened the door to jump down.

The entrance to Pontack's in Abchurch Lane was crowded with gentlemen like Lord Petre and his companion: well dressed and disposed for enjoyment. Inside the tables were set out in rows down the length of a large panelled room, which reverberated with the sound of plates rattling, silver clinking, and voices raised in merriment.

Lord Petre walked ahead of Douglass towards two seats at the central table. Above the din of talk chairs scraped as people stood to greet him. There was a general murmur of "Good day, my lord," followed occasionally by his singling out of an acquaintance. He was pleased that Douglass should witness all of this, and he found himself wishing that Arabella Fermor might have seen it too.

"I see that Richard Steele is sitting on the other side of the room," he said. "What a clever fellow he is—his *Tatler* was the liveliest thing that I have ever read, and the *Spectator* is said to be even more diverting."

Douglass, looking idly across the tables, said, "Your man Steele is with a gentleman whose acquaintance I made recently. A young poet, by the name of Alexander Pope."

Lord Petre was surprised. He had not expected Douglass to be a reader of Steele's literary journals, and was certain that he would not have read Pope's poems. Might Douglass have some particular reason to notice him?

This was the first time that Alexander had been to Pontack's, and the first time that he had dined with the great periodical writer, Richard Steele. He sat very upright, smiling the wide nodding smile of a person who is thinking of a thousand things besides those which his companion is saying to him. Half the restaurant had risen to greet them as they walked in, pressing forward to congratulate Steele on the first issues of his new paper, the *Spectator*. Alexander wondered briefly whether he should offer to pay for their dinner, decided against it, and was then unsure whether to involve himself in the ordering of their food, or to pretend, absently, that he had no interest in the matter. His eyes darted about the room, which he was certain must be filled with well-known figures. Could that be Robert Harley, Queen Anne's chief minister, sitting across from them? And his companion—he was sure that it was—that it must be—he could not stop himself from exclaiming: "It is Dr. Swift! Dr. Jonathan Swift! Sitting with the chief minister."

Steele smiled and said, "Yes, yes; they dine together often. Incomprehensible. Swift is my intimate friend—he wrote for the *Tatler*. But Harley, intractable Tory, the worst chief minister we have had. Can't imagine why Swift sits down with him. But perhaps we can get them over here . . ."

Steele broke off to order their dinner. He chose a selection of dishes that showed his marked preference for meat, richly prepared.

"Your 'Pastorals' made something of a success, Pope. I hope that more will soon flow from your pen to take the town by storm," he said, flapping his napkin about as though in salute to Alexander's adept versification. "If you do, we shall write you up in the *Spectator*. A great many people in London are your supporters; I've heard you spoken of at a dozen supper parties . . ." but Steele was suddenly distracted, and he said, "Oh—I see that the Earl of Kingston is here, dining with that brute of a fellow Clotworthy Skeffington. Kingston probably hopes to exchange his daughter Lady Mary Pierrepont for Skeffington's fortune. How curious. Self-interest leads men into the oddest actions." He laughed, forgetting that he had been in the midst of lavish praise for Alexander's writing.

But Alexander did not mind, for at this moment he felt that his stars were in alignment. Here he was in Pontack's restaurant, as the guest of Richard Steele, founding writer of the world's most fashionable periodical. Steele had mentioned Lady Mary Pierrepont, the lady whose portrait had been in Jervas's studio. Everybody seemed to know of her! His curiosity was piqued, but he was prevented from asking about her by the arrival of a larded chicken at the table, in company with another fowl draped amply in a cream sauce. Steele eyed them both excitedly, and then, seizing a leg of the bird nearest to him, embarked upon a new story, while Alexander continued to smile and nod, somewhat nervous of making his own attempt upon the poultry.

Steele was saying, "And you will particularly enjoy this part of the story, Pope, for she said to me . . ." when he broke off to remark, "Ah! My Lord Petre is here, too, I see."

Alexander looked up and saw the man from Jervas's portrait walking towards him. Steele was on his feet, saying to Petre, "I am here with my young friend Mr. Pope, who is a poet. Perhaps you have met already, my Lord."

Alexander pulled himself up as straight as he could manage.

Lord Petre began to shake his head, and the words "I fear that—" were forming on his lips, when his expression changed abruptly.

"I *do* believe that I have made your acquaintance after all," Lord Petre said quickly. His face had a stricken look, which made Alexander wince. He had remembered the day at Ladyholt. "But when I met you then, sir, I did not know you were a poet of country life," Petre added, smiling graciously, but without at all compromising his air of confident superiority. Alexander saw that he was master of a situation such as this.

Alexander turned to see Lord Petre's companion, whom until now he had noticed only obliquely. To his amazement, he saw that it was James Douglass.

"I, too, have made your acquaintance, Mr. Pope," Douglass said, and Alexander stared, taken aback. But Douglass did not mark it. Was it possible that he was mistaken about Douglass's identity?

"Do you go to the masquerade tomorrow evening, Mr. Steele?" Petre asked affably. "I hope that you will write about it in the *Spectator*, and make us all famous."

"I could write about it, my lord, but I would not make you famous," Steele answered jovially. "Everybody there will be masked, so I cannot say which men and women are present, and which are not."

"That hardly matters, sir!" Douglass interjected. "We all like to be remembered, even when we are disguised. Are not our true selves but rarely seen, even in ordinary life?"

As he spoke, he lifted a hand to his neck, and Alexander knew that he had made no mistake.

Involuntarily, he glanced at Lord Petre, but he was laughing heartily as Steele replied, "You and I think alike, sir. Who cares what a person's character is in point of fact? The way it appears to the world is the only thing of interest to us!" Alexander turned away. Nobody except himself seemed to feel the slightest doubt about this intriguing character Douglass.

When the conversation with Steele was over, Lord Petre walked to his table, Douglass following behind. Robert Harley rose and greeted him.

"How do you do, Harley?" Lord Petre answered. "Congratulations, sir, on the passage of the imports bill. A great victory for our party."

As soon as they sat down, Douglass exclaimed, "That was the chief minister, Robert Harley! Is he well known to you, my Lord?"

Lord Petre looked at him. Had Douglass really doubted his position in society?

"I know Harley a little," he replied. "I see him at court, in Westminster—and here, of course. But you cannot pretend to be surprised by my connections, nor flatter me that you admire them. You wish to make use of them, as well you ought."

Douglass nodded, but Lord Petre did not feel that the matter was settled. "When a person is rich and powerful, he grows used to being of indispensable importance to those around him," he added in a lower tone. "If you did not prize my position in society, I would be as much affronted as a beautiful woman who has been praised for the excellence of her character.

"Look at Dr. Swift, for example. How mightily has he laboured to become a well respected clergyman—but in fifty years, who will recall the dignity of his sermons or the wisdom of his theology? He will be remembered only as Robert Harley's friend, the man who drank claret and ate mutton at Pontack's with Queen Anne's chief minister." But Douglass only shrugged.

Lord Petre motioned to the waiter, and soon afterwards oysters were brought and the wine was poured. Douglass raised his glass and declared, "To the glorious cause, my lord."

His voice brought Lord Petre a renewed thrill. "The most glorious in the world," he replied, and they drank.

Douglass tossed off a couple of the oysters. "An excellent dinner! Let us have a bottle of the Ho Bryan with the geese. It is a new wine from France. Come; this time *I* shall be the one to ask for it."

But before he could do so, they were joined by the very people of whom they had been speaking. Lord Petre was on his feet instantly. "We have just been praising the excellence of your satires, Dr. Swift," he said. "May your mighty wit keep the Whigs out of office for many years to come!"

"I thank you, my lord," Swift replied with a bow. "Though the Whigs' demise is certainly to be wished for, I confess that my efforts as a satirist have been in pursuit of a far loftier object. Whenever *I* am employed in London as a scribbler, my parishioners in Ireland are spared from hearing my sermons—and I am spared listening to my parishioners."

"You are not fond of sermonizing, then, Dr. Swift?" Lord Petre asked, trying to conceal his surprise.

"Not upon matters of religion, my lord," Swift answered with a smile. "My abilities do not suit the subject of faith—especially not of the Irish variety. If a man wants to believe that the flesh of our Saviour is an edible commodity, served up to the nation for breakfast on Sunday mornings, it is beyond the reach of my rhetorical reason to persuade him otherwise."

Lord Petre gave a half-smile, allowing it to be forgotten that he was Catholic. Swift was speaking of Ireland, after all. "But I am surprised that your writings are political in their nature," he returned. "I had believed that the clergy were obliged to write upon theological subjects, if they wished to secure advancement in the Church."

"You are correct, my lord—young clergymen are always trying to get their philosophy printed," said Swift. "Yet there is that part of me that doubts whether an essay called *A Brief Exposition of the Lord's Prayer and the Decalogue, to which is added the doctrine of the sacraments* will become an overnight sensation," he added, and smiled wearily at the group.

"It is hard to describe the absurdities of the clerical life to men who live in the world," he continued. "I might toil for years to produce an indifferent monograph entitled *On the Being and Attributes of God.* It would be published obscurely—a run of fifty at best. But my colleagues in the Church would fall upon it like so many gourmands upon a Bologna sausage. For months to come, they'd gather in the evenings to divide a bottle of wine among eight of them, listen to one of their number perform upon the viol, and chew over my threadbare ruminations on God's essence, all stolen from a treatise of the same name from 1684. A year or so later, one of them would groan out a pamphlet in reply, *Some Reflections*—or perhaps *Seasonable Observations—upon those late remarks, by Dr. S——* and the whole ridiculous performance begins again: the wine, the viol, the interminable talk."

Harley and Lord Petre laughed, but Douglass was restless, bored by the discussion.

"Well I must say that I do find theological disputes rather hard to follow—" Lord Petre observed.

"Hard to follow!" Swift interjected scathingly. "Clergymen idle about, whinnying and neighing at one another in a strange horsy language that no sane person can comprehend, and yet everybody is expected to stand by sagely, pretending to understand every word they say."

"In London, at least, your acquaintance must rather be with literary men than the clergy," said Petre. Swift bowed to acknowledge that this was, indeed, the case.

"We are among literary men now," said Douglass. "A young poet is sitting across the room in company with Richard Steele."

Swift looked behind him at Alexander. "I do not know that young man," Swift replied. "Is he a satirist?"

"Not in the least," Lord Petre replied. "He writes eclogues, like the young Virgil. Perhaps one day he will give us an epic."

"Ah! Well, I have not the serious cast of mind that is required for epic, and it sounds as though that gentleman will not share my inclination to the ridiculous," Swift replied. "I fear that he and I are likely ever to be strangers."

The conversation ended shortly after this exchange. When Swift and Harley had left, Lord Petre said, "Swift did not show much interest in that fellow Mr. Pope."

"I believe that Pope writes about the country," said Douglass, "where he spends an immense deal of his time. Knows all about the condition of the roads and the state of the hunts. I should say that it is just as well if he gets on to a horse whenever he can, for it will be a mighty long time before he ever sits upon a woman. He would have to get astride a whore as he would his mare—with a mounting-block to help him up off the ground."

Petre gave a laugh and motioned to the waiter to bring more wine, seeing that Douglass did not mean to order the Ho Bryan after all.

The next morning, Alexander was to meet Jacob Tonson in his bookshop in Bow Street to hear his opinion of the lines he had composed for a new poem. He was apprehensive about the meeting, not only on account of what the old publisher would say about his verses, but because he had not told Tonson that he had given his *Essay on Criticism* to an old schoolfriend to print. He had done so out of insecurity, but as he walked into the shop, he realized that it might appear to be a mark of his arrogance or indifference to Tonson's good opinion.

A young man in spectacles looked up from the sums and papers on his desk, which he was studying very seriously, to greet him. Making sure old Tonson doesn't pay his authors too much for their copyright, Alexander reflected. The young man smiled kindly, and Alexander bowed in return. Why was the boy greeting him with such gracious condescension? Very likely he knew of some unpleasant tidings that Tonson had in store for him. He noticed that the *Miscellany* containing his poems was displayed prominently upon the table, and was certain that it had been placed there just before he entered.

Tonson's boy saw him looking, and said, "We have sold a great many copies, Mr. Pope, since the *Tatler* praised the volume. Mr. Tonson has been showing it to every customer."

Alexander nodded but said nothing, fearing that he heard a note of mockery in the fellow's tone. His jealous eye was caught suddenly by a stylish new edition of *Paradise Lost*, piled in much larger stacks upon the table, with a card boasting that it was Tonson's ninth edition of the poem in twenty years. Nine editions. Not even Dryden had so many. There were illustrations, too, lavishly engraved.

At last Tonson himself appeared, holding a book that Alexander had not seen before.

"How do you do, sir?" he cried, sitting down, and placing the book so that it was just out of Alexander's sight. "Do you have refreshment? We have tea now, you know."

Alexander said that he would take only a glass of wine, and strained to see the volume that Tonson kept concealed.

"I have read the new lines that you sent to me," Tonson began, "but before we discuss them, I have some elevated compliments to pass on—from a gentleman who calls you the 'Little Nightingale'."

Pope attempted a smile, cursing Tonson inwardly. "Ah, yes!" he said. "My friend Mr. Wycherley. I hope that he is well, sir. He gave me the name 'nightingale' in jest because I sing, you know—like the classical poets. And because I am little," he added, after a moment's pause.

"Wycherley," Tonson replied. "'Tis a shame that he has lost his memory since his illness, for he was the greatest playwright of his age."

"I used to follow Mr. Wycherley about the town with as much constancy as my dog runs after me in the country," Alexander replied.

Tonson glanced down at the little book, and took a drink from his wine.

"Are you fond of dogs, Mr. Pope?"

"I am," said Alexander, warming to his conceit. "My favourite dog is a little one, a lean one, and none of the finest shaped. So 'tis likeness that begets affection. He lies down when I sit, and walks where I walk—which is more than many very good friends can pretend to." Jacob Tonson watched Alexander speak with an even, appraising look, neither smiling nor frowning, but taking keen measure of the young poet.

"Let us turn now to your verses, Mr. Pope," he interrupted. "You have given the title *Windsor Forest* to this new piece, and it seems that you wrote it while in the country."

"At Binfield, yes."

"Quite. Well, I think it has too much of the country in it. Everything in your poem quivers and trembles with the apprehension of death: the pheasants, the hares, the doves, the trout, the deer . . . There is nothing but rustic carnage from beginning to end."

"The first object of country life is to kill as frequently and as prodigiously as possible," Alexander replied with an ironic smile.

"That is too raw a sentiment for my readers, Mr. Pope," Tonson answered. "When one is pent in a great city, one likes to imagine rural delights: the feathered tribe, the scaly breed, the woolly—and so on. One does not wish to be told that they are mown down in their infancy by men with guns and fishing rods. In two hundred lines, you have snuffed out half of Berkshire."

"That was rather my design, Mr. Tonson."

"Country life is too old-fashioned for these days, Pope. What of trade? What of commerce? The spoils of empire, rolling in from the four corners of the earth to London. London! A great city, risen from the ashes of the fire like a phoenix—I leave the details of the composition to you. Yes! What you have written should be but the beginning of a much longer poem. We come from the country, full of—what do you have?—'bright eye'd perch' and 'clam'rous Lapwings'. We arrive in the city, rich with the fruits of the trade winds. Glowing rubies, ripe gold, spicy amber—you know the style better than I."

Alexander flinched at Tonson's mixed metaphors, but he replied as diplomatically as he could. "Sir, in a poem there has to be some vehicle by which the reader is carried from the, the 'woolly tribe' (as you would have it) to the, er, spicy city," he said. "It is absurd to change suddenly from the country to the town without some conduit to make the transition easy. The rules of poetry do not allow it."

"Well, change the rules of poetry, then," Tonson said. "If London does not await my readers at the other end of these verses, they will not care to make the journey through Windsor Forest with you."

Alexander sat quite still in his chair, looking at his publisher. He had been working at *Windsor Forest*, on and off, for four years. It was an exquisitely witty imitation of Virgil's young style, as Tonson understood perfectly well.

"You must give my readers something new," Tonson continued. "Your first poems were striking in one so young, but now it is time to show a more ingenious talent."

Pope bit back his disappointment. "But I have a fondness for the verses of my youth that nothing can displace," he said, trying to compose himself. He feared that if he took a drink from his wine his hand might shake. "The visions of my childhood are vanished for ever, like the fine colours I then saw when my eyes were shut. In those days every hill and stream had—how can I describe it?—the glory and the freshness of a dream. A notion that would make a fine poem, I think."

"Readers in the present day are not concerned with visions of childhood," Tonson answered briskly. "They live in a world in which everything is new. Let them go forward, Pope. Another poet, in another age, will take them back to what they were. Just be sure that you don't give your new verses to that scoundrel Lintot to publish." Alexander laughed a little at this, and at last Tonson brought forth the book that he had been keeping out of sight.

"*An Essay on Criticism.* Printed for W. Lewis in Russell Street, Covent Garden," he read from the title page. "Is this yours, sir? The writer is anonymous, though the style I take to be your own."

His own book! Not just a poem in a miscellany. Alexander wanted to reach out for it eagerly, but he was stricken with embarrassment for not having told Tonson, realizing now that the pleasantry about Lintot had indeed been meant as a reproof.

"Not even I have seen the thing in print yet," he mumbled.

Tonson did not smile. "Indeed, the pages are still warm from the press," he replied. "My man Mr. Watt printed it for your publisher friend Lewis, so he showed it to me. Ours is a small world." Tonson paused again, still stern. "I have read the poem through, sir, and I think it extremely fine."

Alexander smiled. "Oh, Mr. Tonson, I value that opinion highly indeed," he said.

"Not without its faults, you understand me."

"I believe that I do understand you, yes," Alexander replied, gaining confidence from Tonson's words of encouragement.

"Faults that can be corrected in the second edition," Tonson added with a twinkle in his old eye.

Alexander bowed modestly. "But I dare not hope that a treatise of this nature, which only one gentleman in threescore can understand, will be reprinted," he said, hoping that Tonson would correct him.

And Tonson, for once, obliged. "I think it very likely that it will run to a second edition," he said, "for it is bound to create a stir in Grub Street. I fancy that when Mr. Dennis, for one, discovers that you have slighted the school of criticism he regards as his own, he will not rest until he has made one of his usual replies." Mr. Dennis was a famous critic in town, well known for his attacks on writers whom he did not like.

"Mr. Dennis's style of reply is one that cannot properly be answered but by a wooden weapon," said Alexander. "I might have sent him a present from Windsor Forest of one of the best and toughest, in English oak."

Tonson laughed, though Alexander could tell that he tried to look severe.

"Pope, I see that you have a taste for trouble. Mr. Dennis does not care for the fact that you are young and brilliant, when he is old and beaten about like me."

Alexander was unable to suppress a laugh as he replied. "If Mr. Dennis's rage proceeds only from his zeal to discourage young and inexperienced writers from scribbling, he should frighten us with his verse, not his prose."

Tonson smiled at him, and then replied in a stern voice, "You must learn not to laugh so loud at your own jokes, Mr. Pope."

"I laugh loudly only because I am so determined that I shall laugh last," Alexander answered as he stood to leave.

Tonson considered checking Alexander for this final piece of impudence, but shrugged instead. The young man was certain to get into a great deal of strife as he went on in his career. And Tonson had made his fortune by knowing that in the world of Grub Street, this was half the battle won.

Chapter Five

"Stain her Honour, or her new Brocade,
Forget her Pray'rs, or miss a Masquerade,
Or lose her heart, or necklace, at a ball."

Arabella was so used to meeting men who admired her that she did not at first realize how much she herself was affected by the encounter with Lord Petre. She told herself that there was nothing in his attentions that she had not seen before, but then days passed, and she did not hear from him. Other men would have written by now: gallant, supplicating notes begging her indulgence. They would have sought her out, and fixed on her a pleading stare, to confess to their feelings of helplessness. With Lord Petre it was apparent that there was to be no pleading stare.

She tried to put their meeting out of her head. It had happened by chance; she must pretend that it had not happened at all. But before she could forget it she acknowledged that it had been the most enjoyable encounter she had experienced. Never before had she met a man's gaze and seen in it the look of an equal. She thought of the confidence with which he had delivered the parting remark about visiting her chamber. There was nothing of the courtier in his character; he did not fawn. If he were to desire something of her, she was certain that he would never beg for it.

She shrank from acknowledging the place he now occupied in her thoughts. To think of him was thrilling, but it also made her afraid. For all her proud talk, Arabella understood well that the situation in which she found herself was fraught with uncertainty. She was a Roman Catholic. Against that, she was beautiful and she was rich—but she knew she was not rich enough for her wealth or beauty to surmount every obstacle that lay before her. For two years she had been considered the prize most worth the winning in

London, but now Arabella could think only of how greatly she longed to be won by Lord Petre. The longing threatened to overwhelm her, and she knew that she must resist it. She could not allow herself to be overcome by passion—least of all for a man who, she suspected, was governed by complex, contradictory emotions of his own.

On the Tuesday night of the masquerade ball, she sat at her window looking out to the street below. It had been dark for many hours, and the lamps that had lighted up the pavements and shopfronts earlier in the evening were now burning lower. By the time she left, they would almost have guttered. Outside the front door of their house, James prepared the carriage for her, and an under-footman handed him the fur blanket that the family took out in the coach on winter nights. Her window gave a little rattle in the wind, reminding her that she must have Betty fit it more tightly in the jamb. It was getting late, and she turned back to her room to ring the bell.

As she did so, she caught a glimpse of her face reflected in the clear light of the dressing mirror. The glance was unselfconscious, and she looked back at herself with a start, surprised by her beauty, as though for a moment it were not her own face upon which she gazed. But she became conscious again, and began to take note of those personal arrangements that made her appear so charming. She was wearing only a smock, having lately removed her gown from the day. The pins in her hair, which had been snipping uncomfortably at her scalp, had been pulled out, and her lightly disarranged curls fell down naturally upon her shoulders. Her only adornment, aside from the pearls that hung from her ears, was a single beauty patch on her cheek.

She was thinking that this was exactly the attitude in which she would like Lord Petre to see her, when Betty walked into the room carrying Arabella's costume for the evening. She was to be dressed as a swan. A grey gown had been made for the occasion, embroidered with a thousand feathers of luminous white, and a head-dress fashioned into a hood of down, smooth as a swan's neck, with a little turret of grey feathers behind the crown. Her mask, in the Venetian style, was lacquered in jet black and egg-yolk yellow to suggest a swan's beak.

When she had chosen the costume she had wanted to seem imperious, magnificent. But something in her had changed, and now she looked at the dress uncertainly. It was too artful a disguise for her mood this evening. She would appear cold and proud in such unsullied plumage; too pristine for heady pleasure. What she wanted was a costume that might capture the same nice confusion, the disarray that had taken her by such delightful surprise when she caught a glimpse of her face in the glass.

Arabella did not permit herself to be completely honest about the change of attire. At first she reflected that the ballroom would be too warm for feathers, and that she would not be able to dance. She also reasoned that she did not wish to so outshine her cousins Teresa and Martha, for whom it was the first ball of the season. At last she decided that the costume would be too lavish for a public masque, and it would be better to save the dress until she could make a greater show at a private ball. But the consideration that Lord Petre would surely be there, and that in a different costume she would be more likely to catch his eye, was one that Arabella did not articulate to herself. She could not admit the concession.

She sat down to her toilette table, which was still scattered with the girlish clutter of her morning's labours. Little perfume jars with silver tops; an inlaid box lined richly in silk. Jewels and trinkets from India and the Far East, which glistened in reflected candle-light. In front of her mirror was a nosegay of the earliest spring flowers, bought that morning at Covent Garden and delivered to the house by an admirer. There were cases of hairpins, a new box of powder, and a fur tippet, thrown down upon the table as she rushed in before teatime. But when she looked at herself again she saw, in place of unstudied beauty, a glimmer of uncertainty. It came as a shock, and she pulled herself up. She was determined that the world must not see Miss Fermor insecure.

She turned to Betty and said, "I have decided to wear the costume that was made for Lady Seaforth's ball earlier in the season. I shall go as the goddess Diana—with a hunting bow to carry upon my arm. My father keeps one in the stables. We shall put up my hair so that it looks rustic; let us have some clean straw sent up to weave through my plaits."

Betty, who had spent three hours that morning steaming the down upon the swan outfit into a state of perfect smoothness, was somewhat put out by the change of plan.

"But you got the swan made just for tonight!" she protested. "Your mother will be wild with you. There'll be trouble in this house for weeks."

"I can hardly explain it even to myself, Betty," Arabella replied haughtily, refusing her servant's gaze. "But the swan is not for tonight. I will wear it to another ball later in the season, and my mother will be perfectly easy with the change. I shall tell her myself." Her mother would not care, she knew. She took almost no interest in her daughter's arrangements.

"I daresay you're hoping to see some gentleman at this ball, madam, whom you fancy will like you better as a goddess," Betty said.

Arabella did not reply.

Her maid laughed, and pulled roughly at Arabella's locks until she protested, "Pray brush more gently, Betty. I shall have no hair at all if you go on as you are!"

On the Charing Cross Road, at ten o'clock that evening, the way was impassable for the jam of coaches, chairs, and cabs that crowded the cobbles outside the assembly rooms. Arabella had invited Teresa and Martha to ride with her in the carriage, thinking that it would be best to arrive in a party of people. It was a novelty for Teresa and Martha to be out at night without their mother or aunt to chaperon them; Arabella, long accustomed to being without her parents, thought nothing of it. They were attended on horseback by a distant cousin of Arabella's, Sir George Brown, a rotund, blustering individual, whose person was coated this evening, as on all public occasions, in a fine pellicule of snuff.

"Thank heavens I am not a swan, or my feathers would become ruffled by the crowd," Arabella said as she stepped upon the cobbles.

"Deuced feathery bird, the swan," Sir George observed with a tap upon the lid of his snuffbox. Arabella ignored him.

But Martha turned to Sir George with a kind smile and said, "Oh yes! Swans have such a lot of—of feathers."

Teresa looked about, overcome for a moment by the splendour

of the scene. "Look at the dancing bear, getting down from his coach and six!" she exclaimed.

"Sir Paul Methuen, beyond a doubt!" Arabella supplied quickly.

A group of cinder wenches and pastry cooks ran by, laughing loudly, on their way to meet a monk and a friar.

"Will you not catch a chill dressed as a shepherdess, Miss Fermor?" Sir George asked.

"I am not a shepherdess," Arabella replied. "I am Diana, goddess of the hunt. See my bow."

The girls stood in a tight little group. Teresa and Martha looked instinctively to Arabella for guidance, though Teresa tried to appear unconcerned by glancing around at the other arriving guests, as if expecting at any moment to see somebody she knew.

After a short pause, Arabella pointed to the entrance of the assembly rooms. "Is not that fellow over there your friend Mr. Pope, Teresa? He is wearing a ruff."

Teresa and Martha looked up together. Alexander stood with his masquerade ticket in one hand, talking to Jervas, who was dressed as a Roman senator. Martha began walking towards them.

Seeing that Teresa did not follow her, she turned back, and said, "How unlike himself he looks! I wonder who he is supposed to be?" When Teresa made no answer, Martha added, "I shall ask him myself!"

But Teresa said, "Better not to approach him, Patty. I do not think it is done to recognize one's friends at these affairs."

Martha guessed that the prospect of an evening with Arabella made her sister anxious, but she had no intention of slighting Alexander for the sake of Teresa's vanity. "But we have hardly seen Alexander for three weeks, except to borrow his little broadsword," she said.

As Martha rushed forward, Arabella looked at Teresa, expecting her to follow. But Teresa remained where she was. "You are right about Mr. Pope, after all, Bell," she said. "He looks uncommonly silly. Thank heavens we shall be masked, so I need not acknowledge him."

Arabella gave her a sharp look by way of reply, but they walked towards the staircase arm in arm.

Alexander broke into a smile as soon as he saw Martha, and stretched out both of his hands across the crowd.

"Patty!" he exclaimed. "Your costume—it is delightful. You must put your mask on, however. I am not supposed to know you."

"Which character does your costume represent, Alexander?" she asked.

"I am astonished that you do not recognize my disguise," he answered with a cheerful air. "I am the celebrated poet Alexander Pope, arrived in London without a masquerade costume. The ruff is borrowed from Jervas. An excellent touch, do you not think?"

Martha noticed that his eyes left her face as he spoke. He pulled himself up straight and adjusted his coat, and she guessed that he had seen Teresa.

At that moment Jervas came up behind him. "You must make that joke as often as you can now, Pope, for if your poems ever do become celebrated, you will have to think of something new to jest about." Alexander was about to reply when he saw that Jervas was looking at Martha.

"I lament that we are supposed to be *incognito*," Jervas said, "for I cannot ask you to introduce me to your friend here. This is the prettiest young lord I have beheld, and I long to make his acquaintance. I should warn him that there will be a Roman senator at this gathering, intending to flirt unabashedly."

To Alexander's surprise, Martha blushed, looking shyly at them both.

"I believe that I shall have wit and virtue to defend myself against any such attack," she replied with a little smile. "But if those should fail, I shall resort to my sword, which was lent to me by a very dear friend." She began to tie on her mask.

Alexander put his hand on Jervas's shoulder and turned him towards the doorway. As he passed into the room behind his friend, Alexander glanced back to look at Martha again. But she had disappeared in the crowd.

While Martha was speaking to Alexander, Arabella was carrying on an exchange of a different kind. Near where she was standing, a man dashed up the steps pulling on the head-dress of an Ottoman prince. Arabella recognized him instantly as Lord Petre, and though she had been in the act of putting on her own mask, she held off for a little longer. She watched as Lord Petre greeted a friend then turned back to survey the crowd. As he did so, Arabella thought that he caught sight of her. He did not meet her eye, and she did not acknowledge him, but, satisfied that he knew her costume, she covered her face. A moment later Lord Petre did the same, and disappeared into the swell of revellers.

After the men had gone in, Martha returned to Arabella and her sister. "How strange that so many women have come to the ball alone," she observed. "Look at that elegant woman dressed like a Spaniard, and yet without a partner."

Teresa had not noticed—she, too, had been preoccupied by the sight of Lord Petre. The Ottoman head-dress made him look even more distinguished than did his ordinary suit and waistcoat. She had seen him looking into the crowd, and she believed that he had tried to catch her eye. He *had* been impressed by meeting Miss Blount of Mapledurham—she had thought as much. She turned to Martha with an assured expression.

"That is probably a woman of the town, Patty, come in the hope of procuring a mate," she explained. "And in any case, it is accepted for women to arrive at the masquerade alone. Once inside, friends separate, and must give themselves up to the conversation of anybody who addresses them. That is the fun of it. There are rooms to which parties may retire if they wish, and show their faces by consent."

At this moment they were pushed by the force of the crowd through the doors and into the ballroom.

It would have been impossible to prepare for the furnace blast of noise and brightness that hit them. Hundreds of wax candles—a bright dazzle of light—sparkling jewels—sumptuous masks—brilliant smiles . . . but no faces. A roar of talk, rolling across the room upon tides of music; two orchestras on raised platforms at either end. Head-dresses rose from the crowd like birds: peacock's feathers and ostrich plumes. Powdered wigs and towers of hair like confectionery; glittering diamonds. There was a quick clicking of heels upon the boards, a swish of petticoats, a clack of fans flounced—heat, light, sound in billows. Venetians, Turks, Spaniards. Chimney sweeps, cinder wenches, muffin sellers, butchers' boys, coachmen. Admirals, judges, courtiers, and kings. An immense confusion of strangers, disguised in strangers' clothes. And scattered everywhere among them, the black-and-white-clad figures of the dominoes, their heads and faces covered entirely in voluminous silk hoods.

As soon as she entered the room, Arabella saw that she was not the only figure present from classical antiquity. She was greeted by a handsome and attentive gentleman dressed as Phoebus, who she could see was an old acquaintance, Charles Luxton. Luxton immediately invited Arabella to dance, and she accepted, knowing that her costume was likely to show to best advantage in animated motion. Arabella had known Charles Luxton for several years, and she encouraged his public attentions for the sake of his personal attractions, which were well suited to her own. She knew, however, that he would inherit only a small estate in an undistinguished part of the country, and that his bride would therefore be a lady of much less considerable fortune, and somewhat less exalted appearance, than herself.

Shortly after the dance with Mr. Luxton had come to an end, Lord Petre approached Arabella. She became aware of her every movement, and turned her head towards him in an arch gesture, at once invitation and dismissal.

He addressed her with a bow. "Oh, how that glittering taketh me!" he declared.

Arabella was pleased with the compliment. She shivered with excitement, but replied in measured tones, "The remark is not your own, sir. You are quoting Robert Herrick, but you thought I would not know it."

Lord Petre raised his eyebrows. "I hardly knew Herrick's lines myself, until I saw you attired like this," he replied. "At least I did not understand them. But since I have seen you, I can think of nothing else: 'Then, then methinks how sweetly flows / That liquefaction of her clothes.'"

Though she had heard the lines before, Arabella had never liked them so well as she did now. But she turned the subject.

"Since you are from the Ottoman world, you cannot be expected to guess which of the Roman goddesses I represent," she said.

"You, a goddess? I had taken you for a siren."

"Do you not see the bow I carry? I am Diana, queen of the hunt, goddess of chastity."

"I rather thought you had stolen the bow from that Cupid standing by the buffet," Petre replied. "He looks very much in need of one, and as though he will not otherwise manage to pierce a heart all night. Perhaps you will offer him yours, for you surely require no instrument to bring your game to ground." He looked handsome as he spoke, tall and powerful, but she was determined not to acknowledge it.

"It is my experience that game hath a wonderful way of fleeing, just as it appears to have been caught," she answered. She was testing him, she knew, but what it was that she wanted him to say, she could not exactly tell.

"You have a great knowledge of the sport, madam."

"Naturally. So do you, I imagine."

"I know its art very well, but I have seldom seen an object that I thought would be worth the pursuit," he said.

"And yet it is held that the greatest pleasure is to be derived from the chase itself, not from the value of the spoils," was her reply. "Perhaps you should attempt it, as a matter of investigation."

"I believe that I shall. And when I do, madam, be assured that I shall keep this conversation in my mind."

With another bow he was gone. Arabella was disappointed that he had not asked her to dance, and in her moment of discontent she plucked unthinkingly at the string on her bow so that it twanged. Lord Petre heard it above the noise of the room, and looked back at her with a playful smile. He was toying with her, and yet it plainly showed that he, too, had moved away with reluctance. Her spirits rising again, Arabella made her way into the crowd.

Alexander, meanwhile, was walking around the room with Jervas, who had taken a glass of wine and a slice of cake for each of them, and was now observing the comings and goings with his accustomed ease.

"That nymph would do a good deal better if she were not speaking in the manner of pit bawdy," he said. "And behold that Quaker against the buffet, drinking off two bottles of wine at once. Maskers should stay a little closer to their characters, at least until midnight."

They were overheard by a man in the suit of a court jester, somewhat overstuffed as to contents, who bore more than a passing resemblance to Richard Steele.

"I would agree with you, sir, had I not lately given my heart to a lady who danced so gracefully that I took her for a countess," Steele said. "But a few minutes later I observed her at the supper tables, lodging edibles in her bosom and pocket and then sneaking furtively away through a side door. I suspect that my 'fine lady' lives very close to Covent Garden, and that she entered the masquerade in order to smuggle out a week's worth of cold suppers."

Jervas laughed and replied to Steele, but Alexander's attention was caught by a young pageboy walking nearby, whom he recognized as Teresa. How lovely she looked in her boy's suit. She was talking to a Turkish gentleman—Lord Petre! He paused. He was close enough to the pair to hear them speak, but he was fairly sure that Teresa had not seen him.

"Your disguise becomes you well, madam," Lord Petre was saying. "I hope you shall profit by it,"

"I have profited already, sir," Teresa replied in an attempt at the playful style, but with a little too much deference. Alexander felt a pang for her.

Lord Petre replied lightly. "Your choice is capital," he said. "I have a great admiration for *Twelfth Night*." He thought for a moment, and then declaimed, "If music be the food of love, play on / Give me excess of it, that, surfeiting, / The appetite may sicken, and so die."

"You are not inclined to love, sir?" Teresa asked.

"I care not for it. When the hart is being hunted, it seldom wishes to be snared."

All of a sudden, Alexander noticed that he was not the only party listening to Lord Petre's conversation with Miss Blount. A person in a domino costume had also stopped near the pair, just as Teresa said, "I fear that the man in black robes has overheard us. Do you know him?"

Lord Petre turned around to look at the domino. "Oh, that is no gentleman," he said with a smile. "Observe the ribbons upon the slippers—are they not distinct? Indeed, I hazard a guess that she is

Charlotte Bromleigh, Lord Castlecomber's wife. I have seen her wear them before."

Alexander turned away, fearing that Teresa would notice him standing there. So Lord Petre was to be Teresa's object in town! She would undoubtedly be disappointed in her hopes, he reflected bitterly—but then almost immediately he felt a sinking in his heart. Lord Petre had begun the conversation. And how eagerly Teresa had pursued it. Alexander had never seen her so willing to please, nor so flattered by a man's attention.

But not five minutes later, Alexander was startled to see Lord Petre standing alongside the woman dressed in domino robes. The pair were just beyond the doorway of the main assembly space, and the nature of their exchange was easy to guess, for they leaned close together as intimates. But when the black-clad figure walked back into the main gathering, Alexander saw that the shoes had no ribbons on them. It was not Charlotte Bromleigh at all. Lord Petre had been meeting a man! Alexander stared, but the figure soon disappeared into the crowd.

He tried to find him again, but it was too late. The ball guests surged around in a rough swell of movement. As he watched, Alexander saw for the first time that many of them were dressed in the robes of the Catholic Church. He noted that several were attired in obvious mockery of their characters: monks holding bottles of wine; a priest strolling about with a gaudily dressed whore on his arm. But others could easily pass for real clerics. As he recalled the murdered masquerade guest in Shoreditch, he looked apprehensively around at the whirl of faces, their expressions hidden by the blank masks.

Near where Alexander was standing, Arabella had come to the end of a minuet with the dancing bear who had alighted earlier from a coach-and-six. Unbeknownst to her, she was being watched by one of the many dominoes, whose face was obscured by the dark folds of his costume.

Suddenly Arabella sensed the figure behind her, and she wheeled around. Seeing the faceless hood looming above, she gasped.

"I do not know you!" she cried out. "You frightened me!"

For a moment the domino said nothing, but then he pulled off his hood and mask. It was James Douglass.

"Oh!" Arabella exclaimed. "Lord Petre's friend from the Exchange."

"Indeed, Madam," Douglass answered with a bow. "I overheard you speaking just now on the subject of disguise." Arabella looked at him closely, waiting for him to continue. Something about him chilled her, but she was intrigued, longing for what he might tell her of his puzzling relationship with Lord Petre.

"A woman masked is like a covered dish," Douglass said. "She gives a man curiosity and appetite, when, likely as not, uncovered she would turn his stomach."

Arabella took a step backward. What a cruel thing to say. "You have little regard for woman, sir," she answered.

"On the contrary, I consider woman to be of inestimable value," Douglass replied, and his eyes wrinkled into a provoking smile.

Arabella half wished that he would go. But she could not resist her urge to hear more of the baron. "Yet you value only those parts of a person that strike the eye," she insisted, determined not to let Douglass disconcert her.

"That is precisely what value *is*, madam," Douglass answered. "The value of gold is no more than the price that can be obtained for it. So it is with women."

Arabella tried to laugh, and decided to make one final attempt. "I cannot think that you would say the same of men," she said. "Surely you do not judge your friends, at least, by their manner alone. You must want to penetrate *their* deeper characters."

"Deep characters do not interest me," Douglass answered, and he looked at Arabella closely. "A man is defined only by his actions."

"But very often people disguise their true motives and real intentions," Arabella replied. She looked around, taken aback by his sudden seriousness, and wanting to escape Douglass's presence.

But he continued to look at her as though he meant that she should listen carefully. "You are mistaken, madam," Douglass said. "When a man really has something to hide, he will not be so foolish as to appear disguised. Woman are vain, and fancy that they can penetrate men's secrets by intuition alone. But they are always mistaken."

"Nonsense!" Arabella cried, stepping away from him. "A penetrating woman will perfectly understand a man's real character."

Douglass shrugged, nodding towards a group of dancers who were standing before them. Lord Petre was among them, dancing with a woman dressed magnificently in the costume of a Venetian noble. Arabella turned away so that Douglass could not see her face, determined that he would not perceive her disappointment.

Alexander, meanwhile, was still thinking about Lord Petre's encounter with the stranger when Jervas joined him. He stood expectantly, waiting for Alexander to speak. Alexander realized that his disappearance from the conversation with Jervas and Steele must have seemed very abrupt.

"Glad to meet you again, Jervas," he said. And, seeing the Ottoman come past with his dancing partner, he asked, "Who is that lady dancing with Lord Petre? She has a very pretty style."

"If I were to hazard a guess, I would say she is Lady Mary Pierrepont," Jervas answered. "I see a gentleman named Edward Wortley standing to one side watching them, looking as jealous as Othello. He's been trying to marry her for years, but apparently her father won't budge on the settlement."

"Oh—so that is Mary Pierrepont!" said Alexander. "She is as beautiful as your painting would have her."

"Quickest wit, sharpest tongue, and biggest flirt in London," Jervas answered with a laugh.

"Lady Mary Pierrepont is permitted to take liberties that other women are forbidden," said Alexander. "She is a Protestant, and the daughter of an earl."

"Well, she does take liberties, of that you can be sure. I heard Wortley say that she knows every man of fashion in London—some of them far too well."

Alexander wanted to ask more, but his attention was claimed by a delightful new sight. Among the group of dancers in the room were Martha and Teresa, who faced each other, performing the parts of gentlemen in the gavotte that was presently being played. Each was evidently delighted by the novelty of appearing in men's attire. Teresa, as was to be expected, danced rather better than Martha; she was really quite adept in fitting a gentleman's steps to her own spirited gait. Martha was struggling to move around the obstacle of her little broadsword, and each time she turned or bobbed, she became caught in the ribbons of the sword knot. It banged against her repeatedly, making her seem clumsy and awkward in her step, like an adolescent boy learning to dance for the first time.

But absorbed in the enjoyment of the dance itself, she was untouched by a consciousness of being watched; she had the happy look of a girl whose pleasures are still unworldly. The sight struck Alexander so forcefully that it threatened to bring tears of affection to his eyes, but he was forced to collect himself, for the dance was over, the sisters bowed to one another, and Martha dashed up to where Alexander was standing. Teresa was on the point of walking over to them as well, and he felt a rush of anticipation, but she was approached by the man who had just revealed himself to be James Douglass. She stopped to speak to him.

As it was now after midnight, Alexander took off his mask, and Martha did the same.

"How well you and Teresa looked when you were dancing, Patty," he said.

She thanked him. "We are both enlivened by being in town again, though I am sure that Teresa often considers its diversions to be wasted upon me."

"Ah, but you may not return to the country, for I depend on you to praise my jokes," said Alexander.

Martha smiled, and said, "I know that you saw Mr. Tonson a few days ago. Did he like your new verses?"

"Not at all, I am afraid to say," Alexander answered. "But he praised my *Essay on Criticism*."

"Oh! My congratulations, Alexander," Martha exclaimed. "I knew that it would be admired."

They were interrupted by Teresa, and Alexander looked at her with a serious expression. "You are in uncommonly lively spirits tonight," he said.

"Do you mean to compliment me, Alexander?" Teresa asked lightly. "You have a habit of giving praise that is so very weak that I would almost be relieved if you were to come forward and damn me directly."

"A nice conceit. I shall remember it. Miss Blount does not care to be damned with faint praise."

As the pair laughed together, Martha looked left out.

Teresa, oblivious of her sister's feelings, exclaimed, "What a diverting evening this has been. The company is excellent—everybody so happy. I have had more pleasure from one outing in London than from months together in the country."

"That is because the pleasures of the town are new to you," said Alexander, again in a stern tone of voice.

"I do not agree with you, Alexander," she said. "Arabella is enjoying herself excessively, and she is quite used to being in London."

"Miss Arabella Fermor would not be seen with a long face if she were passing the most disagreeable three hours of her life," Alexander replied.

Jervas joined their conversation. "Am I to assume that you have now made Miss Arabella Fermor's acquaintance?" he asked.

"I have not met Miss Fermor, but I have looked upon her—which must supply the happiest portion of claiming her as a friend," Alexander answered.

"Did I not tell you that she was the most beautiful creature alive?" Jervas exclaimed, forgetting in his enthusiasm that the Miss Blounts were standing by. "She is radiant as the sun."

"You have stumbled upon an excellent comparison, Jervas," Alexander said, still feeling censorious, much disappointed that Teresa showed little interest in him. "There is a sameness about Miss Fermor's beauty that does indeed resemble the sun's. Her smiles are without variety; she shines upon all alike."

"You are not quite correct, Pope, for I fancy that she shines rather more brightly upon my Lord Petre than any other person," replied Jervas, who had caught sight of them speaking earlier in the evening.

"If that is so," Alexander answered, "it is because Lord Petre is foolish enough to venture forth when the lady's beams are at their brightest. Other men would stay indoors, for fear of a heat stroke."

Chapter Six

"When to Mischief mortals bend their Will . . ."

As it happened, Lord Petre was feeling out of sorts. He was tired of smiling and talking to women whose faces he could not see. He had not minded dancing with Lady Mary, who was very handsome, and whose company was diverting. But though he had known her for many years, he had never felt a serious attraction—just as well, since her family were Protestants and Whigs, and his were Catholic Tories. She was the cleverest woman of his acquaintance, and since Lord Petre was a clever man himself, this might have proved a powerful allure. Yet he did not share some men's taste for intellectual women, however pretty they might be. There was too much that was restless about Mary Pierrepont's mind; there was a desire for constant provocation that he found tiring.

These were idle reflections, an attempt to tear his mind away from its new preoccupation, Arabella Fermor. He was unnerved by how completely she had captivated him. He replayed their moments together—the glittering, loose gown she wore; the look of absorbed concentration as she had tied her mask; that talk of harts and hunting; her gorgeous smile.

He had known her since she was a child, and even then it had been generally acknowledged that she would be beautiful. But Petre had met beautiful girls before. The attraction that he felt for Arabella made him feel physically hungry. Standing beside her, he had been barely able to suppress an urgent, overwhelming desire to take hold of her lovely form and tear at it like an animal. He had experienced nothing quite like it until now. He felt angry and excited; he felt a sort of desperation. And yet he had no choice but to stand and make the gallant small talk that was expected of him, wrestling his mind away from the overpowering impulse to take her in his arms.

He left the ballroom and stood instead at the card tables, mechanically watching the play as it was carried on. In truth he saw nothing. His mind's eye was entirely absorbed by recalling Arabella's form and figure; the tip of her tongue touching upon her teeth as she spoke; the hair disordered about her face: innocent as a child's, yet knowingly, artfully caught up. Of course it was impossible to do so, but how he wanted to take hold of that lithe, warm, breathing frame and crush it beneath him.

He must attend to the gathering. There were friends here; there were his family's acquaintance; he had to appear himself. There should be nothing odd, nothing remarkable about his conduct, particularly when the real business of his evening was the meeting he had arranged with Douglass later on. He felt in his pocket; the banknotes were there.

But already he was conscious that Sir George Brown was beside him, heavy and dull, though still a friend to whom he owed consideration. Sir George leaned over the card table, breathing so heavily upon the head of a player that he was actually causing the hairs of his wig to move. Lord Petre would have laughed, but he remembered suddenly that Sir George was Arabella's cousin, and experienced a new stirring of longing and passion.

He forced himself to speak. "How do you do?" he asked, and Sir George sprang to a standing position, nearly knocking the player's wig off altogether.

"Tremendous, tremendous," Sir George blustered in his usual style, the light powder of snuff stirring gently upon his person as he spoke. "Never better, my dear fellow. My word, how smart your turban is. Perhaps I should have done something of the same with my costume. But look, it is my friend Dicconson—over there—hello, sir; hello, William!"

Dicconson was another Catholic acquaintance, lately married to a baronet's daughter. He had been to stay at Ingatestone while Lord Petre's father was alive, but Lord Petre had always disliked him. Dicconson submitted reluctantly to Sir George's greeting at last, and walked across to where they were standing.

"My congratulations upon your marriage," Sir George said affably. "Lady Margaret is a charming woman."

Dicconson gave an indifferent shrug. "We were married last

month," he acknowledged. "But you probably heard that she tried to get out of it. She told her father that I drank too much. When he put it to me, I looked at him and said, 'Sir; your daughter whores too much, but I do not object.' He laughed of course—knew it was true as well as I did—and he gave me another thousand. So it all went off without any more nonsense. Excellent arrangement upon the whole."

Dicconson had made no attempt to greet Lord Petre on joining the group, but now he swung around and demanded, in accusatory tones, "When do *you* choose a wife, my lord? There are plenty of girls about, and some of them rich."

Lord Petre made no reply, but Dicconson went on, undeterred. "My cousin, for example, Miss Catherine Walmesley—I am her guardian, you know. Her parents died last year, and there are no other children in the family. She must be about fifteen, I suppose. Pious as the Madonna, and if you looked at her too closely you'd be sick—but she's worth fifty thousand pounds. Dunkenhalgh, the Nottinghamshire seat, is so damn dark you'd never see her anyway. You should marry her."

"At present I have no thoughts of marriage," Lord Petre said, turning away from him and walking out of the room. Sir George hurried along at his side, the lapels of his coat flapping around the stout barrel of his stomach. With an irony that he knew would be lost upon his companion, Lord Petre observed, "Charming family, the Dicconsons. I like the father, particularly."

Sir George agreed.

As they walked back to the supper room they passed by a series of small chambers off the main ballroom. The door to one of these was wide open, and Sir George and Lord Petre glanced in as they went by. A pair of revellers was fornicating upon a sofa, their masks, shoes, and stockings tossed across the floor to the doorway. The woman's skirts billowed around her waist as her lover pressed down upon her in a liquorous embrace; the couple moaned and panted without the slightest consciousness that people might be observing them. The scene was one of joyful excess. As Lord Petre continued walking, the tableau was fixed in his mind: a confusion of white thighs, tangled clothing, and the transported smiles of pleasure. It effected a piercing return of the emotions he had felt earlier, though now with the complicating additional sensation of self-disgust.

The supper room was nearly full. On the far side, a little knot of men was standing in a tightly packed formation around a person whom Lord Petre could not see, but he guessed from the men's attitudes that she must be female—and that they admired her. Curious, he moved closer to see who she was.

As soon as he did so, he smiled. She was a tall woman, with hair dark and sheer as a horse's flank, and high, lean cheekbones that gave her whole bearing a proud, equine reserve. She was listening to the men with a detached, even a bored expression, but she did not fidget. Though she wore a silk domino gown, she had turned down the bahoo, leaving her head bare, and her jawline and shoulders were framed by the luminous black of the fabric. In one hand she carried her mask.

Lord Petre stepped forward so that he would be directly in her line of vision, just beyond the circle of gentlemen. She did not see him immediately, for her companions pressed forward eagerly, their voices pealing out in clear boyish notes. After a moment, however, her glance lifted, and she met Lord Petre's gaze. She inclined her head incrementally, in the barest sign of acknowledgement, her nostrils slightly flared in place of a smile. And then, deliberately, with no alteration in her manner, she stepped through the barricade of her admirers, scattering them like pheasants. Ignoring their dismayed cries, she moved forward in her inky robes, the ribbons on her slippers catching the light. Lord Petre bowed to her.

"My Lady Castlecomber," he said.

"My Lord Petre."

As she spoke, he noticed Arabella enter the room. She saw Lord Petre instantly, and stood stock-still in the doorway, alert as a firework.

But he continued to talk to his new companion. "How does your husband, my Lord Castlecomber?" he asked.

Lady Castlecomber put up a hand to lift the folds of her hood away from her graceful neck, and said, "My husband is in Ireland."

He raised his brows, and repeated, "In Ireland?"

She returned his look with a smile, and said evenly, "Yes, he is abroad for some time."

As they talked, he could feel Arabella's eyes on them; it was as though she were standing close enough for him to feel her breath, and he felt himself blaze up like tinder at the thought of it. The sensation made him reckless with desire, and he asked, "Does my Lady Castlecomber receive visitors while he is away?"

"Only those visitors whom she likes," she replied, in a low voice. Lord Petre took a step closer to her, and put out his hand to touch the little indentation made by the top of her wrist bone, brushing along her hand with the back of his own. She looked down, watching the progress of his fingers.

"Are you going to pay me a visit, Lord Petre?" she asked.

"If you will let me," he replied. She smiled at him again, and he bowed and moved away, taking care not to look at Arabella. He marvelled that, wanting her as violently as he did, something had moved him nonetheless to arrange this meeting with Charlotte.

They had been bedfellows on and off for years, ever since Charlotte had married, and he had met her with her husband at an assembly in town. They were not lovers in the sentimental sense; he doubted that Charlotte had ever been in love in her life. She was not that kind of girl, which was exactly what he liked about her. She fucked him as she did everything else—for love of the moment, with perfect execution and abandon. Lord Petre took a glass of wine from the buffet and drained it in one swift movement, putting it down with too much force.

Arabella, meanwhile, made herself sit down beside Sir George. She turned and smiled at him, hoping that he would say something that would allow her to laugh and incline her head to where Lord Petre was standing. At the very least she hoped that he would look at her with admiration—to confirm to anyone who happened to be watching that Arabella Fermor was irresistible, even to the ponderous Sir George Brown. But, to her dismay, Lord Petre turned abruptly away from the supper buffet, and walked out of the room.

She had been utterly discomposed to find him flirting with Charlotte Bromleigh—Lady Castlecomber now, Arabella reminded herself. She had known Charlotte, or known of her, all her life. Men had always found her handsome, though in Arabella's opinion she looked like a horse. But Lord Petre had actually touched her hand, when he had never attempted to touch Arabella's own. He had not even asked her to dance.

Alexander noticed Arabella's inattention, and guessed its cause. Of all the observations that he had made during the course of the evening, this one interested him the most. If Arabella Fermor had set out to conquer Lord Petre's heart, he reflected, she was not likely to require the support of auxiliary troops, least of all her pretty young cousin.

Just as he thought of her, Teresa entered the room on Douglass's arm, tripping unevenly along and gazing up at him flirtatiously. They sat down together and from the corner of his eye Alexander could see the quick, animated movements of her hands and face. Douglass looked at her as though she were a tempting delicacy—a morsel that he craved, even though he suspected it would not agree with him. On Alexander's other side, Martha was talking to Jervas. Her face was still flushed from dancing, and her hair had started to tumble down around her neck. Every few minutes Jervas picked up a bottle of wine from the table, splashed some of the liquid into his own glass, and then held it up to Martha with an enquiring look. Each time Martha accepted another drink, she glanced unconsciously towards Alexander. He stood up impatiently.

But suddenly his attention was arrested by James Douglass, who sprang to his feet, gave a hurried half-bow, mumbled good night, and rushed from the room.

Teresa was smoothing the front of her coat, her head bent to hide her face, which had gone white. Her fingers worked fretfully at a knot in the ribbon of her mask.

Alexander turned to Martha and Jervas, and said loudly, "Mr. Douglass was certainly in a great hurry to be gone."

Teresa, hurt and self-conscious, heard the note of triumph in Alexander's voice, and said, "That is his manner. He is often like it." She was recalling the day at the Exchange when he had disappeared from the conversation with Lord Petre.

Alexander was about to reply, when a new idea came to him. He scanned the room, looking for Lord Petre, but could not see him. He was no longer speaking to Charlotte Castlecomber, who was now standing at the buffet with the dancing bear. Nor was he with

Arabella. No—he was gone, gone just ahead of Douglass. Alexander walked away as abruptly as Douglass had done, and though Jervas looked towards him enquiringly, Alexander avoided his eyes.

He walked through the ballroom, now empty and cavernous. Only one orchestra was playing, its notes echoing desultory and wooden against the walls. The room was dimly lit by half-candles that had not yet burned out, but he was fairly sure that Lord Petre was not there. Four or five hooded dominoes could be seen in the gloom, long and dark like shadows.

He hurried down the stairs of the assembly rooms, out to where the carriages and coachmen were waiting. Again no sign of the Turk. Though he had no idea what he expected to see, a vague fear came upon him. Perhaps Douglass had taken Petre unawares, and struck him down in the dark. What if Douglass were to find Alexander too? For a second he hesitated, thinking of his father's warnings. But curiosity propelled him. He rounded the side of the building, where only a few carriages were left in the deep night shadows, abandoned by their coachmen. The bored horses stamped occasionally and nudged at their nosebags, blowing their vaporous breath into the morning air. But nobody was about, and he turned to walk back inside. The men had got away.

As he did so, something flashed in the corner of his eye. He swung about: a lantern had been put out, and he realized that somebody was opening a carriage door from the inside. Alexander stood stock-still. He knew that his breathing must be deafening; he was certain that he could be seen and heard in spite of the darkness. A long moment passed. Then two figures stepped out, masked but unmistakable: the sinister folds of the domino and the turban of the Turk's head-dress. Alexander shuddered, and swayed slightly to keep his balance. He was sure that they would find him.

But the night was very dark. He sensed that the men were walking away from each other; he could hear them moving in separate directions, Lord Petre towards the assembly rooms and Douglass down a narrow street. Alexander swallowed, his legs weak underneath him. He waited a minute, and another one, his breath quick and shallow over the drumming of his chest. But the alleyway was silent. He edged forward to the courtyard again.

Suddenly he saw the Turkish head-dress directly in front of him. He stopped short, but a moment later he heard Lord Petre talking to his footman, giving directions for another stop in the carriage. Alexander slipped away out of sight behind the wheels of the coach, and up the stairs of the building.

As he drove away from the masquerade, Lord Petre could think only of the meeting he had just had with Douglass. It had shaken him, and excited him, more than he had expected.

"I thank you, my lord," Douglass had said as he took the proffered banknotes. "We are just in time—I meet our agent tonight."

"There was some trouble in obtaining them," Petre had replied.

Douglass hesitated. "Are they all here?" he asked.

"I believe so."

"When the King is on the throne, you will know that you have played your part, my lord," he said. "Few men will be able to claim as much."

"Few men have the chance," Petre answered. "Many have given their lives to this cause. I have given but a few hundred pounds."

"If our rebellion is to succeed, there are grave times ahead," said Douglass.

"Nothing to what my fellow Catholics have already endured," Petre replied. "You rebel in the name of the Stuarts, Douglass; I in the name of the Catholic martyrs. We have suffered for two hundred years." He paused, and then asked, "Was it an agent that you met at the Exchange the other day?"

For a moment Douglass looked puzzled. Then his face cleared, and he answered, "That man's name is Dupont, a friend. He deals in a commodity that is as precious as ebony, and of a good deal more use to most Englishmen."

Lord Petre was confused. What could Douglass be talking about? But then he understood. "I suppose you mean that he is a slave trader," he replied. "But what has he to do with our enterprise? What business do we have with human traffic, or with a man who deals in it?" he demanded.

"I am afraid that in one respect, my lord, our business resembles Dupont's very exactly," Douglass said. "Like him, we are willing to pay a great price for the safe delivery of our human cargo." They were both silent a moment.

"Are you afraid to continue?" Douglass asked.

"Certainly not," Lord Petre answered.

"I am relieved," replied Douglass, "for the part you play in this drama is destined to be greater, and considerably more heroic, than that of Dupont or any other party. You are to be our liaison in the court."

Lord Petre laughed mirthlessly. "The court!" he said. "Well—you could not have chosen a man who knows that world better, or who admires it less."

"I am glad to hear it."

"There is nothing you could ask of me touching that world of falsehood, hypocrisy, and betrayal that it would not be my pleasure to discharge."

"Nothing at all, my lord?"

"Nothing at all," he echoed.

"What if I were to tell you that there are men in our party who would like to see the Queen killed?" Douglass asked.

Lord Petre drew breath sharply. He ought to have guessed that something of this nature would be planned—if Queen Anne were still on the throne, how could James III be restored to it? But he went cold at Douglass's words. He had assumed that the Queen would be removed by diplomatic coercion.

"But the Queen is a Stuart, too," he protested. "And childless; she has no heir."

"She is in the hands of advisers who do not support the Stuart cause," Douglass replied in a cold voice.

So that was the plan, thought Lord Petre. To kill the Queen before her successor had been decided. For a moment he felt panic rising. He could never be part of such an action. But no: this was the first real test of his resolve. Protestants had murdered his fellows in cold blood. They had forced the rightful king from the English throne. Future ages would remember the Jacobites not as assassins but as heroes—honourable men. The hero's course awaited him.

In a steady voice he said, "If I can be persuaded that such a course of action will achieve the outcome we seek, there is nothing that I would not do on behalf of James Stuart's—His Majesty's—cause."

He then pushed the carriage door open. It was a fraction too soon. A careless slip; Douglass had still been checking the notes. Tonight no one had been about to observe them. Even if they had been seen, nobody would have guessed the cause for their meeting; people did exactly as they pleased at masked balls. But at this moment Lord Petre's train of thought was cut short. He had arrived at Lady Castlecomber's town house.

When Alexander had left the room in pursuit of Douglass and Petre, neither of the Blount sisters paid much attention to him. Teresa joined Jervas and Martha after Douglass's departure, and Jervas continued to talk, turning to one lady and then the other, flattering and charming them. But the girls had grown listless and silent, their happy energies dissipated.

As the supper room began to empty out, Teresa said to her sister, "Shall we ask Arabella for the carriage home?"

And Martha replied, "Perhaps Mr. Jervas will hand the three of us inside." The girls went in search of Arabella, and as soon as they found her Jervas escorted the ladies downstairs.

When the girls' carriage had left Jervas turned back inside in search of Alexander, hoping that he, at least, would not be ready for bed.

Inside the coach, Arabella shook open the fur blanket to spread across their knees. But it was not quite large enough for three, so while Arabella's lap was amply covered, the other two sat stiffly, feeling slightly too cold.

Arabella broke the silence. "I have heard that Lady Mary Pierrepont's father plans for her to marry Clotworthy Skeffington, heir to the Viscount Massereene. But rumour has it Lady Mary told her father she would rather give her hand to the flames than to him."

"I heard that she is secretly engaged to Edward Wortley," said Teresa. "But if she marries him, the earl will cut her off with nothing. Wortley is said to be passionately in love with her, but you know that she is to inherit a fortune."

The carriage hit a deep pothole, and they were all flung

forward. Teresa quickly put up a foot to stop herself falling. She knew that she sat well in the coach, like a rider upon a well-managed horse—much better than Arabella, who was scrambling to regain her seat.

"Only Edward Wortley would presume to imagine himself worth such a sacrifice," Teresa added. "Such a sulky, self-important sort of man."

"Oh, he is the type of person whom women like Mary Pierrepont find fascinating," said Arabella, confident again. "He has no charm to speak of, his dress is dull . . . and his wig ill-kempt—and he talks loudly about how wicked the Tories are and how noble the Whigs, as though it were a universal truth to which everyone must assent. He has no small talk, no light conversation, and he never compliments anybody upon their dress or offers to bring them refreshment. In short, he is the sort of clever man who believes that his cleverness can redeem every other fault—and presumably Mary Pierrepont is vain enough of her own powers to believe him."

"Lady Mary doubtless knows that it is harder to turn away from a life of wealth and luxury than she acknowledges to the world," Martha interjected, tired of hearing Teresa and Arabella showing off their idle bits of gossip. "I imagine that she will not marry Wortley when it comes to the point."

Teresa turned to her with a knowing air. "If *I* were betrothed to Clotworthy Skeffington, the second son of a footman would seem a glittering prize in comparison," she pronounced.

"Wortley is not without attractions," Martha replied firmly. "He is likely to be sent abroad as the English ambassador if the Whigs ever come back into government. To France or Germany perhaps, or to Turkey—a novelty even for Lady Mary. I am sure she thinks of that when she considers Wortley's suit."

By the time the carriage arrived at the Blount girls' house, all three girls were shifting restlessly about, telling each other how tired they were; how eager for bed; how cold the night was. Arabella said goodbye to Teresa and Martha with scarcely a glance in their direction, and began to rearrange the rug around her chilly form.

When she got home at last, shivering and yawning, she handed her cape to the bleary-eyed servant who opened the door and hurried upstairs. She decided not to ring for her maid, wanting to avoid the impertinent questions that Betty always asked when woken late at night. Arabella pushed open the door of her chamber, where she was greeted by the sight of Shock dozing in his little basket beside her bed, and a fire in her grate that flickered low but companionably, like a friend who had stayed half awake to welcome her home. But rather than calming her, these sights restored the spirit of wilful determination which had been quenched by the sight of Lord Petre reaching out to stroke Lady Castlecomber's hand.

They had spoken so intimately, though only briefly. She had been shocked, and yet the shock was accompanied by the jolt of something unexpected. Mingled with the pangs of jealousy and wounded pride had been an illicit attraction. She longed to act as they had; she longed for their disdain for propriety; their careless sophistication; their casual liberties that gave away a longstanding familiarity. Charlotte Bromleigh was the eldest daughter of a wealthy Catholic family, but Charlotte's father, whose Roman sensibilities were of a worldly kind, had decided to remove his daughter from the small, closed circle of eligible popish gentlemen to which everybody believed that she belonged. He had arranged her union with the Protestant Lord Castlecomber, lately the inheritor of an Irish peerage, in need of money to restore his estate. Lord Castlecomber, who cared little for the niceties of religion, had been willing to wed the rich, handsome daughter of one of the oldest families in England, and Charlotte Bromleigh became the wife of a peer.

Arabella liked to believe herself impervious to jealousy, but now she acknowledged that she felt envious of Lady Castlecomber. In part she envied the security that marriage had given her; the knowledge that her wealth and position were assured. But truly she was jealous of Charlotte because Lord Petre had touched her. The intimacy of their relationship was palpable. When she had seen him reach across to Charlotte tonight, Arabella had suddenly known that she wanted him to do the same to her.

Lady Castlecomber was married, however; Arabella was not. A single woman without noble birth had no real liberty. And yet how could a match to a man like Robert Petre be achieved? Arabella had met his mother, and knew her to be a cold, determined woman. She had been charming enough to Arabella as a young girl, but she would be ruthless in protecting her family's position, and no sentimental consideration would persuade her that her son should marry a girl with less than ten thousand pounds.

Then again, Lord Petre was of age. Though he might disoblige his family, they could not actually prevent a match of his choosing. She checked herself again. She had seen that Lord Petre already had access to every pleasure and gratification. What would make him marry Arabella Fermor?

Lord Petre liked the way Charlotte Bromleigh bit his shoulder when she had an orgasm. She didn't make much noise, but when he put his hands on her thighs, which were tucked in tightly and gripping his torso, he could feel the tremor in her muscles. The sides of her waist were still hot from her laced stays. He pulled himself up, and spilled on to her stomach.

Charlotte laughed at him. "If my husband were in town, you could have spent inside me," she said. "I'd far rather that a son of yours should inherit the title than one of his. But then he's a suspicious dog, so he'd probably find us out."

"Oh, I like your belly just as well," he answered. "If we were to change things about now I would miss the old ways." He pressed the full weight of his body on to hers, and lay there for a moment. When she became short of breath he rolled off her with a smile.

"And do you like my mouth?" she asked, continuing their conversation.

Kissing it, he could feel her teeth upon his tongue.

"Yes, it is very fine," he murmured, and kissed her again. Wriggling out from his embrace, she began to move down the bed. He felt a tingling of excitement as she put her hand, and then her lips, around his cock. Oh, but he liked this the best of all, he thought, as he saw her looking up at him.

Afterwards, they stayed together. Charlotte was lying on her back, and he traced the outlines of her nose and eyelids and cheekbones with his fingers.

"I don't believe that you hate your husband so much as you pretend, you know."

She sat up, surprised by the remark. "Oh, I don't hate him," she replied in an offhand voice, leaning back on her arms. "I am indifferent to him. Of course when he comes to fuck me I do worry that I'll catch the clap from one of his whores. But otherwise I don't mind marriage. I never expected that I would marry somebody heavenly like you," she added, catching his eye.

He looked at her, trying to picture married life with Charlotte. They would have been easy with each other, he thought, but he knew that their ease existed because they felt no urgent desire. Although their relations were forbidden, and therefore deliciously enjoyable, he never felt a sick rush of temptation or an exhilarating release of abandon when he was with her.

"I think it would have been very pleasant," he said at last. "I fear that none of the women chosen for me by my family will be endurable. What am I to do about it, Charlotte?"

She pushed her hair away from her face and smiled frankly. "You will do, Robert, exactly as we all expect," she answered. "Marry the person they want you to, and seek your pleasures elsewhere. It is an excellent system, in successful operation for hundreds of years."

"But suppose that I wish to take my pleasures from marriage?"

She laughed. "Then you must expect a very much less pleasurable existence than you are presently used to. But all this goes very much against your character," she added. "To a lady's ear it sounds as though you are falling in love. Can this be so?"

"I should be a fool to fall in love, as you perfectly well know," Lord Petre said after a short pause.

Her reply was ready. "I know that you are not a fool, but I did see you looking foolishly at that shepherdess at the ball tonight. Why was she carrying a bow?"

"She was not a shepherdess," he answered, conceding her suggestion. "She was Diana, goddess of chastity."

"Then it is a costume whose significance you would do well to remember," Charlotte rejoined, "because she looked to me very much like Arabella Fermor—a woman to whom you owe some care."

Now he sat up too, and looked at her reproachfully. "I would not have expected you to take the lady's part in this, Charlotte," he said.

"I take Miss Fermor's part because I see in it a reflection of what my own circumstances might have been," she answered with more severity in her voice than before. "Arabella has not the security of great fortune or noble birth."

"Oh, Arabella can take care of herself perfectly well," he answered quickly. "I need not concern myself with that."

She frowned, and he thought that she would argue with him. But her face cleared, and she shrugged. "In the interests of preserving good humour between us," she said, "I will accept that you are right. Indeed I will say that Arabella's handsome face and composed manners are enough to frighten off all but the most determined suitors."

"For all your bright and laughing ways, Charlotte, you have a great deal of wit and good sense," he said. "My Lord Castlecomber is lucky to have you as a wife."

"Do not forget that I am lucky to have him as my husband," she replied seriously. "I could not have you in my bed if I were unmarried. I should be bent entirely upon safeguarding my reputation from attack."

He stretched out again beside her and put his arms around her waist, kissing the outside of her thigh.

"You will never be safe from attack, Charlotte," he said. "Your face and breasts and thighs offer more temptation than any man can withstand."

She uncurled her legs and lay down too, turning her face upward to be kissed. "Put your hand upon my cunt, Rob," she said. "I want you to make me spend again before you leave." He slipped his hand between her thighs, and she mumbled into his neck, "You see; I am wet and ready for you."

Chapter Seven

"And Secret passions labour'd in her breast"

In the days after the masquerade ball the frost came to an end, and rain began to deluge unceasingly. Jervas walked downstairs to breakfast, tying the sash of his morning gown, his slippers scuffing on the treads of the stairs. A jet of water was pouring on to the cobbles from the guttering above, but he was determined to go out, and not to allow the rain to depress his spirits. He heard a rustling from the drawing-room. Looking in, he saw that Alexander was there already, leaning over a book with a sheaf of papers on a table beside him. It was only half-past nine. It made Jervas feel indolent to be beaten out of bed by his guest.

Alexander looked up as he entered, but did not speak. Jervas walked across to his splendid fire and gave it a big, generous poke; putting his back to it, hands clasped behind him as he surveyed his guest. He could not credit the way that, in spite of his ill health, Alexander could sit so doggedly in one place, reading line upon line of Homer, barely glancing at the dictionary that he kept at one side. He noticed that Alexander did not smile at him. Surely he was not still cross about the business of Martha Blount and the wine. It had been nearly two days ago.

Alexander had indeed been feeling out of sorts with Jervas since the ball, irritated by his endlessly easy manners and cheerful temper. It made him feel even more of an outcast than he already did, ashamed of his earnest labours and urgently felt ambitions. Jervas could never understand what it was to be dependent on the generosity of friends. But the thought made Alexander blush—it was because of Jervas's generosity that he sat here now. He found that he could not help but needle Jervas, however, by making a show of his own diligence and self-discipline. Hearing his host scuffing down the stairs, Alexander had gazed down at his book with increased concentration, pleased that Jervas would see him out of bed and working. He tapped his feet upon the little footstool, and waited for his host to appear in the doorway. There he was, smiling as usual. The same smile that he had bestowed upon Martha while he filled her wineglass. Alexander did not mind Jervas's gallantries to women, nor his joking descriptions of how charming he had been to his friends' maids and serving wenches. But Martha Blount was different. How was she to know that Jervas was always flirting with women, never falling in love? What if she were to form an attachment to him, only to find that he did not return it?

Alexander blew his nose loudly. He had woken with a nasty cold the morning after the ball, which now threatened to linger for several days. How cross Jervas had been when Alexander asked to go to bed at the end of the masquerade. In the coach home he had sat in the corner like a spoiled child, even though the ballroom had been practically empty. Alexander had made no attempt to cajole him, but instead had pondered what he had just seen in the carriage yard. Douglass and Lord Petre had been dining openly in Pontack's less than a week before; why then were they meeting furtively in the darkness now? He could make neither head nor tail of it.

Alexander and Jervas were shaken from their reflections by a servant clattering the chocolate pot and china cups in the next room. Jervas gave a cheerful sigh, his back now warmed by the fire. He looked again at his guest, hunched in his chair, gazing down at his book. But Jervas saw that even Alexander was faltering; his finger had stalled on a line in his text.

"Ah ha! I *knew* you could not be as absorbed as you appeared," Jervas exclaimed, breaking instantly into a smile. "Admit it, Alexander—for all his virtues, Homer is devilishly dull."

Alexander glanced up and saw Jervas squinting down at him like a big hungry badger, tapping his paws on the sides of his gown. In spite of himself, he laughed, and set aside his volume.

"Oh, very well, then, so he is," Alexander said. "But since so much pleasure comes from having read it, the *reading* is a necessary ill."

The two friends stood up, and walked across the hall to the room where their breakfast had been laid out. "But you are no stranger to necessary ills, Alexander," Jervas replied. "You already have more practice in fortitude than men whom we know of twice your age." He threw himself down upon a chair, took a hot roll from the covered dish, and pushed it across to Alexander. "You have had your illness for so long, and yet you bear it patiently," he went on. "Do you not dread the effects of its continuation?"

Alexander smiled back at him. "A headache, a fever, a pain in my back," he said, "sometimes very bad, but often hardly there at all. These symptoms are nothing but the outward show of an illness that we all bear long and patiently—the disease that goes more often by the name of *life*."

"What an excellent notion, Pope," Jervas answered affably. "Your reading gives you a fine way of putting things. I stumble about, sometimes hitting upon the right phrase; more often than not only half-remembering what I have read."

He stood up from the table and walked back across to the drawing-room, where Alexander heard him call out, "This talk of reading reminds me of a paper that I wanted to show you." Jervas burst back into the room brandishing an old copy of the *Tatler*. "I have been keeping it for you," he said. "It is excessively amusing—a satire upon hoop petticoats. Joseph Addison has written the piece in the assumed voice of a judge, passing sentence upon the garment's absurdity."

"I know it well, Jervas," said Alexander. "A celebrated essay."

"But you probably do not recall all the details," Jervas replied. "Did you notice that it is extremely bawdy? Listen to this!" He ran his finger across the page to find the lines he wanted. "'forthwith'—I am omitting some sentences—'forthwith the Petticoat was brought into the Court. I directed the Machine to be set upon the Table, and dilated in such a manner as to show the Garment in its utmost Circumference; but my great Hall was too narrow for the Experiment . . .' Is it not amusing, Pope? Addison is making merry about the lady's intimate parts."

"I do see that, Jervas," said Alexander. "It is a diverting piece."

"You should write in the same style."

"There is a lightness to all that Mr. Addison thinks that makes his prose seem buoyant," Alexander replied. "But the style is not mine."

"You are being a dull dog today, Alexander," Jervas said. "I am determined to cheer you up. There is a piece in the *Daily Courant* about Tuesday's masquerade. What a splendid evening it was. Gaiety unalloyed."

Alexander marvelled that Jervas seemed to have forgotten his dissatisfaction and crossness at the end of the night. When he became angry himself, he remained so until the matter was resolved.

But he answered Jervas by saying, "I enjoyed myself a great deal. James Douglass is an entertaining gentleman. What do you know of his character?"

"His character? I can hardly say. I knew him at school, and he was one of the brightest, brainiest lads in the place. He made his boyish fortune by marking out rings in the dirt, which we were all wild to play marbles upon. And then he hatched a scheme for the village sweet shop; he ran a kind of messenger service back and forth. It seemed a great lark at the time. Curious fellow. He has been abroad for many years—France, the West Indies—and who knows where else."

"His friendship with Lord Petre is unlikely, do not you think?"

"Not really," replied Jervas. "I'll wager that Lord Petre wants Douglass for some business he is engaged in. A joint stock venture, if I were to guess. Douglass is always to be found at the Exchange. But I hope that he will not be taken in by Lord Petre's easy manner. These noble fellows are pleasant enough, but they never forget that you are not one of them."

"My sense of Douglass is of a man well able to look after himself."

"You have the measure of him there, Pope."

Jervas turned back to his paper. "Another slave run away in London," he announced as he turned to the public notices. "'A negro maid, aged about 16 years, much pitted with the smallpox, speaks English well, having a piece of her left Ear bit off by a Dog.' Black servants are never gone long, and someone always catches them quickly, so the reward is trifling."

He picked up his cup and put it down again impatiently. "I wonder what Hill can be about with our chocolate? I gave my footman Andrews and his sister some time away because their father died on Friday, but it appears to have brought the whole house to a standstill." He jumped up from the table. "Will this rain never stop?" he exclaimed. "I cannot bear the rain!" He bustled out of the room to find his servant.

"It is perfectly fine again," Jervas called from the hall. Alexander looked out of the window and saw that the rain had eased briefly, though the sky appeared heavy and sodden. A high wind was blowing, making the hanging street signs creak violently, and the loose tiles chatter noisily on the rooftops. "I mean to have a walk before I go to the coffee-house at noon. My kersey-coat and umbrella, Hill," Jervas finished. "I shall be dressed in a moment."

Jervas had not been out half an hour when the skies opened again and the streets, barely drained off from the last downpour, filled instantaneously with mud and filth that swirled around the ankles of hapless pedestrians. Looking along the street, Alexander watched while a dustman, shin deep in mud, freed a blockage by pulling a decomposing cat from the street drain and throwing it to the side of the road. At last Jervas rounded the corner, his coat sodden, his wig flattened and leaning to one side, his stockings coated entirely in mud.

"Good God!" Jervas cried, coming in, "I never saw anything like it! A drunkard has vomited over our town and then taken to pissing upon us for good measure. The streets are running in sewage, with water over the ankle. I'll swear that I had my foot caught around the puddings of a dog while I was crossing Albemarle Street."

"Jervas, you have dirt even on the back of your cravat," Pope exclaimed, as his friend removed his dripping surtout.

"Some empty-headed fop, employed in the vain attempt to save his shoes, rammed into me with the tip of a muddy cane that was tucked under his dainty arm. A wedge of cold filth, straight down my back!"

The wet articles were removed, and Jervas mounted the stairs to his bedroom, talking all the while. Alexander followed him, and the footman Hill came behind. They entered into Jervas's dressing closet, a cosy space where he sat to read when he wanted to be out of the way of his servants and guests. His little collection of erotic paintings, which Alexander remembered having seen on his previous visit, was displayed on one wall. He wondered where

Jervas had bought them, reflecting sardonically that it would cause quite a stir in Binfield if he were to attempt a similar display on the walls of his own chamber.

"Will's coffee-house is nothing to what it was," Jervas said, turning his back to his guest while he fussed with his wig in the looking-glass. "The coffee is Stygian; Beelzebub himself would send it back. I suggest that we go first to White's, where we can take a cup without mortal fear."

While Jervas and Alexander prepared to go out, Arabella was sitting languidly in her bedroom. She had received the usual round of billets doux from her admirers that morning, men whose habit was to send letters out to all and sundry, hoping that one day the strategy would succeed in springing a mate. Arabella generally enjoyed them as a flattering diversion from the real business of securing her own suitor, but this week the billets had appeared almost malevolent; mockeries of her unattached condition.

For the hundredth time she ran over her conversation with Lord Petre. It had been exquisite but hopelessly brief, and it had given her nothing of substance. She longed to engineer a private meeting between them, but she felt her powerlessness to do so. It would only make her look a fool. As she turned these thoughts over in her mind, the chamber door opened, and Betty entered with a letter.

Arabella instantly recognized the coat of arms on the seal, and her heart gave a leap. Betty was looking at her curiously, obviously expecting her to tear it open then and there. But Arabella was determined that nobody should know what she felt. Drawing herself up proudly, she turned away, telling Betty to leave the note upon the dressing table and to help her with the final arrangements of her hair. When Betty had finished, Arabella asked her to take Shock for a walk through the house, instructing her to pay particular attention to his use of the stairs. Only when Betty had left her bedroom did Arabella take up the letter and open it with more alacrity than she had shown in any other task during the last two days.

"My dear Miss Fermor," Lord Petre began. He recalled the occasion of their meeting at the Exchange, and complimented

Arabella's extraordinary beauty. He lamented that she had not adorned that or any other public place since the night of the masquerade, and he hoped that she would therefore attend the performance of Mr. Handel's new opera in the Queen's Theatre at Haymarket the following evening. To this he added, without any further gloss, a pair of lines from Rochester.

With the arrival of Lord Petre's note, the landscape of Arabella's social and sentimental universe changed in an instant. She had been invited to Mr. Handel's *Rinaldo* by Martha and Teresa, who were going with their dull aunt and their insufferable friend Henry Moore—and until this moment she had not been planning to attend. Now she cast aside the discontent of the last days and found herself overcome with feelings of excitement and anticipation. And yet, for the first time in her life, she was uncertain what would be expected of her; how she ought to behave. She was about to embark upon something altogether new, and it gave her a feeling of delicious restlessness.

Arabella could not bear to be indoors, but there was little to do. She could buy something new to wear when she saw him, yet she feared that it might make no impression. She could prepare herself for the meeting tomorrow night, and yet still be taken by surprise. She could not be steady. After a short time she rang her bell for Betty, and when the maid entered she announced, "There are no more silk stockings in my possession! We must go out to get some the moment that it stops raining."

As it happened, Betty knew that Miss Fermor was well supplied with stockings, having taken a pair of her best to wear to the tavern and the playhouse earlier in the week. But she knew better than to correct her mistress on matters of dress.

Arabella was attired in a pale blue gown. She had been expecting to spend the day indoors, receiving a visit from old friends of her mother's, and the dress was unsuitable for wearing out in wet weather. But although it was still threatening rain, she decided not to change her apparel; it seemed now more important than ever to be faultlessly arrayed when she appeared in public. She asked Betty to bring her new frieze cape and muff. She knew that it was a terrible choice for rainy weather, when the water would ruin the nap of the fabric. But it was new, and she looked well in it, and she could not resist the temptation it presented to her newly roused spirits.

Taking her umbrella from the servant who opened the front door, Arabella prepared to step on to the street. She saw with dismay that the cobblestones were running two inches deep in muddy water, and realized that she would have to change into patten clogs. Their wooden soles would make her look like a horse when she walked, but she was not likely to meet any acquaintances on the streets of St. James's this morning. Still, she kept her frieze cape on, just in case she did.

When she had at last struggled up to Piccadilly, she opened the door of the hosier's shop, looking a great deal less presentable than when she left the house. To her dismay she discovered that Lady Castlecomber had arrived only a moment before, accompanied by two footmen: one holding an umbrella above her head, the other lifting her skirts from the level of the ground. Like Arabella, she was wearing a cape made of frieze, though hers looked quite a lot nicer on account of having remained dry. Arabella looked around the shop desperately, hoping she could avoid speaking. Perhaps Lady Castlecomber would not remember her, Arabella caught herself wishing, before realizing that this would be an even more humiliating turn of events. Then she checked herself. She had nothing to fear. If there was anxiety in the exchange, it should all be Charlotte's: what if Arabella, in a fit of spite, were to let Lord Castlecomber know of the affair with Lord Petre? Smiling, she turned to greet her rival.

"Good day, Miss Fermor," Lady Castlecomber answered. "What a lovely cape you have. *Such* a shame that its nap got wet. No stuff is worse than frieze in wet weather, though I could not resist it, either. Are you going to Lady Salisbury's levee? I hope that you will ride there with me."

"Alas, I have only the shoes that I am wearing," Arabella said. "Much as it would give me pleasure to accept your invitation, I shall not do so." She turned away from Charlotte to hide her expression. She had not been invited to the levee, and she knew that the Salisburys were friends of Lord Petre's. She had seen him speaking to Lady Salisbury at the masquerade.

"I was envious of your pattens the very moment I entered the shop," replied Lady Castlecomber pleasantly. "They are the only thing for a day like this."

Arabella glanced down at Lady Castlecomber's feet and saw that she was wearing a pair of heeled leather shoes, as unspoiled as her coat. She bit her lip, resenting Betty's even stare from the doorway; the maid was so plainly curious to know the cause of Miss Fermor's embarrassment.

She walked over to the counter where the most expensive stockings were displayed, but then checked herself. She must wait for Lady Castlecomber to leave. She felt a fool turning over the goods idly, as though she did not know what to buy, but she ought not be seen making an extravagant purchase on the day before so seemingly insignificant an occasion as the opera; it would give the impression that she was angling for a gentleman's attention. At last Lady Castlecomber said goodbye and quit the shop.

By the time Arabella and Betty left with their package of new stockings, the rain had eased to a drizzle, and they had not gone ten yards down Piccadilly when Charles Luxton, the modestly entailed gentleman with whom she had danced at the ball, drove by in his carriage. Seeing her, Luxton stopped and stepped out of his vehicle into the wet street, insisting on handing her in. He shepherded Betty in behind and then jumped inside, declaring that he would drive Miss Fermor home safely.

No sooner had the door closed upon them than Charles leaned towards her with red-faced eagerness, delighted to see her, and saying that he wanted to speak privately. Arabella, tired out from her morning, moved away from him, a headache beginning to strike at her temples as she pressed back against the carriage side. She had not expected this. She had barely even considered Charles Luxton a suitor—let alone a man on the point of declaring himself. She had danced with him only once at the ball, and she had not seen him for months before that. She could not bear to hear his ardour when she had just been reminded of Lord Petre's intimacy with Charlotte Castlecomber. But Charles insisted upon speaking. Stammering slightly with unaffected bashfulness, reaching towards her, he told Arabella that he was to become the happiest man alive.

"Miss Fermor—I hardly know how to say it—but I long to tell

you!" he breathed. "I can think of nothing else. This morning I applied for permission to marry Miss Emily Eccles, my distant cousin, whom I have admired ardently for many months. And permission has been granted!" His brow, which was damp from the rain, glowed with sincerity and warmth as he spoke, almost causing the windows of the carriage to steam over.

Despite herself, Arabella heard it with a shock. Of course she did not *want* to marry Charles, but not even to be asked! How entirely she had misunderstood his motives for stopping. She attempted to collect herself so that she might respond properly to the news.

"The person who marries you, Mr. Luxton, must always be sensible of the greatest good fortune," she said. As she spoke, she remembered that she had met Miss Eccles once or twice in the country the year before. How amusing that Charles had entertained a moment's doubt of his offer's being accepted.

But Charles, who was always so much kinder and more generous than Arabella remembered, said, "When you become acquainted with the lady in question, Miss Fermor, you will see that the good fortune in this matter falls entirely to my share."

When the carriage arrived in Albemarle Street and stopped outside Arabella's town house, Luxton sprang down and escorted her to the front door. As he bowed goodbye, and returned smiling to his carriage, Arabella felt a most unexpected twinge of regret. What a strange morning it had been. The elation brought on by Lord Petre's note—and the humiliation of seeing Charlotte Castlecomber on her way to Lady Salisbury's levee. It had reminded Arabella once again that her position was precarious, and, for an instant, she wished that kind, good-natured Charles Luxton might have done for herself. To be settled; to be secure. But she knew that it could never have been; even while she watched him return to his carriage, she felt a pricking of amusement to see that he turned his feet out and bobbed his head enthusiastically as he walked. And when she handed the troublesome frieze cape to a footman and instructed him to see what could be done with it, Arabella decided that she was pleased to hear of Luxton's engagement to Emily Eccles. Had Charles inherited a larger fortune, he could have married very well indeed.

Chapter Eight

"The Wise Man's Passion, and the Vain Man's Toast"

White's Chocolate House, at the end of St. James's Street near the palace, was not a place that Alexander would ever visit on literary business. His acquaintances in the literary world thought of St. James's as a sink of aristocratic indulgence that would bring devastation upon any traveller who crossed its bourn. They would often speak of the region and its inhabitants with high-minded disdain: "His poems are trifling, and his prose crude. He lives in St. James's, of course." Their affectation incited in Alexander something very close to rage against his fellow scribblers. Why could they not acknowledge their envy of the rich and powerful, as the rest of the world was content to do?

Jervas and Alexander entered together and were greeted by two schoolfriends of Jervas's, Harry Chambers and Tom Breach. Harry invited them to sit down in a pair of empty chairs, moving his muff off one of the seats with a great smile of accommodation. Tom asked if he could fetch Jervas and Pope coffee or chocolate, glancing doubtfully at Alexander as if to enquire whether he had ever heard of either beverage. Jervas said that he would take chocolate; Alexander, bohea.

They were just settled when Harry remarked, "But your wig is still perfectly curled, Charles, in spite of this devilish weather. Surely you did not buy it from Monsieur Duvillier, you extravagant dog!"

Jervas denied it. "Even I do not travel to Paris for my wigs. But I will allow that it is my second of the day," he confessed. "I was soaked to the skin this morning."

"This is my second shirt!" Harry sympathized. "I wore fifteen last week, and I would not be at all surprised if it were twenty this time." He took out his snuffbox and gave it a careless tap; then he lifted the lid. Tom, who had returned with the drinks, looked at him with surprise.

"It is the fashion to tap the snuffbox before opening, Tom," Harry said with a lazy smile. "I cannot show you here, but if I were to do the same thing at the play, twenty women would turn towards me upon hearing the sound."

"Oh, Harry," Tom replied. "How dedicated a follower of fashion you are. But the gentleman leaning upon the counter has stolen a march on you, for he is already wearing red heels, though it is not the evening."

Harry gave a grunt of disbelief, and craned his head around to look at the offending shoes. "But you will see that he also has a shoulder knot," he added with a meaningful glance at Tom; the man in question was an unspeakable vulgarian.

Alexander was pleased that Jervas had brought him to White's and given him the chance to observe the absurdities of Tom and Harry's conversation. He wondered whether it might be the sort of thing he could work into a new poem—even Tonson would have to admit that readers would be diverted—everybody liked to read about characters whom they recognized. But how could it be done? When people talked in poems, it was not in the colloquial language of everyday speech; indeed he could not think of a modern poem that concerned itself with daily life at all, least of all to laugh at it. Alexander looked at Jervas sitting and smiling at the pair's careless banter, giving every appearance of unironic enjoyment. It would never occur to Jervas, of course, to make fun of men like Tom and Harry. His paintings were not satirical; he was far too reverent an admirer of the fashionable world to mock its absurdities. Jervas asked Tom what news there was from the town.

"I called last Wednesday upon my Lady Purchase, but found her not at home," Tom said with a yawn. "And yet she was standing at the window of the drawing-room, looking down upon me quite clearly while the servant spoke."

"Lady Purchase is at home to visitors only on Tuesdays and Thursdays, so I am not at all surprised to hear that she would not see you," Harry drawled in reply, looking down to smooth his stockings more evenly over his legs. "It is a rule very strictly observed. My Lady Sandwich regards it as such a point of good breeding that on days when she is not officially 'at home,' she denies herself to visitors with her own mouth." He finished with his stockings and leaned back in his chair.

"I can hardly believe that my Lady Sandwich is still able to move her own mouth," Tom rejoined, "she is so varnished over these days with paint and powder."

"Tom—do not pretend to be innocent of the devices of women," Harry bayed in reply. "You are an artist, Charles, and will know how it is done—do not all women wear faces that are painted on in the morning and washed off again at night?"

Jervas knew better than to proffer his own observation, saying instead, "I'd rather hear about your adventures in feminine painting, Harry!"

"Mine are nothing in comparison with my friend Dicconson's," Harry replied, still in the same offhand tone of voice. "Do you know him, Charles? Excellent chap; always ready to buy a man a drink. He swears that he never saw his wife's face until he married her. Her skin is so battered about from make-up that when she wakes in the morning, she scarcely seems young enough to be the mother of the woman he carried to bed the night before."

"A trifle, a trifle!" Tom exclaimed. "I knew a woman with a face so delicately coloured in that I was in danger of blowing her features away altogether if I sighed upon them too lovingly. Being abed with her was like coming into a room newly painted. The smell was intolerable."

Alexander was listening to this conversation, much amused, when Tom suddenly changed course. "Harry," he exclaimed, "there is an elderly gentleman coming towards us in a waistcoat that must have been made half a century ago. I believe that it is William Wycherley."

"Wycherley the dramatist?" Harry answered. "Don't be a fool, Tom. *The Country Wife* was presented in the theatres forty years ago. He must be dead almost as long as Shakespeare."

"No, I believe that it is he," Tom replied. "But though he is not dead, he must at the very least be blind, for he has been sitting at the servants' end of the room without noticing."

Alexander looked over his shoulder in dismay. Indeed it was

William Wycherley walking to their table. He was unmistakable, tall and corpulent, dressed formally in a style now thirty years old. He moved with a distinctive limp caused by his gout, but no doubt made worse by lumbering about town under the weight of so much flesh. By the luckiest stroke, Alexander thought, he had just written to let Wycherley know that he had arrived in London—but had implied that ill health would make a meeting difficult to arrange. He felt particularly ashamed of having used his health for an excuse, knowing that the old playwright was unwell himself. Tonson had said he was losing his memory. He corrected the careless slouch into which he had slipped in unconscious imitation of his companions.

When Sir Anthony Englefield had arranged his introduction to William Wycherley three or four years previously, Alexander had felt more excitement than from any other meeting in his life. But he had realized almost immediately that their friendship would not be what he had hoped. Wycherley had once been the greatest playwright of his age, but even then he was already in a much enfeebled state, and openly craved the admiration of a young, talented poet. Wycherley had asked Alexander to help him prepare a volume of his poems for publication, and although Alexander had known that the verses were inferior, he had nonetheless helped to make them respectable, telling himself that it was an honour to assist so great a writer. He had been so shocked by Wycherley's fallen condition that he could not bring himself to acknowledge it frankly.

"Mr. Wycherley!" said Alexander, springing to his feet as soon as the dramatist was near him.

The old man had grown even fatter since they had met the previous year; his great bulk dwarfed Alexander and his little bow of greeting. Wycherley regarded him in silence. His wig, piled high and ornately, sat slightly awry. He was accompanied by his page, a middle-aged man whom Alexander had met before. Alexander reddened. He knew that they were watched by everyone in the room, and feared suddenly that Wycherley was about to cut him. But the page stepped up to his master and said very quietly, "'Tis Mr. Pope, sir. Your young friend."

Wycherley said immediately, "Ah, Mr. Pope; I do not see so well as I once did. Are you visiting the town with Mr. Caryll?"

"No, sir. I am staying with my friend Charles Jervas, whom I believe you know." Jervas bowed, but stayed clear of their exchange.

Wycherley appeared not to notice Jervas at all. "And how does Mr. Caryll do?" he asked.

Alexander wondered whether he ought to correct Wycherley, and tell him that he had not seen Caryll for three weeks. He could hardly bring himself to look at the older man, aghast at this evidence of his further deterioration. Only a few years ago he had still been commanding; now he was a figure of fun—it was hardly dignified for him to be seen out. How bitterly ephemeral was fame, Alexander thought.

"He is well, sir," he replied, adding, "he remains in the country this year." There was a pause, and Alexander glanced across at Jervas, widening his eyes in a gesture of mute appeal.

But suddenly the fog of Wycherley's confusion cleared away and he said confidently, "I am glad to see you returned to health, Mr. Pope. I feared that you might not be able to enjoy the pleasures of the season. Mr. Tonson tells me that your *Essay upon Critics* is soon to appear." He was entirely unlike the self of two minutes previously. Alexander was astonished.

"*Essay on Criticism*, yes. I am delighted with it, sir, though apprehensive of its reception," Alexander replied, feeling no apprehension at all at that moment, but only relief that Wycherley had returned to something approaching a normal manner.

"When I do have the happiness of reading your new poem, Mr. Pope," Wycherley replied in a mannered voice, "I shall praise it immoderately."

Alexander answered him with as much deference as he could summon. "If you find pleasure in my green verses, sir," he said, "it must be the pleasure a man takes in observing the first shoots and buddings of a tree which he has raised himself. Your compliments will shame me."

"If I displease you by commending you, I shall please myself nonetheless," came the overwrought reply. "Remember that incense is sweeter to the offerer than the Deity to whom it is offered, He being too much above it to take pleasure."

Jervas, sensing Alexander's discomfort and hoping to bring the meeting to a close, stepped in at this moment to ask Wycherley where he was travelling to, and to offer him a ride in his carriage. Wycherley accepted readily, saying that he was going to Will's coffee-house. Jervas took leave of Tom and Harry and they set off immediately.

Alexander could hardly suppress a laugh at three such vastly different men crammed into a small London coach, struggling to appear at ease while their mismatched forms were compacted ever more tightly together. Alexander and Jervas were wedged in on either side of Wycherley as if to protect the safe passage of the larger man. Being, Alexander suspected, the only person in the carriage who still had unrestricted access to his respiratory system, Wycherley began the conversation. "Why does our friend John Caryll come to town so seldom?" he asked Alexander.

"Caryll's family is of a retiring temperament, sir," he replied, thinking that Caryll came more frequently than Wycherley probably knew. "They do not enjoy the bustle of London, and Caryll would not think of coming without them."

Wycherley gave a scornful humph, which served to stuff the two other men still more firmly into their corners, and countered, "I think it is because the family's fortunes are still not recovered from his late uncle's foolish extravagances. Caryll cannot afford to be in town."

Alexander believed that this guess was nearer the mark, but he had no intention of gratifying Wycherley's appetite for gossip by admitting it. "I would not describe old Lord Caryll's misfortunes as extravagances, sir," he said in as prim a voice as his position allowed. "He was unfairly imprisoned for the Popish Plot—although he manifestly played no part—and then he lost his lands over an assassination attempt that he knew nothing about."

"Knew nothing about it; what nonsense! Lord Caryll was a Jacobite. He confessed it openly. He more than confessed it; he lived in France when James II's court was exiled there. I have even heard that he was the exiled king's secretary of state. He was undoubtedly involved in plans to bring James back to the throne."

In a more pious tone than he would normally use, Alexander said, "Whatever his uncle may have done, John Caryll has suffered wrongly at the hands of those people who wish harm to the Roman Catholic Church."

"I did not think you were a defender of the Jacobites, Mr. Pope."

"I am defender of my friends the Carylls, sir."

"And of the Catholics, I wager. Well, I suppose you cannot help it. But why did John Caryll not stay out of the affair altogether? I heard that he actually went to prison for it—and now his whole family are held to be traitors."

"Caryll's imprisonment was only for two weeks, and he was unjustly convicted," Alexander argued in an impassioned tone.

"Well, if they were my fortunes, or my family, I should have become a Protestant long ago," Wycherley said complacently. "All of Caryll's troubles might then have been avoided."

"I do not think that Caryll ought to be censured for protecting his family," said Alexander. "Nor old Lord Caryll for being a Jacobite. His generation of Catholics suffered cruelly. If the Catholics are safe now, it is only because they—we—have learned to keep silent."

Alexander was surprised by how angry Wycherley's attack had made him. He had certainly never considered himself a defender of the Jacobites, nor even of his own religion, but Wycherley had forced from him a loyalty that he had not known before. After all, Alexander had been barred from attending university, stripped of his right to property and position. It was easy enough to forget now that he was staying with Jervas in Westminster, but only a few weeks previously it had seemed to blight his fortunes. He felt a perverse pleasure in seeing Wycherley stumble as he lumbered out of the carriage at Will's. Barely able to mutter a goodbye, Alexander turned away from his old friend and slammed the coach door.

Jervas was in a good temper on the way home. "How luxuriously comfortable we are without Wycherley's immense bulk in here," he said. But Alexander was scowling and quiet, staring out the window and kicking his foot against the seat. After a while Alexander's kicks began to grate on Jervas's ear, and he exerted himself to pull his friend out of his brooding silence.

"Were Wycherley's remarks about your friend Caryll true, Pope?" he asked.

Still looking out the window, Alexander replied, "Oh, true and yet untrue. Old Lord Caryll was a Jacobite, but I do not believe that his nephew is involved. Even if he were inclined to the Jacobites' cause, it would be too dangerous, since his family is already suspected."

"What a strange, old-fashioned world it seems," Jervas said. "Plots, counter-plots, imprisonment, treason. Old Lord Caryll, Wycherley, even your friend John Caryll seem like men from another time to me."

Alexander replied sharply. "Happy for you that they seem so, Jervas. But the taint of popery still hangs over me as well; I shall probably never shake free of its deadening grip."

"I cannot understand the attractions of Jacobitism," Jervas replied. "It renders rich people poor and sane people mad. It is perfectly plain that James III will never be installed upon the throne, and yet, year after year, men cast their fortunes, and their family's fortunes, into the Channel, believing that they will wash ashore in France and lure him back."

"That is not precisely how the Jacobites arrange their affairs," Alexander said in a censorious tone. "To you, the Jacobites seem merely diverting lunatics, for you have nothing to lose by their actions. But suppose that the persecutions begin again. I might find that nobody will print my poems."

Jervas wanted to laugh at Alexander's determined gloominess, but he kept himself from smiling, and said instead, "You think that because it is raining and we have not yet dined."

But Alexander was not to be consoled. "When I am with men like Wycherley I find that my energy for poetry ebbs away entirely. Their verses and plays are as feeble as ass's milk—but how can I succeed, if I cannot be like them?"

Jervas looked at Alexander in alarm. He never knew what to say to these outbursts of his friend's, and his silence merely goaded Alexander to further outrage.

"Most writers are insufferable, always complaining of their failures: that the style of their verse is not in fashion; that they have not the patronage to succeed; that they are not rich enough, not poor enough; that they have not a loud enough voice to be heard. Anything, in short, except that their talents are insignificant, their writing of the meanest kind."

"But your verses are not mean, Pope," said Jervas consolingly. "Has not Jacob Tonson said some flattering things to you?"

"I will not be beguiled by flattery!" Alexander answered furiously, biting back the words *as you allow yourself to be.* He saw Jervas shrink back from him; he knew he was behaving badly, but the sight of Jervas's anxious, conciliatory face made him feel more frustrated still. It was not his fault that he could not be easy with everybody, and find all the world charming, as his friend did.

"Do you not long to show the world its vanity, its hypocrisy?" Alexander barked. "When you find yourself doing the portrait of some vain, idle whimperer, do you not want to crush him with the strokes of your brush? No! You do not. I have never known you to judge the subjects that sit before you, Jervas."

"But I am not a judge, Pope; I am a painter. Thank heavens!" Jervas gave a little laugh, looking warily at Alexander for his response. "I would not care to be a judge, though my father thought the law might do well for me. What right have I to determine the merits of those I paint? My patrons pay me to show them as they would have the world see them—not as I happen to feel on a wet morning after too many oysters the evening before!"

"But I am a *poet,*" Alexander replied, with such a combination of pride and uncertainty in his voice that Jervas nearly laughed again. "Nobody pays me to praise them." He paused, and then, unable to stop himself, said, "The trouble with men like you is that you hesitate to be bold. You only ever *hint* at a person's faults; you hesitate to suggest anything so forthright as enmity. I believe that you are afraid to strike!"

He looked defiantly at Jervas, half hoping, half dreading that he had provoked him to anger at last. But Jervas looked back at him composedly, and said, "It has nothing to do with fear, Alexander. It is because I have no desire to wound."

Alexander sank back in his seat as Jervas spoke, suddenly ashamed of his outburst, and wishing, far too late, he knew, that he had shown more self-control.

But after a minute or two, Jervas put out his hand to Alexander and said, "At home there will be beef and mutton and cheese waiting for us, and pudding and a fire to warm us through the evening. Enough of this ranting and raving, Pope. I command you to cheer up!" Alexander smiled gratefully, and gave Jervas's arm an apologetic shake.

Some days earlier, Martha and Teresa Blount had invited Alexander to visit, but with his cold and the bad weather he had not gone. When the sun came out on the day after his argument with Jervas, Alexander decided that he would pay a visit to the girls.

"So you are come at last," Teresa said as he was shown in to the sisters' sitting-room. "Patty believed that you had commenced an amour with that little milkmaid to whom you were speaking at the masquerade." She stood up to kiss him on both cheeks.

Alexander wondered why she was in such a good mood. Was it the effect of London, or had she seen Lord Petre again?

"You have been ill, Alexander—I am sure of it," Martha said, looking at Alexander's troubled face.

But Alexander, still thinking of Lord Petre, wanted to show Teresa that he, too, could be gallant when he chose. "Yes, I suffered a constant ache at being apart from you both, and a dreadful fever from longing to see you once again," he said. "But having brought the condition upon myself, I cannot be nosing about for sympathy."

"Have you been busy writing poetry, Alexander?" Martha asked.

"Only the commonest, meanest kind, having no muse nearby to inspire the higher sentiments," he replied.

"It would be a shame were so much wit not to be recorded for posterity," Teresa said in her old tone of teasing challenge.

In spite of himself, Alexander took the bait. "If I do have wit," he answered, "I had better *write* to show it off than not. For as any lady who has seen me will attest, I have nothing to show that is better."

"If you pass the plate for compliments too often, Alexander, you will collect fewer than you deserve," Teresa answered. "I am happy to praise your verses—and Patty is willing to compliment your person—but only when you do not clamour for it."

The door opened, and a footman announced that Miss Arabella Fermor was waiting for the ladies in her carriage. The mood in the room changed immediately.

"Heavens, I had forgotten that Bell was coming this morning," said Teresa, jumping up to look at herself in the mirror. "I must buy a head-dress to wear to the opera tonight. Patty, you said yesterday that you would come." From the glass, she looked commandingly at her sister.

"But Alexander is here, and we have not finished our sewing from this morning," Martha replied, testily meeting Teresa's reflected gaze. "I believe that I shall stay behind."

At this Teresa wheeled around, saying in an accusatory voice, "Oh, do not start talking in that tone, invoking Alexander and the sewing as though it were an offence against religion to be seen in a lace head-dress."

Alexander had risen also, and was standing stiffly between the two girls, not knowing which of them to turn to.

But he wanted Teresa to leave the house feeling well disposed towards him. "Madam, though there may be pride and vanity in the wearing of a lace head-dress, your friends will consider it one of the highest acts of charity that you can exercise," he said.

At this Teresa gave Martha a triumphant smile, and gathered her things for going out.

Wishing to be even-handed, Alexander turned to Martha. "But you need not worry that Teresa will become too much accustomed to pleasure, Patty," he said. "She will return soon enough to the country, with its cold, old-fashioned halls, morning walks, and three hours of prayer a day."

"I shall not!" Teresa replied defiantly. "But if we are to do nothing in London but sit about the house sewing, we might as well go home directly. Why do we come to town, if not to attend balls and plays and assemblies? And why go to those, if not to look handsome?"

"You should take care, Teresa," said Martha sharply. "Some winters hence your face about the town will be like a rich old-fashioned silk in a shop, which everybody has seen and nobody will buy." Alexander suppressed a smile, and Teresa shot him a resentful glance.

"Oh, very witty, Patty!" she answered. "But in your conceit I should be more like a richly admired brocade—far too good to be cut and made up to suit just anybody's humour."

With this riposte she swept out of the room, leaving Martha

and Alexander standing awkwardly side by side. Martha looked at Alexander and he reached out as if to take her hand, but then, suddenly, changed his mind.

Martha gave a sigh as she sat down. "Teresa is catching Bell's habit of believing that she can persuade any man into admiring her," she said. "She does not seem to understand that where there is no fortune, there can be no persuasion."

Alexander smiled at her. "I can only say in reply that if your sister's stubborn nature were to be set against ten thousand pounds, I would call them pretty evenly matched. Any man that she cannot overcome by argument, she very likely will by temptation."

Martha looked grave. "You do not suppose that Teresa could be so foolish as to fall into an affair, Alexander?"

He was about to answer glibly when he suddenly noticed that he was enjoying the exchange; there was a substance to Martha's conversation that Teresa's lacked, and he reflected how much he might come to depend on her judgement and advice. He wondered how long this had been the case.

"I hope that even your sister has sense enough to avoid that fate," he said. "But if she does not, our constant proximity to all her scenes of pleasure will remove any residual risk." He smiled reassuringly.

But Martha replied in a low voice. "I only wish that Teresa could be happier. She seems always to be striving for something that she can never have."

"Were I of an ecclesiastical temperament, I should offer you and your sister as well as myself a piece of advice," said Alexander. "To aim not at joy, but rest content with ease."

Martha looked up at him in exasperation. "You are always giving advice in which you do not believe, Alexander," she answered, but smiled as she said it.

"Well—perhaps aim *not only* at joy," he conceded. "But I do have a great regard for ease. I should have been born a baron, for they seem the easiest men alive. Lord Petre has nothing at all to do, and yet he appears constantly occupied," he added. "Your brother knows the Petre family, does he not, Patty?"

Martha's answer was ready, as though she had thought about the subject a good deal. "There was talk at one time of his going into business with Lord Petre's father, but Michael had not the capital for it," she said.

"What business would a baron have with your brother?"

"Stock-jobbing," she answered. "There is a venture called the South Sea Company that will make everybody very rich, and Lord Petre's father hoped to begin another like it," she said. "But investors do not like to put their money with Catholics, so it went no further. I suppose that Lord Petre wanted Michael for our family's good name."

Alexander was surprised to find Martha so assured on the subject of her brother's interests. They had never spoken about it before. How could she have such a firm grasp of financial affairs? Teresa did not, he was sure.

"Why would Lord Petre's father have cared for Michael's name?" he asked, feeling naive.

"The Blounts have never been Jacobites."

Alexander was puzzled. "But neither have the Petres, surely."

Martha hesitated for a moment, cautious, and again he was amazed by the new side of Martha he was seeing. He wished he had listened more closely in the past to his father when he had tried to explain the complexities of the Jacobites and their politics.

"Do you recall that Lord Petre's former guardian, your friend John Caryll, was involved in retrieving an estate confiscated from his uncle?" Martha asked.

"I was speaking of it to Jervas only yesterday," he answered. "But it had nothing to do with the Petres."

"That is not so," she said. "Old Lord Caryll had been imprisoned for trying to defend five Catholic lords arrested in the Popish Plot. They were all to be tried together, and likely beheaded. Do you recall the names of the other lords who were imprisoned?"

Alexander shook his head. That Martha had never let on until now!

"Lords Stafford, Powis, Arundell, Bellasyse, and Petre," she said.

"Petre!" he echoed. "Lord Petre?"

"The present baron's grandfather. He died in the Tower, a known traitor. The Petres bear the black mark upon their names, just as the Carylls do."

"So the Petres are Jacobites."

"*Were* Jacobites, Alexander," she corrected.

Alexander was arrested by a series of thoughts. "But I begin to understand—Lord Petre is constantly with that man James Douglass, yet I do not believe that they are friends. They are of such opposing manners; from such different families. But I saw them in secret after the ball; they were hiding together in an empty carriage."

Martha laughed. "I do not understand a word of what you are saying, Alexander."

"I do not understand it myself, Patty. Whenever I see Douglass, he gives the appearance of being underhand, of having always something to conceal. But until this moment I could not fathom Lord Petre's involvement."

"Alexander, I cannot follow you."

"What if their friendship were founded upon political self-interest? Suppose that it were a matter of treason. A secret indeed," he said.

"Alexander! You are being ridiculous," Martha exclaimed. "You let your jealousy of Lord Petre encourage you to the most preposterous fancies." She paused, regretting her choice of word. Collecting herself, she added in a calmer voice, "Even supposing this talk of secret meetings were true, which I do not believe, think what would happen if he were to be exposed. The family would lose everything; Lord Petre would be imprisoned, and probably executed. It is impossible!"

She broke off, and the pair of them sat in silence for a moment.

"Have you told Teresa what you have told me?" he asked. "Perhaps you should do so."

As she watched him, Martha felt a wave of sympathy. How well she understood his feelings—his desire to discourage the affection for Lord Petre that Teresa seemed to bestow so unfairly. Was that what this whole exchange had been about? What a temptation it must be to reveal that Teresa's admirer, Douglass, was a blackguard, and her favourite, the baron, a traitor!

With a sigh, she replied, "I am sure that your suspicions are unfounded—Lord Petre is not a traitor. In any case, I do not think such advice would dissuade Teresa, and she might well tell him about it in an attempt to gain his attention. I believe that you must keep your speculations to yourself."

Alexander looked abashed as she spoke. Supposing she was right, he reflected ruefully. Perhaps it was jealousy that made him so curious about Lord Petre's business with Douglass. When he compared his wild speculations to Martha's real penetration and insight, he was embarrassed.

"You understand your sister well, Patty," he said. "And how thoroughly I suspect you understand me. I shall say nothing to her. Instead I promise to watch over her like a guardian sylph in Romance, protecting her from harm as she faces the tribulations of the fashionable world."

"In that guise you shall soon enough be occupied," Martha answered with an ironic note in her voice. "Teresa is to go to the opera tonight, an event well attended by the society of which you speak, drawn up magnificently in lace, brocade waistcoats, and sword knots. She is not likely to appear well fortified in comparison."

Chapter Nine

"The glance by day, the whisper in the dark"

That evening hundreds of people were gathered outside the theatre in the Haymarket, jostling to get inside. A jam of carriages and sedan chairs had accumulated at either end of the street, and ladies picked through the dung and straw in their silk slippers to reach the theatre. A fur tippet fell to the ground, and a lady's footman struggled with the filthy street urchin who darted in to steal it. Chair carriers battled to deposit their passengers under the arcade of the building, ramming the carrying-poles into the backs of unsuspecting theatregoers. A hog-man, not knowing or not caring that it was an opera night, turned into the street with a snorting, scuffling pack who smeared their flanks across the ladies' fronts, ruining silk stockings with each kick of their muddy trotters.

At the doors of the building the attendants, liveried in scarlet since it was the Queen's Theatre, bumped against the oncoming crowd, shouting at them that no food or drink could be brought in. Orange sellers stood beside them, hawking rotten fruit for the gallery to throw on to the stage when the pace began to flag. Two men stood before the doors and called, *"No arms to be worn in the theatre! Gentlemen to leave all swords outside!"*—and were roundly ignored. With much bell ringing and yet more shouting, the fireman's carriage arrived with engines full of water in case the lights set fire to the stage during the performance.

Alexander and Jervas had come to the theatre in a hackney carriage. Jervas had not only forgiven Alexander for his outburst the day before but seemed indeed to have forgotten it altogether, and they were walking together affably, getting along better now than they had done since he came to town. They arrived just as

Richard Steele did, and Alexander greeted him energetically, hoping that he would be disposed to talk.

"Can't abide the Italian opera," Steele began as he led Alexander up the stairs towards the men's box. "Why do so many people turn out for an evening in which the understanding can play no part in their pleasure?"

Alexander laughed. His friend was obviously in a good mood. "That nobody can make sense of it is an opera's first recommendation," he replied wryly. "It frees the audience from all constraint. Whether they have attended or not attended, the conversation afterwards will be just the same. This is true of every public entertainment, of course—but the Italian opera, which is entirely formed of nonsense, suits the fashionable world the best of all."

"There would be no opera at all without the fashionable world," Steele said, putting his hand on Alexander's shoulder and looking back to wave to an acquaintance farther down the stairs. "Were the nobility not clamouring to pay a guinea apiece to show off their finery in the superior illumination of theatrical lighting, this Mr. Handel would doubtless still be giving organ lessons in Germany."

Alexander laughed again and asked, "If you dislike the opera, Mr. Steele, why do you come?"

"For our readers, Pope, our readers," he said with a sigh. "We must tell them about it so that even those who have not attended at all may join the conversation afterwards in confident voice."

Alexander had bought a copy of the opera book that day in Covent Garden, and he flipped through its pages while he and Steele settled themselves. He wondered where Jervas had got to—he always knew everybody at these outings. He must still be at the bottom of the stairs. "Even if they do play the work in English," Alexander observed to Steele, "it will be no more comprehensible, for I see that the libretto is by Aaron Hill."

"Yes. Hill has no talent whatsoever for making himself understood," Steele assented. "A shame, for he might otherwise write well. Might I see the book?"Alexander handed it over, and Steele perused it.

After a minute or two he chortled with amusement. "Mr. Hill tells us in his preface that he wishes for a drama to display the excellence of the music and 'to fill the eye with more delightful Prospects, so as to give Two Senses equal pleasure'," he said. "Which two senses do you think Hill has in his mind?"

"Not the same as the two I have in mine," Alexander replied. "But since he is the manager of this theatre, there is one very delightful prospect that must stimulate him to continually higher efforts: that of being one day able to claim credit for somebody else's dramatic talents."

"But Mr. Hill is in charge no longer," Steele said with relish, delighted to find someone to whom he could impart the news of the theatre manager's demise. "Did not you hear? He has been suspended since the beginning of this month—the set builders were not being paid, and there was an outcry after the episode with the birds."

"Birds?" Alexander echoed. "I heard nothing of it." He wondered how Steele came by his information. Perhaps people came to him with gossip, hoping that he would write about them in his periodical.

"It was a *most* diverting episode for those of us who would prefer to see the Italian opera make a triumphal return to its native land," Steele explained. "Some weeks ago I was in Covent Garden with Joseph Addison, when we saw a boy walking along with a great cage of sparrows. Addison, with whom you are yet to be acquainted, asked him where he was going with them, and the boy informed us that they were for the opera. 'For the opera?' said I, 'What, are they to be roasted?' thinking that at last Hill had stumbled upon an idea that would make him some money. But no! The boy replied that the sparrows were to enter the stage after the first act."

Alexander bowed, sensing that Steele's story was building to a climax.

"You might imagine my astonishment upon hearing the news. But my surprise was nothing compared to that of the ladies in the audience when they found that the birds were, by the third act, already making nests in their head-dresses. There was yet more confusion the following night, for the sparrows did not seem to understand Mr. Hill's telling them that it was a different play. They continued to make entrances at very improper moments, putting out the candles as they flew about, and causing great inconvenience to the heads of the audience. In the end I think we can conclude that it was the sparrows who beheld a delightful prospect, and Mr. Hill who was roasted."

By the time Steele reached his punch line the box was nearly filled with operagoers, and there was hearty laughter at the conclusion of the tale. Amid the bustle of people arriving and sitting down, Alexander saw that Jervas had appeared with a large crowd of friends and acquaintances. Lord Petre, Robert Harley, and Jonathan Swift were all gathered around him, as well as a friend of Swift's whom Alexander knew only by sight from the coffee-houses. Steele stepped directly up to Chief Minister Harley and introduced himself. Lord Petre hastened to the front of the box and began looking out into the audience, paying little attention to what was passing among his friends.

By this time the opera had begun, but the fact had very little impact upon most of the audience, who continued to talk and walk around just as before. Jervas rejoined Alexander, taking up position in Steele's old seat.

"Dear me," said Jervas, looking over the edge of the box. "What a sound they are making down there. 'Tis hard to know which noises are writ by Mr. Handel for his drums and cannon, and which rendered by Mr. Hill's assistants as they drop the scenery backstage."

"It makes no difference to the audience, so long as they can take snuff, smoke, and stare at the ladies' boxes," Alexander replied. "Presumably it does make some difference to Mr. Handel, who I can only hope is not present to witness the scene."

"I rather regret that I have the advantage of Mr. Hill's playbook," Steele said, returning to his perusal of the performance. "I am promised here that the King of Jerusalem is to be drawn in a triumphant chariot by a team of white horses. Yet it is perfectly plain from the scene now going on that he is obliged to arrive from the city on foot."

Alexander stood up to look at the stage, and decided to try to work himself around to near where Dr. Swift was standing, hoping that he would at last have a chance to meet the famous clergyman. He longed to tell him how much he had admired *A Tale of a Tub*, but feared that Swift might think him gauche. Perhaps he should talk instead about the opera. The renowned Italian castrato Nicolini was presently making a sedate crossing of the stage in a pasteboard boat, singing of violent tempests in both heart and mind. Swift was looking over the side of the box, a disdainful expression upon his face, and Alexander moved to stand beside him for a few minutes, pretending to watch the performance. As Mr. Handel's music reached a crescendo, Dr. Swift let out a cry of irritation. Alexander saw it as his chance.

"Do you not admire the entertainment?" he asked.

Swift answered him without hesitation, not seeming to care, or perhaps even to remember, that they had never been introduced. "My enjoyment is overthrown by the sight of my fellow clergymen, sitting in the front row of the theatre with the music open on their knees," he said, pointing down scornfully at a little group of clerics sitting below. "Behold them there, posturing as men of judgement and refinement. They watch with such a serious air, as though it were only by nodding and beating time with one's fingers that a person could show himself able to listen to music. I should think them funny, were not their vanity so wretchedly on display. Instead they fill me with a savage indignation."

Alexander was so surprised by Swift's outburst that he forgot to be guarded in his answer.

"But why should their indignity turn *you* savage?" he asked.

Swift stopped abruptly to look keenly at the young man beside him.

"I do not believe that I know your name, sir," he said.

Alexander faltered, and looked around anxiously to make sure that no one had seen him speak to Swift out of turn.

"My name is Alexander Pope, sir," he replied.

"I heard of you some time ago, Mr. Pope," said Swift, "and it made me curious. I have heard that you write poetry."

Pope blushed and mumbled, "Hardly! A few verses; only one of them printed." He looked down at his feet. Then, cursing himself for almost throwing away an opportunity such as this, added, "I do have another poem coming out very shortly, sir. Next month, I hope." He hesitated again, fearing that he would seem to be showing off, or begging some favour from the more famous writer.

It must have been Steele who described him to Swift, Alexander speculated.

But Swift resumed their conversation about the clergymen below. "You pose an excellent question," he said thoughtfully. "Why *do* those men affect me? I suppose because their indignity is a reminder of a still greater loss of dignity in myself. I stoop to be among them; like those paltry parsons with their music, I flatter and bow and scrape, seeking preferment that I do not really desire. And rather than turn away from the Church, I resort to despising my fellows. I become savage, sir, when I see that I cannot escape my own ill nature."

Alexander listened with an expression of wonder, even of delight, as he spoke. Swift's words reminded him of his own outburst at Jervas. "I believe that I understand you, Dr. Swift," he cried, meeting the clergyman's eye. "I too am beginning to perceive the consequences of belonging to a profession in which one feels entirely at odds with all fellow practitioners."

Swift met his speech with a corresponding energy. "We are all of us vain—but if a man would be proud, I wish he would swagger about as though he were ten times the size of his fellows, peering at them through a glass. This at least would justly represent his feelings of superiority. But these fellows show their vanity through the pains they take in reading and study. It is intolerable pretence."

Alexander said, hoping that he would not sound ridiculous, "You must be every day reminded, Dr. Swift, of how very different the path that you tread is from that of your fellow travellers. But so does orthodoxy beget heresy."

"Tell me sir: are you a conformist in point of religion?"

Alexander was surprised by the question—he had not expected Swift to raise the subject of religion when he must know he was a Catholic. Steele would hardly have omitted that detail. But he resolved to answer Swift frankly. "My family are pious," he replied, "and when I am with them they say so many prayers that I can make but few poems. I call myself an occasional conformist. As I am drunk and scandalous to suit my company in town, I am grave and godly at home, for the same reason." He tried not to laugh at his own joke, but it slipped out nonetheless.

Swift was laughing too, and did not notice it. "You are witty, Mr. Pope. My Lord Petre told me that you are no satirist, but I believe that he was in error."

"I shall not correct him," Alexander replied, interested to hear that Lord Petre had spoken of him at all. So it had not been Steele. He noticed that they were being overheard by a third party. It was Swift's friend, the short, chubby fellow, whom Swift introduced as John Gay.

"I know that you are a scribbler, Mr. Pope," Gay said. "I have read your verses, and admired them exceedingly."

"Mr. Pope should more properly be called a poet than a scribbler," Swift corrected him. "He has learning, and will one day write an epic in the manner of Virgil."

But Alexander shrugged this off. "Your recommendation makes me into a dull, dry scholar," he said laughingly, "the sort whose dearest ambition is to write a treatise for *The Works of the Learned.*"

Gay smiled. "*The Works of the Learned!* Is that really a periodical?"

"Most certainly. Unreadable from start to finish."

"I like its title very much indeed," Gay enthused. "Entirely absurd and overblown. I hereby make a proposal. I move that we three begin a society in vehement opposition to dull journals and dull men. Our publication shall be called *The Works of the Unlearned.* We shall publish as infrequently as possible."

"An excellent plan," said Alexander, carried away with the pleasure of his success with Swift. "We shall be remembered as the great unlearned wits of the age."

"How much better that, than to be forgotten as its most learned sages!" Swift rejoined.

The music of the opera sounded a particularly strident blast, and the attention of all parties was momentarily drawn back to the action.

Gay, who had been following the drama with even greater merriment than Steele, exclaimed boisterously, "Dear me, I fear that the undertakers have forgotten to change the side scenes. We now have a prospect of the ocean in the middle of a delightful grove. I must own myself astonished to see that well-dressed young fellow in a full-bottomed wig, appearing in the middle of the sea, and without any visible concern taking snuff."

Throughout the merriment caused by the opera, Lord Petre remained uncharacteristically silent. He stood in the corner of the box, trying to concentrate on the performance, but in truth all of his attention was focused on the ladies' boxes and fidgeting with the buttons on his coat. He had noticed Robert Harley glancing towards him, probably wondering what was the matter, but he could not bring himself to care, either for that, or for his obvious inattention to the performers. All he wanted was to know that Arabella was present, and, more important, present because he had requested that she come.

He told himself that it would be only a few minutes until the first act was over. He would leave the box with the other men—neither rushing ahead nor lingering behind as though he were embarrassed. He would greet a few others, and then he would approach her. The thought of Arabella Fermor's standing within reach of him made his throat close over slightly. It felt a little like panic, but it was pure excitement. He would be permitted to kiss her hello, first one cheek, and then the other. It was the fashion.

But supposing she were not there—it would be torment to stand and make conversation. There would be no one else to flirt with; nobody he could bear to make the pretence of flirting with. If Arabella was not at the opera he would have to leave.

He paid no attention to Richard Steele, who was crying out with ever-increasing exuberance, "The birds! The birds! I do believe they have already got into Lady Sandwich's head-dress!" The whole party was laughing and peering over the box to watch them, but Lord Petre stood impatiently in his dark corner, longing for the act to be over.

Arabella was seated beside the Blount sisters' aunt. From her position in the ladies' box, she could see Lord Petre quite clearly on the other side of the theatre, standing with the men in his party. Why *did* men always stand? she wondered. To appear impervious to the charms of the Italian opera, presumably. They were achieving that effect without difficulty.

She watched as he moved apart from his friends, turning to look into the audience. She was certain that he was looking for her. How delightful. She had taken care to sit well back, where she could not clearly be made out.

The door of Arabella's box opened, and two elegantly dressed women walked in: Lady Salisbury and her fashionable friend Henrietta Oldmixon. She looked up and smiled as they came forward, hoping that they would acknowledge her. They nodded back and seemed about to speak, but then caught sight of friends seated among the little crowd of women at the front of the box. Arabella saw that this fashionable group included Charlotte Castlecomber and Lady Mary Pierrepont, and disappointed she watched as Lady Salisbury and Henrietta Oldmixon moved forward to greet them, leaving her behind.

On her left, she could hear the Miss Blounts making a fuss about their friend Alexander Pope. Martha was saying, "I believe that he is enjoying himself, though he struggles to pretend not to. I wonder who that clergyman is? Alexander is looking up at him very eagerly."

"Alexander's eager look is rather trying, do not you think?" Teresa replied. "If he could learn to view the world with greater detachment, he would find himself a more general favourite."

Aunt Blount interrupted her eavesdropping.

"What think you of Lady Tewkesbury, Miss Fermor?" she asked. "What colour would you give to the lace at her breast? Is it golden or yellow? It looks well beside the rich painting on her face, does it not? And what age would you say she is, Miss Fermor?"

Arabella turned to old Mrs. Blount with a patient smile. She must give an appearance of interest, of course. She answered that the lace appeared more gold than yellow; that the effect of her paint was fine, and (biting back the temptation to say that she could not be a day more than a hundred and twenty) guessed that Lady Tewkesbury must be something under forty-five.

When she came to the end of this speech, Aunt Blount smiled and said, "I perceive that I am boring you, my dear."

Arabella started, hoping that her surprise, at least, was imperceptible to her astute companion. It had not occurred to her that Mrs. Blount could be so observant.

"But you bear yourself with so much charm and gentility, Miss Fermor," the old lady continued, ignoring Arabella's discomposure, "that I cannot doubt your future happiness. You have not, for example, glanced more than once at the gentlemen's boxes in the last half-hour—which is more than can be said for my poor niece Teresa."

Arabella hardly knew what reply to make. Mrs. Blount smiled and said, "But look; I see that the singers have finally paused for breath. When it comes to making noise, an audience will always outlast the performers in point of stamina."

Arabella had no time to consider how seriously she had misjudged this exchange, for the act had ended and the box was astir. There was a general current of movement; she caught sight of Mary Pierrepont, Charlotte Castlecomber, Miss Oldmixon, and Lady Salisbury walking towards the supper room, and, beside her, the Blount girls were standing up to follow them. She was about to see Lord Petre. For a moment Arabella sat motionless, and then slowly, appearing to give much attention to adjusting her fur stole, she walked alone to the salon in which the company was assembled.

Lord Petre had positioned himself by the buffet with Robert Harley, who was describing a bill about cattle imports from Ireland soon to be read in Parliament. Hardly conscious of what he was doing, Lord Petre took two glasses of wine from the waiter and offered one to Harley—only to find that he was holding one already.

"So much the better for you, my lord!" said the chief minister with a laugh. Lord Petre smiled back at him mechanically and turned to face the gathering. He wondered whether he should attempt to explain his inattention.

Then he saw her.

In his mind he had imagined and reimagined Arabella—as she had appeared at the Exchange; in her goddess costume at the masque. By day he remembered her in bonnet and gloves; at night he imagined her as she had been as Diana: hair gathered loosely at her shoulders, stray tresses across her face. But she was a hazy figure in his reconstruction, beautiful and yet without features that could be clearly imagined; alluring and yet with a form that he did not precisely recall. As he looked across the room, however, he beheld the Real Being standing at the entrance.

Her beauty was shocking. There was no whimsy about her dress tonight: her mantua gown was exquisitely composed and cut to her figure, the brocade petticoat full to the ground, the sleeves adorned with gorgeous furbelows, the *décolletage* deliciously full. She was tall, yet not too tall; her bearing bespoke a confidence and power that would never yield, yet the curve of her face and the freshness of her skin promised sweet consolation.

Both Arabella and Lord Petre had told themselves beforehand that they would not look directly at each other when they met. Arabella reminded herself of this even as she turned into the salon. But each saw the other at exactly the same moment; neither had time to turn away unseen—and as their eyes met the impulse that would have made them move apart fled. Arabella's eyes flashed; she parted her lips—to smile, to speak (though there was nobody by to speak to)—but found that she could go no further. She stood motionless at the entrance, waiting for him to come to her.

At last he was by her side. She found herself holding one of his two glasses, but neither of them lifted the drink to their lips for fear of a shaking hand.

Lord Petre broke the silence. "How did Miss Fermor enjoy the first act?" he asked her.

"I was hardly able to look away from the stage," she said in reply. "The drama between the lovers was very powerful. I am wild to know how it will end."

"The lovers are compelling, are they not?" he echoed.

"Exceedingly, my lord." She smiled, but could say no more.

"We are a large group this evening," he observed.

She inclined her head, but again found herself speechless.

He was ready with another question, however. "Did you arrive with the Miss Blounts?" he asked, "I saw them in the box."

"I came in their aunt's carriage," she answered.

In his new awkwardness, Petre realized that he had failed to kiss Arabella in greeting. It was too late, the chance lost. He stood in brooding silence, while Arabella looked about the room with an attempt at nonchalance.

They were rescued by Richard Steele and Robert Harley, who approached with a view to sharing in more merriment at the expense of the singers and the audience. Then Teresa walked over with her friend Margaret Brownlow and asked Arabella whether she knew the name of the gentleman standing talking to Sir George Brown. With immense effort Arabella looked over at the person they described.

"Yes," she said shortly, "it is Francis Perkins."

"Are you acquainted with him, Arabella?" Teresa asked, determined to take her attention away from Lord Petre.

"I have met him once or twice." But instead of Teresa's voice in reply, she heard Lord Petre's.

"You danced with Mr. Perkins at the masquerade, did not you?" he asked in a low tone. She only just stopped herself from turning to him instantly.

"My Lord Petre has an excellent memory," she said to Teresa with a light laugh.

There was more talk, more laughter. One moment Arabella thought that he would walk away with the other men. The next Lord Petre feared that she would turn back to the box with Miss Blount, and that his chance would be lost. The chance for what, he could not say. Neither of them heard a word of the conversation; each of them looked for a reason to address the other. They both wished, vainly, that everybody else would go away. At last, as the audience began returning to their seats, they found themselves face to face. Lord Petre stood mute, looking at Arabella intently. She struggled for a pleasantry to break their silence.

Finally she said, a little too loudly, "How eagerly I look forward to the next act."

Lord Petre continued to stare, and she had time to feel an instant's anger towards him for taking no action—when, abruptly, in a low voice, he said, "I must see you."

It was Arabella's turn to be silent.

"Will you allow me to find you?"

Arabella might have answered, Shall we go back to our seats? What a delightful evening this has been. And had she done so, Lord Petre would have checked himself. If she put a stop to it, he told himself, he would withdraw instantly. But Arabella, very much to his surprise, and somewhat to her own, did not.

"I am not in hiding, my lord," she replied, and turned to join the approaching figure of Mrs. Blount, who was walking back to the box.

Seated again, Arabella thought back over each detail of their conversation. Their exchange had been deliciously fraught, conducted by two persons who thoroughly understood the habits, the small nuances of flirtation. Nothing had been overstated—except for his thrilling, urgent cry: *I must see you.* How unlike the mewling suitors she had endured hitherto, with their hesitant approaches and weak compliments. A warning voice told her that she must not see him alone. But in her heart she knew that she had already gone too far to turn back.

The players had begun again and now their music was delightfully sweet. At last the audience was quiet, captivated by the story. Over on the men's side, even Steele's protests were silenced as the hero vowed to endure all dangers to save his beloved. But his bravado was of a most fragile order, and sure enough, he was soon tempted. A Siren sang to him, and he was powerless to resist her call. Unheeding of his companions' cries, Rinaldo abandoned his heroic journey. The beloved was forsaken; the hero had fallen.

Very much against his wishes, Alexander found himself enthralled in the drama. He had not noticed until now that the composer and librettist had found a story so well suited to the present situation in England. It was an episode from Tasso: the Christians' siege of Jerusalem. An apt choice, for the story was fraught with the drama of religious enmity. Yet how cleverly it was done, he saw, and felt the prickling agitation of jealousy. What a superb aria the Siren sang: how simple, how truly surprising—but menacing, with its steady, relentless rhythm. He acknowledged, with a sinking feeling, that it was superior to anything he himself had written. This Mr. Handel must be a clever fellow, German or no.

In her box, Arabella leaned over to the Blounts' aunt and said, "I am in need of some air. I shall return presently." Her companion, assuming Arabella meant that she needed to find a chamber-pot, nodded and turned back to the performance.

Arabella stood up, walked out of the box, and leaned back against the wall in the dark passageway. How could she endure the rest of the night? Lord Petre's question had promised such exquisite relief, but here she was once again, pressed between Martha Blount and her aunt, with nothing but more conversation, more standing about, more tedious gallantry to follow. He would leave with the men, she with the women. And they would meet each other in a fortnight's time, as good as strangers again.

Seeing that the men were all attending to the drama, Lord Petre withdrew from his seat. He knew that the right thing to do was to have a piss and return to the performance. But how could he shake off this sense of anticipation? He could attend to nothing. He walked into a room just off the passage. He might have known that a crowd would be waiting there for the chamber-pots, but felt that he couldn't bear to stand for twenty minutes watching people urinating noisily in front of him. He walked out on to the street and opened his breeches in the alley beside the theatre. Probably not a very sensible thing to do, he reflected as he came back inside.

At the top of the stairs, he paused before turning back to the men's side. He might just go to where Arabella was sitting and look in. Nobody need see him. He would put his head around the doorway, and leave immediately.

But she was standing in the passage.

"My lord!" she exclaimed as he walked up to her.

"Bell," he said, and gave her the kiss that he had missed out on before. His hand was on the back of her neck, his thumb pressed to her jaw. With his other hand he took hold of her shoulder, so that she could not turn away. The kiss was brief; had they been in public it would hardly have drawn notice, but for the force with which he held her.

"Forgive my rudeness earlier. I came to render the debt I owe you."

"An oversight, my lord. There was much to distract you."

"There was but one thing to distract me."

She smiled.

"Bell, will you come with me now?"

She froze. Even now she could withdraw from this with dignity; nobody need know what she had felt this evening—what she had felt ever since she had seen him. But it was impossible. She knew that she must refuse him, yet found that she could not.

"My things," she stammered, "they are within—the Miss Blounts will—"

He held a finger to his lips to silence her. "I shall take care of them," he said, and walked into the box.

Bending down to the girls' aunt, Lord Petre whispered, "I found Miss Fermor outside. She is unwell—faint with the heat. I shall send her home with my footman. It is fortunate that I happened to see her, but do not be alarmed, madam. Do not thank me; I shall return before the act is over. Will you hand me her things?"

Teresa, overhearing the exchange, leaned forward to speak.

"My poor cousin!" she whispered. "I wondered why she had not resumed her seat. I shall—I must—accompany her, my lord, to see her safe home."

But her aunt put a hand on Teresa's arm as she began to stand.

"You will stay here with me, my dear. Miss Fermor is in the safest hands." She looked at Lord Petre with a smile that he knew not how to interpret. "You are kind, my lord," she said.

"It is my great pleasure, madam."

He returned to Arabella and offered his arm. Lucky that Teresa had not been allowed to come outside with him, for Arabella now displayed an animation that spoke of not only excellent health but excellent spirits.

"Let us go, madam," Lord Petre said.

She gave one of her proud, impenetrable smiles, and replied, "By all means, my lord."

Chapter Ten

"Beware of all, but most beware of Man!"

This would not be the first time that Arabella had ridden in a gentleman's carriage late at night. It was customary for girls to be driven home by their admirers, and as she walked down the stairs beside Lord Petre, Arabella recalled past coach rides, which generally took place after the gentleman accompanying her had had a good deal too much to drink. The journeys had therefore followed a predictable pattern of hastily confessed ardour and urgently executed seduction. But when Lord Petre handed her into his carriage, he did not spring in behind her, and for a moment, Arabella believed that he really *was* going to send her home alone with his footman. He had merely gone to give directions to his driver, however, and she sat bolt upright, smiling very brightly at him as he finally climbed into the coach. He took his seat opposite her, but made no attempt to close the window coverings, so that they could clearly be seen to drive away together in the direction of Arabella's house in St. James's.

The movement of the coach caused them to sway to and fro, making it difficult to concentrate. Lord Petre did not seem concerned as he looked out the window at the lighted buildings they were passing by, but Arabella tried to meet his gaze, to show herself, as much as him, that she was not afraid. Now that they were alone together, she was conscious of having moved beyond the orbit of the familiar. In previous late-night encounters, this would have been the moment in which her admirer would tack amorously across the carriage towards her, murmuring in a thickened voice that he had never beheld such beauty as hers, nor such exquisite charms. Taking hold of whichever part of her person would admit purchase, he would press his lips to her own, and, with uneven proficiency of execution, would fondle her person for as long as she was willing to support it. This was usually very little time at all, and the episode would conclude in a resentful silence that lasted until the carriage arrived at Arabella's front door.

Lord Petre, however, did not lean in fervently, but sat opposite, swaying to the motion of the carriage and looking at her with an unhurried air. "I trust that Miss Fermor is not, in fact, indisposed," he said eventually.

Arabella smiled, but her heart beat quickly against her stays—how strange that she should feel so much more agitated by Lord Petre's steady gaze than by the overtures of her previous suitors. "Miss Fermor's disposition depends upon the circumstances in which she finds herself," she answered with a smile, hoping that he could not see how quickly it faded. "I will confess to feeling a little faint," she added. "The carriage is somewhat close."

"Allow me to open a window, madam. That will make you easier." He did so, with another smile, and she wondered if he might be laughing at her.

After a few more minutes, Arabella realized that the lights of shops and buildings were no longer visible outside; they had turned down a narrow, unlit laneway. She felt her fingers pricking and her throat tightening with alarm.

She tried to steady her voice as she said, "I fear that your driver has lost his way, my lord. We are in a secondary street, some distance from my family's town house."

She thought she saw Lord Petre smile again, but in the dark shadows of the carriage it might just as well have been a sneer. He made no attempt to stop but said instead, "I believe that you are right. If he does not regain the proper course shortly, I shall ask him to pull up."

Arabella felt a rising sense of panic. What was she to do? Not a soul knew where she was.

The carriage jangled to a halt; they were in a deserted alleyway. Lord Petre's footman sprang down from behind and opened the door, the catch giving a sudden, loud click that made Arabella jump again. Lord Petre leaned out of the door, saying quietly, "Will you take her in, Jenkins?"

As the footman put out a hand to help her down, the lantern he was holding cast a pool of light over the damp ground below the carriage door. She tried to spring down lightly, conscious that Lord Petre was watching her, but she lost her footing on the step and stumbled. She gave a little cry, and the footman's hand closed tightly on her arm to steady her. His grip was painful, and she looked up at him with an expression of fear that she was unable to conceal. He took no notice, but with his hand still closed around her arm, led her around the back of the carriage and towards an opening in the alley wall. Arabella squinted, trying to make out the dark forms that were obscured by the glare of the lantern.

They went through the low doorway, and Arabella was surprised to find herself in a stable yard. Jenkins now walked ahead of her, and the altered position of the light made it easier to see. There was a much larger gateway for carriages to come through, and Jenkins was now helping the driver open the wooden doors that were closed across it. As she stood alone she began to shiver, but at last Jenkins returned and led her to the back of the house. He hung up the lantern, taking a night candle instead, and showed her into the dark kitchens.

It was a relief to be inside; the low-ceilinged room was warm from the ovens, and Arabella's little heels walked more securely on the flat stone flags of the floor. Jenkins gestured to a doorway at the side of the kitchen, where there was a flight of stairs. They began to walk up, Jenkins's candle making hollow shadows on the white walls, prompting Arabella to look behind her. These must be back stairs; she was surprised. They had not been built since the Great Fire, except in large mansion houses of the last century. The Petres were even grander than she had thought.

The way up, of course, was empty, but as they passed the ground floor of the house, they heard a clatter of footsteps. Jenkins stiffened, and pressed himself against the dark wall next to the doorway. Arabella stood stock-still, dreading that he would put out the candle and leave them in darkness. The little flame seemed the only familiar sight in this strange place. But the footsteps faded away, and the house was quiet again.

They climbed to the second floor, and Jenkins turned into a door on the left, which let into a tiny bedroom, sparsely furnished. Arabella surmised that it was his own, and walked quickly through.

A door at the other end of this closet gave on to a much larger bedroom, handsomely appointed. With a shock, Arabella realized that it must be Lord Petre's. She looked around quickly, noticing a high-beamed ceiling and dark wainscoting—the house was old—forbidding in the dim light. There was a large high bed with draped curtains—like Arabella's own, in fact, though upholstered in a dark brocade—but she quickly averted her eyes lest Jenkins see that she was curious. A large fire burned in the fireplace, but it was far from the bed, and it seemed far from Arabella, too; the room was chilly, and she hurried after Jenkins, her heels ringing on the old wooden floorboards.

He opened another door, and they entered an adjoining sitting-room. A rush of warm air enveloped her, and she saw a large, bright fire in the grate. It blazed up, crackling from a recent tending. The room was lit with wax candles, their flames glowing against the walnut grain of the furniture: a fine carved desk, a pair of tables, a long sofa, and two armchairs, upholstered in the new style. But nobody was there.

The servant withdrew, and Arabella sat down on one of the chairs, upright, too awkward to lean back. She could hear a ticking clock and the spitting fire, but nothing more. She had no notion at all of what to do—the gleeful spirit of contest that had once so possessed her was gone. Being alone in a man's chamber was quite different from the harmless coach rides she had known so far, and the flirtations that she had mastered in the ballroom seemed absurdly out of place here. She was struck anew by the enormity of what she had done; how foolish she had been to imagine that she could be in command of the situation. She had known of unmarried girls who had been ruined by doing exactly this—she thought of Maria Granville, whom she had ridiculed to Teresa at the Exchange. She sat with tightly clasped hands, her knuckles squeezed white.

But to her relief the spark of rebellion that had prompted her to come did not desert her entirely. She made herself unlock her hands and lean back into the arms of the chair. After a moment or two she stood up, and walked over to look at her reflection in the large mirror hanging above the fireplace.

The warmth of the fire began to relax Arabella. She put her

hands up to her face to pinch colour back into her cheeks, rubbing and sucking at her lips to make them bright again. She stroked her hair, arranging the two curls on either side of her neck, and smiled at her reflection, faintly at first, but then with more assurance, as she walked back to her seat to wait. Again she asked herself why she had come. Was it a momentary whim, an instant of madness? She did not believe so. She had taken a great risk, but in spite of that she did not regret her actions. For the first time in her life she felt that she had found her way to adventure, and the discovery made her realize how much, and for how long, she had dreamed of it.

The door opened from the hall without, and Lord Petre entered. He walked over to the sofa by her chair and sat down on its edge, one leg folded under him, the other stretched out in front to steady himself. He tucked his sword in neatly beside him and leaned towards her.

"I cannot believe that I have you here," he said, smiling. To her relief she saw that it was the boyish smile again, the one that had so attracted her at the Exchange. He got to his feet again and poured out a glass of wine for each of them.

He handed her a drink. "How are you now?" he asked.

"Quite recovered," she replied, taking a sip. It flowed through her pleasantly, reassuringly, making her forebodings appear foolish. Lord Petre did not appear to be agitated in the least.

"I am glad to hear it," he said. "Had you been faint, I would have suggested that we loosen your stays."

She said nothing, but felt a renewed tremor. As she took another sip of her wine she wondered if perhaps this feeling could be anticipation. He caught her eye. He was smiling again, but devilishly, and she wondered if he had guessed her thoughts. He took the glass from her hand and put it down on the mantel.

"I wonder if we had better not do so in any case."

Do what? thought Arabella. Oh! Loosen my stays. So this is how it was done, she reflected, and the word *seducer* flashed across her mind. She felt another rising of anticipation, and recognized that the feeling, far from being alarming, was pleasant.

"I would be inconsolably disappointed were you to faint, now that I have you here," he said, as he took her hands and raised her up to stand beside him.

She smiled, this time archly, and answered, "I am afraid that I have no experience of unlacing my own stays. Betty is always by to help me."

He was very close to her now; she could feel his breath on her cheek. She thought that he would kiss her, and she lifted her face towards him, but he said, stroking her on the neck, "What does Betty generally do? Can you recall?"

"As a rule, I am seated upon a stool," she said.

He took her by the hand and led her to an upright chair.

She shivered—it was certainly excitement now. "Yes, somewhat like that one," she said. "She unbuttons my gown—" Arabella felt his fingers on her back. They moved quickly, and she knew that he had done this before. But where she would have expected to feel jealousy, she felt a twinge of gratification—perhaps even pride—that he was so adroit.

"Then Betty unties my petticoat," she continued, "and helps me to unlace the stays. It is a delicate task, but I suspect that you will be equal to it."

He stood behind her, and the palms of his hands arched over her shoulders, his fingers stroking the white skin of her throat. He pressed his thumbs into the hollow of her collarbone, and she felt him lean over to trace, lightly, the swell of her breasts made by her stays. She could hear him breathing quickly, now, and her own heart was pounding. She wanted to touch his hands and his face, but she sat still, letting him take hold of her.

At last he lifted her face up to his, and began to kiss her. Not the clammy touch that she had known in the past, but hungrily, without restraint. She knew that his skill must be the product of practice, but, curiously, that made it all the more pleasurable. The power that she had noticed when he moved and spoke was now concentrated upon herself, and though his lovemaking seemed impulsive, she also admired its deliberate force. He was in command of the situation, and she arched up towards him, infected by his desire and determination. He pulled her to her feet.

"Bell, you are the most beautiful girl I have ever seen," he said. "Would that I could keep you always just as you are in this moment." She felt his hands under her stays, on her skin, as he explored the curve of her waist; his fingers pressed into the little space beneath her ribs. "I pray that you may never change," he mumbled.

He pulled her close to him, and her gown and petticoat fell to the floor around her body. He folded his arms about her and kissed her again, and she felt, with a shock, the outline of his penis. It was hard—it startled her—she had never felt a man's member before. But she noticed that he was not self-conscious at all as he began to push her backward towards his chamber. She stepped over the little barrier made by her outer garments.

His room seemed nicer now. The fire had burned up brightly, and a candle was flickering next to the bed. Jenkins must have put it there before he retired, Arabella thought with surprise. Lord Petre lifted her on to the bed. The cavern made by the bed curtains was warm and comforting. He kicked off his shoes and knelt beside her, his hands on her legs.

"What a delicate silk your garters are, Arabella," he said as he plucked at the bows. "And how easily they can be untied," he added, looking at her to be sure that she did not want him to stop. She felt the ribbons sliding off and the touch of his hands on her skin as he peeled down her stockings. "These are delightfully pretty," he said. "I believe that they have golden thread through them." Her legs tingled as his fingers touched them. With a playful smile he said, "We had best get them off, for otherwise I shall be hopelessly distracted."

Arabella thought that she had never felt anything so exquisite, so private, so intensely pleasurable as this.

Lord Petre buried his face in the folds of her smock. "Your shift is very alluring," he went on, "so we shall leave it on you for the moment." He was kneeling before her now, laughing at her flushed, eager face. "Now, these troublesome, troublesome stays," he murmured, pretending to examine them. "Good Lord! How can you bear to be trapped inside them, all day long? Let me see—but I cannot untie the ribbons, for you are lying upon them." He kissed the space between her breasts, and her neck. "How pretty your robings are. They match your gown. What a gorgeous creature you are, Bell."

Half believing that he really was unable to work the ribbons, Arabella sat up and started to unlace the whalebone frame that surrounded her torso. Her face lapsed into an expression of fierce concentration, which made him smile. With a charming lift of her eyebrows, she looked up and said, "There, I believe you can finish it now."

"Yes, I think that I will."

When Arabella was dressed only in her smock, and this garment could not be described as "on" her in the strictest sense, she said to Lord Petre, boldly, "Will you show me how to unbutton your breeches?" But she blushed as she said it, suddenly shy. She looked up at him, and she saw, for the first time, an expression of concern on his face. She wondered whether it was for himself or for her.

He smiled at her and asked, "Have you not undressed a man before?" and she shook her head, gravely.

He took her hands and put them on his waist; she tucked them under the tails of his shirt, feeling his skin with her thumbs. She felt him twitch—she had tickled him. "I will show you," he said, "but after that we shall have to be very careful."

"Careful of what?"

He looked at her as though he wished that he could sink his teeth into her neck and devour her. No longer able to resist speaking candidly, he replied, "Careful that I do not drive my cock into you up to the hilt, which is what I would like to do, and get you with child."

Lord Petre was true to his word, and when Arabella left his house at the end of the night her chastity was preserved. His carriage deposited her at her parents' town house and she skipped inside, exhilarated by what had just passed. She ran up to her bedroom, surprised to see that the fire had burned out and that the sky was lightening in the little eastern corner of her window.

As Arabella thought back on the night with mixed emotions of gratification and astonishment, Lord Petre felt surprise of a different kind. When he had walked in to discover her seated on the chair by his fire, her look of nervous apprehension had taken him aback. How different she had suddenly appeared from the Arabella Fermor of the ball and the opera: that proud, controlled creature whose beauty and self-possession filled him with longing. At first he had not known what was the matter; he thought perhaps that she was ill . . . but then he had realized, with a shock, that she was afraid. Not wanting her to see that he knew, he had walked over to pour a glass of wine, hoping that she would compose herself. She had, of course.

But though her assurance and confidence had aroused him, that glimpse of her vulnerability had drawn forth emotions that he had never known before. He felt the desire to protect her, to keep her from harm: he imagined himself as her champion, secretly carrying her colours between his armour and his heart. His fancy took flight, and he pictured himself returning from the troubles and travails of the world to find her at his fireside, the proud smile that she wore in public turned inward to a sweet, imploring look of appeal. This new image of Arabella, at once the siren who sang to him and the maiden who ministered, gained swift purchase on Lord Petre's imagination, propelling him to even more vehement, and now exquisitely poignant, pangs of desire.

The pangs, however, he was shortly required to set aside. He was awoken at eleven o'clock the next morning by Jenkins, who came to tell him that John Caryll, his former guardian, had arrived in town. He had called at the house for Lord Petre at ten, but was in a hurry to be gone, and had instructed Jenkins to have Lord Petre meet him in White's coffee-house at noon. Lord Petre sat up wearily, reluctantly taking the velvet morning-coat that Jenkins held out to him, and sliding his feet into the slippers that had been placed beside the bed.

"I suppose I must go," he said, deducing from Jenkins's silence that his footman agreed. "But I cannot leave the house without breakfast," he added. "Will you get me some toasted bread and bacon, Jenkins? And I do not think I can face my chocolate this morning. I shall take a mug of ale instead."

He pulled on a pair of stockings and breeches and tied them into place, wondering which coat he should wear. Perhaps just his blue one. Mr. Caryll would hardly notice, and there was not much chance of seeing Arabella out this morning. He thought of Arabella's curls falling over her face as she untied her stays, and felt an erection stirring in his trousers. But Jenkins came in with the bacon, and he was calm again.

*

When Lord Petre arrived at White's, he was relieved to discover that Caryll's friend Mr. Pope was there too. He ought to have expected it, he reflected, remembering with some embarrassment the meeting at Ladyholt when he had made the unfortunate discovery of Mr. Pope's crippled frame. Mr. Pope did not seem to recall it, thank heavens. But now he would not have minded if Pope had ass's ears and a monkey's tail, so long as he made small talk with Caryll.

Caryll stood to greet him, clapping him on the back. "How are you, my lord? Well? Splendid—you look tremendous."

He had forgotten Caryll's enthusiasms, more familiar with the prickly officiousness that had been habitual when he was his ward.

"You remember my young friend Pope, do you not, my lord?" Caryll was saying. "Alexander Pope, the celebrated poet?"

"Not celebrated," Pope was mumbling, looking awkward. Lord Petre gave him a sympathetic glance, remembering the days before he inherited his title, when people were always introducing him as the next Baron of Ingatestone while he protested furiously. Of course nobody had cared in the slightest.

"Nonsense, Pope," Caryll was saying. "Your *Essay on Criticism* is to be sold next month—you told me that Tonson believes it will go to a second edition."

Alexander frowned with embarrassment, making Lord Petre want to laugh.

"What brings you to town, sir?" Alexander asked Caryll. Immediately the gentleman's face became serious.

"I am here to see about a bride for my son," he answered.

"Is not your son to marry Lord Arundell's daughter?" Lord Petre asked without thinking.

"In the end I did not favour the match," Caryll said stiffly. Lord Petre recoiled, looking at his former guardian with curiosity. How strange he was: one minute effusively friendly, the next like ice. He would certainly not want to be out of favour with him—nor reliant on him for anything either, he thought. He hoped that Mr. Pope did not depend upon him for his progress in town.

But Caryll had started to explain. "Lord Arundell would not

agree to the settlement—he was greedy on his daughter's behalf. The arrangements I proposed were fair, but he would not have it so. I parted company with him. But I believe that I have found another lady who will suit my son better. Lord Throgmorton's daughter. Do you know her, my lord?"

Lord Petre shook his head, motioning for the waiter's attention. John Caryll was a beady fellow, and he could well imagine old Lord Arundell blanching at the settlement. But he wished Caryll no ill; he had such a large number of children for whom he was expected to provide.

He was pleased when Caryll turned to Pope and said, "I have brought a letter from your father, sir. I hope that it contains his blessing for you to remain in town."

Alexander took it from him quickly, with a nervous smile. "I should be astonished if it were to contain his blessing, but I do hope that he will understand my wishing to continue here," he said, looking apprehensive as he broke the seal.

Lord Petre was beginning to frame a question about Caryll's wife and children, when Pope burst out, "It is just as I thought. He does not like it, but he gives permission. I believe I have you to thank for this, sir." He smiled up at Caryll, and Caryll looked gracious. Lord Petre glanced at him sceptically. He could not imagine Caryll interceding on anyone's part, let alone for little Alexander Pope.

But Alexander was exclaiming again. "Good Lord!" he cried as he ran his eyes down the page. "That man *was* a priest!" The two others turned to him in surprise.

"What are you speaking about, Pope?" asked Caryll, prickling instantly at the mention of Catholics, Lord Petre noticed.

"The masquerade guest! The fellow who was murdered in Shoreditch," Alexander said.

Lord Petre went still.

"His name was Francis Gerrard," Pope said. "A Catholic from Lancashire. There was a notice about it in the *Daily Courant.* My father is an avid reader of the newspaper," he explained to Lord Petre.

"Francis Gerrard," John Caryll echoed, and he glanced quickly around the room. "I knew him. He was indeed a priest, accustomed to visit the embassy on clerical business. He expected to be taken for a masquerade guest that night and ignored."

Alexander and Lord Petre both stared at him. Who had Caryll heard this from?

Caryll continued to speak. "Gerrard had long been an ardent supporter of the Jacobite cause, very active at the time of my uncle's arrest. Some time ago, I believe, he discovered that there were traitors among the Jacobite agents in London. I was told that he went to the embassy that night to tell the ambassador's secretary what he knew."

"You were told, sir?" echoed Alexander. "You know of this already! He was killed deliberately?" Alexander felt himself grow cold. He had allowed himself to forget the fears he had had when he first came to London. Martha had put his mind to rest, too, dismissing with calm good sense his suspicions of Lord Petre. But he had only to glance at Lord Petre's face now to guess that they had been well founded.

"Nobody knows," Caryll answered. "Nothing more has been discovered of the murder."

Lord Petre knew that he had gone white. "But where did you hear of this, sir?" he asked.

Caryll looked around the room again. "From an old friend," he said quietly. "The Jacobites of my uncle's generation are still closely connected."

Lord Petre played with the buttons of his coat, pretending to be distracted by something the waiter was saying. He was stunned by Caryll's news. What was the meaning of it? Was Caryll giving him a warning? He wondered whether Douglass had heard the story. He must be told immediately. Perhaps Caryll had even engineered this meeting to tell him about Gerrard. And yet it had been Mr. Pope who raised the matter.

Could Caryll still be with the Jacobites? Lord Petre looked across to him, searching for some sign of mutual understanding. The glance was not returned. But Caryll had already been imprisoned for suspected treason, Lord Petre reminded himself. He could not risk further involvement now. Once again he tried to catch Caryll's eye, but he had turned to greet another acquaintance who had just walked into the coffee-house.

*

Alexander was relieved to be gone from Lord Petre and John Caryll's company as he walked back to Jervas's house that afternoon. He wanted nothing to do with the Jacobites, and though he did not believe that Caryll could himself be involved in anything of a treasonous kind, the glimpse he had been given of secret communications and clandestine meetings had repelled him. Jervas was right—it was another world, one that he had supposed to be long gone.

Of course, for as long as he was living with Charles Jervas he would be safe; the very idea of Jervas letting anyone sneak around after dark in a cassock made him laugh. But it had been astonishing to observe Lord Petre's countenance when the subject of Gerrard was raised. He had tried to hide his confusion—it had seemed that Caryll had noticed nothing—but he had gone white at the news. Alexander smiled, gratified to have seen Lord Petre at a disadvantage for once. At first he had swaggered into White's, his sword swaying as though he were a knight-at-arms returning to the banquet after a hard day's jousting. But he had slunk out at the end with his tail well between his legs, no doubt reflecting that there would not be much jousting to be had if his body were tied to a cart and divided into four bloody pieces.

Chapter Eleven

"With varying Vanities, from ev'ry Part,
They shift the moving Toyshop of their heart."

"Arabella's petticoat had no flounce," Teresa announced to her sister as they sat together one morning about a week after the opera. Martha was working at her sewing; Teresa holding a letter.

"Who is your letter from, Teresa?" Martha asked, ignoring her sister's observation, which she had heard several times before.

"Our grandfather," she replied. "But he has nothing to say—he only asks how we do, whether our aunt is recovered from her cold, and if Alexander has been to call on us. Alexander has probably sent him the news by now. He loves to write long letters showing off about some author or other whom he has read."

She walked over to the looking-glass to study her face. Martha watched as she turned her head one way and then the other.

"Do you know, I think my profile is just as nice as Bell's," Teresa observed, as much to herself as to her sister. The day before, she had returned from a morning levee at Arabella's looking crestfallen, and had sat alone in her room for nearly an hour. When Martha had asked about it she said, "Arabella had new friends there, whom I had not met before. She must have been going about visiting without me." Martha guessed it was why Teresa was worrying about her dress today.

Teresa examined her profile again. "I was watching Arabella talking to Lady Salisbury yesterday," she said, "and her nose turns upward at the end. But somehow she always manages to stand so that one does not see it."

"What is that package on your desk, Teresa?" Martha asked.

"Oh, something from Alexander, I believe," she answered, not looking at it.

Martha glanced over at her sister sharply. She must have decided that Alexander was not a smart enough friend for Arabella and her new set. But surely Teresa had never dreamed that Arabella would take an interest in a young poet anyway. How wilfully naive she could be, Martha thought.

"From Alexander?" she echoed. "What is it?" She stepped over to look at the parcel.

"I don't know—it looks like a book of some sort," Teresa said. "He has probably sent that Frenchman Boileau for us to read. Alexander made a joke about him the other day, which I did not even pretend to understand. He said he would give us a volume."

Martha took up the packet and turned it over in her hand. "Boileau? I think not—I believe it is Alexander's new poem. He said that he would send it, even though it is not yet in the booksellers' shops."

"Well, I think he might have waited at least until everybody else is reading it too! What is the use of struggling through fifty pages of poetry if nobody else is doing the same?"

Martha laughed, exasperated, and said, "Teresa, do turn away from that mirror!"

She did not turn away, but she glanced at Martha's reflection, which she could see in the glass behind her own. "Why do you not open it, since you are so eager?" she said.

But Martha had already sat down and begun to untie it, and she found the same little volume that Jacob Tonson had shown Alexander a couple of weeks before. She opened the front cover.

"*Essay on Criticism,*" she read. "How fine it looks. Alexander does not put his name on the title page, though—what a shame."

"Probably because he knows how desperately dull it is," said Teresa, and she turned to look at her sister. As soon as she had spoken she regretted it. It was the sort of remark that they would once have shared a smile over, when Martha had been quite happy for her to tease Alexander about his foibles. But lately, she and her sister had not shared in the jokes of the past. A thought struck her, and she looked at Martha wonderingly. Surely Martha did not imagine that *she* and Alexander could make a match? Unconsciously, she shook her head at her reflection.

Returning her sister's glance, Martha frowned. "This is the first book that Alexander has published on his own. The 'Pastorals' were merely in Tonson's collection, but if the *Essay* is well received, he will have made a name for himself. Do you not want to see him famous?"

Martha knew a lot more about Alexander than she herself did, Teresa noted. They must have been spending more time together than she had realized.

"Alexander has been talking about this *Essay on Criticism* for years, and I am heartily sick of it," she said. "Why does he never write a poem that is witty and diverting?"

"The *Essay* is an ambitious new work, and serious," Martha answered. "This poem could be the making of him. And yet if John Dennis reads the poem, he may likely try to slander Alexander's reputation. I know that he is apprehensive."

Teresa did not like to hear Martha speaking on Alexander's behalf.

"Who is John Dennis?" she asked as she examined the hem of her gown.

"Teresa!" Martha exclaimed in reply. "Don't pretend that you don't know who John Dennis is. He is the most famous critic in London."

Teresa did not, in fact, know who Dennis was, but she said nothing, preferring to let Martha think she had been trying to provoke her. Until this conversation she had not been aware of the extent to which she had fallen out of touch with Alexander. She had forgotten that he had a new poem coming out—and suddenly she wished that she had remembered it. She paused, aware that she was unfairly cross with Martha. She ought to have known that Alexander and her sister would spend time together while she was with Arabella—yet she resented their friendship.

Martha picked up the note that Alexander had included with his poem and read it.

"Alexander has sent us both a billet-doux. It is very charming," she said with a smile.

Teresa jumped up and grabbed the note from her sister. "Let me see it!" she exclaimed. "It was meant for me, Patty. You should not have read my letter!"

"But Alexander addressed it to us both, Teresa," said Martha quietly.

Teresa was distracted, however, when the door opened and a servant brought in a nosegay of flowers. She was at his side in an instant.

"Oh!" she exclaimed as soon as she saw that they were for her. "How lovely! And from the hothouse, for it is far too early for hyacinths from the garden. Is there a note, Jones?" she asked, but the servant shook his head and retired, closing the door with a bang.

Martha was deflated. She had told Alexander that Teresa liked white hyacinths, and guessed that he had sent them to accompany the poem. Of course, Alexander knew Teresa better than to hope she would admire him for his verses alone. Martha shook her head ruefully. Alexander's affections were unchanged.

"Who do you think they are from?" she asked Teresa.

Much to Martha's surprise, Teresa was evasive. She fell silent a moment, considering the possibilities. "I know not," she said at last. "My first thought was James Douglass. When he danced with me at the masquerade I happened to say that our house was next to Lord Salisbury's in King Street." A little spark of excitement appeared in her eye, and she added, "But now I am wondering whether Mr. Douglass might not have mentioned it to Lord Petre. He smiled at me very kindly when I left Arabella's levee yesterday, and said that he was sorry I was leaving so soon."

"Whoever sent them must know the sort of flowers you like, Teresa," said Martha. She paused, and then added, "Perhaps it was Alexander."

"Alexander? Oh, I don't think so." Teresa's face fell, and she looked away. The sight checked Martha in her desire to scold her sister for the outburst over the letter. Her own hopes for Alexander were not so dissimilar to Teresa's for Lord Petre. Was not her own pleasure at Alexander's book as wilfully misled as Teresa's reaction to the flowers? She wondered now whether he had addressed the letter to both girls merely as a necessary gesture, required in the interests of politeness. Not for the first time since they had been in London, the sisters remained together without speaking, neither able to confide the feelings of disappointed hope that so occupied her mind.

*

Lord Petre's private meetings with Arabella were quickly established. When Arabella held the morning levee from which Teresa had returned out of sorts, Lord Petre attended with a group of his friends: the Duke of Beaufort, Henrietta Oldmixon, and Lady Salisbury. His hope was that they would begin to include Arabella as part of their intimate circle, thereby making their clandestine meetings easier to arrange. Arabella was delighted by the development. When Lord Petre's party arrived, a servant led them upstairs to her chamber. She was sitting on her bed drinking chocolate, wearing a loose nightgown and jacket, her hair not yet put up. Teresa was there already, with two other girls whom Lord Petre knew by sight. Arabella's mother had appeared briefly to greet Teresa, but as soon as Lord Petre and his grand companions appeared, she left her daughter to pursue the friendships free from constraint.

The chocolate pot was on a silver stand, the cups ready on an inlaid table, and fresh flowers were on the mantel, sent that morning from Covent Garden by Lord Petre. Seats were found for the new arrivals, the chocolate was poured, and they sat talking for nearly an hour.

Just after noon, the door opened and Betty announced that Miss Blount's carriage had arrived to collect her. Teresa left with obvious reluctance—Lord Petre guessed that she had ordered her carriage before she had known that others would be visiting. He felt a small pang of remorse; perhaps he and Arabella should not make use of poor Teresa as an unwitting alibi in their secret arrangements.

But about ten minutes later, Henrietta Oldmixon sighed and said, "I have an appointment with my dressmaker—I wish that I had not made it so early in the day. How very diverting your levee has been, Miss Fermor; I shall certainly come again if you will have me."

Lady Salisbury rose too, saying, "Indeed, Miss Fermor. How glad I am that Lord Petre has introduced you into our little group."

Arabella smiled, leaning across the bed to kiss them both goodbye, and then said, "But I cannot bear to sit while Betty does my hair without anybody to talk to. Lord Petre—I hope that you and His Grace will remain with me a few minutes longer."

The Duke of Beaufort looked as though he would like to accept Arabella's invitation, but, with a fearful glance at Henrietta, he said, "I regret that I must leave too, Miss Fermor. An appointment at my club . . . Next time, I trust . . ."

Lord Petre bowed and said, "I do not dine at Locket's for another hour, Miss Fermor. I should be happy to stay." He shot her a secret smile of understanding.

The others left, and Lord Petre closed Arabella's chamber door behind them.

"Betty will not come for twenty minutes at least," said Arabella. "I am glad that you are here to entertain me."

She sat down in front of her dressing mirror, wearing a loose gown that permitted Lord Petre's hands a very free range over her person, but which would also enable them to be withdrawn the instant Betty opened the chamber door.

When they met again a couple of days later, it was Lord Petre's turn to arrange the encounter.

"I shall likely require your assistance this afternoon, Jenkins," he said to his servant as he dressed in the morning. He knew that Jenkins would understand. He had always been discreet during the days of his involvement with Molly Walker and, more recently, Charlotte Castlecomber.

Jenkins bowed, and said nothing.

"I shall be bringing Miss Fermor to my apartments later on," Lord Petre said, "but I do not want my family to know that I am at home. Would you advise the servants that I am out of the house this afternoon?"

"Certainly, sir," said Jenkins, and waited for Lord Petre to reach into his pocket.

Lord Petre handed him a guinea. As he turned to leave, Jenkins took a letter from his jacket, and asked Lord Petre whether he meant it to be delivered.

"Ah, there it is," said Lord Petre. "I am glad that you noticed it, for I thought it was misplaced." He felt in his coat for more coins. "Buy some flowers from the market as you go, and take the letter to Miss Fermor with my compliments." He gave Jenkins the money.

Jenkins pocketed it. "Thank you, my lord."

Lord Petre departed, and Jenkins duly bought the handsome posy that Lord Petre was accustomed most days to send to Arabella. But he did not pay for the flowers with the money his master had given him, instead putting them on the account that Lord Petre kept with the florist. He saved the coins for his personal use—as he did with most of the money for little purchases that he was given. He considered it one of the few advantages that a servant could be said to have over his master in the present age of credit.

A few weeks later, Arabella was paying an afternoon visit to Lord Petre's apartments. She sat in an armchair beside the fireplace, and he lolled opposite her on the long sofa. He stood up to stir the fire, glancing at her as he did so. She was reading a volume of French poems, and the arc of her neck curved gracefully over its pages. Beside her, on the floor, lay her little heeled shoes, one of them tipping on to its side. Lord Petre looked at them as he turned back from the fire, noticing that the silk damask with which the shoes were covered matched Arabella's jacket. The colour of sea in winter, he thought, as he bent to pick one up. How many hours she must spend each day getting ready, making sure that her garments were all in perfect order.

"These are very pretty, Bell," he said, and she looked up with a smile.

Lord Petre's shirt hung untucked from his breeches, the loose sleeves covering his hands. He tossed the shoe back on to the floor, and Arabella stopped herself from leaning forward to straighten it. Instead she took one of his hands, sliding her fingers up under the awning of the cuff.

"What does a baron do all day?" she asked. He sat lazily on the sofa, pulling her across towards him.

"That is an excellent question, Bell, and easily answered," he replied. "A baron does nothing." He put his hands behind his head and leaned back. Arabella knew that although he liked to deprecate himself in this way, he also liked to be contradicted.

She laughed. "But what about when you are at Ingatestone?" she asked. "Surely then there is much to attend to."

"Oh! In the country—that is a different matter entirely. I had assumed you were speaking of the town. In the country I am constantly occupied. In the summer I fish, in the autumn I shoot, and in the winter I hunt. I frequently dine at greater length and even more heartily than I do here, and it is not at all unusual to travel an hour to a neighbour's for dinner. Now that I describe it, I wonder that there is any time at all left for gambling and drinking."

Arabella frowned at his flippancy, certain that he did not believe his own words. "I do not believe you to be so very idle," she said.

"You are quite right, Arabella. On Monday I dined with James Douglass and on Tuesday with Robert Harley. Last week I went to see a hanging at Tyburn. 'Tis a wonder that I am not entirely exhausted."

"You have been to a hanging?" she echoed.

"Of course," he replied, leaning back on his sofa, trying to look careless. "It is widely considered the most diverting spectacle in London. But I did not enjoy it so much as I had been promised," he added with a laugh that rang hollow. "The man who was being hanged did not die immediately—his wife and children had to pull at his legs to spare him the agonies of a slow death. I did not think it was so wholly entertaining as to justify the attendance of almost an entire metropolis."

Why should he have raised the subject of the hanging when he had disliked it? Arabella thought. She guessed that he did not want to be thought a coward, and yet he told his story in such a way that he could not be accused of being a brute. She said nothing, puzzled by these contradictions in his character.

"Ah, Bell, do not be cast down," Lord Petre said, misinterpreting her silence. "Wretches hang; jurymen dine: 'tis the way of the world."

Arabella looked up at him directly. "Oh, I know *that*," she replied. She paused, and then burst out, "But why are you being so strange and secretive about what you do all day?"

He sat up from his reclining position on the sofa and returned her look without smiling. "Ah—now you are being serious." He walked over to the fire again and gave it a prod with the poker. But then he stepped abruptly to the side of her sofa, knelt down, and looked up at her. His face was earnest, ardent. Arabella's heart began to pound.

"I am at present engaged in business that I cannot speak of," he said obliquely. "When I dine with Mr. Douglass it is not what you think."

It took Arabella a moment to register that he was not after all proposing marriage to her, and when she did, she looked at him incredulously. What on earth could he be talking about? This was not what she had expected.

"I am engaged in—have been for many months engaged in—an affair that is for . . . for the public good of our country," he finished. Arabella said nothing. He was speaking sincerely, but she did not understand him at all.

"It is a plan that involves our queen," he said. "If we are successful, we will make England the strongest nation on earth. And I shall make a name for myself. Not because I am the seventh Baron of Ingatestone, but because I am Robert Petre, an Englishman." His tone was thrilling. "But it is a most confidential matter of state. I can say no more, and should not have said so much. Will you keep my secret?"

She still did not grasp what he was saying, but she listened with more interest than she had expected to feel. It was not the substance of his remarks that caught her attention, it was the sight of him inflamed with the fire of passionate ideals. Behind his charming manner, Lord Petre longed to be a rebel, a hero. This, then, was the basis of his friendship with Douglass. They were firebrands. He took her by the hands, gripping them very tightly.

At last Arabella felt that she had the measure of him. She leaned towards him equally ardently, admiring his courage, his idealism.

The thrill that she perceived in him became real in her, too. His passion was contagious—and it filled her with daring. Leaning forward further still, so that the breath of her whispered words was on his cheek, she said, "Will you take me to bed, Robert?"

Lord Petre felt a rush of exhilaration. His confession had not made her afraid, then! He saw that she was flushed with excitement.

Her breath was still on his skin, and his heart thundered in his chest. He longed to give way, but he hesitated. Protect her and keep her safe. Until today he had thought what he felt for Arabella was violent physical desire, but it was more than this. He was beginning to love her.

Arabella felt him pause, and she pulled back. "I have not the slightest doubt that you have fucked all the married woman you have been abed with," she said.

He felt a thrill as she spoke the word. Protect her! She was fearless. Laughing, he replied, "Married women are a different matter. There is scarcely a man in London whose father is the person to whom his mother was married. Nobody expects married women to be chaste."

But Arabella did not answer. Standing up, she stepped around him and walked towards his chamber.

At any other moment, had he not been so fired up with thoughts of rebellion and adventure, he might have been able to stop himself, though it would have required an immense effort. But the circumstances proved too much for him.

Afterwards he was happier than he could ever remember being. It was so easy, and he wondered why he had had such scruples—such fears—about taking her as his mistress. This was not like his relationship with Charlotte, where they were natural with one another because they felt no disarming passion, nor like his involvement with Molly, where their desire had been entirely physical. With Arabella it was a complete absorption. Although he had just been with her, he still desired her; he felt a lingering anticipation that made him want to be with her always.

Arabella was infected with a spirit of playfulness. Her eyes flashed triumphantly and her smile burned brighter than ever. She sat up, saying, "I am fond of your bed, but its aspect is unvarying. I propose a change of scene. What is that door over to the right? No, not Jenkins's chamber—the other one."

He replied, smilingly, "That is my closet."

"I hoped that you had one! May we visit it?" she asked.

"I suppose that we may," he replied, and then added, with pretended severity, "But remember that a gentleman's closet is his sanctuary. You must not move my things about in there, nor urge me to make it look tidier than it is."

"Of course I shall not!" said Arabella, springing off the bed.

Lord Petre's closet had a window at one end, and two looking-glasses with japanned lacquer frames, which gave the room a cheerful brightness in the mornings and snug comfort in the afternoons. There were two high-backed armchairs, an ottoman, and a small writing-table. Three sides of the room were lined with oak bookshelves, containing his library, and the fourth wall was covered in paintings, cartoons, and engravings. The window was draped in richly brocaded silks.

She looked over his bookcases. "I see that you have Milton and Shakespeare well placed, to make visitors believe that you read nothing but fine literature," she said, as she ran her fingers along the spines of the books, reading their titles. "But I am not fooled. Where do you keep your French pamphlets and your poems by Lord Rochester?"

Lord Petre did not answer, but sat down in one of the chairs, watching her indulgently.

"Aha! What is this?" she cried. "*L'Académie des dames* and *L'École des filles.* These are spoken of in reverent tones in every girls' school in Paris, but I have never seen a real copy. I am wild to look inside." She opened the volume and examined it, leaning her shoulder back against the bookcase. He could see the outline of her figure under the light fabric of her shift.

"Good Lord!" she exclaimed, looking up at him boldly. "The clergyman is fornicating with two women at once."

He laughed. "Since you have found me out, you might as well know all," he said. "Lord Rochester's *Poems* are on the shelf to your right."

"I knew you must have them, for you sent me his lines in your letter. But those were not at all lewd, though Rochester is the most notorious poet in the world. I suppose then you were trying to make me think you a man of delicacy . . ."

He threw his feet over the arm of the chair and said with a chuckle, "I was hoping that you might one day make a visit to inspect his verses more thoroughly. But I had not imagined that it would be so transporting an event as it is. The sight of you sitting in my silk armchair in your shift with *The Imperfect Enjoyment* open in your lap is worthy of my Lord Rochester's warmest lines. Why do not you read some of them to me now?"

"Very well," she said, and began to recite the opening of Rochester's poem.

"Naked she lay, clasped in my longing arms, / I filled with love, and she all over charms."

She glanced up at him.

"There's a much better part, a few lines on," he said, walking over to lean on the back of her chair.

"Where?" she asked. He bent his head so that it was beside hers and pointed with his finger. "Oh!" she said, and read aloud: "In liquid raptures I dissolve all o'er, / Melt into sperm, and spend at every pore. / A touch from any part of her had done it: / Her hand, her foot, her very look's a cunt . . ."

From where he stood, he could see down the opening of Arabella's smock. He put his arms around her neck and felt the contours of her breasts and belly.

"You are enflaming me again," he whispered. He rubbed his hands over the skin of her stomach, excited by her unembarrassed pleasure; the way she shivered when he touched her.

Arabella, too, was amazed by the force of her arousal. When people in town gossiped about scandals among their acquaintance, there was never any mention made of pleasure. And yet she had never enjoyed herself so much before in her life. Being with Lord Petre had transformed her—she was carried away with instinctive, unalloyed delight. It was like liquor; no, it was better: it made the boredom of daily existence bearable. She could while away the long days of polite conversation by thinking of the delicious hours that she had spent, and was going to spend, with him. It was not only physical pleasure, it was the pleasure of companionship, of a character so evenly matched with her own. Even if she had felt that it would be politic to do so, she could not now bring herself to stop.

It had grown dark, and the streetlights were brightly lit when Arabella asked, "Is there anything to eat in your rooms? I am rather hungry."

"Not a scrap. But I have an idea. I shall take you to a place that you have never visited, and which will give you something new to tell your friends at the tea table. But we must go out through the stables."

"It is a great nuisance always to come and go from the rear," she said. "It would be nice occasionally to enter in the proper way."

"Now Bell, have we not just spent many enjoyable minutes being told by Lord Rochester that you are mistaken? To enter by the proper route is to make no entrance at all." She laughed, and walked over to where her clothes lay, putting her arms through the vest of her stays. He came up behind her and kissed the back of her neck.

"We shall have no more complaint from Miss Fermor," he said, pulling her lacings tight and tying the ribbons. He gave the whole corset an expert tug, settling it on her hips. "We are going out," he announced, and picked his breeches up off the floor.

The pair went down the back stairs, Lord Petre warning Arabella to be quiet lest his mother and sister were in the parlour. There were no servants in the kitchen but there was a lantern burning on the table. It illuminated a patch of plaster on the ceiling where a servant had written his name on the whitewash with candle smoke beside the initials of his beloved.

Lord Petre glanced up at it, looking irritated. "The youngest footman," he said. "He is always entertaining a grand passion, usually here in the kitchen when he thinks that we are out."

As they walked into the stable yard an altercation could be heard between the butler and the night-soil carter, who had only just arrived to remove the contents of the septic vault.

"Well I 'ad to go first to the market, didn't I?" the night-soil man was saying.

"To the market! Be good enough to tell me why," replied the butler.

"So's I could unload *your* sallets and *your* roots afore I fills up the cart wiv *your* turds," said the man pithily.

"Our butler has taken to speaking in a most dreadfully affected manner," Lord Petre remarked as they passed. "The other day I told him not to have the servants bring the chamber-pots down the front stairs when guests are in the house, and I very nearly thought he would correct my grammar. He and the footmen pick up preposterous habits in the coffee-houses."

Petre handed Arabella into the carriage, and gave directions to the cookshop in Chancery Lane. "I hope that I shall one day take you to a most luxurious dinner," he said, "but I assure you that you will never have one tastier than this."

Arabella guessed that Lord Petre had chosen a place where they would not run into their acquaintance, though she had heard that other girls dined with young men to whom they were not yet engaged. But usually in little groups, she reflected, and at more reputable establishments. But when she saw the shop she realized that Lord Petre had chosen a perfect end to their day of adventure.

A small crowd was gathered outside when they arrived, chatting as they ate their penny dinners. Lanterns hung from long steel hooks and warmth burst forth from the shop's ovens to greet passers-by. The front counter on the street was packed with a miscellaneous collection of men and women, calling out to each other between their mouthfuls of food. The diners were mostly shopkeepers and tradesmen, or servants with coarse napkins tucked around their necks to save their livery. The crowd stood back as Lord Petre and Arabella stepped down from the carriage. One or two people bowed; there were murmurs of "M'lord", "M'lady", and a cheeky "Look out: Quality's here", perfectly audible.

Along one wall of the shop a fireplace held five spits of gleaming meat, and there was a wooden counter where the proprietor and his wife, Mr. and Mrs. Thomas, laboured mightily with hot knives, mustard, and rolls. A boy with sweat gleaming on his pink young forehead stood next to the fire to turn the roasting joints. Between turns, he played with the cookshop dog, whose job was to make sure that the floorboards were kept clean. It seemed likely to Arabella that this was the only surface of which such a claim could be made. The proprietor's daughter stood sulkily at one end of the counter while Mrs. Thomas directed her to clear the tables of tankards and wooden plates, but she sprang to life each time a male diner walked past with a friendly wink and a "Hello, Poll!"

Arabella smiled at Lord Petre as he led her to the counter.

"What a delightful place!" she said.

"Choose whichever meat you have a fancy for, and Thomas will carve you off the part that you like best," Lord Petre said. Mr. Thomas stood in front of Arabella with his wig plastered to his forehead, his red cheeks squeezing out beads of sweat as though through the mesh of a sieve. He drew his gleaming knife slowly across a sharpening steel. Instinctively, Arabella took a step backwards, but seeing Lord Petre shake him by the hand and give him a shilling, she came forward again, a little chagrined.

"What are the meats today, Thomas?" Lord Petre asked.

Mr. Thomas laid down his steel and gave his forehead a hearty wipe with a cloth that was tucked into his apron. "Beef, mutton; very nice veal, my lord," he announced proudly. "Our own pork, very tender, and then that's beef again at the end." The meat rotated above the fireplace, dripping juices into pans below that fizzed merrily on the flames. The flesh was glossy with basting, crackling along its roasted sides.

"I shall have pork, Thomas," said Lord Petre, "and veal for the lady," he added when Arabella had chosen. From the rear of the shop a guest called, "Two more bottles of beer, Poll, and sharpish."

Lord Petre glanced over at the man. "A regular diner, Thomas?" he asked affably, as the host began to slice the joints.

"Every week, my lord, and always in a new coat." Lord Petre craned his neck back a little to observe the gentleman's attire. "Made his money in slaves, so they say," Mr. Thomas continued. "But he's always bringing some nasty foreigner in here to spit on my clean floors. Tonight it's a Frog—last week it was a fat Dutchman who stank of cheese."

Mrs. Thomas gave her husband a shove to silence him, and called out, "You heard the gentleman, Polly! Peter, mind you watch the fire and don't be feeding good meat to the dog." She turned back to her customer. "Yes, Mr. Watkins, what can I do for you today?" she asked with a smile.

Thomas deftly sliced great quantities of flesh on to a wooden salver, sprinkled it with a little salt, and added a spoon of mustard from a large pot. On a separate plate he put four or five bread rolls, warm from the oven, with a wedge of butter.

Polly leaned against the wall near a hogshead of ale, talking to a girl whom Arabella recognized as Molly, the wench from Fowler's glove shop. Mrs. Thomas looked at the girl resentfully, and Arabella guessed that Molly was a regular visitor, but one whose friendship was not much encouraged. The pair giggled volubly, and whenever a customer called out for more refreshment, broke into fresh laughter. When she turned around to look at a young man who had called out from the other side of the room, Molly's gown fell open from her petticoat, revealing that she was pregnant.

That was why Mrs. Thomas was unhappy about the girls' friendship, Arabella thought. Naturally, they would not want their daughter getting into the same sort of trouble. It was strange to think of girls like Polly Thomas having parents who would decide that Molly Walker was a bad influence, or who would make sure that their daughter did not stay out too late at night. It was more than her own parents did. She supposed that girls from her station were expected to know how to behave on their own. She wondered fleetingly what her maid Betty's mother and father would be like, but her imaginings were broken off when Lord Petre took her arm to lead her to a table.

Polly sashayed up to them as soon as they were seated, and slung two mugs of ale on to the table. Lord Petre gave her a penny, and she shot a saucy look in Arabella's direction. Arabella ignored her.

"Eating with fingers—how novel," she said. "What a charming place this is."

"Charming because you are here, Arabella," Lord Petre answered, looking at her with renewed admiration. "It is a wretched enough spot when one dines at noon in company with fellows from the Exchange. But now I shall always think of you sitting here in a blue silk manto gown, eating oiled veal with your fingers and drinking a mug of ale. I shall henceforth be happier in this little corner than anywhere in London, for I have been happy here with you."

At that moment, Arabella thought that she had never in her life tasted nicer meat, nor drunk sweeter ale, for as she heard this speech, she knew that Lord Petre must be in love with her.

Later, as they left the cookshop, two familiar figures stepped through the door: Charles Jervas and Alexander Pope. They were deep in conversation; Arabella could hear Alexander saying "—but if it runs to a second edition, I shall have to see that booksellers other than Tonson begin to stock it," and it looked at first as though they would not stop.

But Jervas saw her and called out cheerfully, "Good evening,

Miss Fermor! I commend your bravery in visiting such a spot. Barely one woman in a thousand would attempt it, but your courage was well answered, I'll wager."

Arabella curtsied to him, and as she did so, he addressed Lord Petre. "How do you do, my lord?" he said, with a low bow. "Miss Fermor has been well championed in her adventure, I see."

Alexander had been standing to one side, but now he stepped forward and bowed to Lord Petre. "Good evening, my lord," he said.

"'Tis a shame that we are this moment leaving, for we might have dined together," Lord Petre replied. But since the shop was crowded, and hungry diners on either side jostled them, Arabella and Lord Petre made their exit.

In the carriage, she said, "If we had to run into our acquaintance this evening, I am glad that it was only them. Mr. Jervas will be discreet, I think, and Alexander Pope will have nobody to tell except my cousins."

"Well, *I* do not mind if the whole world knows that I sat in Thomas's cookshop with Miss Arabella Fermor," Lord Petre said with a complacent smile. "Everybody who sees you is half in love with you—if I am the lucky man who takes you to dinner, so much the better. You may be sure that little Alexander Pope thinks that you are beautiful. He was probably jealous!" Arabella laughed at the idea.

It was not until he drove home alone later on that Lord Petre reflected on the incidents of the day, which served to fix the momentous one—Arabella's glorious seduction—more firmly in his memory. The scene with the butler and the dung carter, the man calling aloud for beer in the cookshop, and Mr. Thomas's comment about his companion, "the Frog". The Frog had looked oddly familiar, though Lord Petre had not been able to place him. And it was strange, too, seeing Molly Walker and Arabella side by side once again. Now he felt a possessive pride in Arabella, and Molly had seemed like a stranger. He felt nothing of the old *frisson* when Molly caught his eye. Their affair was long in the past—thank God! Molly looked as though she would burst; she must be close to her confinement. He thought about who the father of the child might be. She had been abed with a man named Fitzjames immediately after their own affair was ended; it was probably he. He wondered idly if Douglass was among Molly's recent bedfellows.

Douglass—of course! That was where he had seen the Frenchman before. He was Douglass's friend Dupont, the slave trader, the man from the Exchange. *He deals in cargo that is as black as cinder*, Douglass had said, or some such phrase. And he had been dining with another slaver tonight, the man with many coats. Lord Petre kicked himself that he had not thought of it until now, but it made no difference in any case. He would hardly have introduced Dupont to Arabella, though he could not help but laugh to think of the conversation that would have ensued had he done so. The image made him want to see Arabella again as soon as possible.

Chapter Twelve

"Ev'ry eye was fix'd on her alone"

Several weeks passed. March became April, and April early May. The sky rolled off its sodden tarpaulin to reveal the pale blue of spring, a delicate net of high cloud ruffled by the breeze. The grass once more began to breathe; birds darted from twig to twig; the river ran strong and full. Along the edges of the great squares, through the parks, and in the fields and meadows, trees shook out their early leaves, crumpled little rags of tender green. Daffodils bobbed their heads, their ears blown back by the spring air. Blossoms enveloped the trees like overnight snow, hanging crystalline upon the branches, only to fall in heavenly scented drifts that whitened the ground. Windows opened; coats were thrown off precipitously. Deer leapt, cowbells jingled. Summer was on the march.

On a glorious morning in late May when the sun came up bright and warm, St. James's Park was at last in full, perfect leaf. Its walks were filled with ladies and gentlemen of the court grouped in threes and fours. Stands of women blazed like tulips in their bright silk gowns, lapdogs darted like butterflies, and gentlemen stood as though they were gardeners looking in rapturous admiration at the blooms that their lavish attentions had summoned forth.

Arabella had arranged to walk that morning with the Blount sisters. She had suggested St. James's Park because Henrietta Oldmixon and Lord and Lady Salisbury were to walk there with Lord Petre, and Martha announced that she and Teresa would meet Alexander and Jervas there too.

When the girls had been walking for about twenty minutes, Alexander and Jervas appeared from behind a group of trees. Alexander was talking away animatedly, heedless of the fact that they were walking near the low branches of a spreading elm. Jervas turned to avoid them, but Alexander walked on, slipping under the boughs easily, and continuing to chatter brightly to the now absent Jervas. Arabella laughed at the sight.

But she stopped smiling almost immediately, for Alexander had walked straight up to Lord Petre, who approached from the opposite direction with Lord and Lady Castlecomber. Lord Petre wore a suit of cream-coloured silk, embroidered with a pattern of crimson tulips—how great a contrast it made with Mr. Pope's coat, she thought, cut from a blue material that had been briefly in fashion two years before. They bowed to one another: Lord Petre's elegant swoop; Pope's awkward little bob. To her disappointment she saw that Henrietta and the Salisburys were nowhere in sight.

As she walked closer she could hear Lord Petre saying to Pope, "I see that you are still in town, sir, with or without your father's blessing.

"But tell me, Mr. Pope," Lord Petre continued, "when will you write a poem about your friends? We long to read great verses about ourselves!"

Pope smiled, and swaggered a little, obviously delighted to be considered Lord Petre's friend. He stumbled out a gallantry in reply, and Arabella almost felt sorry for him. She hoped he realized that the baron was only being charming; of course they would never be more than polite acquaintances.

At this moment Arabella caught Lady Castlecomber's eye, and Charlotte came to greet her. But when she asked Lady Castlecomber how she did, Arabella thought that she detected a note of superiority in the other's response, and felt a sudden jealous impulse to say something spiteful.

"I did not see you at Lady Salisbury's levee last week," Arabella said. "Was not she once a particular friend of yours?"

"And is so still," Lady Castlecomber replied with distinct reserve. "But I was with my husband in Ireland. Lord Castlecomber travels a good deal," she added, and then, "Do you travel often, Miss Fermor?"

"I was at school in Paris for many years," Arabella replied.

"Ah, then you have not been there recently," Charlotte countered, smiling as Lord Petre joined the group.

He shot Charlotte a warning glance and offered Arabella his arm.

"What need have we for Paris when we have St. James's Park in the spring?" he asked, and led Arabella away.

Alexander watched this little exchange with interest. He had wondered why Lord Petre excused himself so quickly from their own conversation—now he understood, and admired the baron for his swift action. For the first time Alexander felt an impulse of sympathy for Arabella; even she needed to be rescued occasionally. He recalled the expression on her face when they met in the cookshop: until then he had not thought that Arabella Fermor was capable of looking discomposed.

She appeared to have supplanted politics as the focus of Lord Petre's interest. When Alexander greeted Lord Petre, there had been no trace of the consciousness and anxiety that he had betrayed in the coffee-house with John Caryll. And though Douglass was in the park this morning too, Lord Petre seemed to take no notice of him. Alexander felt a moment's thankfulness to Martha for stopping him from telling Teresa about the Petre family's Jacobite past.

Teresa had positioned herself on the edge of Lord Petre's circle, obviously hoping to join his conversation with Arabella. But she was left standing alone and Alexander saw her glance around to see if her exclusion had been noticed.

He caught her eye. "Will you take a turn with me along the Lime Walk?" he asked.

She smiled gratefully. "Alexander!" she exclaimed. "I am so pleased to see you." She was about to take his arm when they heard a gentleman's voice behind them. Alexander turned to discover Douglass standing not five inches away.

"Come for a walk with me along the lime-tree avenue!" Douglass commanded Teresa.

She hesitated, torn between the two men. Then she saw Arabella glance over from her position beside Lord Petre. The look decided her.

"I thank you, Mr. Douglass," she said, and took his proffered arm. But suddenly she turned back, pulling away to put a hand on Alexander's arm. "I am sorry," she said. "I wanted you to come, but—"

Douglass impatiently drummed his fingers on his thigh.

"Do you mind?" Teresa said to Alexander, but then her face cleared. "Here is Martha just come up!" she said. "Why do not you walk with her?"

Martha looked stricken. "I did not come to ask—" she began, but Alexander cut her off.

"Enough, Patty," he said, offering her his arm. "The morning is too glorious to waste upon trifles. Will you walk with me to the water garden?"

With a smile divided between resignation and pleasure, Martha took Alexander's arm.

Between Lord Petre and Arabella, meanwhile, anticipation had been gathering like a heat haze. Already Arabella had noticed other women watching them, curiosity and envy stamped on their faces. By rescuing her from the exchange with Lady Castlecomber, Lord Petre had declared himself publicly to be her champion.

"I see that our friends have deserted us," he observed with an ironic smile, as soon as they were out of earshot. "'Tis hard to know whether they are motivated by feelings of malice or kindness. But from what I know of them, I venture to guess that it is the former."

"Shall we ramble about the park, as they do in Lord Rochester's poem?" Arabella asked.

"I don't believe that they were rambling, strictly speaking," he answered.

"Well, I did not think that *we* would ramble, strictly speaking."

He raised an eyebrow at her. "Shall we walk in the shade of the avenue?"

"There are so many people about; it is like Covent Garden on a Monday morning. The meadows are more . . . rustic."

"If we are secluded, my imagination will turn to country pleasures," he said.

"I have never known any pleasure in the country," Arabella answered. "I assume, however, that you are making coy reference to the rustic indulgences of nymphs and swains—not to mornings spent visiting the Catholic cousins."

"Your Catholic cousins are unlikely to approve your wandering in the meadows of St. James's Park," he replied. "Indeed we know of at least two of them walking nearby, who would object strenuously to your straying from these familiar paths. Were I a gentleman, I would deliver you safely into their hands before further mention of rural sports provokes me to run you to ground in plain view."

The large open meadows around St. James's Park were used as a pasture for dairy cows. The grazing land extended out beyond Buckingham House towards the village of Chelsea, and north beyond Piccadilly, where the fields of Hyde Park joined the Pasture Grounds above St. James's. Morning and evening, herds of cows were brought in for milking in the sheds dotted around the pasture, where by day the milkmaids, clad in white aprons and caps, laboured to produce pails of milk, packets of butter, cream, and fresh cheese.

They walked for about fifteen minutes until they reached a pretty spot under cover of a spreading oak.

"Ah, here we are at last," said Lord Petre. "Miss Fermor is to be seated upon this low milking stool, to prepare herself for country pleasures."

He removed his coat and stood in only his shirt, waistcoat, and breeches. Arabella looked around to see whether they were observed.

"The prospect is so very *open* here, my lord. I do not think that this is the place to linger."

"Oh, but it is perfect," he said. "A happy rural seat. And look! A milkmaid, just come into view. I shall ask her to join us."

He smiled at Arabella's look of alarm, and walked over to the young lady. He spoke to her in a low voice, and she smiled and nodded as he handed her some money. She disappeared behind a low cowshed. A moment later she re-emerged carrying a little tin pail, which she handed to the baron. The pail was full of fresh new milk.

Arabella laughed, and Lord Petre smiled down at her.

"You did not imagine that I had any darker motives in mind, did you?"

"Of course!" she answered. "Be assured that I think nothing but the worst of you."

The milk was soft and dense with cream. They sat together drinking it until the maid returned to claim her pail and stool, and then they walked on, coming shortly to a small hay shed. Lord Petre poked his head in at the door, and Arabella stepped in beside him, looking up at the piles of grassy bales. Without warning, Lord Petre grabbed her by the waist, swung her about to face him, and fell backwards dramatically on to the cushions of hay, with much laughter and shrieking from Arabella. The cloth cap she wore quickly fell off, as did Lord Petre's hat. He leaned towards Arabella to kiss her, but just before he could she threw a handful of hay at his face. "A caution against swiving in St. James's Park!"

Spluttering loudly, he picked up his own handful of hay and did exactly as she expected, with the result that both parties were hopelessly dishevelled and rusticated before any swiving had even begun. But it now began in earnest.

He kissed her mouth and neck, pausing to look at her for a moment, the current of attraction palpable between them. He put his hand between her thighs and she opened her legs as he stroked them—her lack of resistance bringing him even sharper pleasure. She strained to bring his hands closer, biting at his lips. He pushed her down into the hay, lifting her legs so that he could see the round curve of her buttocks. He jammed his cock inside her and sank down against her thighs, pinning her arms back with both hands.

He licked the salty cleavage between her breasts and kissed her mouth and mumbled, "I must not spend inside you."

"If you stop I will scream," she whispered, and it made him push down on her harder. Her breath was quick as she came, and a moment later he did too, kissing her face and lips in rapture.

Afterwards they lay watching the shafts of dust made by the sunlight that pierced the wooden boards of the wall. Outside there was silence. Lord Petre picked little pieces of hay from Arabella's hair, blowing them off his fingers.

"You have very nice hair, Bell. One of your best features."

"Betty took an hour and a half this morning to arrange it. It is a terrible trouble."

"The trouble is worth it. Did I mention that you are very lovely?"

"That is better. You have been speaking too much in the language of Lord Rochester of late."

"And you do not always find that Rochester is to your taste?" he asked with a smile, kissing her forehead. "Would you like something better suited to our present mood? I offer something from Dr. Donne.

"'Now good morrow to our waking souls,'" he declared, "'Which watch not one another out of fear. / For love, all love of other sights controls / And makes one little room an everywhere.'"

Listening to these lines spoken by the young, handsome nobleman with whom she was lying in the hay, Arabella felt a charge of delight. No doubt it was partly because "The Good Morrow" is one of the great short lyrics in English, and she felt an instinctive appreciation of its virtuosity. But also because—as Alexander had guessed earlier—she sensed that Triumph, riding in a gilded chariot and drawn by a team of white horses, was now but an easy distance away.

The return to Lord Petre's carriage, by contrast, fell short of expectations. The pair hastened through the fields feeling hot and out of breath, and every bit as itchy as Teresa might have wished. Anxious to avoid seeing anyone they knew, they cut up along the outside of the avenue, trying to stay out of sight behind the trees. When at length they reached the carriage they were swiftly enclosed within by the patient footman Jenkins, who pocketed the guinea Lord Petre handed to him and instructed the coachman to go directly to Miss Fermor's house.

When Alexander and Martha had turned off towards the water garden for their walk, they saw Lord Petre and Arabella setting out for the meadows. Alexander watched Lord Petre's strong gait and confident smile jealously, wishing that he too were leading a young lady off into the hayfields, all smiles and excited anticipation, while his rivals looked on longingly. Then he realized, ruefully, that he would not have known what to do next. His crumpled body made him ashamed. But would it have mattered less to him had he been the baron, and Lord Petre the draper's son? When Dame Fortune dealt her cards, why must it always be with such a cruel hand? He glanced at Martha, who looked dejected too.

"Wherever they are going, I am sure they are enjoying themselves no more than we are," he said, and her face brightened at the compliment.

Alexander thought about Lord Petre's suggestion for his next poem. This scene would certainly make a fine satire. A hunchbacked knight-at-arms with a damsel on his arm—both looking enviously after the heroic lord and lady as they rushed off for a tryst in the meadows. He smiled and made a mental note of the image, then remembered with a frown that it had been two days since he had looked at his writing. The weeks were slipping away—it was nearly June. He wondered whether people were buying the *Essay on Criticism* yet. Tonson was probably hiding it away in the back of his shop. He must go by and urge him to put it on display.

"Do not despair of making a name for yourself, Alexander," said Martha suddenly. Alexander looked at her. How had she known his thoughts?

"You must remember that whatever people appear to be in public, their private selves are different. Lord Petre, I believe, is a serious man, capable of reflection and judgement, however he might carry on with Arabella. And the other men of your acquaintance are the same; I feel sure of it."

"My dear Patty," Alexander replied. "You are right, I fear, that my reputation will ultimately depend on the opinion of men like Lord Petre. The fashionable world looks to the wealthy for its judgements; they are willing to forget that the Baron of Ingatestone is a Roman Catholic."

"The world is willing to overlook any fault in a person who possesses a fortune," Martha answered.

"Well, if I *do* write a poem about Lord Petre's circle, everyone must appear in the most heroic light. This is clearly no moment for candour."

She laughed. "Perhaps not in poetry, but in life there could not be a better. Some firm words with my sister, perhaps, telling her not to walk alone with men like James Douglass."

"Douglass! What a blackguard that man appears."

"Caution, Alexander!" Martha warned. "He may be nearer than you think—we have come to the Lime Walk."

Alexander was about to speak again, when Martha burst out, "But there she is! Upon the bench ahead. And I believe that she is crying. What can be the matter?" She broke away from Alexander and rushed towards her sister.

Alexander looked at Teresa. She sat beneath the dappled shade of the limes, the bright leaves making half-transparent shadows around her; the light tinting her silk dress a delicate green. Her hands played restlessly with the ribbon of her wide-brimmed straw bergère, and the attitude in which she sat made Alexander think of the day in the garden at Whiteknights, so long ago. He knew that she would not look up at him with a happy welcome now.

Martha was sitting on the bench beside her, a hand upon Teresa's. "What is wrong, dear?" she asked. "What happened?"

"I thought you were in the water garden," Teresa said with a sniff.

"Where is Douglass?" Martha demanded.

"He is gone. Just this moment gone. I said that I would stay to rest—I am rather tired."

"But Teresa, you have only been walking for half an hour in the shade," said Martha. "You could not be tired. Why did Mr. Douglass not wait with you?"

"As soon as we had walked away Mr. Douglass said, 'I'll wager you would rather be Miss Fermor than Miss Blount at this moment.' You know how he speaks. I said something foolish. Then Mr. Douglass began to pay me a great many compliments about the superiority of my person to Miss Fermor's—and I started enjoying myself. It does not seem fair that Arabella should be the only one of us to receive compliments from men. But some of Mr. Douglass's remarks were very free indeed, and so of course I asked him to stop."

Her distress brought Alexander a return of all his old emotions: tenderness, affection, disappointed hope. How long they had troubled him, though of late they had become more a matter of habit than of real compulsion. But how powerfully he felt them now, reminding him that his love for her was as much a part of him as his crooked back and frail body.

"Mr. Douglass made a great many promises, Patty," Teresa was saying. "There was something very charming about him—and when he begged me to come away in a carriage, I thought that it might be an adventure. But then he told me that Bell is Lord Petre's mistress." Her voice reached a high-pitched crescendo.

"He said—" she gave a tearful gulp—"he said that I should give up all thoughts of Lord Petre until he tires of Bell! Then he added something very lewd indeed about our going in the carriage together—and when I pulled back from him he walked away."

Alexander snapped out of his reverie. Lord Petre and Arabella! How much mischief that pair would cause before the season was over.

He stepped forward and extended a hand to Teresa. "You must congratulate yourself for standing firm against Douglass's advances," he said. "You have shown strength of character. Far more strength, it seems, than your cousin Miss Fermor."

Martha glanced at him gratefully.

Teresa drew herself up and said, "If I were Arabella, I should not become Lord Petre's mistress. I should choose to be chaste." But she started to cry again. "So Alexander thinks it is true, Patty," she wailed. "He believes that they *are* lovers. What if Lord Petre marries her? She will be a baron's wife."

"If he has promised to marry her, Teresa," Alexander interjected, "I fancy that your cousin Bell has not reckoned with the objections of Lord Petre's family. And until that obstacle has been overcome, she is nothing but plain old Miss Fermor."

"If Arabella has become Lord Petre's mistress, then it is *her* heart that we must be concerned with, not the baron's," Martha added.

Teresa said nothing, but Martha continued, "We must go home immediately. Will you be so kind as to hand us into our carriage, Alexander?"

Alexander did so, and then turned back to the park, puzzling over the feelings that the day had produced. During the last weeks he had been thinking of Teresa less and taking solace in Martha's companionship more. But when Teresa had cried, his feelings for her had been as powerful and vivid as when he was a boy. Perhaps, then, they would never leave him—even when he looked at her in anger, it would always be with the anger of love. His affection for Martha was founded on respect and real understanding. But having felt all that he had for Teresa, how could he ever think of preferring her sister? He would be untrue to both of them at once.

As he walked along the main avenue that extended out to the pasturelands in the west, he saw Lord Petre and Arabella sneaking back from their tryst. They looked out of breath and uncomfortable, and there was a good deal of hay adhering to the back of Miss Fermor's dress and hair. Lord Petre helped Arabella into his carriage, and, as Alexander watched them, all the subtleties of his reflections were set aside. He felt instead a jolt of envy and pure longing.

Arabella had failed to remember that her mother had told her to be home half an hour ago, until she was in Lord Petre's coach. She was so unused to her parents paying her any attention that the request had barely registered when it was made, but she now recalled that her mother had arranged for her to have a carving lesson. Learning to carve a joint of meat was a feature of every well-regulated English girlhood, but Arabella had managed to escape it by being sent to Paris at the age of twelve. Only belatedly, therefore, was she to acquire the ancient art. She wondered why her mother had suddenly decided upon such a course, and speculated that it was because she had finally noticed that her daughter had been three seasons in London without a husband to show for it. Arabella smiled to think that the expediency of the carving lesson was already unnecessary. But she supposed that it would do no harm; even as a baron's wife she would carve the joint at dinners.

When she entered their town house her mother called from the parlour, "Arabella, is that you? You are late for your lesson, and your father wishes to see you immediately."

Making no reply, she gave a cheeky smile to the footman and pressed her finger to her lips. As she sprang lightly up the stairs her mother called again, "Arabella? Arabella!" Her footsteps were heard in the hall as she came to look for her daughter, but she soon retreated again to the parlour.

Arabella arrived in the parlour ten minutes later in a clean cap and gown to find her mother just coming to the end of a tirade against the butler: "—and I know that the footmen merely shake the spilled salt back into the cellar at the end of dinner, to serve again tomorrow," she was saying. "'Tis full of crumbs, and it will not do. And the knives and forks are to be *removed* from the cloth before it is bundled up. I saw you shake the tablecloth on to the street so that the beggars could have the scraps of our meat and bread. That is all very well, but you need not give them cutlery to eat it with!"

"Though it would be more convenient for the beggars," Arabella's father interjected, and her mother shot him a hard look. They always conducted themselves in this way in front of the servants—her mother barking out directions and her father making mocking rejoinders. She felt a little sorry for her mother as she saw the butler yawning to suppress a laugh.

But Mrs. Fermor did not notice it, and began to give instructions for their dinner party the following day. "For the first course a fillet of veal," she said, "a fricassee of lamb, a dish of peas and a sallet of herbs. Then we shall have beefsteaks and a game pie, with asparagus—"

"My dear, I do not think that the company will be expecting peas as well as asparagus," Mr. Fermor cut in. "They will think it indigestible. A joint of beef will do very well instead."

His wife ignored him. "There shall be peas and asparagus, bought tomorrow from the market," she said. Mind that there are three whole pigeons in each pie, for otherwise it shall make but a paltry dish. We shall have whipped syllabub, orange cream, and strawberries for the dessert."

When the butler left, Mrs. Fermor said to her husband accusingly, "You were rubbing your teeth when we dined at my Lord Leicester's on Tuesday." He frowned at her in response. "Mrs. Molyneaux saw you, and mentioned it to me," Mrs. Fermor continued. "And 'tis not civil to be twice in one dish. I observed that the Duke of Bedford was twice in the ragout, but that does not serve you for an excuse. Arabella, do not scratch yourself."

"I did not, ma'am," Arabella replied, feeling little pieces of straw itching her back. She remembered Lord Petre's face when she threw the hay at him, and smiled. But her father turned and spoke to her in a severe tone.

"Arabella, I hear from the butler that you have been ordering bottles of water from Islington," he said. "What do you propose to do with it?"

"I propose to drink it, sir."

"To *drink* it? What an absurd notion." Arabella reflected that it was only to be expected that her parents would be opposed to her new scheme.

She scratched herself again, and her mother said, "Do *not* be scratching, Arabella." She scowled at them both. How could she make them see that she must have water to drink if she had any hope of being thought fashionable?

"Lady Salisbury daily drinks spa water and says that she was never healthier," she said.

"What need is there for you to drink water," Mr. Fermor asked scornfully, "when there is plenty of small beer in the larder?"

"On the subject of drinking, Mr. Fermor," his wife interrupted, "the habit you have caught, of throwing down your liquor as though into a funnel, is an action fitter for a juggler than a gentleman."

Once again, Mr. Fermor made no reply. He turned back to his daughter, and said in a voice that would brook no argument, "If my Lady Salisbury believes that the drinking of water will improve her constitution, I congratulate her," he declared. "And when you are married to a baron, and have an establishment of your own, you may drink as much water as you please. But for the present, you will follow the regime that has kept your mother and me healthy these twenty-five years."

Arabella smiled indulgently in reply. Little did her father know that her situation would resemble Lady Salisbury's much sooner than he could possibly imagine.

"Arabella, I would like you to attend more carefully to your skills in carving than you have been doing," her mother said. "When I was your age, I was carving the joints for large parties at dinner, twice or thrice a week."

"Young ladies now do not follow those habits so much as they used to," said Arabella obstinately. "They are regarded as old-fashioned, ma'am."

"Whatever you might like to believe, Arabella, the habits of married life are not subject to fashion. If a girl wishes to marry well, she shall be handsome, genteel, chaste—and accomplished in keeping a household. Men do not like lazy wives, even in the year seventeen-eleven."

Arabella was not at all chastened by the rebuke, for she knew that her mother was mistaken. She repaired to her carving lesson, thinking how very much less affectionate and open-minded were the married lives of her parents and their acquaintance than her own was going to be.

*

The next morning Alexander paid a visit to the Blount sisters to see how they did, only to find that they were not at home. He told the footman that he would wait until they returned, and he sat down in the parlour, asking for a sheet of paper. He wanted to make note of a new idea that had come to him on the way there, which he was afraid he might otherwise forget. The footman shot him a look of surprise, obviously thinking him eccentric, but Alexander paid no attention.

In due course, he heard the sound of a carriage outside and the echo of voices in the hall. The parlour door was thrown open, and Teresa bounded in.

"Hello, Alexander—we were expecting to find you here. Oh, you are writing. You are always writing—'tis a dreadful affectation." She put her parcels down on the floor and handed her bonnet to the footman. "Do you know that we saw your friend Jervas coming out of the *bagnio* near Covent Garden half an hour ago? Since he was alone, we guessed that you had either drowned in the hot bath, or come to pay us a morning visit."

"I see that you have recovered your spirits, Miss Blount," he said censoriously, sorry that the subdued Teresa of yesterday was gone.

"Oh, quite recovered," she rejoined, collapsing into an armchair and fanning herself energetically.

"What a diverting morning we have had," she added in a tone that came much closer to Arabella's languid accents than Alexander had heard before. "Martha bought gloves," she continued, "I bought lace, and we saw many friends. I have forgotten the episode with Mr. Douglass already, there is so much else to entertain us. Indeed, it is fortunate that I discovered him to be a rascal—for when he met me today he was just as attentive as ever—but I was not taken in. He was in company with Henry Moore, Mr. Chettwin, and the Duke of Beaufort. My Lord Petre was there too, being very charming. We are to form a pleasure party with them tomorrow in Hyde Park."

"That makes it sound as though the party were intended for us," said Martha. "But they were making the plan when we met them, and so Lord Petre invited us to come," she explained to Alexander.

"It was very civil of him. Perhaps he will have invited Mr. Jervas, too," she added.

"Lord Petre is to bring champagne," said Teresa.

Alexander returned home after only a short visit, regretting that Teresa's experience in St. James's Park had not cured her of her boundless capacity for misguided optimism. Hope springs eternal in Teresa's breast, he thought sardonically. She never *is*, but always *to be* blessed. He laughed out loud, and wrote it down. The visit had supplied him with a good couplet, at least, if not very much else.

When Jervas came home later in the day, he burst into the room where Pope sat writing, and announced, "There is to be a pleasure party tomorrow in Hyde Park, Pope. My Lord Petre asked me to bring you with me. Indeed," Jervas added with a cordial smile, "I half believe that he invited me solely in order to secure you! He is a great admirer of your poetry, and is determined to be instrumental in your becoming famous." He walked over to the sideboard and poured himself a glass of wine. "Mind you, Pope," he continued, "the nobility are altogether too fond of declaring that they will make the reputation of this person or that, so I should not set much store by what he says. But you may be sure that he means to flatter you."

With an ironic smile Alexander thanked Jervas for the encouragement and turned back to his verses.

Chapter Thirteen

"When offers are disdain'd, and love deny'd
Then gay Ideas crowd the vacant brain"

The party in Hyde Park the following day was very cheerful. Lord Petre arrived with Jenkins early in the morning and marched about the meadows for half an hour, directing his footman to set the baskets down first in one spot and then another, before finally settling on a small patch of rising ground. Jenkins had brought two under-footmen, a groom, and the cook's help, and the five of them set to work with hammers and wooden stakes to make an awning under which Lord Petre's guests might sit. Then they set up trestle tables and seats, covered the tables with damask cloths, and laid out glasses, napkins, plates, and silver. Lord Petre himself carried the basket of champagne from the carriage, leaving the bottles lying in the straw that had protected them on the journey over from France. Jenkins had been to Covent Garden market that morning, and brought baskets of strawberries: little red *fraises* peeked from a nest of leaves and flowers. There were dishes of clotted cream, plum cake, and bread and butter for the ladies, a roasted sirloin for the men, and two pyramids of fruit.

Alexander arrived at the party with Jervas, Martha, and Teresa. They were among the first of Lord Petre's guests; Lord Petre could be seen talking to the Duke of Beaufort, but he rushed out from under the awning to greet them as Jervas's carriage pulled up. His clothes were already a little rumpled from his morning's efforts, and his chestnut curls had strayed from the ribbon that tied them back. His look, Alexander decided, was that of a nobleman striding across his fields with a bouquet of grouse—though happily he had no actual birds in his hand. Lord Petre bowed to them all, offered both Martha and Teresa an arm, and led them forward to the marquee.

"You see it is not a formal party," he said, waving his hand across the general landscape. "Comfort and pleasure are our guiding principles. Will you take a glass of wine, Miss Blount? There are strawberries by the dozens—I have heard that ladies are fond of them—and cherries too. A cherry for Miss Blount!"

Teresa was mightily gratified by his attention, and she looked about with a wide, complacent smile, just as she had seen Arabella do in St. James's Park.

"Few ladies can claim the distinction of being intimate friends not only with the town's foremost painter, but with its foremost poet too!" Lord Petre exclaimed, very nearly tipping him a wink, Alexander observed with amusement. Teresa looked somewhat less delighted with this remark than with his previous attentions, but she still smiled graciously, pleased at least to be the foremost poet's favourite. The foremost painter, meanwhile, had walked over to the sirloin, and was helping himself to a large slice while he chatted to the Duke of Beaufort, whose picture he had made some months previously.

Lord Petre turned from the girls to Alexander, and said, "I am honoured indeed to have you here, sir. I have been told on good authority that your *Essay* is superior to Dryden's on dramatic poesy."

Alexander wondered on whose authority he was relying—it sounded like the sort of exaggerated remark that he himself would make as a joke to Martha—but he bowed cordially. Lord Petre pulled out a chair for Alexander to sit upon, saying, "You will have some wine, sir, and a slice of meat, perhaps? Or a strawberry. Pray, take a strawberry." Alexander did as he was told and sat back in his chair; he was enjoying himself more than he had expected.

Teresa exclaimed, "How sweet these cherries are! Nicer than any I have had before. Alexander, I hope that you will have one of my cherries." Alexander smiled to hear her, and turned to take a cherry. But Martha was sitting between them at the table, and Teresa leaned directly across her sister to offer the dish to Alexander.

Alexander stopped her. "I will not take cherries, Teresa, but I hope that Martha will. Come, Patty—I have not seen you eat anything. Let me give you a slice of cake, too." Martha smiled at him, and began to eat some of the fruit.

"What do you think is making Lord Petre so gracious today?" she asked Alexander in a wry tone.

Before he had time to reply, he heard a new voice beside him. It belonged to a lady he did not recognize, though she seemed familiar, as if he had seen her before.

"My Lord Petre describes you as the town's foremost poet, Mr. Pope," she said to him. "Do you write satire? I hope that you are not one of those wits who laughs at everybody except himself."

Alexander looked up in surprise, and hastily rose to his feet. The lady was young and pretty, elegantly dressed, but displaying a charm and animation that took away the imposing air she might otherwise have had. When he studied her more closely, he saw that she was more than pretty: she was a beauty. He wished that he knew her name.

"Be not afraid, madam," he said. "Necessity will force my hand. Unless I laugh at myself, I shall have nothing at all to write about—which would render me ridiculous indeed. Ten thousand men cannot yield so much satire as ten minutes' reflection upon one's own follies."

"Ah! But ten thousand women might supply the need," she answered with a flash of laughter.

"Are you a satirist yourself, then, madam?" he asked. Caught up in the conversation, they had unconsciously stepped away from the others. Alexander hoped that the tête-à-tête might continue, at least until he had discovered her identity. "Wit comes to you more readily than to two-thirds of the men who make a living from it," he said.

"I am a woman of fashion—which amounts to the same thing," she answered, also obviously enjoying the exchange.

"You mean that you live by your wits?" he asked.

"Indeed—and like most satirists, I live beyond my means." She met his eye, and smiled. It exhilarated him.

"Then you must live more extravagantly than anybody I have met," he rejoined. "Your wit is prodigious."

"A compliment indeed from the famous Mr. Alexander Pope," she said with a bow more like a man's than a woman's.

"Since my name is known to you, madam, I beg that I might know yours," he said.

"I am Mary Pierrepont."

Mary Pierrepont! The Earl of Kingston's daughter. He took a step backwards, and said, "I am relieved that I did not know it before, my lady, for I might have been too afraid to answer you."

She laughed. "You do not seem a timid man, Mr. Pope."

"My timidity is well concealed. I am very shy beneath all this bluster."

She responded readily. "Then you are not shy at all, since shyness is a matter of manner, not of character."

Alexander bowed. He was dazzled by the speed with which her conversation moved.

She stopped to think for a moment, and then said, "But I shall allow that you may be reserved. Is that what you meant, Mr. Pope?"

"Your correction is just, my lady."

As they talked, Lady Mary grew increasingly animated, her cheeks flushed and eyes engaged. Her manner was uniquely delightful. She was confident, not simply of being clever, which might have repelled him, but confident in the pleasure that her cleverness gave. He knew that she had a reputation for being "intellectual," but such a description belied her nature. She was animated by her beauty, her energy, and her intellect all together.

They were prevented from continuing by the arrival of a carriage bearing the Salisbury coat of arms. It pulled up not far from where the group was situated, and Lord Salisbury, who was riding on horseback beside the equipage, sprang down and stood by the door, waiting for his lady and her friends to descend. A pair of footmen threw open the doors and the heads of all Lord Petre's guests swung around to watch the new arrivals.

Lady Salisbury stepped down first, a plume of ostrich feathers nodding on the top of her bonnet as she took her husband's arm. Next came Henrietta Oldmixon, in a dress of apple-green silk, richly brocaded in gold leaves. She passed a lapdog to one of the footmen to carry across to the marquee. Finally the third member of the party appeared, smiling as she waited to be helped down: it was Arabella.

Lord Petre had arranged for her to come to the gathering in the Salisburys' carriage. He strode across the grass alongside the Duke of Beaufort, and as Arabella appeared at the coach door both men were ready with their hands to assist her. She sprang down, kissing each of them in turn. The three girls then took off across the grass together, and Lord Petre, Lord Salisbury, and the duke hurried along behind, with the footmen following at a respectful distance.

Henrietta was describing the difficulty they had had in finding the party. Her clear voice rang out across the grass—she did not trouble herself to turn her head to address anyone in particular. "His Grace said 'under a pair of oaks,'" she trilled, "*not* the most useful direction to give when we are to meet in a park!" The three girls laughed, and the men followed suit.

"*I* am astonished, madam, to see you out of bed at this inhumanly early hour," the Duke of Beaufort answered her. "You were still at cards when I left the assembly at four this morning."

With a roll of her eyes, Henrietta drawled, "It cost me no small difficulty, Your Grace, let me assure you. I am ravenous for a cup of coffee and toast—though I daresay that we are too rustic for that this morning." There was more laughter. Alexander turned to Lady Mary but saw that she had moved away, distancing herself from the new arrivals. He wished that Teresa might have shown the same disdain; instead she was leaning forward eagerly, hoping to be noticed.

"Oh, very rustic indeed!" said Lord Salisbury. "I see that there is nothing but two dozen bottles of champagne, thirty yards of damask, and half the silver plate in London."

"Will you take a glass of champagne wine, Miss Oldmixon?" Lord Petre asked.

"It seems that there is nothing else to be had," Henrietta replied, raising her eyebrows as she dropped into the chair that had been held out for her by a footman.

Martha watched their arrival, amazed by the spectacle of Arabella and her new friends. These must be the people Teresa had seen at the morning levee, she thought, noting that the defining trait of all successful girls seemed to be their refusal to show the faintest surprise or pleasure in their surroundings, however remarkable they might actually consider them. While they settled into the splendour of Lord Petre's luxurious arrangements, the three of them carried on their conversation as though they had done nothing more than walk from the sofa to the tea table at home. They talked of parties attended, jokes passed, remarks made, all of which were vastly entertaining—and from the enjoyment of which the other guests were subtly, but determinedly, excluded. Lady Salisbury and Henrietta Oldmixon had been schooled in well-bred indifference from the nursery, but Martha owned herself to be impressed by Arabella's performance. The mirthless laugh, the world-weary smile, the disdainful air: she had made them her own.

All three of the principal men in the party flocked around Arabella.

"Will you take something to drink, Miss Fermor?" Lord Salisbury asked.

"Can I bring you refreshment?" offered the Duke of Beaufort.

"I fear that Miss Fermor is too much in the sun," said Lord Petre, with an ironic smile. "Is there something that we can do to relieve her?"

As he watched them fawn upon her, Alexander entertained for an exquisite moment a fantasy of Arabella asking the men to move the tent so that she could better enjoy the view. He believed that, had she done so at this moment, her request would have been honoured.

But she merely said, "I thank you, Your Grace, I shall take a glass of the wine. And a strawberry or two, my lord," looking not at Lord Petre but Lord Salisbury, "though without any cream," she added, just as he put a spoonful over the fruit.

Martha watched with a mixture of amusement and dismay as they scurried around Arabella like eager dormice. Her beauty was the kind that men found particularly attractive, but Martha had never entirely understood the attraction. Today, however, she saw what it meant to describe a woman as frighteningly beautiful. It was literally true. The gentlemen were hypnotized by Arabella's mere presence, and at the same time they were terrified of her. They seemed to sense that she might ask them to do anything, and that if she did, they would be powerless to refuse her.

Sitting beside Martha, Alexander wondered what Lady Mary made of the trio. It was clear that she had no desire to be thought of as part of their set; she was seated on the other side of the awning, talking to a man whom Alexander had never seen before. He glanced back at Arabella, noting that the uncertainty she had betrayed during the conversation with Lady Castlecomber in St. James's Park was gone, replaced by an ever more steely self-confidence. But his opinion as to the cause of her magnetism differed somewhat from Martha's. It did not derive simply from her extraordinary good looks. He believed it came rather from her knowing that one day her beauty would cease to hold sway in the way that it did now—and that her power, though formidable, was of short date. This was what infused her actions with their remarkable force, giving them a suppressed urgency that no performance in languor and indifference could entirely efface.

But these subtleties, perceived by Martha and Alexander, were lost upon Teresa, who reeled from two stinging discoveries. The first was that Arabella had excluded her from the new friendships with Lady Salisbury and Henrietta Oldmixon. And the second, seemingly insignificant, but of the greatest importance to Teresa, was that all three ladies had arrived at the party wearing riding habits. She could not believe it! Arabella had specifically said that she rode only pillion when she was in town, whereas she, Teresa Blount, had been acknowledged in the same conversation as a very fine horsewoman. This might have been the one opportunity she had to outshine her cousin, and yet no one had bothered to let her know that there was to be riding. The unfairness of it was hard to bear, and as Arabella sat in her new habit, surrounded by the concentric circles of her aristocratic admirers, Teresa thought that she had never tasted such bitter gall.

While the Blount girls and Alexander were busy with their thoughts, Lord Petre made conversation with Lord Salisbury—they had been edged away from the ladies by the Duke of Beaufort, who was determined to claim the lion's share of their attention.

"You have land in Barbados, do you not?" asked Lord Petre.

"Sugar," Lord Salisbury replied with a complacent smile, reaching out to take a handful of cherries. He threw a couple into his mouth and removed the pits, dropping them carelessly on to the tablecloth near where Martha was sitting. He ignored her upward glance and continued to speak. "It has made my fortune, and required almost no exertion on my own part."

"Indeed!" Lord Petre exclaimed. "How can that be so, my lord?"

He looked down at Martha with a sympathetic smile and moved the cherry pits.

"I need never go out there," Lord Salisbury mumbled through a mouthful of fruit. "My slaves come from a reputable trader, who travels to Africa himself. He always gets me excellent men; women too, I believe. The plantation never gives me a moment's anxiety, and it costs me nearly nothing when I think of what it costs to maintain the estate in England."

"But slaves are said to be quite expensive," Lord Petre replied with casual confidence. "'Black Ivory,' are they not?" He was pleased to have remembered the phrase Douglass had used.

Lord Salisbury looked suspicious at the note of challenge in Lord Petre's question. "It is all about having the right trader," he answered, sounding put out. "Edward Fairfax got me into a scheme out there. We pay the trader, and he delivers the slaves to us directly, with no grasping middlemen to swindle us along the way. Fairfax tells me that is the key."

Lady Mary Pierrepont, who had been standing to the side of their group listening to the conversation, asked, "But what if something should happen to his cargo?" Lord Salisbury gave her a hostile glance, but Lady Mary ignored it, blithely unconcerned about his opinion.

"Nothing does happen to the cargo," Lord Salisbury said irritably. "We pay him for three hundred slaves, and he delivers them. Well, he delivers about two hundred and fifty in the end; we lose a few along the way."

"You lose a few slaves?" Lady Mary repeated with a laugh. "Where do they get lost, between Africa and Barbados?"

"Some of them die on the voyage over," he replied. But he said it somewhat vaguely, Lord Petre thought. He wondered whether anybody had questioned Lord Salisbury about the arrangement before now. "I daresay they are sickening before the boat sets out from Africa," he added. "But the captain throws any dead slaves over the side, to stop the disease from spreading."

Lord Petre and Lady Mary both nodded. "It sounds a capital scheme," said Lord Petre. "But there is one detail in your account that puzzles me. How can three hundred men fit into a boat the size of a slave ship? I do not think it possible."

"Oh, they stand in rows—like books on a shelf," Lord Salisbury replied airily. "They do not need much room. They are chained together, of course, for otherwise they try to make trouble. The crew has beds, I suppose, but I imagine those are strung from the rafters or some such."

"Good Lord," said Lady Mary. "Three hundred men back to back, with fifty of them on the verge of death. The smell must be infernal."

"Well, the traders grow rich enough from it," said Lord Salisbury, defensively. "We pay them amply for their pains."

Lord Petre was about to ask him how this could be consistent with his claim that the plantation cost nothing to run when their conversation was interrupted by Henrietta Oldmixon, who sprang energetically to her feet and turned to the duke.

"The champagne is making me restless," she announced. "And Your Grace has promised me riding. Will you take me to the Ring?"

"By all means, madam," the duke replied with a bow. "I came equipped expressly for the pleasure, with a second horse, saddled for a lady." And he led them away.

Lord Salisbury promptly offered his arm to his wife, and they walked off to mount their own horses; an additional horse for Lady Salisbury had of course been brought. This left Arabella and Lord Petre, on whom all the eyes of the party were now trained. Alexander noted that Lady Mary had already retreated to her nearby carriage.

"I know better than to offer you a horse, Miss Fermor," Lord Petre declaimed. "Your refusal ever to ride when you are in town is famous. But I should like to offer myself as your cavalier, and invite you to sit pillion with me."

Even now, Teresa hoped that Lord Petre might recall that, in the very conversation to which he had just alluded, her own excellence as a horsewoman had also been discussed. But Lord Petre either did not remember, or did not wish to acknowledge Teresa's skill.

The three couples rode away in the direction of the Ring, and Jervas, Alexander, Martha, and Teresa were left under the trees among half a dozen empty champagne bottles and a threadbare collection of guests. Jervas did his best to cheer the girls up, but the wind had gone out of the morning's pleasures. Teresa proposed a walk along the promenade that joined Hyde Park to the Palace in Kensington Village, and the others agreed to it. Alexander offered Teresa his arm, and was happy to find that she took it with a grateful smile.

When Arabella and Lord Petre arrived at the Ring, it was filled with carriages and equipages of every description. Coats of arms shone on the bright side panels of the doors; liveried footmen bristled to attention and nodded haughtily to servants in other coaches. Doors opened to unload their fashionable cargo in a bright shimmer of feathers and silks.

Into the midst of all this splendour rode Arabella and her cavalier. They entered with a confidence that spoke of their absolute certainty of being the most handsome and enviable of the people gathered there. Lord Petre turned to pass a pleasantry to her, bowing his head close enough to make their intimacy unmistakable. Arabella was exquisitely conscious of it. But she displayed exactly the degree of self-assurance required to suggest that although she knew she must be constantly observed, she was indifferent to public attention.

After a couple of circuits around the Ring they dismounted to greet their friends. Lady Salisbury and Henrietta Oldmixon saluted them with peals of laughter from atop their high-gloss horses, and the Duke of Beaufort and Lord Salisbury approached on foot with other acquaintances whom they had met while riding. Everybody was talking merrily when Lord Petre touched Arabella on the elbow.

"Will you excuse me a moment?" he asked. "I see that my friend James Douglass is on the other side of the Ring."

Arabella followed his glance to where Douglass was standing, and observed that he was watching them closely.

"Of course!" she said though aware that she disliked Douglass's steady, piercing gaze. She guessed that the meeting must have something to do with the plan Lord Petre had talked about on their memorable day in his rooms, and she looked at the others self-consciously, expecting them to ask her why Lord Petre was leaving. But they were distracted by the Duke of Beaufort's friends, and had not noticed.

Lord Petre had known all along that Douglass would be in the Ring that afternoon. They had arranged to meet. Whenever he had looked across while he rode with Arabella, Douglass had returned the look, nodding discreetly so that Lord Petre alone would observe it. For the first time, Lord Petre found that he did not want to see him. He was loath to part with Arabella, suddenly aware that by involving her in the secret meeting he had unwittingly placed her in danger. But he knew that he must hear Douglass's news.

As Lord Petre rode up, Douglass said, "You are handsomely mounted today, my lord."

Lord Petre ignored his jaunty tone of voice. "Have you been waiting long?"

"Since the hour arranged," Douglass replied. "I passed the time making love to my Lady Sandwich. As she has never received more than ten minutes' attention from another man in her life, I fancy that she doubted the sincerity of my advances." He laughed. How cruel it sounded. "I thought that Miss Fermor would never tire of sitting on your horse's rump and smiling at the crowd," Douglass finished.

But then his mood changed abruptly. "I received today a message from Lancashire," he said quietly.

The baron instantly became grave. "Is there news from France?"

Douglass seemed about to reply, when his face clouded over; he caught sight of someone over Lord Petre's shoulder. "I shall meet you tonight," he said quickly. "The Pen and Hand in Shoreditch. At nine o'clock." And he was gone.

When Lord Petre turned around he saw Lady Castlecomber waiting to take his arm.

"You seemed in mighty spirits earlier, my lord," she said.

"Hello, Charlotte," he replied, disconcerted by her sudden appearance. "I had not seen that you were here." He wondered whether she had overheard the exchange with Douglass.

"I attribute your good humour rather to the influence of Miss Fermor than to your companion with the chestnut horse," she said. "For I assume that it is Arabella that you came here to see—not him."

Lord Petre was relieved, and chose not to answer her directly.

"James Douglass makes better company than you might suppose," he replied.

"Ah, so that gentleman is James Douglass," she said. "According to my husband, he is still in Africa. One shudders to imagine what he does there."

"He returned to England many months ago. News travels slowly."

"Some news more slowly than others, I think you will agree. In any case, I must upbraid you for keeping company with Mr. Douglass. I had not thought you would have such unsavoury friends."

He looked at her sharply, but saw from her face that she meant nothing serious by the remark. "It has not been my custom in the past, as you know," he said.

"Nor do I imagine that it will be your habit in the future," she replied. "Let us call your present situation an unfortunate interlude."

"Shall I ask whether you refer to more than my relationship with Mr. Douglass?"

"Not if you wish me to be candid with you, Robert."

He smiled.

"It is pleasant to see you, Charlotte."

"And to see you. But I will not flatter you further by saying that I miss you, for ours is a friendship that must withstand the trial of periodic interruptions."

"You have always expressed yourself felicitously, Lady Castlecomber," he replied, as they joined the group in which Arabella was standing.

When Teresa and Martha left the picnic spot with Alexander and Jervas, they were in pairs—Teresa and Alexander in front, Martha and Jervas behind. Martha was not so fast a walker as her sister, and she had far less impatience to be gone from the picnic ground, so she and Jervas meandered behind the others.

Teresa was relieved to be away from the party, and glad to have Alexander to take her arm. The sight of Lord Petre and Arabella riding together had left her feeling very low. She did not know exactly what the degree of their relationship was, but it was apparent that they were intimate. She could deceive herself no longer: she was not the object of Lord Petre's attention. The truth was all the more bitter for her feeling that she should have admitted it long before now.

In a much-subdued mood, she began to cast her mind back over the recent history of her friendship with Alexander. She remembered the ill-fated day in St. James's Park—he had rescued her at the very moment when she felt most alone after being slighted by Arabella and Lord Petre. The memory embarrassed her. She should not have hurried off with James Douglass. When Alexander had seen her crying in the Lime Walk, her feelings of humiliation had been all the more acute for knowing that she had behaved meanly towards him earlier. She was relieved to see Lord Petre paying attention to Alexander at the picnic today; his professed admiration must be real. Alexander deserved that, at least.

Where were they gone, the old, easy days of their friendship? She forced herself to admit that she had behaved badly on almost every occasion that she and Alexander had been together since coming to town. When he visited her on the day after the episode with Douglass, she had slighted him, showing off because Lord Petre, in a moment of perfunctory hospitality, had invited her to his picnic. Alexander had been hurt, she was sure, but in spite of this he continued to attend her, walking beside her without so much as a chastening glance.

Alexander interrupted these disconsolate reflections by saying, "I believe that Lord Petre has not been admitted to the pleasure of seeing you ride."

"He has not," Teresa replied, startled to hear him speak. "But how did you know?"

"Had he seen you," Alexander answered, "he would not have allowed such an opportunity to pass without begging you to perform once again."

"You are kind, Alexander," she replied sincerely. She paused, and then added in a modest voice that was very different from the tone he was used to, "I do ride well, and it pleases me to hear you say it. And yet I feel that it is impossible to have any share of notice when my cousin Bell is by. She simply does not allow it." She hesitated again. "But then, Arabella is so very handsome, and always so lively. She makes excellent company."

Alexander understood the effort it had cost her to say this, and he replied lightly, sparing her feelings.

"The fires of Miss Fermor's beauty burn too hot for my constitution," he said. "Were I to approach any nearer, I should be in danger of incineration. I also think that she has too much hair," he added.

Teresa smiled at last, but said, "Her hair is generally thought very fine."

"Neither Miss Fermor's hair, nor any other part of her features, has for me one tenth the loveliness of your own person, madam," Alexander replied.

Teresa could almost hear him holding his breath. Awkwardly, she replied, "I thank you for saying so, Alexander."

"It is a mean enough compliment," he said, looking at her closely. "I am like a poor fellow who makes his rich landlord a scurvy, worthless present, hoping to receive one of infinitely greater value in return."

She hesitated, not knowing what to say, and answered at last, "Your present is worth a great deal to me."

They had come to a natural halt as they talked, and they looked back to see how far Martha and Jervas trailed behind them. It was in fact some considerable distance, for the pair had sat down on a low bench at the entrance to the walk. Teresa looked at Alexander. The sight of his familiar form at her side, when she felt so much in need of being admired, brought a sudden lump to her throat. But how complex, how contradictory were the emotions accompanying the tears that started to her eyes.

They were tears, she admitted, of gratitude—that he had not left her, despite every provocation. But they were tears of pity, too. Was not there something pitiable in a creature who continued, as Alexander did, after he had been beaten and abused? He stood beside her now, demeaningly dependent but fiercely proud, like a precocious child. And she was crying out of disappointment: in herself, as much as in him. She knew that she should love him in spite of his physical frailty; indeed that she should love him because of it. But she recoiled from him. She could hardly bring herself to think it: his crippled body repelled her, and the thought of his embrace made her cold.

"Oh—the others are nowhere near," she exclaimed in dismay.

Alexander was looking at her evenly. When he noticed the change in Teresa's manner today, the flames of hope had sparked within him, almost against his will. He feared that it was, as ever, misplaced hope. But he could not help but feel it.

"I see that you will not ask what sort of present you might make me in return," he said.

She coloured—already she regretted having allowed the conversation to come so far. She adopted their old, teasing style. "I have long ago learned that your wit is not meant to be answered, Alexander," she said. "You present it as a collector might exhibit a butterfly, or an insect caught in amber. As a marvel, requiring admiration. It would spoil your display if I were to bring a specimen of my own to show."

To her relief, this answer seemed to divert him from his thoughts of romance. He considered what she had said for a moment, and then replied, "The notion of an insect captured in amber is clever. And you are right, it resembles my wit exactly. Neither rich nor rare—only causing much puzzlement as to how it came into being." Again a pause, and then, "You stand alone above your sex, Teresa."

The mawkish finale of this speech caused a renewed agitation in her breast. "Come, Alexander," she said severely. "Stop this pretended modesty immediately. It is exceedingly unpleasant, and makes me wish to return to my sister."

"Then let us walk together a little more, and I shall do nothing but boast of my abilities," he replied.

His answer relieved her; she hoped that the ardent exchange had been brought on by heightened emotion that had now passed. They walked more easily, but after a few minutes Alexander asked Teresa if she was tired, and she replied that they ought to get back to Martha. When they turned around, Teresa breathed comfortably to think that the moment of crisis had passed.

"How beautiful London is in the summer," she observed, "and yet it fills me with a kind of dread. In August Martha and I must return to my grandfather's house at Whiteknights."

"The town will be desolate without you," Alexander answered, in his old tone of teasing gallantry. "But why will you leave in August?"

"The Queen's summer levee at Hampton Court is at the end of July, and Martha and I have plans to attend it. Then we shall go," she said. "But if I had the means to live in London all the year, I should do so," Teresa added.

"When *I* am rich," Alexander replied, "I shall live in some bucolic spot upon the river, from where I may choose to be in either the country or the city, according with my taste."

"You seem very sure of your success, Alexander."

"Success has far more to do with being sure of one's talent than it has to do with being talented," was his reply. "Though whether or not that will work to my advantage I leave you to say."

She smiled, and they continued to walk companionably.

Before long, Alexander spoke again. "Your sister is waving to us, and we will be with her in just a few minutes," he said. "How much pleasure I take from your company, Teresa. My only wish is that I might be instrumental in seeing you settled."

Her heart beat quickly again, but she answered him steadily, "You do everything in your power to take care of us, Alexander."

"There is yet more that I could do," he said urgently. "I could offer you a home. I could promise that you would come to London enough even for your taste. I could make your life easy and Patty's secure."

Not meeting his eye, Teresa said, "And how would you bring these miracles about?"

She prayed that he would not say anything he would regret.

"By declaring myself sincerely as your lover," he burst out, "and making you an offer of marriage."

She could not bring herself to look at him, but, prodding at the gravel path with the toe of her shoe, she said quietly, "Then I was quite right to say that a miracle would be required."

He looked at her, aghast. "Do you doubt my sincerity?" he asked.

"Not at all," she replied. "But I am somewhat sceptical of your abilities as a lover." In her nervousness she giggled a little.

Alexander pressed on. "Then you doubt every part of my

being," he cried, "for you have only ever known me as one who loved you."

Because she knew that it was true, it made her angry. "Had I not known you many years," she said coldly, "I would take your last remark for an affront. If I had ever suspected your intentions, I should certainly not have permitted the attentions you bestowed."

At last he stopped being gallant. Looking directly at her, he said harshly, "Teresa, do not insult me by pretending not to have understood me."

She looked around, not knowing how to respond. His foolish intensity made her more angry. "Pray, sir," she answered, "do not insult *me* by suggesting that there is anything like an understanding between us."

"Insult you?" he said, incredulous. "You call me presumptuous for singling you out as the loveliest woman I have known?"

Unable to control her feelings of vexation, she returned, "It is a distinction that I had rather you had not thrust upon me. I came to London without any thoughts of attachment—entirely free to choose—to be chosen. I considered myself a woman without obligation, and I assumed that this was the light in which I was generally regarded."

He stared at her, incomprehension stamped on his face. It merely goaded her on.

"But now I learn that you have marked me out as your own," she said, feeling a sob rising in her throat. "Perhaps you have even boasted of it to others—and put it about town that I am already attached. Am I to understand that you have presumed to speak as my champion, though I have never permitted it?" She knew now that there was nothing true in what she said, but she went on regardless. "I have never given you the slightest encouragement. I loathe the merest idea of an arrangement, an attachment, being formed to a person who—with . . ."

His face was quite still as he finished, "With *me* is what I believe you are saying."

This roused in her a fury of self-reproach. "You think me cruel, unthinking, selfish—a thousand things—I know." She broke off; she must hold her tongue, she must not bring Martha into it, but it was too late. "Why do not you marry Martha?" she cried desperately. "You would do well with her. But do not blight my chances by appointing yourself as my lover, least of all when we are among such acquaintance as these."

"You are referring, I assume, to Lord Petre," he answered. "You are a fool if you do not see that he would hold a woman such as you in contempt." He paused and weighed his words. Even now he was generous. "Not because *you* are contemptible, Teresa, but because he is," he added.

"He! How dare you presume to know what he, or any other gentleman, thinks or feels about me," she stormed. "You know nothing of men or of the world. You are a cripple, as small in thought as in stature! You see nothing, you hear nothing, Alexander, but what is lowest to the ground."

He stepped back with a look of disbelief. "Then you cannot blame me, madam, for having paid such long and devoted attentions to your person."

They had nearly reached Martha and Jervas, and Alexander saw that they had been overheard. Already the pair were standing to meet them, Jervas's legs braced awkwardly to confront him, Martha white with anxiety. The four of them stood for several moments in ghastly silence.

Martha finally spoke, ending the pause.

"The sun has tired me and the glare has given me a headache," she said. "Mr. Jervas has been sitting with me so kindly, but I must go home."

"We have already been here far longer than we ought," Teresa added brusquely. "Give me your arm, Patty—let us hurry to the carriage."

"I shall accompany you," said Jervas, before Alexander could speak.

But Teresa replied curtly, "We prefer to walk alone." And she pulled her sister forward without another word. Alexander held Jervas back, letting them go on.

Anger, misery, and disappointment were the prevailing emotions of the afternoon. Alexander was not prepared for such bitter sensations, largely because he had not prepared himself for the conversation at all. He knew perfectly well that Teresa had no wish to hear his avowals. He had not even meant to make them. Only a short time before, he had been thinking that she occupied less of his attention than in the past. What had made him declare himself now? He had thought that she would refuse him, and indeed, had she accepted the offer, he believed that his feelings would have been divided. Some strange, perverse vanity had led him on, a contrary sort of pride. Just as he felt his fatal weakness for Teresa abating, he had been tempted into declarations from which the former intensity of his feeling had hitherto made him shrink.

And he had been punished for it. The cruelty of her response! It was as though she hated him—and yet he did not think that it was hate she felt— how could it be? There must be some part of her that responded in kind to his affection. But there would be no more of such thoughts. He would not ask himself, over and over, whether she loved him. She would not marry him. He had seen her cruel, cold, selfish, angry. He could not continue to admire her. He, too, must be cold.

Teresa had never imagined that sorrow would figure in the aftermath of a proposal from Alexander, but now she, too, felt its thorn. The feeling surprised her. She was sorry that Alexander had spoken and that there had been such a scene. She wished that she had not become so angry; she wished that she had not been driven to say things she did not really believe. But she would not take back what she had said, and run the risk of opening the discussion again. She was sad, she was vexed—but she would not feel regret.

And yet, despite all this, she was disappointed that his declaration was over. She had long planned that if Alexander should ever propose she would refuse him. But the knowledge that he admired her had been a precious consolation—even if it was one that she never admitted. Now that her refusal had been given, she was left with the fact that it was the only offer she had received. Natural, then, that Alexander, who had forced so unwelcome a reflection upon her, should become even more markedly the object of her resentment.

A week passed without contact between Alexander and the Blount sisters. During this period a considerable share of unhappiness fell to Martha, who had no feelings of indignation to modify her lowness. She was cut off from her two dearest friends, neither of whom made any attempt to draw her into their confidence. Since she did not understand precisely what had happened, she feared the worst: that Teresa and Alexander would refuse ever to be in the same room again, and that she would be forced to choose between them.

As Martha sat alone in her room thinking over the sad state of affairs, she sighed bitterly. There would be no real choice, of course. She would have to take her sister's part. Why must it always be thus—would there never be a moment in her life when she could do, or even speak, as she truly felt? Although she was angry with Teresa for having spoken harshly to Alexander, she was conscious, too, of a secret pleasure. No longer could he persuade himself that Teresa was the superior sister. In the face of such bitterness, such selfishness, Alexander must see Teresa clearly at last. Wretched, perhaps—deserving of sympathy and care—but wilfully cruel to the people who loved her most.

In thinking about Alexander's part in the crisis, Martha surprised herself. She found that she resented him, too. Had he given any thought to it, he must have known that a breach between himself and Teresa would also end his friendship with Martha. And yet he had not thought of that at all, obviously. In the past, it would have caused her unspeakable hurt. But now she was angry. However clever he might be, Alexander had behaved like a fool.

At nine o'clock on the night of the picnic, Lord Petre went to meet James Douglass in the Pen and Hand. The tavern was on a dark and dirty street in Shoreditch, some distance from where Jenkins had left him in the carriage.

"What possessed you to bring me into this part of town?" Lord Petre demanded. He couldn't help but be apprehensive as he walked along the desolate streets, fearing that someone might be watching him from the alleyways.

"Your fellow papists say Mass in this garret after dark. I am surprised you do not know it, my lord."

"Catholics of quality do not come here to pray," he replied. "They would likely be knifed to death. You should not have asked me here."

"I am to meet an agent later."

Lord Petre said nothing.

"In seven or eight days' time four of our men will enter London from the north," Douglass said in a low tone. "A fifth will come by water, alone. He will be at your house between two and three o'clock in the morning. Can you be ready?"

Lord Petre leapt to attention, forgetting his anger. "I can," he answered.

"The agent will be carrying documents from France. You are to offer protection for two days until he sails again."

"I cannot keep him in my family's house, but my servant will take him to a safe place."

Douglass nodded briefly. "And the other matter?" he asked in a lower voice.

Lord Petre took a packet from his coat and handed it across. It contained three hundred pounds. Douglass looked around the room quickly, and shoved the package into his surtout.

"I must tell you to take care with those, Douglass," said Lord Petre. "You know that traitors have been discovered among us."

"Have your rich friends been filling your head with rumours again, my lord?" Douglass asked mockingly.

Lord Petre knew that this indifference was pretended. When he had told Douglass the news about Francis Gerrard's murder, months ago now, he had gone white.

"Traitors in our ranks!" Lord Petre recalled him saying. "Gerrard must have told Caryll before he died."

"Not directly," Lord Petre had corrected him. "He told one of the leaders. The night he was killed, at the embassy." He remembered Douglass's aghast expression clearly.

But today he took Lord Petre's caution lightly. "Gerrard was killed months ago," Douglass said. "Nothing has happened since. Your friend Caryll got his story wrong. We have nothing to fear from traitors."

Lord Petre pushed his chair away from the table, angry again. "I am certain that Caryll was not mistaken," he hissed. Douglass could be as careless of his own safety as he pleased, but the money was Lord Petre's. He was determined they would not lose it.

"Steady there, my lord," Douglass urged him in a low voice, glancing around the room. "Remember where you are. I am sorry to have baited you just now," he added, as Lord Petre composed himself. "As you say, Caryll's word is sound, and your connections are indispensable. We could not go forward without you."

Mollified, Lord Petre reached out to shake Douglass by the hand before he left the tavern.

Chapter Fourteen

"Clubs, Diamonds, Hearts, in wild disorder seen"

Henrietta Oldmixon had planned an evening gathering with dancing, cards, and supper. Oldmixon parties were famous: the year before they had given a Roman banquet, where the guests dressed as senators and emperors and reclined on low couches to dine. In the winter Henrietta had arranged a medieval feast at which a flock of starlings was released from a pie just when supper was served, and acrobats and jugglers played tricks among the dancing couples. This assembly, held nine days after Lord Petre's picnic in Hyde Park, was to be a masquerade. But since all her guests would be known to one another, the caution that accompanied encounters at the public masquerade could be suspended.

Arabella Fermor was to be the guest of honour, the newest addition to the charmed group of Henrietta's friends. The town's wits and intellects had been summoned for the occasion, Charles Jervas and Alexander Pope among them. The Blount sisters were invited because of their relation to Arabella.

Before the picnic Teresa and Martha had been looking forward to Henrietta's party a good deal. But Alexander's unwanted declaration, Lord Petre's attentions to Arabella, and Teresa's discovery of her cousin's fashionable new friendships meant that both girls were now preparing for it with more dread than eagerness. They would go, nonetheless; it was unthinkable that they should miss such an occasion. Jervas's carriage collected them shortly before nine on the night of the party. Arabella had not offered to drive them. The coach ride with Jervas and Alexander was awkward, and even Martha, who generally tried to smooth over such moments, sat proudly silent.

Since it was a private party the guests wore evening dress

rather than full masquerade costume. Teresa and Martha were dressed in silk brocade gowns with Venetian masks over their faces, and when they arrived at the house they found that others had done the same. Some of the masks were elaborate: animals and carnival figures; ornate jewels and feathered head-dresses. Three of the guests, however, wore full disguise—the plumage of birds—a falcon, a peacock, and a swan. Their costumes were magnificent, all the more so because they did not, in fact, conceal the identities of the wearers. It was apparent that Henrietta Oldmixon was the falcon and Lady Salisbury the peacock; the swan, needless to say, was Arabella.

For each of the three nights before Henrietta's party Lord Petre stood for many hours in the dark stable yard of his house on Arlington Street, waiting for the agent to come. But he did not appear, and there was no news of arrests, or any other signal that something in the plan had gone awry. Lord Petre was sure, therefore, that he must keep waiting. But he was growing tired of these lonely vigils, and he longed to see Arabella again, so he decided to go to the Oldmixon party and return home just after midnight. He would give the appearance of going to bed, as he had done on the other nights, and would then sneak down to wait for his night visitor. When their business was accomplished, Petre planned to have Jenkins take the agent away to his own family's house—loyal Catholics as the Jenkinses were, Lord Petre knew that they could be trusted.

When all Henrietta's guests had assembled, a stand of fireworks was let off from the yard below, and the maskers crowded into the front rooms to watch. As the display came to an end, Teresa discovered that Arabella had come to stand beside her, and in a moment they were joined by Henrietta.

"You know Miss Oldmixon, of course," Arabella said to Teresa.

Teresa was surprised when Henrietta greeted her warmly. Until now she had not even bothered to acknowledge Miss Blount as an acquaintance.

"This is a charming gathering, Miss Oldmixon," Teresa replied in a determined effort to imitate her companions' insouciance.

"I am glad that you are come," said Henrietta. "I hope that you and your sister will be diverted. Did I not see you both the other day at my Lord Petre's pleasure party in the park? I did not know you were acquainted with him."

"He is a friend of the family. Our brother is often at Ingatestone," Teresa replied untruthfully, but she was pleased that Henrietta smiled by way of reply.

"I don't suppose that anybody was long in the park after Lord Petre and I were gone," Arabella said. "Oh—but you were attended by Mr. Pope and Mr. Jervas, Teresa. Perhaps you remained behind."

Before Teresa could answer, Henrietta interrupted. "Well, I must say, Arabella, that *you* were gone from the party pretty hastily," she said. "And when you are seen to act with eagerness, we must conclude that alacrity is now the fashion, and that indifference is a habit of the past. Do you know your cousin's reputation for being more fashionable than any other girl in London, Miss Blount?"

Teresa was sure that she heard a note of sarcasm in Henrietta's voice, and she echoed it in her own reply. "Arabella's reputation is well known," she said. "We hear of it even in the country."

Arabella turned away from them with a look of unmistakable irritation and a reproachful glance at Henrietta as she went. Teresa was surprised again. How gratifying it was to discover that the jealousy she felt towards Arabella existed also within the charmed circle of London's belles. She began a more confident circuit of the room, feeling that her fortunes had improved. Lord Petre, standing to one side of the gathering wearing a mask and a cockaded hat over his long curls, no longer seemed a figure whom she would pass by bashfully. She might even smile to think of his weakness for Arabella, since it appeared to have won her cousin fewer friends than had at first appeared.

She walked up to Martha, intending to make up for some of her recent thoughtlessness. But Martha, accustomed to Teresa's approaching only when she was in need of reassurance, said, "Did Henrietta Oldmixon say something unkind to you?"

"Certainly not!" said Teresa. "You need not be concerned for *me,* Patty."

"Oh, I know that," Martha replied, quickly recognizing her sister's mood. "I am only passing by on my way to the supper room. Will you accompany me?"

"If you would like me to," said Teresa, pleased, in truth, that Martha was there. They left the assembly room to cross the entrance hall. As they did, Martha caught sight of a swan's plumage disappearing rapidly up the stairs. Her eyes followed its progress, and Teresa saw it too. There was a short silence between them.

"She must know the house," said Teresa.

But a moment later a tall man, wearing a black mask and a cockaded hat, followed the same course. He made not the slightest effort to greet them, for his eye was trained upward, following the flight of the feathered bird. Martha looked at her sister; it was clear to both that Arabella and Lord Petre had arranged an assignation.

In the main assembly room, Alexander had watched the little exchanges unfold between Teresa and Henrietta, and then with Martha. He followed them to the supper room, trying to meet the sisters' glances. Teresa looked at him coldly; he was not surprised. But, with a shock of dismay, he saw Martha turn away. Alexander felt as though he had been struck down. Never had he imagined this! His first impulse was to rush towards her, but she had begun to talk to Charles Jervas and was seemingly absorbed by what he was saying. Alexander felt winded.

But Richard Steele and John Gay were standing before him: Gay asked how he did, and Steele filled his own plate with ham and urged him to take some. Alexander barely heard them, for he was thinking over and over of Martha's rebuff. But he knew that he must recall himself. Steele and Gay were discussing the dramatic production of *Dick Whittington and his Cat* that they had just seen at Drury Lane.

"Capital, did not you think? A rousing, spirited sort of fellow," finished Steele.

"The cat was not so distinguished on the night that I saw the performance," Gay replied. "There was too much of interest for him behind the stage in the way of rats, and only rarely was he present when Whittington wished for his company."

"I heard that the manager of the theatre was wild about it," Steele answered, "but there is nothing to be done. Pope!" he exclaimed, suddenly. "You should write something of this sort for the town. We would give you a tremendous fanfare in the *Spectator*."

Alexander forced himself not to frown. "I thank you, sir, but I have no tale that would lend itself to the introduction of either cats or rats. I favour rather those dramas which concern themselves with people. But your audience might feel that a little too closely for amusement."

There was laughter at this, more than he had expected. He noticed that many people in the room were observing him, smiling and murmuring in low tones. He wondered why. Their stares seemed to contain admiration. Might they have heard of the success of his *Essay on Criticism*? As he glanced around he saw Henrietta Oldmixon coming towards him, bringing with her the Duke of Beaufort, to whom she had been speaking.

The duke had unmasked, and his expression put Alexander in mind of some furry, earthbound quarry, lately surprised by a bird of prey that he had not seen approaching. Naturally, Henrietta did not actually hold the duke in her beak, but his limp, slightly bedraggled demeanour conveyed well the nuances of their relation.

"Mr. Pope!" Henrietta exclaimed. "We speak of nothing but your *Essay on Criticism*. You are the most celebrated writer in London."

Alexander suspected that the compliment was not strict in point of fact, but he took it in the spirit with which it was delivered.

He bowed. "I thank you, madam. Since you are the town's most celebrated giver of entertainments, I am gratified indeed to receive praise from one who understands so well the nature of diversion."

The Duke of Beaufort, who had the bruised appearance of having been dropped unexpectedly from a considerable height, collected himself and said, "My congratulations, too, Mr. Pope, upon your success. You shall receive a great deal of notice."

Alexander bowed.

"His Grace judges properly, Pope," Steele rejoined. "Your writing goes from strength to strength. Is there talk yet of a second edition?"

"Hardly," Alexander replied, smiling broadly. A large group had now gathered around him, wanting to hear what he had to say. "I have received many good wishes on account of the poem's excellence so far, but not from any party who might reasonably be suspected of having read it—and far less of having bought a copy." There was a loud burst of laughter at this. "Talk enjoys a reputation for being cheap," Alexander continued, "and happily for my fame, though not my purse, that circumstance encourages people to indulge in it very freely." He thought for a moment that the room might actually break into applause. He had never received so much attention before in his life. How bitterly ironic that tonight, when at last the success Martha had prophesied was coming so delightfully to pass, she would not share in his elation.

Richard Steele spoke. "There is one person, however, who *has* read your poem—and who is doing everything in his power to prevent your ever writing another."

Alexander knew immediately whom he was talking about. Just as he had feared, John Dennis had written a cruel attack, and though Alexander had not expected to feel wounded, it had hurt him considerably. He wished that Steele had not mentioned it. "You are speaking of Mr. Dennis, I imagine," he said. "His essay was exceedingly ill-natured, but I confess that I had anticipated it." After a moment he added, to make it clear that he took Dennis's criticism lightly, "But Mr. Dennis's slander is of the kind that rather amplifies one's reputation than diminishes it."

As he spoke, he saw that Teresa was standing very close to the group.

"I am surprised to hear you say that his attack did not affect you, Mr. Pope," she said. "His description of you was well calculated to be remembered. How did his essay begin? 'As there is no creature so venomous, so there is nothing so stupid and impotent as a hunch-backed toad . . .' Is not that correct?"

He was not sure how many of the people in the room had overheard them, but he stepped back from her, embarrassed. Why had she approached him, to add fresh injury to his regret and vexation? He knew that he should not blame her entirely, but as he remembered Martha's coldness towards him, he felt a flash of anger that he could not control.

"I need hardly tell *you*, madam, that on that one score at least, Mr. Dennis was in error," he replied. "A creature cannot be both venomous and impotent at once. The venomous animal is to be feared precisely because it does not hesitate to bite."

Steele cut in quickly, obviously regretting what his remark had engendered.

"Dennis is a fool, and everybody knows it. You need not trouble yourself with him, Pope."

And Henrietta said, "We are wild to know what you will do next, Mr. Pope. Is it to be a tragedy? Or perhaps an epic?"

"I believe I shall turn next to satire," Alexander replied, reflecting that this present scene would supply as good a place as any with which to begin.

Much to his relief, he saw that people had begun other conversations again, and that the room was quickly becoming just as rowdy as it had been before the interlude with Teresa. She was nudged out to the edge of the gathering, as Henrietta's guests pressed forward to meet the man whom their hostess had praised as the liveliest wit in London. Alexander did not understand how it had happened so suddenly, but everybody seemed to know who he was. He felt a rush of gratitude, then a feeling of elating self-confidence.

Looking up, he saw that Lady Mary Pierrepont stood beside him.

"Mr. Steele has told me that you have considered making a translation of the *Iliad*," she said. "What an undertaking! The greatest poem ever written. I long to ask you everything about it: your preparations, your methods, your manner of proceeding. Do you puzzle over each passage, or translate freely in the spirit of Homer's verse?"

Alexander felt a thrill. "I long to do Homer justice," he replied, "but I fear that I never shall."

"Nonsense, Mr. Pope!" she answered. "I do not believe that you have the slightest apprehension on that score. You think yourself the equal of Homer—and why should you not? Nobody was ever great who was afraid of great men who have come before!"

Alexander was delighted. Lady Mary's approach at the picnic had not been a moment of rashness after all. She wished to pursue the acquaintance! His anger with Teresa, even his regret over Martha, began to fade. A noblewoman—the cleverest woman in London!—had sought him out.

"I long to know which parts of Homer are your favourites," she said. "My own is when—"

But before she could finish her sentence she was interrupted by a man whom Alexander had not previously noticed. The newcomer faced Lady Mary squarely, bumping Alexander out of the way with his strong, stocky body.

He addressed her peremptorily. "When you have finished speaking with this gentleman, madam, I pray that you step aside a moment," he said.

Alexander heard a tremor in her voice that seemed out of character. "Do not you know Mr. Pope, Mr. Wortley?" she replied.

So this was Edward Wortley, the gentleman to whom Lady Mary was reputed to be secretly engaged. Wortley looked at Alexander with a malicious sneer, and said, "I congratulate you on the *Essay*, Mr. Pope. I hope that your readers will turn first to your poem before consulting Mr. Dennis's remarks upon your personal defects."

"Dennis himself would do well to follow your advice," Alexander answered, with an attempt at humour. "His attack is so full of remarks upon my person that he has hardly space to censure my *Essay*."

Wortley replied by peering down at Alexander in an exaggerated way, as if wanting to show him that he was so insignificant as to be barely visible. "He had space enough to call you a Jacobite," he said rudely.

His rudeness made Alexander all the more determined to be charming, wanting to show up Lady Mary's suitor as the petulant boor that he was. "In so doing, Mr. Dennis shows his talents as a storyteller as well as a critic," he said. "Neither my self nor my writings can possibly give him reason for the charge."

But Wortley was determined that Alexander would suffer. "His accusations will do you harm in the present climate," he said.

"I am not afraid of it, sir," Alexander replied, hoping that he could bring the conversation to a close, and indeed, Wortley did not answer him.

"I will meet you on that sofa beside the window, Mr. Wortley," Lady Mary said. Alexander was astonished by her tone of voice. He had expected her to be as forthright with her suitor as she had been with him. Wortley glared at her for a moment, but she said no more, and neither did Alexander. After another pause he stalked away and sat staring at her pointedly from his position on the little sofa.

"Forgive Mr. Wortley's manner, sir," she said, in a low voice, afraid of being overheard. "There is a matter—I mean that we had arranged to speak this evening—and he thought that I did not remember. He is not himself. When you see him again he shall be in much improved spirits."

"You should go to him, madam," Alexander replied, confused by her unexpected submissiveness.

As she walked away, she turned back with some resumption of her former sparkle. "When next we speak, Mr. Pope, I shall expect you to be ready with passages from the *Iliad*, translated by your own hand," she said smilingly, and he replied:

"I shall be prepared, madam."

As Alexander made his way back to the supper table, people whom he had never seen before came up and congratulated him. He was thrilled. Until now he had hoped that his writing would bring him an invisible kind of fame, so that nobody need know of his deformity. But he found that he liked this attention after all. It was Dennis's attack that had done it—the very words that Teresa had spoken aloud tonight were making his celebrity. The Toad of Grub Street. It was as such a creature that he was destined to become famous.

After supper, the guests were invited to repair to another large reception room on the first floor of the town house for cards and conversation. When Alexander reached the room it was already crowded. White candlelight blazed from every bracket, and in the corners of the room were great urns of fresh flowers: striped tulips, pleated opium poppies, tuberoses, and sweet jasmine, filling the room with a powerful, overblown scent. The windows at each end of the house were wide open, but there was no breeze blowing; the air was close.

Everybody was crowded around a game of cards played between Henrietta Oldmixon, the Duke of Beaufort, Arabella, Lord Petre, and—Alexander saw with surprise—Lady Mary herself. He caught sight of Martha standing across the room from him; and this time when their eyes met she did not turn aside. His first impulse was to rush over to her, but something held him back. He was ashamed of his behaviour in the park, and he feared that if he were to stand before her now he would see only her disappointment and disaffection. He turned back to the card game.

They were playing Ombre. The three ladies responsible for the play held the hands of cards; the two gentlemen stood beside Henrietta and Arabella, ready to place bets on their behalf. It was apparent from the handwritten bills in the centre of the table that considerable sums had already been staked on the outcome of the game. The cards were dealt, and Henrietta, to the left of the Ombre, led the betting.

"Upon Miss Oldmixon's success, I stake a hundred pounds," the duke announced and looked around the room with a wide smile, making sure that the lavishness of his outlay had been noticed.

"I answer His Grace by venturing two hundred pounds upon Miss Fermor's behalf," Lord Petre answered immediately.

There was a general sensation in the room. The guests began to whisper among themselves, crowding more nearly around the table to see what would happen. The gathering became quieter, though people halfheartedly attempted to continue their conversations.

An expectant silence fell as the players turned to Lady Mary, the last to place a bet. Alexander noticed that Edward Wortley had slunk away, hoping to avoid spending money, he surmised.

"The baron and the duke play boldly for the ladies' sakes," Lady Mary said in her clear voice. "But I answer them by betting three hundred pounds that I will beat you all."

And she threw a note of hand into the centre, without the slightest trace of agitation or heightened feeling. Alexander was dumbfounded with admiration.

When the hands were played out, Lady Mary was declared the winner. She wore no expression of exultation or excitement at the outcome, but said simply, "I thought that I would have the best of the cards."

The dealer cleared the table at the end, and she added to Lord Petre, "Your bet was rather foolhardy, my lord."

"'Tis only a game of cards," he replied, with as much indifference as he could muster. "What is lost on one night is easily to be gained on another. That is the best of Lady Fortune. Capricious as she may be, she is with us as often as she is against us." But as he turned from her he wiped his brow.

Henrietta Oldmixon seemed entirely unaffected by the fact that six hundred pounds had just been staked on the outcome of a single hand of cards, and picked up a conversation where it had been left off moments earlier.

"What extraordinary news about the Duke of Newcastle's death," she said to Arabella. "The fortune has gone to his daughter, Lady Henrietta Cavendish Holles. His wife is left with very little, of course."

Alexander noticed that Arabella had gone rather white at the end of the card game, aghast at Lord Petre's throwing away so large a sum of money on her behalf. But she collected herself quickly and turned to Henrietta with only the faintest trace of anxiety around her eyes. "I heard two gentlemen the other day praising Lady Henrietta for her great beauty and sparkling wit," she said with a dull smile. "When I heard her thus described, I knew that the duke must be gravely ill. But I did not think he could already be dead." Alexander could not help but admire her capacity for self-possession, though her dispassion was chilling.

"He fell from his horse and was killed instantly," Miss Oldmixon answered carelessly. "His daughter is a nice enough girl, though, as you say, not handsome. I hope that the match made for her will not be too irksome."

As Lady Mary Pierrepont stood up from the table and moved away, telling the men that her winnings might be brought to the house in the morning, Alexander stepped forward to compliment her on the boldness with which she had played.

"You are the Achilles of the present age," he said. "No need for new translations of Homer when epic battles are to be won and lost at the card table."

To his dismay, her reply was distant.

"I am glad that you have enjoyed the evening's assembly, Mr. Pope," she said, and turned away coldly.

Alexander kicked himself for speaking. Once again he had been naive, thinking that he could presume on so insubstantial a friendship. With all her wit and cleverness, Mary Pierrepont had made him forget that she was the daughter of an earl. She was at liberty to speak to him, and she delighted in so doing, rejoicing in her ability to flout convention. When she had addressed him earlier, it had no doubt been partly in an attempt to make Wortley jealous. He had been a fool not to see it—not to see that however unsatisfactory a suitor Wortley might be, his intimacy with Lady Mary was well established, hardly likely to be dislodged by the son of a Catholic textile importer. The night had delivered a good number of lessons in folly to himself and to others alike. But though he knew that he should have been ready for it, Lady Mary's slight piqued him—the attentions paid to him this evening had spurred his ambitions. Now that he had been noticed at last, he could not bear the thought of being insignificant once again.

Martha watched with interest while these events unfolded. She saw Arabella's face go white when Lady Mary won; she saw Lady Mary collect the money from Lord Petre without a flicker of apology. Their reactions prompted her to reflect that even if Lord Petre had fallen in love with Arabella, the gulf between the nobility and commoners was profound, perhaps deeper even than that between Catholic and Protestant. She wondered whether Arabella would ultimately possess the iron nerve required to succeed in Lord Petre's world. But then Martha watched as she left the card tables, laughing as Lady Salisbury put a hand on her arm, glancing neither right nor left. Perhaps she would have what was needed after all.

As she watched, Alexander walked up to Mary Pierrepont and spoke to her. To Martha's surprise, Lady Mary slighted him—Alexander stepped back with an embarrassed, confused expression. Instinctively Martha felt for him: his face crumpled into a fierce twist of self-reproach, and she guessed that he was scolding himself for having spoken.

Something about Alexander's expression made her realize that she could not remain angry with him. Alexander might be foolish, he might be proud and selfish, but he would always be his own severest critic. Tonight, after all, he had tried to catch her eye to show that he was sorry; it had been she who had looked away. But Martha decided that she could not approach him in order to re-establish the friendship. She was determined to make a new beginning in her dealings with Alexander. She would wait for him to seek her out.

The room was very warm, and her head had begun to ache. To recover, she removed herself to a seat that had been placed close to an open window. The night air was refreshing, and, since the room made a lively spectacle, she was happy to be apart from it for a time. She had been sitting there for only a few minutes when Alexander caught sight of her pained expression. He guessed that she was feeling faint, and hurried to the buffet to bring her a glass of wine. As he came over to her seat, Martha turned to him with a little heightening of colour in her face. He smiled shyly, finding that he, too, was awkward.

He did not ask her whether he might sit down, but did so at once. He handed her the glass, and she raised it to her lips. For a moment they sat together without speaking.

"Thank you, Alexander," she said.

"How are you now?"

"I feel very much better," she said, not quite willing to tell him how pleased she was that he had come. "But I should like to stay seated a few minutes more," she added.

"Of course. I hope that we may sit for a little while at least."

Though she hesitated to do so, aware that it would mark a change in their relationship, she forced herself to raise the subject of Teresa.

"My sister has been troubled this evening, do not you think?" she said after a short pause.

"She has," he answered. "Your sister is not, perhaps, a person capable of being sincerely happy. She cannot find a way to be at rest."

Apprehensive of Alexander's reaction, Martha steeled herself to speak candidly. "And yet she is happier than you would like to believe her," she replied. "You are sometimes unwilling to accept that her pleasures take a form that is very different from your own."

Alexander looked at Martha with surprise. It was not the sort of remark that he expected from her. His first impulse was to dismiss it angrily, but he made himself pause. "There is one respect in which I do believe that we are alike," he replied. "She, like me, would be happier if she were not so bent upon being admired by people for whom she feels no real regard—and who are themselves incapable of disinterested feeling."

For a long time, Martha had suspected that Alexander took this view of her sister. She knew that she could not lose this chance to articulate her real feelings.

"It is very important to Teresa that she feel part of the fashionable world. In a curious sense, I consider it a mark of bravery," she said. "She will not submit to being less than our cousin Bell, or any of the other girls. I cannot reproach her because it is a part of her character that I admire."

"But it is a kind of courage that proceeds from being frightened," he insisted.

Martha stood her ground. "Is not all bravery an attempt to overcome fear?" she asked with a frank gaze.

In a voice that made her think he understood what she was saying, he replied, "In matters of the heart, I am at last coming to understand that Teresa is determined to choose; she will not be chosen."

"But I hope that she *will* be chosen, for it is of the greatest consequence to her."

"You are never swayed by wilful inclinations or transient passions, Patty," said Alexander, after a thoughtful silence. "Why should those things fall only to your sister's part? Could not you both have taken more even shares in good sense and folly?"

"Teresa is not so foolish as she seems to you," Martha answered severely. "I do not care to choose for myself. I wish to be chosen." She was conscious of breathing quickly. The silence before Alexander answered was wretched.

But at last he said, "Ah! Well, that requires nothing more than that you be endlessly patient and infinitely wise."

Martha feared that he was making fun of her, but his face was solemn as he said, "Remember that a man values only the prize that it has cost him trouble to obtain—nothing that comes easily could be worth the winning. And your misfortune, Patty, is to be just such a prize. So must you be patient until your hero—a vain, idle, misguided fellow, whom you shall watch despairingly as he loses his way and his nerve a thousand times—finds his path to you with infinite slowness. Few women have the stomach for such sluggishness, and they take matters into their own hands. But I know you to be a different sort."

Martha felt a thrill when she heard Alexander's words, but it was followed immediately by a sense of deflation. "That is a gallant way of saying that if I will wait to be chosen, I must accept that I shall be chosen last," she said. But she was determined not to be low. "But I do not think of you as an idler, nor a flatterer, Alexander," she continued. "I am surprised to hear that you have wasted time in seeking admiration from those you do not admire. I am not sure that I believe you."

"When I am in the town, Patty, I have no choice but to become such a person," he said with a shrug. "In London a man is everywhere but at his own house; he minds everything but his own business; he kisses everybody but his own wife. It is the fashion. I spend my time in anything but that which should employ me, and I spend whole days talking to men I have no value for."

Martha relaxed, and their conversation continued in this way for a little longer. Towards the end of their exchange, Martha said, "Do you know that Teresa and I return to the country at the end of next month?"

He nodded. "You sister has told me," he answered, "and I warned her that I shall follow you both close behind."

He meant to be charming, but she knew that he had hoped to write a new poem before he returned to the country. "Yet the town becomes you better than the country in many ways," she replied. "You are able to enjoy so few rural diversions."

"Indeed I am no hunter," he answered her, "but I am a great esteemer of the sport; unhappy only in my want of constitution for it—and for drinking, of course."

"These are the chief pleasures of the country! It is a pity you are so sickly."

"It is a pity everybody else is so healthy."

Martha laughed. "This talk of hunting makes me sad to think that the summer will dwindle away so soon. The nights are long now; it will begin to grow light almost before we are in bed. But soon the days will grow shorter again."

"Then we must make time stand still a little longer," he said in reply. "An idea has come to me, Patty; tell me if you like it. Did you ever see the Lambeth Gardeners upon the river in the mornings, bringing their wares to market?"

"I did not."

"It is said to be a fine sight; a river of barges filled with fruits and flowers. If this morning is light, the water will already be in early sun by the time they come. What do you say to a trip upon the river at sunrise?"

Her face lit up. "Oh, but I have longed for many weeks to see the boats coming into market from Lambeth," she said excitedly. Then she paused, and asked, "But what of your health? You are delicate, and will catch cold. It is not wise."

"Wise it may not be—but I am saving all of my wisdom for when I am so much crippled that I cannot leave the house. Ours is no age for being wise! Now it is midnight. I shall come for you at five. Four hours is sleep enough for any person less than twenty-five."

Chapter Fifteen

"All that I dread, is leaving you behind!"

The Blount sisters were gone from the party, Jervas and Alexander with them. Lord Petre was gone too—indeed the only guests remaining were hardened gamesters, friends of Miss Oldmixon's brother, who had settled in to play until dawn. Henrietta, Arabella, and Lady Salisbury were sitting together around the remnants of the tea table, congratulating their hostess upon the great success of her assembly. Henrietta had invited Arabella beforehand to stay the night, so she was still there, but conversation was desultory, and there was much yawning.

"Do you know, Henrietta, I think that I shall go home to bed after all," Arabella said. "It would be great fun to stay here, but my costume will be a difficulty in the morning, and it is too much of a trouble to send a servant now for other clothes. I shall ask one of the footmen to find me a chair."

"But your parents believe that you are to spend the night here," Henrietta protested, being one of those girls who do not like anybody to alter a plan she herself has decided upon. "Their house will be closed up—it is nearly one o'clock."

Arabella was adamant. "A night servant is always about," she said. "I shall not have trouble getting in. At least my cousin Teresa will not rouse me early in the morning, since she will believe that I am here with you. She often asks me to accompany her on morning visits and trips to her dressmaker. Very tiresome—it *almost* makes me long for the country, where there is nothing to do."

She arranged with the footman to have a sedan chair ordered, and set about freshening up her plumage, which had lost some of its fullness while she was sitting. The chair arrived, and Arabella was handed in.

The chairmen started out towards the street in St. James's where Arabella lived, but shortly before they would have arrived at the Fermors' town house she tapped on the box and asked that she be taken instead to the Petre family's house on Arlington Street. When they arrived, her chair was carried around to the stables. The back of the house was in darkness, but at the sound of the chairmen's steps, Lord Petre's footman appeared from within, carrying a candle.

"Miss Fermor!" he whispered, sounding surprised. Arabella wondered who else he could be waiting for at such an hour, and concluded that the worthy Jenkins must be anticipating a meeting with his own mistress. Jenkins took her inside, and she followed him up the back stairs, now so familiar to her that she hardly needed a light. They walked silently, Arabella having learned to place her feet exactly where the boards would not make a sound. Jenkins pushed on the door of Lord Petre's chamber, and Arabella saw Lord Petre spring forward, a look of alarm shadowing his features.

"Arabella!" he exclaimed, and the whole expression of his face changed from apprehension to excitement. It was gratifying, and Arabella had no desire to enquire too closely into the reasons for the original apprehension. "You are here! My darling girl," he said, "I thought that you would never come." Almost before his servant had withdrawn, Lord Petre took Arabella's face in his hands and kissed her violently.

"How desperately I longed to spend inside you at the assembly tonight," he murmured. "With my arms around you in that dark gallery, I could barely contain my ardour. The sight of you in all those feathers—"

She drew back and held her hands against his face, pushing the curls away from his eyes. "Had I let you have your way with me a moment longer," she said with a smile, "Sir Anthony Vandyke would have crashed down on top of us both. The frame of the picture was directly against my back when you pushed me on to the wall. One should not stumble about in the dark in other people's houses."

"One should not, but I am helpless when you are in sight."

"Not *quite* true, my lord—for you could not see me."

"But I can see you now, and so I shall take you by force or fraud, whichever is quickest." He pulled her to the bed, trying to remove her dress as they went. "If we are to accord with the characters in mythology, *I* should be the swan, and you a naked maiden. Zeus appeared to Leda thus disguised before he ravished her." He threw her down on the covers. "Let us get at least one part of the tableau right," he said, biting at her neck. "Off with the swan!"

Arabella laughed, protesting that Lord Petre was removing the clothes too forcefully.

"You are pulling at my feathers," she said, standing up to help him. "No; it is like this." She turned around. "Take care with the silk or you will tear it. Yes; very well." The dress came off, and she stood in her shift.

"Now you are in character," he said as he pulled that over her head as well. "Though you looked so enchanting in the costume that Zeus would have taken you feathers and all."

"Shall I put it back on?" she asked with a smile as he pushed himself down upon her.

"Certainly not," he mumbled, wrapping her legs around his waist.

Afterwards, when they were lying together in the darkness and Arabella was settled softly and quietly in his arms, he whispered gently that he would return in a moment, and Arabella murmured an incoherent reply.

He withdrew to his servant's closet, where he dressed by the light of a candle that had been left burning and joined Jenkins in the stable yard.

Jenkins was keeping a drowsy watch. He started as Lord Petre came in, and stumbled to his feet.

"Nothing yet, my lord."

"It is near three. I shall stay with you here." Lord Petre shuddered.

"Are you cold, my lord?" Jenkins asked.

"It is a little chilly, is it not?" Lord Petre gave a low laugh, though not a very hearty one. A few minutes later, a tremendous clatter was heard in the dark. Both of the men jumped. There was a distant laugh, and muffled tones of recrimination.

"The next yard," said the servant. "The drunken groom dropping a lantern."

Again there was silence.

At last they heard a scuffle of footsteps not used to the rough cobbles of the alley. Lord Petre stood, motioning to his servant to keep back, as a man came into the shadowy court.

"Who goes?" he asked sharply.

"Messenger for the baron," said the stranger.

Lord Petre took the man's arm and led him into the stables.

"Who are you, and whence are you come?" he demanded, shining his lantern up into the man's face, forcing him to shield his eyes as he winced at the light.

"Menzies, my lord," he said, struggling to stand further back from Lord Petre's lantern. "Just arrived from Scotland."

"I am the baron," said Lord Petre.

Menzies handed him a packet of papers.

"Within are named the other men, and details of the action. The King's troops are ready on the coast, and the northern bands will be in position. Is the Queen certain to be present on the occasion?"

"She is."

"Your role is described within."

Lord Petre nodded.

"You will hear of the arrest of other agents tonight, entering from the north. None of them carried papers of value. These are the proper directions. I came by water for safety's sake. Am I to remain in this house?"

"My servant will take you to a place," said Lord Petre. "You will receive two days' protection there."

"Very well. Good luck, my lord. In the name of the King."

"In the name of the King."

A moment later Menzies was gone with Jenkins. Lord Petre turned inside and crept back to his apartments, locking the package into his desk. It seemed incredible that the rebellion would take place at last. He was struck afresh with amazement that it should be happening to him; that he, of all people, should play so pivotal a role. He longed to know the details of the plan, but the papers would be in code, and he knew that he could not leave Arabella for as long as it would take to read them. He undressed to his shirt and slipped back into bed beside her, naked and relaxed in slumber. It was nearly four o'clock.

Just before five, unable to sleep, Lord Petre shook her awake and lit a candle.

"No—it cannot be time yet," she murmured. "It is still dark. My parents believe that I am at Henrietta's."

"I have a surprise for you," he said, unable to bear his pre-dawn solitude any longer, and wanting a distraction from his thoughts of the impending action.

One eye opened warily.

"Of what kind?"

"Of a kind that necessitates your rising from the present position," he said, pulling her to him.

"I cannot," she answered, pushing him away, though not very earnestly.

"It will soon be light," he insisted. "We shall go by boat on the Thames to watch the sun rising. It is among the finest sights in London. But we must be gone before the house is astir."

"But I have only my swan's costume," she said, sitting up and rubbing at her eyes.

"Put it on again," he said. "I will give you a cape to cover it when we are in the boat."

When Lord Petre returned to bed after the meeting in the stables, Jenkins delivered Menzies to his parents' cottage on the outskirts of town. By the time he got back to Petre's house it was time to begin the new day's work; he had not slept at all. Walking into Lord Petre's chamber to light the fires for morning, he saw that the pair had already gone out. But he noticed irritably that they had left the floor by the fireplace strewn with little white feathers. It would take him at least half an hour to pick them up, and he would be late to work downstairs. The butler, envying his position as the baron's footman, would surely use the chance to give him a sharp rebuke. Angrily, Jenkins walked over to the fire, and began tossing little piles of feathers on to the flames. But just as he gathered up the last handful, he changed his mind, and crammed it into his coat pocket. With the faint trace of a smile, he went downstairs.

When they arrived home from the party Alexander asked Jervas if he could borrow the carriage for the morning trip with Martha. His host protested that the expedition would prove disastrous for his health.

"You are determined to make me an invalid," Alexander argued, "but I will not submit to it before my time is come. You, who have nothing to fear on that score, might wish to play the valetudinarian as a novelty. I, for whom every ailment and discomfort is near to hand, need not pretend to be ill in those rare moments that I am well."

Jervas walked unsteadily to the sideboard and poured himself a drink. "Very well, then, my dear Pope," he said. "But you must get some rest immediately, though I think I shall stay and have another little glass of wine."

Alexander came down again before dawn to find Jervas snoring in the chair, the fire gone out, and the empty bottle on the rug beside him.

At a quarter to five, with less than four hours' sleep, Martha did not welcome the servant who told her that Mr. Alexander Pope was waiting outside. But she came down more quickly than Alexander had expected, and stepped into the coach with a sleepy, melancholy air. Alexander gave her a blanket to tuck about herself, for the morning was chilly, and they set off through the half-dark streets.

After a couple of yawns, Martha said, "I confess that I do not have the dew of youth resting lightly upon me this morning. I feel something closer to a fog."

Alexander concurred. "In the early morning one feels that being young is overrated by the poets," he said, passing a hand across his face. "Youth is but a betrayer of human life, too—only in a gentler manner than age."

As their carriage rounded a corner they were presented with an unobstructed view of the River Thames, and despite their tiredness neither party could help exclaiming, "Oh! How fine it is!"

And so it was. The sweep of the river curved down towards the city, its banks sleek and gleaming in the morning light. The first sun upon the water made little tucked shadows between the waves, giving them an appearance of constant and brilliant animation. Along the embankments the flanks of buildings shone like mirrors. Rows of summer trees, planted in twos and trimmed to salute the sun in one even line of green, softened the view, making the landscape into a pleasure garden that shimmered with fresh life. The sky was wide and clear, polished brightly by the sun's first warmth on its canopy. It seemed newly washed; refreshed with a delicious lucid vapour. The blue was uninterrupted, save for a few sweet, scattered clouds that drifted lightly and daintily across the canvas of the scene.

Coming out of the cool, shadowy streets to behold such a sight was exquisite. Their carriage soon jangled to a halt, and the pair jumped down, longing to be in one of the little craft drawn up on the shores to carry travellers, and upon the water. Alexander handed Martha in, and settled himself.

"Towards Greenwich!" he told the lighterman, and they pushed off into the sparkling current.

Around them the air moved so lightly, so gently, that it could scarcely be called a breeze. And yet it played upon their hands and faces as though it were the breath of Summer herself, warming and cooling together, whispering of pleasure and of passing time. Their boat skipped along on water that was neither rough nor smooth but ruffled into perfect liveliness.

And the river was so full! It was as though the Thames's green banks, now overflowing with the bounty of summer, had poured forth their profusion of growth into the very barges as they passed. Boxes of lettuces, leeks, cucumbers, and asparagus; onions and carrots and herbs and broad beans; cherries and strawberries and ripe melons, whose scent could almost be thought to infuse the balmy air like incense. There were flowers, too, nodding their bright erect heads to the sun: roses and sweet peas; nasturtiums, pinks, and larkspurs; peonies full blown and stained with crimson dye, or tightly curled in soft white-petalled globes.

The gardeners called out to one other as they passed, greeting their friends and cheerfully abusing other purveyors of the same wares, but there was no real resentment in their tones. The morning was affecting all alike with the sense that they had entered a Paradise, and that the day and its delights was a second Eden.

Alexander and Martha were dazzled, and they sat for a time in happy silence.

They passed by a barge filled with roses, alongside which a lighter craft had drawn up. A gentleman was buying a posy for his lady, and as the gardener lifted the blooms into the air, a shower of dew drops flew up and turned to vapour in the sun.

"Oh, Alexander! Thank you for showing this to me," Martha exclaimed.

"I had not imagined that such a place could be," Alexander answered her in a rapture, "least of all in the city. The air shimmers as though a million invisible spirits were about us, flicking their wings in the light."

"It sounds as though you are thinking up verses, Alexander."

"My imagination is greedily hoarding every picture that the morning presents, nearly surfeited, and yet I long to take in more. I compose quick lines at every discovery, as an artist struggles to sketch a fleeting impression even as a new one rushes upon him. Every sight is gone in an instant, and I have only my mind's eye in which to keep a mean copy of the glorious original."

They were quiet again, then Alexander burst out, "I have long wanted to write a poem about an earthly Paradise, and the present scene is one that even Milton's matchless imagination could not conjure. And now suddenly I have an idea for who can inhabit the place. As in Milton's poem, there will be mortal creatures, but divine beings too. Angels are too grand for my verses—I shall have lesser spirits; nymphs that live upon air. Delicate and magical, like this morning itself. You'll see," he said grandly, "Milton will not outdo me."

Martha watched him silently. Had Teresa been there, Martha knew that she would have laughed at him for being so earnest—and there was indeed something laughable about Alexander with his bright, darting eyes and eager movements. But when he boasted that he would not be outdone by Milton, she saw that he was entirely serious. The world was full of men whose ambition was to write a poem as great as *Paradise Lost*, but perhaps, just perhaps, Alexander would actually do it. It was an extraordinary thought, and she shivered, as though she had caught a glimpse of something uncanny.

Alexander broke into her thoughts, leaning forward and speaking in a rush: "What do you think of this, Patty? It is a description of the invisible spirits on the Thames: Some to the sun their insect-wings unfold; waft on the breeze, or sink in clouds of gold. Transparent forms, too fine for mortal sight—their fluid bodies half dissolved in light. Loose to the wind their airy garments flew; thin glittering textures of the filmy dew, dipped in the richest tincture of the skies, where light disports in ever-mingling dyes. While every beam new transient colours flings; colours that change whene'er they wave their wings."

As he spoke, it seemed to Martha that the air was filled with magical sounds, the ethereal music of poetry that is not quite of this world. She looked at Alexander with a kind of awe. She knew, with a calm detachment that had nothing to do with knowing him personally, that the young man sitting opposite her was destined to be a very great poet indeed. He was more than merely talented; he was—and even as she thought it she felt a thrill—he was a genius. She looked into his shining, faraway eyes, and saw that he knew it too, and that this was what gave him the unearthly quality she now sensed.

She struggled to put her thoughts into words. "Alexander, I feel . . . I don't know what to say," she said helplessly. "I feel as if you've given me a present that I long to show to others, and yet which is a precious jewel that only I will ever see. Your genius will make you famous; nothing can stop you now." Something made her go on. "But I know that we shall always be dear to each other."

Alexander's description of the fairies had loosened her tongue, and she spoke more freely than she had believed herself capable. Her heart overflowed, and she had admitted her most secret thoughts. But she feared that this enchantment would be of short duration.

"Dear to each other!" exclaimed Alexander. "Patty, I have realized that yours is the dearest friendship of my life. I could not live without it. Surely that is clear to you; you, with such remarkable understanding."

Martha looked down; she could not meet his eye. She had imagined this conversation, or a version of this conversation, a thousand times, and now it was actually unfolding. She was overcome with embarrassment.

"I fear that I cannot be very clear when it comes to understanding you, Alexander," she said quietly.

Alexander studied her face intently, and was surprised by what he saw. For the first time, he realized fully what it was that Martha felt for him. She saw him opening his mouth to speak; her heart beat wildly. But then he stopped abruptly. She knew that he was struggling to frame the right words in reply. The silence was unrelenting.

At last he spoke. "You know that I keep a portrait of Milton beside me when I write," he said, "hoping that it will keep me humble, for I am otherwise liable to become puffed up with pleasure in my own cleverness."

Her heart sank; he would not answer her plainly. Why was he talking of poetry—of *Milton*—again, at this most heart-wrenching of moments? Did he mean to be cruel? She could not believe such a thing. "I know it, Alexander," she answered slowly, "but what has it to do with this?"

"Because a passage from *Paradise Lost* came suddenly to my mind," he replied. "When Eve learns that she must leave the Garden. The fault is her own, but her lament is bitter."

"I do not recall it."

Alexander quoted the lines.

"'How shall I part, and whither wander down into a lower world? / How shall we breathe in other air Less Pure, accustomed to immortal fruits?'"

Martha held her breath as Alexander finished Eve's sorrowful cry. For a minute she made no reply; she felt unspeakably sad. She had always believed that if he never loved her it would be because of Teresa, and she knew that she had come to take consolation, even pleasure, from gathering up the light, discarded threads of his affection for her sister. But in the end it would not be Teresa who kept him from her. It would be his writing.

The discovery was more bitter than she could have imagined; she felt utterly alone. She thought back over their morning together and wanted to cry. The glorious enchantment; her realization that his genius could transform the ordinary world; the breathless exhilaration of hearing his verses as he composed them—would they serve only to leave her abandoned, forlorn, and alone, while Alexander found fresh woods and new pastures?

"Are you saying that you have grown accustomed to immortal

fruits, Alexander?" she asked as lightly as she could, aware of the strain that was audible in her voice.

Alexander looked at her steadily; she saw that he wanted to speak truthfully, and she met his gaze, though it hurt her to do so.

"I begin to see that to follow poetry as one ought, one must forget father and mother, and all other mortal loves, and cleave to it alone," he said. "If I am to succeed as a poet I cannot wander freely in this world, though I know it to be filled with earthly delights, and able to bring great happiness. Will you believe me when I tell you that it makes me desolate to tell you so?"

"I do believe you, Alexander," she said, choking back tears. "But you must pay frequent visits, for I cannot do without your friendship."

He took her hand. "You will never need to," he said gently.

He went on in a stronger voice, "In any case, Patty, my recent experience of the world has made me sceptical of passionate attachments. Real affection holds fast to the very end, for it does not expect too much from human nature. But romantic friendships, like violent loves, begin with disputes, proceed to jealousies, and conclude in animosity."

She laughed bravely, blinking back a last stray tear. They had come to a landing stage just beyond the stopping point for the markets at Covent Garden. It was half-past eight.

Alexander let go of her hand, and looked around at the wharf. "Shall we alight, and walk to the market for breakfast?" he asked. He smiled at her, warily, and then added in his usual teasing tones, "I should like to be thinking high thoughts of Virgilian hexameters and Homeric similes, but I dwell instead on low thoughts of chocolate and hot rolls, and coffee with egg and bacon."

Martha assented, presenting as bright a face as she could manage. They were almost at the landing when she exclaimed in surprise, "Look, Alexander. We are not the only parties to have hatched this plan! It is my cousin Bell—and with *Lord Petre*!"

Alexander turned to look. Sure enough, the other couple was coming in to land at that very moment, Arabella holding a bunch of roses in her lap and smiling jauntily at her companion. She was quite unaware of their presence, but it looked as though Lord Petre had seen them. Martha looked down, horrified to catch Bell out in an expedition so obviously unsanctioned. Perhaps she is engaged to him, she thought with wonder, but neither the Fermors nor the Petres would be disposed to keep secrets of the nuptial variety. She looked apprehensively across to Alexander, who was surveying the pair with a cool, ironic smile.

Chance dictated that the two boats reached the landing platform almost together. To Martha's astonishment, though rather less to Alexander's, Lord Petre saluted them before they were even docked.

"Miss Martha Blount—Mr. Alexander Pope! Is not this a magnificent morning? Miss Fermor and I were on the river before sunrise, so we have seen the glorious pageant unfold from the start. We came directly from Miss Oldmixon's party. I insisted upon it—Miss Fermor had never seen the Lambeth Gardeners from the water."

Alexander looked back at him, and said, "We have not the energies of you and Miss Fermor, my lord. A short sleep was required to fortify us for the spectacle. I called for Miss Blount at five."

"Then I fear you missed the finest part of the morning! That interval between darkness and dawn, when the sun first appears upon the river."

"Was not Miss Fermor rather cool in her plumage?" Alexander asked. "Even the swan, well adapted to the aquatic climes, is known to huddle closely to its fellows during the early hours before dawn."

"She felt nothing," Lord Petre replied. "Miss Fermor is of a robust constitution, and happily I had taken the precaution of bringing an extra cape—a provision that few swans are able to call upon."

Arabella listened to Lord Petre's flippant speech with annoyance. He seemed determined to call further attention to the ludicrousness of her outfit—which that awful little Pope had so impertinently noted—and to the improbability of their having come straight from the party. What had Lord Petre been thinking of, bringing up the cape? Of course they would not have been on the water before dawn! She disliked the way that Pope looked at her so knowingly, as though he understood her situation more completely than she understood it herself. But was not he himself out with another woman—and Teresa's sister, of all people! If Martha Blount were out alone with a man, it could not be so very wrong, she reasoned.

This unwelcome meeting made her feel naked and exposed. What if Martha guessed that she and Lord Petre were bedfellows? Not that she should mind, of course; she knew that he meant to marry her. But Martha's shocked face, all white and withdrawn under the hood of her cape, made Arabella feel suddenly self-conscious. No, it was more than that, she admitted to herself. It had made her feel humiliated.

When Lord Petre spoke, Alexander and Martha looked at Arabella. But she would not meet either party's eye, and seemed in a great hurry to be gone, though she had been laughing very pleasantly only a short time before.

"I am rather cold now, as a matter of fact, my lord," Arabella said stiffly. "I should like to be taken home immediately. The sun will shortly be high in the sky; my parents will be anxious for my safety. I had not imagined that our trip would take so long."

She nodded quickly to Martha, ignored Alexander altogether, and rushed into the carriage that was waiting by the landing. Lord Petre bowed a good deal more ceremoniously to both parties, and followed.

Lord Petre left a silent and morose Arabella at her parents' house. He regretted the way their encounter had ended, particularly after such a splendid trip on the river, but he knew that this was not the moment to worry about a trifling misunderstanding. There would be plenty of time for apologies later. He went directly to bed when he got home, and slept until evening. He got up, took a late dinner of pie and asparagus in his rooms, and prepared to read Menzies's papers. It was time now for serious matters. He had just embarked upon the task when Jenkins came into the room. He walked quietly about, lighting the candles and drawing the curtains, but when he was finished he did not leave. He stood, instead, beside Lord Petre's desk. "May I speak, my lord?" he asked.

"By all means, Jenkins," said Lord Petre, not looking up. "What is it?"

The footman said nothing.

Lord Petre glanced at his servant quickly and saw that Jenkins was grave, plucking nervously at the lace trim on the pockets of his livery.

"Is something the matter, Jenkins?" Lord Petre asked, putting down his pen and pushing his chair back slightly from the desk. It occurred to him that something had gone awry with Menzies, and he felt a leap of fear.

Jenkins cleared his throat. "I would like to speak about my sister, my lord."

"Your sister!" Lord Petre replied, almost with a laugh. Thank God, he thought. "Is she in want of a place, Jenkins?" he asked pleasantly. "I am sorry to say that we have no needs at present."

"No, sir," Jenkins answered quickly. "She is not looking for work." He hesitated, clasping his hands first behind his back and then in front of him. "She is—you see—" he broke off again, blushing deeply.

"Quickly, Jenkins, what is it?" Lord Petre asked, growing impatient.

"My sister is with child, my lord," he said finally. "She is soon to be confined."

Lord Petre leaned back in his seat, looking at Jenkins with what he hoped was avuncular concern. "Is your sister a married woman?" he asked. He felt like a country alderman, caring for his wayward parishioners.

"She is not married, my lord," Jenkins replied. Of course she is not, Lord Petre thought, repressing a smile.

"I believe, indeed, that my sister is known here, my lord," Jenkins added angrily.

Lord Petre groaned inwardly. This was really becoming too much. Was he to become the Jenkins family's patron? "Known?" he repeated listlessly. "Who is your sister, Jenkins?"

"Her name is Molly Walker, sir," he said.

Molly Walker! Good God. Confused thoughts assailed him. Had Jenkins not known of their affair? But of course he had—he had seen Lord Petre with Molly many times. He had even helped to arrange their meetings. Why had neither he nor Molly said something when it was going on? Perhaps Jenkins was ashamed of what his sister had become. Lord Petre was horrified by the revelation.

His mind racing, he asked, "Why is Molly's name not Jenkins?"

"My mother's first husband was called Walker," came the explanation.

But Lord Petre hardly heard him. He remembered that Molly had been visibly pregnant that day at the cookshop. Could Jenkins be about to beg him to duel with Molly's seducer? A preposterous idea. Then a dreadful thought struck him. Might the child be his? But no, it was impossible. It was now late June, and his affair with Molly had ended last August.

But as though he had read Lord Petre's mind, Jenkins said, "My sister says that you are the father of her child, my lord."

Petre leapt to his feet. "But you know that is not so, Jenkins! Our intimacy ended too long ago. Why did you say nothing before? You of all people know it—you must defend me."

"I am here to defend my sister, my lord," Jenkins answered.

"But your sister is lying," Lord Petre exclaimed, and he saw a look of possessive anger in his footman's eye. In a more careful voice, he said, "I have not seen Miss Walker since August," and he sat down again.

"Molly says that the child is yours, my lord," Jenkins repeated coldly. "She asks that you support it." As Lord Petre watched Jenkins, a suspicion dawned on him. Had Molly and her brother been planning all along to trap him?

But he was determined to remain in control of the interview. "I cannot do that, Jenkins," he said firmly. "I am sorry for your sister's condition, but the child is not mine." He had heard of situations such as this—wenches claiming noble fathers for their children—but he had never imagined it happening to himself.

"I am sorry to say that you and your sister are taking advantage of your position in my house." It was too bad that Jenkins should charge him with the offence at a moment when he knew so much that might damage him.

"My sister is not a liar, my lord," said Jenkins, unrelenting.

Lord Petre looked up at him coldly. "And I am not a fool."

But as he observed Jenkins's face, he realized that this would not do. Molly had put him up to it, he guessed. Jenkins was a decent fellow, the sort of man who would always look after his family. Suddenly an image of Molly came into his mind: that proud, defiant bearing. She must be desperate to go to such lengths as this.

He began to regret what he had said.

"Wait a moment, Jenkins," he said as the footman began to leave the room. "I shall give you a hundred pounds for your sister," Lord Petre continued. "But I cannot assume responsibility for a child that is not my own." He hesitated, and then said, "In all likelihood I am shortly to marry."

Jenkins's face was flushed as he walked back to Lord Petre's desk to take the money. "I thank you, my lord," he said.

"You need not fear for your own position, Jenkins," Lord Petre added. "I will not mention this matter again."

Jenkins bowed, but his face was still hardened with anger. After he left the room Lord Petre sat for a few minutes, thinking of what had passed. The matter was an annoyance, but at least it had made him articulate his desire to marry Arabella. The thought exhilarated him, but reluctantly he pushed her from his mind, and returned to the papers on his desk.

Chapter Sixteen

"Oh thoughtless mortals! ever blind to fate"

The following day Alexander and Jervas sat at the breakfast table. Their conversation was desultory; Jervas tucked into his meal, and Alexander read his letters.

"Thank heavens I have an appetite again," Jervas said, biting into a slice of thickly buttered toast. "I was as sick as a dog after the Oldmixons' party—the punch must have been stronger than I thought."

"I'm sorry I was not aware of it, Jervas," Alexander replied, cracking the top of a boiled egg that had been sitting with a little cover on the eggcup to keep it warm. "I spent the day in bed myself."

"I told you that you had no business to be venturing out on the water, Pope," Jervas said. "That sort of vigorous early-morning exercise is only for men of strong constitution."

Alexander dipped a piece of toast into his egg and changed the subject. "I am reading a letter from John Caryll," he said. "His eldest son is to be married at last to a lady by the name of Mary Mackenzie—daughter of Kenneth Mackenzie, first Marquis of Seaforth."

Jervas swallowed with much nodding of his head, and then said, "Caryll must be relieved to be rid of one of his brood." He took a drink of his coffee. "There is such a prodigious number of them—neither the daughters pretty nor the sons rich. Awkward. But I thought young Caryll was to marry one of the Throgmorton daughters."

"They were too much inclined to enter into nunneries," Alexander answered. "Caryll could not be sure that the lady would share his son's bed, and feared that she might wish to live in France."

Jervas laughed. "Not ideal in a wife," he replied. "But awful as married life must be, it must surely be preferable to a French convent." He ate a slice of bacon.

"Well, a match has been achieved," Alexander said, "and Caryll comes to London soon to make the arrangements. Indeed, I see that this letter was wrongly directed, so he may be here already."

"Kenneth Mackenzie, Marquis of Seaforth," said Jervas. "He sounds rather grand. Will the happy couple require an artist to paint their picture, I wonder?"

Alexander smiled. "I should not be looking to Mackenzie for a commission," he replied. "They are a noble family, but impoverished. The marquis is a Jacobite."

"A Jacobite! Good God—what is Caryll thinking of? I thought he had just managed to struggle out from under the traitors' yoke with his uncle."

"Caryll says that the Mackenzies are not spies or conspirators, Jervas. Merely supporters of the Jacobite cause. To tell the truth, though, I do not understand it myself. I suppose he did not think a better match could be achieved." Alexander finished his egg, looking thoughtfully into the depths of the cup. "At least, I hope that they are not spies and conspirators, because Caryll has asked me to accompany the young couple from London to Ladyholt at the end of July. I should not like to be arrested on the road home." He laughed. "My father would be far too pleased."

Jervas laughed too. "Yes, his worst fears would be answered, and he would have nothing left to wish for."

Alexander thought about the journey. It might be a good idea, after all, to return to Binfield for a time. He had done almost no work since being in London, and the poem he had begun to compose on the water begged to be written. He wondered whether he should surprise his father and mother by arriving unannounced.

His attention was reclaimed by Jervas, who had started to pace about the breakfast room.

"If you insist on travelling about the country with young John Caryll and his Jacobite bride, you are doing yourself no favours."

"The Caryll family are old friends of my childhood. I cannot abandon them merely upon political grounds," Alexander replied, though he wondered whether Jervas might not be right.

"'Tis as good a reason as any to abandon one's friends," Jervas replied, walking back to the table. "But you see that I grow restless, Pope, and begin to tease you. Let us go out to Will's and hear the news of the town."

They were not the first to arrive at the coffee-house that day. As they walked in the door, Alexander was saluted by his publisher Tonson, who was drinking coffee with Jonathan Swift and John Gay. On the other side of the room Jervas's friends Tom Breach and Harry Chambers leapt to their feet and called him over. The murmur of talk was louder than usual—there was a palpable air of excitement in the room—and Alexander felt certain that something important had happened. As he watched Jervas walk over to Tom and Harry he saw that James Douglass was there, too. Their eyes met, and Douglass raised a brow, but Alexander looked away.

But his attention was claimed by Tonson, who had jumped to his feet. "Have you heard the news, Pope?" he cried, thrusting a copy of the *Daily Courant* into his hands. "A party of Jacobites was arrested. They were trying to enter the city last night."

Involuntarily, Alexander glanced back at Douglass, who was still staring at him. Could Douglass know his suspicions? Perhaps Douglass and Petre *had* seen him the night of the masquerade. Caryll had told Lord Petre the truth about Francis Gerrard. He must have repeated it to Douglass. What if Petre had mentioned that Alexander had been at the coffee-house that morning, too? But he set aside his speculations and replied to Tonson lightly, hoping to change the subject.

"What a curious enterprise to be involved in," he said, glancing at the paper. "If a person wants to be hanged, there are easier ways of achieving it than by treason. A trifling theft, for example, will have one upon the gallows in no time, with much less trouble to the criminal."

"Ah," said John Gay, "these days every nobleman and politician in England makes his living by stealing. It is called 'going into debt', and is held to be a mark of good breeding. No: for a man of good birth and character, treason is the only remaining path to a hanging."

But Tonson was not to be deflected. "The Jacobites are on the march again," he said. "It will be a blow to their forces to lose these men to a single night's operation."

Alexander wondered what Tonson's view of a rebellion would be. The old publisher was adept at keeping his political opinions to himself.

Tonson interrupted his reflections. "Why do not you write a satire upon the scandal, Pope?" he asked.

Alexander saw that Tonson's expression was serious. But he knew that Alexander did not write political poetry. Perhaps he was trying to tell him, once again, that he did not think *Windsor Forest* worth printing. Or was he still resentful that Alexander had taken his *Essay* to another publisher?

"Satire relies upon the making of witty comparisons," Alexander replied abruptly. "It has been discovered that a band of desperate traitors was plotting to bring James Stuart back from France. They have been stopped, but everybody wonders whether others may still be at large. This is the stuff of tragedy, not of satire."

"It is the stuff of great public interest—which is why you would do well to compose a poem about it," Tonson said curtly.

"Scandals concerning the court and the fashionable world are where readers are to be found," Alexander said. "Nobody cares for the escapades of a few obscure Scotsmen who will soon lose their heads."

"Mark my words, Pope," Tonson declared. "It is the way to fame and fortune."

"What do you think of all this talk of plots and counter-plots, Dr. Swift?" Alexander asked.

"I think it becomes the patrons of Will's better than their usual subjects," Swift replied. "They generally converse upon literature, a subject ill suited to men of no information. But nobody has the least idea as to the facts when the talk is of spies and traitors. What could be better?"

Alexander smiled. "But the denizens of Will's coffee-house enjoy a reputation for being the most learned and the most literary men in town."

Swift replied with a twinkle in his eye. "That, sir, is merely another way of expressing my own view, that Will's is the place in which I have endured the worst conversations of my life."

On the other side of the room, Jervas was still sitting with Douglass, Tom, and Harry. Alexander wondered whether they were speaking about the arrests. Jervas could not be relied on to remember the conversation, and he realized he was curious to know what Douglass would say. Impulsively, Alexander left the conversation with Tonson and the others to join Jervas's group.

"They were arrested last night, Charles," Harry was saying, seemingly less concerned by this than he had been by Lady Purchase's refusal to receive him some weeks before. He took a lazy sip of coffee. "The fatal tree will be pressed into service again, for there is no doubt that they will hang."

Douglass looked sharply at Alexander as he sat down. "What a credulous fool you are, Harry," Douglass cut in. "I'll wager a hundred pounds that these three men have been arrested for outward show. The government is trying to make people think that it is in control of the Jacobites, but it is not. A rebellion is coming."

"Oh, the Jacobites cannot last long," Tom replied laconically. "They do not have enough money or men."

"Their *eventual* failure is certain, of course," Douglass said. "When people are prepared to give anything for the sake of their beliefs, they are sure to be taken advantage of."

Tom gave a guffaw. "If you had the nerve to be as unscrupulous in action as you are in conversation, Douglass, you would have become rich long ago," he said. "I know your type! Principle always gets the better of you in the end."

Douglass scoffed at this. "If being unscrupulous was all that was required to become rich," he answered, "Will's coffee-house would be filled with the greatest lords in England. But success in financial enterprise needs something more. Let us call it good luck."

Alexander came away from the conversation more confused than before. Douglass had cheerfully prophesied rebellion! The man became more opaque each time he appeared. He was Jervas's schoolfriend, a person of respectable family, seemingly of good fortune. And yet there was still nothing familiar about him, nothing certain. How could it be that a man with so powerful a presence left no lasting mark of his character behind?

Lord Petre, too, paid close attention to the news of the arrests. He knew that they had been arranged in order to conceal the action. He had finished reading the papers Menzies had given him, knew that Jacobite troops were beginning to gather north and south of London, and that he was to give Douglass another five hundred pounds at the end of the week—money to raise a guard to bring the King from the coast to London. The moment was approaching. The directions were clear. He was to meet the other agents in Greenwich in a week's time, when the command would be given to mobilize the armies. He had been told to make sure of the Queen's whereabouts for the remainder of the season. But he was as yet unsure what role he would play in the actual assassination. This part of the plan continued to unnerve him. Even now it was vague, and Douglass had been no more specific than at the first discussion, long ago. Every time Lord Petre pressed him for information he was evasive, claiming to be no more than a conduit for directions from the leaders. But Petre was tired of being always in the dark. He decided to press Douglass for details when he saw him.

The night before Lord Petre was to give Douglass the money, he returned home early from an evening of cards at his club. He was tired, and had taken too much to drink, and he ran quickly up to his chamber, hoping that none of his family would be disposed for conversation.

But when he entered his apartments Lord Petre discovered that a man was seated in a chair next to the fire. He stopped short.

"Who are you?" he called out from the door.

The man turned to face him. To Petre's astonishment, it was John Caryll.

"Caryll!" he exclaimed. His old guardian had not stood up to greet him, and sat staring at him silently from his chair. The casual air he had adopted at their last meeting was gone. "How did you get here?" Lord Petre asked, suddenly uneasy.

"I arrived this evening from the country," Caryll replied in too calm a voice. "I have spent the evening with your mother."

"I am surprised to see you," said Lord Petre, superfluously.

"I am here to speak upon a matter of business," Caryll said. He looked sinister in the half-light of the room, sitting in the chair as watchful as a cat. Nervous, Lord Petre began to walk towards the fire.

"Pray close the door," Caryll said.

He did so, then moved to sit down. But before he could, Caryll began.

"Five hundred pounds in bank bills are in your desk," he said. His voice was clear and deliberate.

Lord Petre froze. But he was determined to give nothing away. "May I ask why you were looking in my desk, sir?" he asked. "I keep that article locked."

"I was with your mother," Caryll replied. "She asked that I look. Your man Jenkins opened the desk for us—he appeared to know that you kept the money there."

Lord Petre struggled to comprehend what was happening. Could John Caryll be one of the agents involved in the plan? But if he was here to reveal that fact, why did he speak so coldly—and why had he said nothing before? And what of his mother? It was inconceivable that she could be complicit. She had a horror of the Jacobites. Lord Petre shuddered. What was going on?

"It is not customary to have such a large sum upon one's person, my lord," Caryll said. His calm was menacing.

"I was not aware that my private affairs were subject to scrutiny," Petre answered. "The money is to pay a gambling debt."

"To whom do you owe this sum?" Caryll asked with a cold smile. "Perhaps I can assist in delivering it more promptly."

"I pay my debts myself," Lord Petre replied. He paused, uncertain, wondering how he might force Caryll to show his hand. "I owe the money to James Douglass, a gentleman with whom you are not acquainted."

"Douglass!" John Caryll exclaimed in a mocking voice. "Your taste is not so nice in point of friendships as in other matters, I perceive. Why do you owe James Douglass five hundred pounds?"

So Caryll knew of Douglass.

"As I have said, it is a gaming debt," he said, playing for time. Caryll still stared at him. He even seemed to be enjoying the exchange, smiling as he drew taut the line of Lord Petre's nerve.

"I must ask you not to lie to me, my lord," Caryll said. "Let me speak more frankly. We know that you are involved with the Jacobites."

Lord Petre felt his heart drop into his boots. His mother knew. How had they found him out?

"You start at the news, as well you might," said Caryll. "Indeed it is a foolhardy plan. But there is worse to come. We have learned that you are in a plot to kill the Queen. I can hardly believe it possible."

"May I ask how you acquired this information, sir?" Lord Petre said, doing his best to remain calm. "Are you still with the Jacobites?"

"Certainly not," Caryll answered. "Your footman told me."

Jenkins! He had betrayed him. But Jenkins was a Jacobite too—he would not abandon the cause, least of all at such a moment. Lord Petre began to stammer. "My footman! He is a Loyalist. I cannot believe it! And the day at White's coffee-house . . ." Lord Petre continued to murmur. It must be connected to the business with Molly. But he had already given Jenkins money. "You knew about Francis Gerrard. I took it for a warning to our men. Are you not an agent, sir?"

At this, Caryll's eyes lit up with anger. "*I* an agent?" he spat out. "You have witnessed the misfortunes that fell upon my family because my uncle was suspected—merely suspected—of treason," he said. "The circumstance has blighted my children's whole lives, not to mention my own. I would be a madman to associate with them. And yet you have done this to your own family. You have subjected your mother and sister to the worst of dangers."

"Then how did you know about Gerrard?"

"You were always naive, Robert. My connections with the Jacobites are historical. They are men of my uncle's generation. My oldest acquaintance—my friends. I am no traitor, sir."

Lord Petre said nothing.

"You have imperilled every possession in the Petre family's name," Caryll went on. "And you were a fool to trust your man Jenkins."

Lord Petre was still reeling from this discovery. "I cannot understand why my servant deserted me," he said.

"Jenkins is considerably more astute than you have been," Caryll answered. "Had he blackmailed you alone, he was afraid of what you might do to silence him. By coming to me, he has assured his own safety, as much as his sister's protection."

"But he will destroy our hopes for rebellion."

"Jenkins put the interests of family ahead of political ambition," Caryll answered. "You can be in no doubt as to what he told us regarding his sister."

"The child is not mine!" Lord Petre exploded. "It is an unscrupulous falsehood!"

"That is the one aspect of this affair in which I take your part," Caryll said. "But as Molly Walker has rightly perceived, the child's real paternity is neither here nor there. Jenkins will expose the plot, and your part in it, if you fail to assume financial responsibility for Molly's child."

"The action is embarked upon, sir," said Lord Petre. "I will not betray my men." His voice was hoarse with emotion.

Caryll was unmoved. "I am sorry to say that you will have to," he replied drily. "To save your family, I will not hesitate to expose you."

Lord Petre was silent. He began to see that Caryll had outmanoeuvred him.

There was a pause, and Caryll said as though it were an afterthought, "Your mother has one demand to make of you."

Lord Petre looked at him, dread in his heart.

"She has chosen you a bride," Caryll said.

Lord Petre was incredulous. "A bride?"

His mother entered the room. She had been a beautiful woman in her youth, and she now carried herself with the distinguished, imposing manner of a person accustomed to wielding power. With her son she had always been distant. But she was attached to her daughter, Mary, and Lord Petre knew that the risk to his sister's reputation and marriage portion would be uppermost in Lady Petre's thoughts.

Both men had risen when Lady Petre entered, but now they were seated again, and Caryll continued.

"The marriage is to be with a person whose family connections will withstand the most scrupulous examination," he said.

"How do you imagine that you will bring such a match about?" Lord Petre asked.

"We have already done so, Robert," his mother replied. "It has been arranged."

He blanched. "May I enquire as to the lady in question?"

"Her name is Miss Catherine Walmesley," she said. "She is fifteen years old, and very devout. She also has a fortune of fifty thousand pounds."

"Catherine Walmesley! You cannot be serious," he cried, real despair in his voice.

"I was never more so in my life," his mother replied.

Until he heard his intended named, it had not occurred to Lord Petre that his relationship with Arabella might be affected by all of this. Caryll and his mother meant to strip everything from him. The discovery made him recoil.

"The match is objectionable in every particular!" he appealed. "Her family is barbaric. Miss Walmesley herself—hardly more than a child—a girl of no education, no cultivation, no personal charm."

"She is somewhat unfortunate in her appearance," said his mother. "But that merely worked to our advantage in securing the arrangement with her guardian."

"William Dicconson!" Lord Petre snarled. "Everybody knows what sort of a man he is. Madam, you and Mr. Caryll have played a low trick upon me tonight. You have engineered this match for Catherine Walmesley's fortune, and you are using my helpless position to force me into a marriage to which I would not otherwise submit."

His mother looked at him in silence. It was not necessary to affirm this description of their actions.

"This is intolerable," Lord Petre moaned.

Neither party replied. "There is a rumour," Caryll began instead, "though not one that I have heard, I hasten to add, that there has lately been an involvement between you and Miss Arabella Fermor."

Lord Petre flushed. "There has been nothing improper in Miss Fermor's relation with me," he said. "It is a malicious slander, put about by those who envy her."

"That was naturally our assumption," said Lady Petre. "But Mr. Dicconson has asked that some public measure be taken to make clear that the relationship will not continue after your marriage."

"Public measure!" Lord Petre exclaimed. "What do you mean? Does he intend that I should embarrass Miss Fermor?" He remembered Dicconson's loud, leering voice at the masquerade ball. *Your daughter whores too much, I said.* He had been describing his own wife. Pure malice was pushing him to this, Lord Petre was sure of it—he was jealous of Lord Petre's own successes.

But he was deeply shaken nonetheless. "What does he propose that I should do?" he asked.

"A trifle!" his mother said with a laugh that grated on Lord Petre's ear like steel. "A mere gesture to show that you are not intimate, nor ever likely to be. Something playful. Miss Fermor will think nothing of it, if you are not in fact lovers." She smiled at her son.

"I refuse to compromise Miss Fermor," he said.

"But I fear that you have already done so," Caryll said. "There is a circumstance . . . an unfortunate circumstance. Your servant has admitted that he is in possession of certain items that would place you in a most difficult position were he to show them to Dicconson."

"What the devil are you talking about?" Lord Petre returned.

"I have not the faintest idea as to its significance," Caryll answered smoothly, "but your man has shown me a parcel of feathers, which he claims to have found in your bed and on the floor around it. I know not what to make of them. They have the appearance of swansdown."

Lord Petre dropped his head into his hands. It had been promise of gain that made Jenkins abandon the Jacobites and turn to Caryll. He thought of the hundred pounds, of his footman's anger as he took it. Who knew how long Jenkins had planned this?

"God damn him," Lord Petre hissed. "God damn you all." He got to his feet. "I will do nothing to harm Miss Fermor," he declared.

"You are not being asked to harm her," his mother said. "A public act cannot tarnish her reputation if there is no arrangement existing between you."

He banged his hand down on the mantel, and cried, "I will forsake my commitments to the Jacobites in an instant! But I cannot marry Miss Walmesley. I am bound in honour to Arabella. We are all but engaged; if I fail her she will be ruined."

His mother was manifestly unmoved. "It is rather too late in the day for such sentimental considerations." she observed.

"But I am devoted to Arabella, madam. I love her!" he wailed.

"What do you mean, you love her?" his mother replied, real surprise in her voice. "That has nothing to do with the matter. A baron does not marry for reasons of affection, as you perfectly well know. Your father and I could not abide the sight of each other, but we married nonetheless." With this remark she brought the exchange to a close, and Lord Petre was left alone with his thoughts.

Towards ten o'clock the next morning, he asked his mother and John Caryll if he might speak to them.

"I have considered my situation," he began, with an attempt at hauteur, "and I see that there is no choice but to submit to your demands. I will sever relations with the Jacobites and marry Catherine Walmesley. In return for this, will you allow me to manage matters with Miss Fermor in my own way?"

"That was not our design, Robert," his mother replied. "Your own way has not been particularly effective thus far."

John Caryll spoke. "There is one other matter on which I should like to offer a word of advice," he said, "and then my offices as your guardian will be over. How much money have you given to Mr. Douglass?"

Lord Petre went white, but said quietly, "About—I have given him seven hundred pounds."

"I hint to you that it would not be wise to give him any more," said Caryll. "You are unlikely to see a return."

Lord Petre laughed scornfully. "I hardly imagined that I would," he said. "The money is to pay a standing army in support of the King."

Caryll appeared not to have heard him. "I told you that Francis Gerrard knew of traitors among the Jacobites. He had heard that they were losing money to a group of their own, men posing as Loyalists. Such thefts cannot be prosecuted, of course, because

Jacobite operations are clandestine. It is a cunning arrangement. I would guess James Douglass to be involved in something of the kind."

Lord Petre denied it. "James Douglass is not a thief, sir! He was as shocked to hear about Gerrard as I was." But Caryll gave him a brief paternal squeeze around the shoulders, and departed in company with Lady Petre.

When they were gone, Lord Petre paced around the room for several minutes, righteous indignation boiling in his breast. His dreams of heroic distinction were dashed. Terrible enough, but when he thought of losing Arabella, tears came to his eyes. Why must he be doomed to forsake the lady he loved, compounding all his other woes? He remembered the happy picture that had sustained him as he had thought of the battles that lay ahead: the vision of Arabella by his fireside, looking up from her needlework to welcome him home. He had lost everything, but he knew that he was right to defend Douglass against Caryll's charge.

He took the bank bills in his desk and turned them over in his hands. He was determined to discharge this one action left to him. This much, at least, he could do. As he looked at them, he thought back to the night of the masquerade, when he had met Douglass and given him the first five hundred pounds. He had told Douglass to put out the lantern, but he had not finished counting the money. Lord Petre had always kicked himself for opening the carriage door a moment too soon; their light might have been seen.

He hesitated. He thought again of that night, of Douglass's face as he fingered the money, and he felt a gleam of doubt. Why *had* Douglass counted the bills in the carriage? Why had he not trusted Lord Petre? They were working together to save the man they believed should be king. At the time he had been so concerned about hiding the light that he had not thought about it. What if Caryll were right? *Losing money to a group of their own men.* He realized how little he know about what Douglass did with the money that he gave him, nor why he had needed it so urgently on the night of the ball.

The more he thought about what had happened, the more wary he grew. The look on Douglass's face when he told him that

Gerrard had found the traitors. He had thought it was concern for the cause, but now he suspected that it had been concern for himself. And who was that fellow Dupont? What need had the Jacobites for the help of a French slave trader? Douglass had said that he would help to bring the King back across the waters—but the papers from Menzies had not mentioned such a person at all. He found that he was afraid of the meeting with Douglass that afternoon, and changed his mind about the banknotes.

He wrote to Douglass instead, telling him that his financial affairs had fallen unexpectedly into disarray, and that he would not be able to produce the money, nor play the role that had been planned in the forthcoming action. The letter was delivered to a coffee-house in Leadenhall Street where Douglass received all his mail, but Lord Petre received no reply. A day or two later John Caryll arranged for him to meet William Dicconson and Catherine Walmesley, and plans for his marriage began.

Somewhat to his surprise during the next few days he gave almost no consideration to the Jacobites or to the heroic role that he was to have played in the action. He thought very little of Jenkins, or of Molly Walker. But Arabella was constantly in his mind. He did not know what to do. Only now, when the prospect of losing her loomed so horribly before him, did he realize how deeply he had fallen in love. But he was powerless. He had been trapped in a diabolical pact—and he saw no means of escape.

He longed to see her again, but feared that if he were to do so, a servant would inform his mother. At last he contrived a meeting on an afternoon when Jenkins had left him at his club. Sneaking away, he hailed a hackney carriage and drove to Arabella's house.

"I thought that it would make an amusing novelty," he explained when she asked him why he had not come for her in his own coach. "We shall drive to Hackney-Hole, pretending to be out for a Sunday drive."

"But it is not a Sunday," Arabella protested.

"That will make it all the more pleasant," he assured her. "The roads will be clear."

As soon as they were alone he could not keep his hands off her. Taking hold of her face he kissed it ravenously, running his hands through her hair, stroking her neck, her breastbone, her shoulders;

touching the curve of her arms, her white hands. He took her face in his hands again and kissed her eyes, her mouth. He pulled her on to his lap, pushing his hands under her skirts.

"Lovely Arabella; my greatest happiness."

The urgency, the physical force of his feeling as he made love to her was overpowering. Never had he been quite like this, Arabella thought.

Later on, when he was calm again, he was more himself, the Robert that she knew well.

He touched her neck. "May I beg some token of you, in lasting remembrance of your charms?" he asked.

She pushed him away. "I shall refuse you," she answered, though her smile belied her words. "A lady does not wish to have her charms remembered, but actively admired," she said.

He smiled and tried to kiss her again, but still she pulled back. She could not be sure whether or not he was in jest.

"If you will not grant me so trifling a favour I may be reduced to stealing one," he said, twining his fingers through her curls. "Would not it be a romantic gesture for you to give me a lock of your hair?"

"Ridiculous practice!" she said. Her voice was cold. "Why would any woman sacrifice her toilette to bestow so useless a gift?"

Arabella was taken aback. What a strange favour for Lord Petre to ask. Surely he must know that such a gesture would be ludicrously out of place. Locks of hair were exchanged only in the courtship rituals of the very chaste or the very young.

She remembered an occasion when she had been about fifteen, and had sent a lock of hair to a young man whom she had met at a country ball. She had received in return for the favour a tender sonnet of his own composition, and she had thought herself very sophisticated; the young man had been eighteen, and had subsequently married the third daughter of a marquess. She and Lord Petre had moved far beyond the moment for such tokens. Far more radical an action was called for from him now. She could not understand it.

Lord Petre made no further mention of the lock of hair, and when, after a little while, he took her in his arms again, she did not resist.

"How you captivate me, Arabella," he whispered as he kissed her, and the drive ended as it had begun: in silence.

While Lord Petre was thus occupied, James Douglass turned in at the door of the cookshop that the amorous couple had visited some months before. The fires for the spits of meat, which had been cheerful on a winter's afternoon, disgorged infernal heat and stench into the summer's evening, and Mr. Thomas and his family crackled and gleamed with so much sweat that they could hardly be distinguished from the haunches of flesh. Douglass peered into the hot gloom in the rear of the shop and perceived that M. Dupont, the slave trader, was waiting for him.

Douglass sat down and called for a mug of ale from a lacklustre Polly Thomas.

As soon as she brought it, Dupont began. "So your man has lost his nerve," he said. "What of the banknotes?"

"Gone," Douglass replied angrily. "And the baron with them. I believe that his part in the conspiracy must have been found out. The whole action is to be abandoned." Dupont, however, had little interest in the affairs of the Jacobites.

"You have no money for me, then," he said.

"No money," Douglass repeated, drinking off a mouthful of the ale. "And no prospect of getting any. My advice to you, Dupont, is that you forget the five hundred pounds, and leave England immediately."

"When I met you at that coach stop on my way to Liverpool, you said that he was good for two thousand. What the devil went wrong?"

"I cannot say. The plan was sound—he supported the cause ardently—he had not the slightest suspicion of me."

Dupont laughed at this last claim. "So your man was an imbecile," he scoffed. "But then who but an imbecile would give two thousand pounds to a group of madmen he has never met, to save a king he has never seen?"

"You know nothing of Jacobite affairs," Douglass snapped in reply.

"Neither do you, I might say."

Douglass said in a fierce whisper, "You would not have had any money out of him, had he not believed that I was true to the cause. But beware, Dupont—I learned that Francis Gerrard told his secret before he died."

Dupont shrugged. "Our scheme is ruined. The little priest was not lying to us that night when he warned us we were too late. You killed him in vain."

"*You* killed Gerrard, Dupont," Douglass said.

"You handed me the knife," answered Dupont quickly.

Douglass stood up. "You need to leave England. I shall go to Liverpool tonight."

"You sail for Jamaica?" Dupont asked.

Douglass nodded.

As he walked out of the cookshop, he reflected that he had probably not seen the last of his French friend. After all, their scheme was cunning—his own idea, of course, but it could not go ahead without Dupont. Douglass lacked the connections to pursue it on his own. And Dupont was ruthless. He thought again of the night when they had killed Gerrard; Dupont had slit his throat as though he were opening a sack of flour.

The trouble with Dupont was that he was not clever. It had been Douglass who thought of the masquerade ticket. He remembered running back down the alley to find Gerrard's bloody body after Dupont had scurried off in the opposite direction. He had pulled the ticket out of his own pocket, and put it into Gerrard's as neatly as he could. It had not been easy, with the dead weight of the corpse falling against his legs. But it had bought them time. Gerrard was still known to most as the poor devil from the masquerade.

As he walked into the night, Douglass shrugged. He did not much care that the plan with Lord Petre had gone awry. He was tired of being in England, and longed to escape abroad again.

Chapter Seventeen

"The conqu'ring force of unresisted steel"

Less than a week later came the day appointed for Queen Anne's levee at Hampton Palace. It was to be the crowning event of the summer season, the one to which Teresa had looked forward so eagerly, and for which she and Martha had remained in town. The day would be spent drinking tea, playing cards, and talking of the pleasures of the season. Her Majesty would make a brief appearance in the afternoon, encircled by those courtiers with whom she enjoyed the most favourable relations. Court dress was the order of the occasion; Teresa and Martha had ordered new gowns of pink and pale green silks; the colours of a magnolia tree in the flush of its spring colour. Arabella's dress was of white damask, with birds and flowers embroidered in gold on the skirts. Her shoes were covered in fine ribbings of golden thread, and she carried the ostrich muff that she had ordered from Molly Walker many months before.

The guests were to arrive at the palace by water. Arabella travelled in a boat up the Thames with Henrietta Oldmixon and Lady Salisbury, whom she met on the banks of the Strand early in the morning. It was sunny but not yet hot, and all three ladies wore light summer shawls around their shoulders. The seats of the vessel had been covered in silk cushions to protect the ladies' gowns, with additional pillows and rugs behind them. A delicate shade was suspended like an awning above to preserve the ladies' fair complexions from the brightness of the day.

As soon as they were settled, Henrietta asked, "How are we to bring my Lord Petre to the point? He has been dithering far too long."

"To which point must he be brought?" Lady Salisbury asked languidly in reply.

"He must make Arabella a proposal," Henrietta declared. "I think it would be fitting if he were to speak today."

Arabella did not want this sort of talk. She was still confused by Lord Petre's strange request in the carriage. "Flirtation is far too pleasant to be thinking of marriage," she interjected. "The baron would be a man of little taste if he were to make his declaration just as we have at last arrived at easy intimacy."

Lady Salisbury flounced her fan open. "Ah! So you do expect to hear from him," she said.

Henrietta cut in briskly. "Of course she does. They are constantly together."

Arabella, sitting as far forward in her seat as the angle of the boat permitted, corrected her. "We are in each other's company but once a fortnight."

"But that is in public, my dear," said Lady Salisbury sweetly. "Henrietta is speaking of your private hours."

Arabella was silent, unsure as to what response she should make to this, and Lady Salisbury, taking her silence as a tacit admission, continued to speak.

"Well, Arabella," she continued, moving her fan back and forth. "I am glad to hear that you still expect an offer, for I have just heard that Lord Petre is to marry Catherine Walmesley—and none of us wishes to have *her* as a friend, of course."

"You mean William Dicconson's ward?" Henrietta interrupted in astonished tones. "But she cannot be more than sixteen! Lord Petre must want her for her fortune."

She looked across to Arabella, who had gone rather white. "Be not alarmed, Arabella," she said. "Miss Walmesley may be worth seven thousand a year, but in every other respect you are her superior."

Arabella did not have an answer for this, and she was glad when Lady Salisbury spoke. "I hope that he does marry you, Arabella," she said. "You have been a delightful member of our party this year, and we should be sorry to lose you."

Arabella smiled in reply, but like the sun, her smile was more brilliant than it was warm. She saw Henrietta and Lady Salisbury exchange a confidential glance. Meaning to show that she was indifferent to what had passed, she reached lazily over the side of the boat to trail her fingers in the water. But the surface of the river was farther away than she had expected, and she was forced to withdraw her hand in a quick, jerking motion. She gripped the sides of her seat in an undignified pose, conscious that the others were smirking, though they pretended to look around at the view.

She was staggered by Lady Salisbury's news. It could not be true—Lord Petre would have said something when they met. To be sure, Catherine Walmesley was worth many thousands of pounds a year, and Arabella's own marriage portion was only four thousand pounds in all. But though she had never met Miss Walmesley, she knew that she was considered dull, and not at all pretty. Lord Petre liked to pretend that physical beauty did not rate highly in his catalogue of virtues, but Arabella believed that he did not mean it. It was a position that he maintained only when he was in the company of very handsome women. Besides, he had told her that he loved her. A proposal could not be far off.

When Arabella's party arrived at the palace, the gardens were already well supplied with the ladies and gentlemen of the court. They strutted about in fringe, gold lace, and feathers, with as great a quantity of hair powder and paint as could be carried off without obscuring the identity of the wearer. The peacocks seemed drab beside them.

Arabella walked up the path from the river with her two companions and came face to face with Lord Petre.

He swept her a low bow, declaring loudly, "Miss Fermor! Your beauty is as a zephyr upon a blazing day, bringing exquisite relief and refreshment to the weary traveller."

Arabella disliked him in this mood. The conversation in the boat had made her nervous. "On what account are you weary, my lord?" she asked tersely. "Did your oarsman expire upon the river, and oblige you to row yourself to Hampton Court?" She saw a familiar flash of laughter in his eyes, but he restrained it, and bowed formally again.

He turned to Henrietta. "Miss Fermor is high-spirited, is she not, Miss Oldmixon?" he said. Henrietta looked at him with surprise, and was about to speak, but Lord Petre stopped her. "Miss Oldmixon looks displeased," he said. "I hasten to assure her that her spirits are every part as high, and her beauty just as brilliant as her companion's."

He was gone as soon as he had spoken, hurrying to greet Lady Mary Pierrepont and her sister, who came up the walk behind them.

At first Arabella attempted to take Lord Petre's conduct as a matter of course, reminding herself that she had seen his concern for the opinion of others before; it was no surprise that on this most public of occasions he should abandon the intimacies that he permitted himself when only close friends were present. She did not number indomitable strength of character among her lover's signature traits. But as she watched him, she perceived a nervous unsteadiness in his movements that contrasted sharply with the authority and control of his usual demeanour. Normally when he saw her in public he would catch her eye, sharing the secret of their connection. She wished she could find a way to speak to him away from everybody else.

Out of the corner of her eye, she saw Lord Petre walk up to Teresa and Martha Blount. This was strange; he had paid them very little attention in the past, except when their friend Mr. Pope was by, which he was not today, she was pleased to see. Lord Petre bowed to Teresa—no doubt she would be grateful for the attention. Arabella could only surmise that he wanted to show off his acquaintance with so ancient a family as the Blounts, although everybody knew that they were heavily encumbered by debt.

"How charming to see you and your sister," Lord Petre said to Teresa, as he kissed each of the Blounts in turn. "I was speaking of you but a few days ago when a gentleman of my acquaintance praised the beauties of Mapledurham. I told him that even so lovely an estate as that was not one part so charming as the ladies who belong to it: Miss Teresa and Miss Martha Blount."

Martha looked apprehensively at her sister, expecting her to receive this new attention with fawning enthusiasm. But, much to her surprise, Teresa greeted the baron with a wary smile.

"We can hardly be said to belong to it any more, my lord," she replied. "Mapledurham is now my brother's seat."

Martha took Teresa's response as a sign that, finally, her sister had accepted that her interest in the baron was never to be reciprocated. She wished that Alexander might have been there to observe the spectacle, and wondered what he would make of it. Alexander had always understood Lord Petre very thoroughly.

Teresa did not wait for Lord Petre to reply to her last remark, but said instead, "I am so unaccustomed to seeing you without Miss Fermor, my lord, that I would fear she had taken ill—but she is standing twenty feet away." She gave a little tinkling laugh, not unlike one of Arabella's.

Lord Petre looked nervous. "Oh! Miss Fermor and I are such established friends that it would be tiresome for me to hover about her on an occasion like this," he said. "Nobody wants to be hindered by old acquaintance when they are in pursuit of new." At this, the girls stared at him with open astonishment.

Lord Petre, seeing that they were at a loss, forged on. "You are not with your friend Mr. Pope today," he said. "A pity—I would like to have improved my acquaintance with him. I fancy that he will be sorry to have missed an occasion that could have supplied him with so much diversion for his pen." He chuckled to himself, appearing not to mind that the girls still said nothing. Martha wondered whether he might be drunk.

As Petre walked away Martha stole a quick glance at Arabella. She flicked her head around as soon as she saw her cousin, but Martha caught, nonetheless, a look of alarm.

The girls' attention was taken again by Lord Petre, who was being addressed in the clear, unmistakable accents of Lady Mary Pierrepont.

"I am surprised to hear you describe Miss Fermor as an old friend, my lord," she was saying. "The general understanding is that your acquaintance with her is of a different kind altogether."

Teresa smiled to see Lord Petre's face when Mary Pierrepont delivered her observation, and wished, not for the first time, that she too had been the daughter of an earl. He looked around to see if they had been overheard, then collected himself, and replied with something close to his former self-confidence. "Miss Fermor would be dismayed to know that so scandalous a rumour has circulated," he said. "A lady of her unrivalled beauty and charm would not permit an association with a person so inconstant, so uncertain, as myself."

Lady Mary looked closely at him. "But the general expectation is of an engagement between you," she said. Again he started visibly.

"The person who marries Miss Fermor must be a more deserving gentleman than I," he finished, and quickly extricated himself from the exchange.

He joined a party of girls in pale blue and lilac silks, whom Teresa had never met. They were several years younger than she and Arabella—she had seen one of them at a levee that she had attended with her mother. She had given the impression of being very silly. Soon after Lord Petre had joined the group, the girls could be heard laughing in shrill, excited bursts, and Lord Petre's own distinctive baritone rang out after them.

"Lord Petre's remarks puzzle me," said Martha to Teresa, as they followed his movements. "Arabella seemed sanguine about the match, and I cannot believe her to be mistaken. Perhaps this is the line she has instructed Lord Petre to take with respect to her until they are publicly engaged."

"Hardly!" Teresa replied. "Not even Arabella would wish to be thought so beautiful that Lord Petre did not deserve her."

They were interrupted by the hurried arrival of Margaret Brownlow. She had remarkable news to deliver.

"Eliza Chambers says that Catherine Walmesley is to marry Lord Petre!" she exclaimed breathlessly. "But I told her that it could not be true. Is not the baron engaged to your cousin?"

Martha gasped; Teresa, too—but she collected herself quickly.

"That seems rather to depend on which of them you ask," she said with a tart smile.

"We had believed that an arrangement would soon be in place between them," said Martha hastily, covering over Teresa's sharpness. "The Fermor family has been expecting it—and ours too, indeed. But if my Lord Petre is to marry another lady, I hope that people will not think Miss Fermor has been treated unhandsomely."

"Oh! Arabella Fermor will not mind," said Margaret. "Every man in London is wild for her. But Miss Walmesley! Who can believe her good luck?"

Arabella, who was beginning to mind a good deal more than Margaret would allow, was walking in the grounds between Lady

Salisbury and Henrietta. She knew that people had been talking about her, and she wished that she could find a way to stop Lady Salisbury from discussing the subject of Lord Petre now.

Lady Salisbury did not trouble to lower her voice as she said, "If Lord Petre cannot obtain his family's permission for the match, you might still marry in secret. An arrangement about the money can always be made later on."

It would be futile to try to silence her, so Arabella responded in an equally strident tone. "I would never consent to a secret marriage," she declared. "It suggests that the lady has something to conceal. There is but one situation in which that arrangement is allowable, and that is where a woman wishes to avoid a husband chosen for her by being already married to somebody else."

But it was apparent that her friends had no wish to discuss the general subject of matrimony. Their concern was with the specifics of Arabella's relation to Lord Petre, and they were determined to pursue the topic as loudly as they could.

"Lord Petre is prodigiously cavalier today," said Henrietta. "Look at him playing the flirt with Clarissa Williamson and her friends. He flatters them—see how Miss Williamson blushes." But Arabella, who had already observed the scene, did not look in their direction again. "I think that he might be more gallant towards you, Arabella," Henrietta added.

Arabella called upon the sturdiest reserves of her self-discipline. "I had much rather that my Lord Petre made Miss Williamson blush, than me," she answered, as another burst of laughter came from Lord Petre's quarter. "What a noise those girls are making. I have never known the baron to be thought so entertaining before."

Lord Petre's laughter was loud indeed, but, as he reflected bitterly, it was no more heartfelt than Arabella's could be. All morning, whenever he caught sight of her, he had felt a cruel smart of anguish. While he spoke cavalierly to others he did so with a surge of shame. When she had lifted her hurt eyes to meet his own, he had felt an overpowering tenderness. She was to him as a wounded deer, which holds itself proud and lithe, even as it pants to escape the mortal blow. How he longed to speak to her; to tell her the truth of what had happened. But if he did tell her he feared that she would quit the levee, and his undertaking to Caryll and his mother would remain undischarged.

He told himself that, in not warning Arabella of her fate, he was being strong—and after a while he really began to feel that this was true. His conviction was not that of a man who knows he must fight to defend the woman he loves, but it was powerful nonetheless. It was the conviction born of self-preservation, and in Lord Petre's noble bosom that ancient instinct had taken firm occupation. He believed that he would hang upon the gallows if he did not obey his family, and his distaste for such an outcome meant that he did not linger long in deliberation. His course of action was clear. He had no choice but to forsake Arabella, and so, when he looked at her this morning, it was with the eyes of a modern Aeneas who abandons his Dido—his one true love—to face the perilous waters of chance alone. The baron knew which way his duty lay.

When Lord Petre put the matter to himself, it was of course without any trace of irony. He believed that for the sake of his family and his fellow Jacobites he must make a public break with Arabella Fermor, and he did not stop to consider that in so doing he chose one betrayal over another. But he was also beginning to feel that he deserved something of a reward for his sacrifice. Since he had been forced to give up all hopes of heroism, since he had agreed to marry Catherine Walmesley, should he not retain Arabella as his treasure? He was the victim of a devil's bargain. Arabella was bold, she was worldly; she liked to laugh at the conventions of their society. Why could she not remain his mistress after the marriage? Why should he not keep that consolation?

His thoughts were interrupted by Sir George Brown, one of the members of the party in which he was standing.

"Miss Fermor and her friends are looking towards us, my lord," Sir George was saying. "If you flirt too outlandishly with these young ladies, Miss Fermor will begin to suspect that she has lost her admirer."

Lord Petre perceived that this was a chance to move the conversation in the direction that was required.

"Miss Fermor does not lose admirers; she only gains them," he replied. "If I am always at Miss Fermor's side, I shall appear a proud, conceited fellow who believes that he is the only man worth a lady's notice. But if you desire me to play the flirt with Miss Fermor, I will willingly do so."

Clarissa Williamson, who obviously did not desire it, gave a pretty shake of her hair at this point, and said, "Then the rumour is not true, my lord, that you and Miss Fermor are engaged?"

He smiled down at her. "I am a mere mortal!" he replied, with a dramatic toss of his own curls. "One does not ask a goddess for her hand in marriage. She would laugh me away."

"I do not believe that you can be so very afraid of her, my lord," Miss Williamson replied with a charming giggle. "I have seen you at her side on many occasions. But we shall devise a task to test your mettle. Sir George! What mighty labour can we give my Lord Petre to show his fortitude?"

Sir George gave a cough of nervous excitement, wondering whether Clarissa Williamson might be flirting with him.

"'Zounds!" he exclaimed, tapping his snuffbox. "Let us send him on an errand," Sir George continued, feeling, for the first time, what it was to play a part in a battle of wits, however few his lines. "A plague on it, my lord! How am I to flirt with Miss Williamson and her charming friends when you are by?" he asked. "You must make love to another woman instead, while I try my luck with these ladies, by gad."

"I shall make love to any woman you choose," said the baron with a smile.

"Then let it be Miss Fermor!" said Sir George. "You shall show Miss Williamson that you are not afraid of her!"

Miss Williamson looked somewhat disappointed in the outcome of this exchange, but, having styled herself a girl of pluck and energy, could hardly retreat now.

"Indeed, my lord!" she cried. "You shall be bold—I command you to defy the goddess Arabella Fermor before the afternoon is out." Lord Petre knew that this was precisely the excuse he required to discharge his actions towards Arabella. Fearful that Clarissa might withdraw the direction, he stepped away from her group, taking advantage of the fact that Lady Mary Pierrepont was passing by.

"My lady!" he exclaimed. "Ever since Miss Oldmixon's

assembly I have meant to compliment you on your daring at the card table."

Lady Mary looked at him, surprised at this abrupt speech. "I show great daring at all times, my lord," she replied.

He bowed to acknowledge it. "But I was particularly struck by the boldness of your bet," he added. "One is not accustomed to see such pluck and talent in a lady—least of all in a lady who plays alone."

"When one is gambling for high stakes, it is always best to play alone," she answered. "I have found that a partner is seldom to be trusted. Do you not agree with me?"

Lord Petre made no answer.

During the afternoon, the guests began to move indoors. Some of them played cards while the others sat talking in small groups. Clarissa Williamson bounded up to Lord Petre, who was standing next to one of the big windows, a little apart from his acquaintances.

"What do you gaze down upon so wistfully, my lord?" she asked, following his gaze. "Ah! The goddess Fermor, sporting in the garden. I hope that you will not neglect your undertaking."

For a moment he made no reply, but stood silently, deep in thought. Then he roused himself and answered, "By no means, madam. I am merely considering my best approach."

William Dicconson, who stood nearby, overheard this last remark. He stepped up to join them, and Lord Petre caught a draught of the strong, sweet smell of liquor on his breath.

"Are you afraid of a woman, my lord?" he asked with a leer. Lord Petre took a step backward and glanced at Clarissa, wondering whether she would guess that Dicconson's remark was meant as a provocation.

"Miss Williamson and I have been exchanging a joke, sir," he answered. "I said earlier that I should be afraid to flirt with a lady so beautiful as Miss Arabella Fermor."

"And I said that he must test his courage—by flirting with her openly," Miss Williamson rejoined.

"Have you considered how so bold a step might be brought off?" Dicconson asked, turning away from Miss Williamson and speaking to Lord Petre in a voice that was edged with aggression.

"I believe that I have a plan in view," the baron replied.

"Then you must execute it swiftly," said Dicconson, in the same unpleasant tone. "Or the day will be over—and then it will be too late."

Arabella came in from the gardens alone, for Lady Salisbury and Henrietta had remained outside, wanting to take a turn in the parterre. They had not invited her to join them. As she entered the room, several people turned to look at her, but spun quickly away when she met their stares. Martha and Teresa sat on a sofa near the doorway, and Martha invited her to sit down with them. She accepted, and took her seat quietly. She thought that the laughter in Lord Petre's group had increased in volume since she had arrived, but she pushed it from her mind, telling herself that it must be a nervous imagining.

She heard Martha talking about Alexander, relieved that it was a subject on which they knew she had nothing to say; she had no energy for conversation. Lady Mary Pierrepont was sitting just across the room with Lady Castlecomber, talking confidentially. It appeared that they, too, had turned their heads to avoid her eye.

"Lord Petre was right—" Arabella heard Martha say, and her head turned in instinctive reaction to the sound of his name. She saw immediately that Teresa had noticed it, and wished that she had taken more care to conceal her interest. "—when he said that Alexander would enjoy this spectacle," she concluded. Arabella dropped her gaze again listlessly. "I do wish he had been asked," Martha added. "We must remember all the details for him."

Teresa was about to answer, when there was a particularly boisterous gale of laughter from Clarissa Williamson's part of the room, and all three of the girls turned around to look. They saw that with a lot of fanfare and dramatic movement, Lord Petre was beginning to move away from his party. He stopped and looked back at them, wanting to be sure that everybody was watching. Arabella saw that Clarissa Williamson raised a hand to point in her direction, but she dropped it abruptly when she caught Arabella's eye. The sound of their laughter had brought all of the conversations in the room to a halt for a moment, and people glanced around to see the source of their merriment. There was a hiatus, but then the noise began again, mounting steadily.

Martha and Teresa had just started to talk when Arabella saw that Lord Petre was walking towards her. His eyes were upon her, but she forced herself not to turn or look. She could feel that his progress was watched by all his companions, and that Mary Pierrepont and Lady Castlecomber were watching him too.

For a second she thought that he was coming to speak to her privately, but then she realized that it could not be so. He was walking purposefully; he was nearly in front of her. Teresa and Martha, who had been speaking softly, unconsciously fell silent.

Her eyes were in her lap, but she saw from under her lashes that he was standing before her. She made herself look up at him, and found that he was smiling—smiling at her—it was the old, familiar smile of their secret intimacy. She exhaled loudly, and felt a rush of relief. She glanced aside to Martha and Teresa, and saw that they were smiling too. The room had grown quiet. The seconds seemed slow and deliberate while she sat and waited; then he bent down, one knee raised in front of him. She caught a glimpse of Lady Salisbury and Henrietta walking in, watching and smiling too. She felt glorious, exultant: her anxieties had been needless. Lord Petre was kneeling before her. All eyes were on her now, but she did not mind.

So this, she thought triumphantly, was what it felt to be a baron's wife.

He put his hand into his pocket, and drew something out. He had closed his fist around it—but Arabella saw a flash and the point of a blade. He reached towards her and she felt the touch of his fingers on her neck—so familiar, and yet she started in shock. There was something cold.

It felt like steel. For a terrifying moment she thought that he carried a knife, and that he was going to kill her. She shrieked—she could not help it—in her panic she hardly knew that it came from her own mouth. She heard the sweep and click of sharp blades coming together, and then she felt a lock of her hair falling away. Lord Petre snatched it up.

"My prize!" he called aloud. "A trophy from Miss Arabella Fermor—I have stolen a lock from the goddess Diana."

To her amazement, the room began to applaud. The sound was tremendous. It was mingled with laughter; at first uncertain, then unrestrained. She stared at her hands in confusion. With an ache of straining muscles, she forced herself to look at him—he was brandishing the lock in the air, smiling idiotically at Miss Williamson, who clapped and squealed. The room around her was a blur of jeering faces. Alarm, embarrassment, shame overspread her features; she could not prevent it.

There was a brief ebb in the general laughter, and Clarissa's voice rang out clearly: "Even the goddess of chastity can not resist the baron's conquering steel!"

Arabella shrank from the artless cruelty of her remark. Good God, she thought—that Diana costume. How vainly she had bragged of being the goddess of chastity. She regretted it bitterly now.

In a low voice, though not so low that Arabella could not hear it, Henrietta quipped, "Would that he had confined himself to seizing those hairs less in sight."

There was more laughter, another scattered shower of applause. Arabella tried to laugh too, but she was frozen. She must not cry, but the tears were smarting behind her eyes. She put her hand up to feel the place where Lord Petre had taken the lock. There was a blank space where the hair had been: a gap, with short stubby ends that felt prickly to her touch. Martha and Teresa were staring at her with anguished faces.

"A trifle, a trifle," she murmured. "'Tis but a trifle."

For a few more minutes, though they felt like an hour, she endured the sound of laughter. At last she saw the room turning back into little groups, embarking upon new stories told in lighthearted merriment. Could it be that they thought so little of what had just transpired? It was the greatest agony of Arabella's life. But they were forgetting her already. Lord Petre himself was talking to Clarissa Williamson again, and he did not meet her eye. Finally she thought that she could trust herself to stand. She got to her feet.

As she left the room, people looked round at her again. They smiled good-naturedly, but to her it seemed malevolent. She smiled faintly in return, the muscle of her lip twitching. For an instant she relaxed her face, but the tears rose in her eyes, and she knew that she must pull up the corners of her mouth again.

At last she was in the gallery. Martha and her friend Margaret Brownlow were beside her. "Are you unwell, Arabella?" Martha asked. Her face, close to Arabella's own, was full of feeling. Arabella reached behind herself for a seat, and Martha took her arm to help her to a low upholstered bench. She sat down on one side of her, and Margaret Brownlow sat on the other.

"There, Miss Fermor!" Margaret said. "He means to make you his wife. There can be no clearer proof. The taking of a lock of hair—'tis a prelude to a far greater step."

Arabella was grateful to Margaret for understanding so little. But she said, feeling her face tremble as she did so, "He does not mean to make me his wife. Otherwise he would not have let the world know that I am his mistress."

The girls were shocked, but she hardly cared. She would regret it later, but at this moment she was concerned only that they should remain beside her on the seat. She could not go back into that room.

Martha was, indeed, looking at Arabella in amazement. Until now, she had still not been sure that the rumours Teresa repeated from James Douglass and the girls in town were true. When she had seen them on the river she knew that her cousin must have spent more time alone with Lord Petre than she ought to have done; she had guessed that there had been some inconsequential intimacy, which she knew most women allowed. But the discovery that Arabella had actually been his mistress, when their engagement was not certain, stunned her. She did not censure Arabella for it, but she could not help but think that she had been a fool. Arabella had shown even less common sense than her sister, she reflected.

Even so, she did not feel that much harm could come of Lord Petre's antics today. The matter would be soon forgotten, and it would do no lasting damage to her cousin. Arabella felt his gesture as a cruel rejection, but Martha did not think that others would see it as such. They sat together for about fifteen minutes, Arabella hardly speaking. At last Martha suggested that she accompany her home.

Arabella agreed, but said, with something of her usual spirit, "I must go back into the room again. I cannot have them think that he has destroyed me."

After Arabella walked out, Lady Castlecomber, who was still sitting with Lady Mary Pierrepont, remarked, "Were I Miss Fermor, I should ask for the lock back."

"Ah—the sad truth about hair!" Lady Mary replied. "A curl that has been cut can never be restored."

Across the room, Lady Salisbury took Henrietta confidentially by the hand and pulled her down to Arabella's empty sofa.

"If I were Miss Fermor, I should be wild," she said. "What can the baron be thinking of? Everybody will know now that they are lovers. It is a blemish on her honour."

Henrietta was hardly listening, looking anxiously instead at the front of her dress. "Take care! You nearly made me spill my tea," she said. "I might have stained my new brocade." Then she registered something of Lady Salisbury's last remark. "What did you say of Arabella's honour?"

"It will be blemished for ever," Lady Salisbury pronounced. She paused dramatically. Then in a loud voice she asked, "*Do you know what I have just heard, Henrietta?*"

As she had intended, her voice was audible to the entire room. "Lord Petre does not mean to marry Arabella at all," she exclaimed. "William Dicconson just told me—in confidence, of course—that the rumour about his ward is true."

Arabella returned to the room just as Lady Salisbury's voice rang out:

"Lord Petre has been engaged these several weeks to Miss Catherine Walmesley."

Lady Salisbury and Henrietta watched Arabella coolly as she came towards them, very pale. They made no move to accommodate her on their sofa.

"Oh—I did not know you were returned to us, Miss Fermor," said Lady Salisbury with hauteur.

Arabella opened her mouth to speak, but nothing came out. She stood quite still for several moments, and then tried to walk out of the room again. But as she began to move away she fainted.

Every man in the room rushed towards her, and the women crowded around behind. Henrietta and Lady Salisbury remained seated, watching disdainfully. Lord Petre reached her first. He dropped down on to his knees beside her and snatched her into his arms. The crowd gasped. He lifted her limp form on to a chair, and one of the ladies pressed her fan into his hands. He waved it in front of her. Gently, he pushed the hair back from her face, and instinctively reached down to the ribbon of her stays, but checked himself. He glanced up, and saw that William Dicconson was watching him.

One person pressed in to offer snuff, another a glass of wine, then a cup of tea. But Arabella's eyes remained closed.

At last she began to come around, opening her eyes in a weak, fluttering motion. She became aware of a low murmur of whispering around her, and then a crush of people pressing in. She realized that she had fainted, and she gripped the edges of the sofa in alarm. Had she looked undignified when she fell? She wondered how she had been moved to her present position. She blinked her eyes open again, and saw Lord Petre kneeling beside her. She imagined what must have happened: he had lifted her up, insensible, and placed her on the sofa as though he were embracing her. But then Lady Salisbury's words reverberated in her head: *engaged these several weeks to Miss Catherine Walmesley.* She felt as though the shame would choke her. How dare he presume to touch her in such circumstances—how greatly did it exacerbate her humiliation.

She struggled to sit up, recoiling from Lord Petre's attempt to help her. "Please leave me, sir," she said in a clear voice. "I have no desire to receive your attentions."

Now Lord Petre looked pale; he tried to appear affronted, as though he had merely been attempting a courtesy. He rose to his feet, glancing around anxiously to see how many people had heard.

Martha knelt down to her cousin instead. "We are ready to take you home," she whispered. "A boat is waiting on the river." She took Arabella by the arm and began to lead her from the room.

Teresa, however, made no attempt to follow.

There are people who, no matter how dearly they have longed to witness the humiliation of a rival, will nonetheless wince if the spectacle really should come to pass. Teresa Blount was not among them. Arabella's distress did not move her. In the past, Arabella had seen *her* unhappy and uncertain too, but such sights had not softened Arabella's temperament, nor disposed her to behave more generously towards her cousin. Teresa did not imagine that, had Arabella not existed, Lord Petre might have married her instead. She could not change Arabella's outcome by feeling compassion for her now. Both Arabella and Teresa understood that they belonged to a world that set no particular store by the virtues of fortitude, charity, and humility. Yet neither of them had ever been tempted to forsake it for another.

So, when Martha turned back to her sister and said quietly that they should accompany Arabella home by river, Teresa replied, "No need for both of us to go, is there? I am going to be presented to Her Majesty."

Martha remonstrated with her by alluding to Arabella's misfortune. But Teresa shook her head fiercely and answered, "*I* do not intend to give up my last day's pleasure because Arabella did not get her own way with Lord Petre. Anybody might have told her that it would turn out thus. Attend to her if you wish, but you will not be thanked for it afterwards."

Chapter Eighteen

"Love in these Labyrinths his Slaves detains,
And mighty Hearts are held in slender Chains"

The next day Martha told Alexander what had happened.

"That is quite a tale, Patty," he said when she came to the end of it. "What I wouldn't give to have seen Miss Fermor's face when the baron snatched away her hair. Nor your sister's when Miss Fermor fainted. What a mighty spectacle it must have been."

"It was most unfeeling of Teresa not to accompany Cousin Bell home," said Martha, wanting to make sure that Alexander had noted this part of the story.

"Perhaps not so unfeeling as you think, Patty," he replied. "Arabella may not have wished Teresa to be there either. She is not the sort of person who would want her rivals to see her languishing in the Cave of Spleen."

"The Cave of Spleen?" echoed Martha. "How fanciful your speech is sometimes. Arabella *was* very dejected on the way home, it's true. If I did not know you better, I would begin to think you felt sorry for our cousin Bell."

"I should be a hypocrite indeed were I to feel sympathy for her now," Alexander replied. "But one does not wish to see Miss Fermor in her fallen condition—it is so much at odds with the character she shows the rest of the world."

"I have never known you to defend Arabella before," said Martha. She looked at Alexander suspiciously. "What can be the reason for this change of heart?"

Alexander looked back at her with a guarded expression. "No, no—no change of heart," he said. "But there was something flawless about Miss Fermor's poise," he continued. "She wore her beauty as a knight wears his armour. I had not thought it could be so easily dented."

Martha laughed at this, feeling more like Teresa in her desire to make fun of him. "Angels, fallen women, knights at arms! Dear me, Alexander," she said. "What a confusion of ideas this tale has roused in you. You need only add an epic battle to your narrative, and you could take on Homer, Spenser, and Milton in a single morning!"

There was a glint in Alexander's eye, and she wondered if he would reach for pen and paper then and there.

"Mind you give me proper credit," she added with a teasing look. She was beginning to enjoy the new footing on which they stood. Once again she wondered what it was in Alexander's character that made people want to taunt him. Perhaps all ambitious people were the same, she considered. Or all successful people, she corrected herself, reflecting that however gratifying it might be to mock Alexander or Arabella, there was not much pleasure to be gained in poking fun at Teresa's unrealized hopes.

Two days later, Martha and Teresa left London to return to Mapledurham. A week after that Alexander departed likewise. His adieu to Jervas was delivered with a mixture of relief and regret, to which Jervas replied in his customary manner.

"I am not suited to melancholy, Pope—I do not like feeling sad. So I shall not say that I will miss you, but rather that I am looking forward to your return."

Alexander pressed his friend's hand, and thanked him sincerely for all that he had done. "I shall return as soon as I have a poem to sell," he added.

Jervas said goodbye with a cheerful wave.

After the events at Hampton Palace Arabella thought that she would never show her face in public again. It was not merely the fact that Lord Petre had abandoned her that was so shaming—the riskiness of their romance had always been a reminder that she might not attain her end. But if she had imagined their parting, it was as a private affair, engendered by his family's refusal to permit the match. She had pictured it as tearful and anguished on his part, regretful and dignified on hers. Of course, she had believed that he would defy his family's prohibition to marry her anyway.

When she thought about what had happened, she was certain that Lord Petre's family had demanded a public separation, wanting to be sure that the relationship would never be resumed. She wondered what leverage had been used to force him to agree. The motive must have been powerful. She was firmly of the belief that his passions in the past had been motivated by sentimental rather than moral feeling, which was inconsistent with the resolve and cold ruthlessness with which he had acted. It was out of character.

As the days passed, her feelings of mortification and betrayal gave way to an unexpected relief. She realized that everybody had known of their affair; even if it had been broken off privately she would have become an object of pity, the pathetic dupe of a wealthy, charming nobleman. But as things stood, it was *he* who came off badly—making use of the protection offered by a public setting to perform so dishonourable an act. Had he married Arabella, he would have declared his real nobility, showing that he was rich enough to marry for love and confident enough to marry as magnificent a creature as Arabella Fermor. She hoped that society would view the marriage to Catherine Walmesley as a feeble retreat, a naked attempt to line his family's pockets through marriage to a woman whom nobody cared for.

If Arabella managed her situation well, she might become even more distinguished a prize. She decided to quit London for a season, go instead to Bath, and return to the capital the following year, by which time Lord Petre and Miss Walmesley would have been married long enough to have begun the unglamorous business of breeding.

She was invigorated by these reflections and her decision. But she couldn't help a bitter underlying disappointment that afflicted her private hours. The nature of this regret surprised her; she had told herself that she was pursuing Lord Petre because she wanted to be a baron's wife—and for the adventure of it, which thrilled her. She saw in hindsight that the affair had been exquisite because of more than his rank and fortune; her motivating ambition had been displaced by more complicated emotions. Their regard for each other had been reciprocal. There had been no need for her to indulge in flights of romantic fantasy when they were in fact united by real understanding and likeness.

But as soon as she acknowledged her feelings of attachment to him, she experienced a sudden release. She was amazed. How could it be that by admitting that she had come to love Lord Petre, she had been spared the lashings of remorse and longing that she had expected to overwhelm her? For the first time in her life, the workings of the human heart astounded her. In spite of these new discoveries about herself, however, she did remain in one fundamental sense true to her former character. She would never discuss the episode, or her feelings about it, with any of her friends, who wondered at Arabella's unflaggingly cheerful disposition and the resumption of her determined social manner. Since they had no insight into the intricacies of her heart, they concluded that she had recovered so quickly because she was not capable of deep feeling.

She was relieved to leave town with her parents, who decided that their daughter's best chances for success in the next season depended upon her being removed immediately from the present one.

Lord Petre's emotions were of a different order. He missed Arabella even more now that their separation was complete, and he reflected how ironic it was that he, most enviable of creatures, should have to suffer the unfairness of losing his one true love. But he decided that he would not seek Arabella out after his marriage to Miss Walmesley, despite his earlier desire to keep her as his mistress. He told himself that it would be up to Arabella to make the first move, and that if she did not, he must submit to his ill-fate.

In due course he would hear that Arabella had returned to society more beautiful and triumphant than ever, and the news would intensify his sense of heroic exile—he alone was doomed to unrequited love; Arabella's passion had obviously been superficial in its nature. If they were to be united again, he reasoned, it would be not as god and goddess but as mere mortals, and Lord Petre was rather afraid of the demands that mortality might make of him. As he sensed her drift away, magnificently self-possessed as ever, he vowed that he would always honour her as the great love of his life, even if he should one day find himself in the arms of another mistress.

In the meantime, however, Lord Petre and his family returned to Ingatestone to prepare for the wedding.

On the day that he left London, Alexander stopped at John Caryll's house at Ladyholt; he was to be collected there by his father's little carriage the next morning. After breakfast the following day, Caryll invited Alexander to walk in the gardens. As they passed through the well-tended borders, looking out on to the gentle summer prospect of grass and grazing cows, Alexander felt a tide of relief wash over him. He had been pent up in the city for too long. The view also reminded him of his poem *Windsor Forest*, of the verses that awaited his attention when he returned home, and of the very few weeks of summer that now remained. He had meant to send another poem to Tonson by the autumn. As he watched Caryll's slow, wandering step he felt impatience. He was stricken with the thought that he might get no more work done in the country than he had in the town.

At last Caryll began to speak. "I heard recently of a rather sorry affair," he said. Alexander wondered if his host had brought him outside expressly to discuss it. He turned to him with an interested expression, but said nothing.

"The matter concerns two families who are very dear to me," Caryll continued. "The Petres and the Fermors. Two of our most ancient lines. Devout, of course."

Alexander was greatly intrigued; he longed to hear Caryll's account of the events. He did not confess to having heard the tale already, wanting Caryll to tell his version of the story without interruption. Perhaps Caryll knew more about why things had turned out as they did. He was curious.

Caryll knew that his young friend was thinking of writing a new poem, and he hoped that he might use Alexander to compose a public record of the events. "The Petres and the Fermors have long been intimate," Caryll began. "There was once some talk of a match between the eldest Miss Fermor and my ward, the baron. Her fortune is not large, and there are seven younger sisters still to be provided for, but I had always thought it an excellent notion to unite two such ancient houses. But lately a coolness has arisen between them."

He paused, correcting himself. "It is more than coolness; there is anger. The Fermors are angry with the Petres, perhaps implacably so. And upon so trifling a basis! Lord Petre, in a moment of high animal spirits, stole a lock of Miss Arabella Fermor's hair. The jest has been taken too seriously. It has caused an estrangement between the two families, though they had lived long in friendship before."

"I am grieved to hear it, sir," said Alexander. "As you observe, it appears a trivial thing to cause such dire offence." He suspected still that Caryll knew more than he was letting on, and he was about to insist on hearing the details. But he stopped himself.

"Amorous causes too often give rise to mighty contest, I fear," Caryll said. "But I believe that you may be instrumental in providing a cure, Pope."

"I, sir? How so?" Alexander dreaded to hear what he would be asked to do.

"I desire you to write a poem to make a jest of it, and laugh them together again."

Alexander's heart leapt. It was a brilliant idea!

"A poem upon Miss Fermor's stolen lock," he answered slowly, not wanting to appear too eager lest Caryll wonder why he liked the idea so much. "The subject is slight," he added.

"But perhaps you will find that more might be made of it than meets the eye," Caryll suggested, slyly. Alexander was grateful for this interjection, and, once again, decided not to enquire too closely as to its cause. What did it matter if Caryll knew something more about Arabella Fermor's ravished hair? It would be he, not Caryll, who would set the episode in writing.

"I have affection for Miss Fermor and her family," Caryll continued, "and I should like to see her happy again. Particularly when the offence is founded upon so insignificant an episode."

"As you justly observe, sir, that is what lends the subject its peculiar charm," Alexander answered.

As they walked back into the house, he thanked John Caryll for his suggestion, and promised to give the idea thought. But then he felt a pricking of compunction. Caryll lived far from the court and the town, thought Alexander; despite his bravado about travelling to London, he enjoyed a retired life, surrounded by a loving family and old friends. Caryll had probably made this proposal out of affectionate solicitude for people whom he knew to be devout Catholics and respectable landholders. Ought Alexander to let his friend know that there had been a more intimate involvement between the two parties than he realized? How differently might his friend feel if he knew all the details? But he decided against speaking out. He did not want Caryll to change his mind about his writing the poem, as he undoubtedly would if he was apprised of all the facts. He reasoned that Caryll need never learn the truth of the affair.

Caryll watched Alexander carefully. He had thought, for a moment, that Alexander was looking at him awry, almost as though he guessed the secret. But Alexander's face cleared, and Caryll concluded that he did not suspect. He decided against telling Alexander what had really happened. Poets, after all, were not to be trusted with the truth. He knew that Alexander longed for fame—he would be far too tempted to make the story into a scandal—which was exactly what Caryll hoped to avoid. He glanced at Alexander again, benevolently. His fears were needless; Alexander probably suspected nothing.

It took Alexander three weeks to finish the first draft of the poem. He spent hours in his room, blocking out the noises that constantly threatened to distract him: the housemaid treading up and down the staircase with her mop and brooms, the cook and kitchen boy calling to each another outside in the yard, his mother talking to his father from one room to another. He broke off for meals, thankful to have a reason to lay down his pen, and yet anxious to be back at his desk as soon as he was away from it. The worst moments in the composition came at the beginning of each couplet, when all he had were two words or a snatch of a phrase that he wanted to make rhyme. He struggled to recall the thoughts he had had about the episode when Martha first described it to him. He paced about his room, lay on his bed for long periods, read his lines over and over until they made no sense. He realized, when he had finished the first canto of the poem and was beginning work on a second, that he could no longer remember which of the lines had been funny when they had first come to him, and he wished that he had put a mark next to the words that had seemed particularly inspired.

Each day he would take long walks with his father, but while they were out he was constantly thinking of ideas and trying to find ways to remember them.

One morning, Alexander's father asked him what his new poem was about.

"Oh, it is a satire, sir," Alexander replied, dreading his father's reaction to the news. "On the court and the men and women of fashion," he added, hoping that this description might modify what he knew must be coming.

"A satire!" his father replied in surprise, disapproval edging his words. "You told me that you were going to write a sacred hymn called *The Messiah*."

Pope hesitated. He remembered mentioning such a poem when he had written to ask if he might stay in town longer. He had never imagined that his father paid the slightest attention to what he was doing—but he should have guessed that this particular detail would be remembered.

"I have been writing the *Messiah*, sir," he said, trying not to sound guilty. "But Mr. Caryll has asked me to break off from that work to compose the present verses. They are intended to help two Catholic families to become friends again."

"Mr. Caryll!" exclaimed Alexander's father. He paused, and then he added in an appeased tone of voice, "He would encourage you in nothing that was wrong." Another pause, and then, "Who are the two families?" Alexander knew that this was his trump card. "The Petres and the Fermors," he said. His father nodded, savouring the names. Alexander smiled to himself, but felt a sting of conscience.

By way of atonement he decided to divulge something that he had been planning to keep to himself. "I have been thinking, sir," he began, "as I reflect on all that I did and saw while I was in London, that I do not properly fit into the world of the town. I wonder if I ever will. I am so very different from Charles Jervas and Richard Steele—and from Lord Petre, of course."

"Well, you are not a baron's son, that's certainly true," his father replied.

Alexander looked at him and saw that his father was embarrassed, refusing to meet his son's eye. It had not occurred to him until now that their lack of position might be why his father so resisted Alexander's joining the fashionable world. He felt a pang of remorse for his own failure to understand.

"But then I should not want to be, sir," he replied.

Mr. Pope was silent for a moment, and Alexander thought that he was going to upbraid him for dismissing social privilege so lightly. But instead, revealing the train of his thoughts, he said, "I hope that you will one day have a house of your own, Alexander. When you do, I believe that it will be very grand." Alexander did not reply, much surprised by the insight into his father's private reflections.

"Be not too quick to cast aside those things that make you very different from your fellow men," Mr. Pope continued. "If you look and think and dress exactly as they do, nobody will remember who you are. I have always known that you were exceptional, Alexander," he added to close the conversation. "I hope you will learn to accept it too."

When Alexander was on the point of finishing his new poem, he received a letter from Bernard Lintot, a well-known publisher in London and Jacob Tonson's great rival. Lintot wrote to say that he had admired Alexander's *Pastorals* and the *Essay on Criticism*. He was sorry not to have printed them himself, and he wondered whether Alexander might have any new material for him to see. Alexander knew that Lintot paid more than any other publisher in London, but he had half promised his next piece to Tonson, and he reasoned that he should not change publishers now; he had no desire to be thought of as a troublemaker. But then he reconsidered. Perhaps that was exactly what he wanted people to think. And Lintot offered to include Alexander's work in a new volume he was preparing, which would have a much larger circulation than Alexander had previously hoped for.

But he did not as yet have a title. He had been thinking of it all along as *Lines, Upon a Young Lady Recently Deprived of a Most Important Possession*, but that would not do. Absurd and verbose. He decided that it must be called *The _____ of _____* . That was how all the best titles were arranged. *The Merchant of Venice*, *The Jew of Malta*, *The Way of the World*. But perhaps they only sounded so well because they were famous.

It must also be something to tempt sluggish schoolboys a hundred years hence. *The Baron and the Belle*? He would feel that he needed to apologize for that name every time he said it. No schoolboy would spend two minutes reading such a document.

The poem sat on Alexander's table for a week or so, untitled and unsent. But the days ticked by, and Alexander began to fear that if it did go not go off, Lintot would print his *Miscellany* without him. He looked through his books, but inspiration did not come. He asked his family, but of course they had no suggestions to make.

At last an idea came to him in the middle of the night—he thought it brilliant, and got out of bed to write it down. But in the clear light of morning it seemed idiotic. Overwrought and hysterical—his poem would sound as puffed up as anything that Dennis might have written. But more time passed, and he could not think of one better. So he scribbled down his foolish title and sent it off, hoping that Lintot might improve on it.

A few days later, as Bernard Lintot received the morning's mail he walked out of his shop door to Will's coffee-house. There were a dozen or so letters, and several larger packages—manuscripts, he guessed—all addressed to Mr. Bernard Lintot, at Cross Keys between two Temple Gates in Fleet Street. He picked up the pile and walked out. While he drank his coffee at Will's he sorted through the mail, coming at last to a package containing fifteen or twenty pages of writing, copied in a meticulous hand, with a covering letter signed "A. Pope". Lintot remembered Tonson's hunchbacked client, to whom he had sent a note some weeks previously. He snatched up the poem eagerly, and began to read.

Moments later, he sprang up from his chair, holding aloft the pages of verse.

Good God! he thought. This poem will make my fortune!

The patrons of Will's looked up simultaneously, smiling and nodding at the great Mr. Lintot. Every one of them was imagining, wildly, that he had somehow got hold of their own half-written doggerel and perceived its brilliance.

"Alexander Pope has sent me his new satire," Lintot cried victoriously. The poets all looked down again, crestfallen. Alexander Pope, they were thinking bitterly. The venomous, hunchbacked toad. But they had better be civil to him next time they met.

Charles Jervas was among the men present that morning. He had been at a loose end since Alexander had returned to the country, and today he had come to meet Harry Chambers and Tom Breach, who had lately appointed Will's as the setting for their morning's idleness. Upon hearing Lintot's enthusiasm Jervas hurried over to claim Alexander as his old and dear friend and Tom and Harry followed closely behind.

Lintot wrung Jervas by the hand, as though he were Alexander himself. "It is the first poem of its kind to be written," he exclaimed, clapping him vigorously on the back, and turning to greet Tom and Harry, too. "I thank God Tonson did not get his hands on it," he declared. "Your friend Pope is to be congratulated for showing the good sense of sending it to me. And the title is splendid! *The Rape of the Lock.* That alone will sell a thousand copies."

Lintot hurried away to write to Alexander, and Jervas was left to the conversation of his old schoolfellows. They all sat down again, and Harry opened a new topic.

"What do you think of this trouble in Barbados, Tom?" he asked.

"Barbados?" Tom repeated with surprise. "I have not the slightest knowledge of it. I am hard enough pressed to keep pace with last week's gossip at Lady Sandwich's levee. There is not time in the day to think of other people's troubles as well."

"But this will amuse you, for it involves Lord Salisbury—whom I know you dislike."

"Awful man," Tom agreed. "I recall his boring me one evening with a brutal tale about his slaves. Tell me of his misfortune."

"Oh—it involves the slaves, as a matter of fact," said Harry, a little put out that Tom had already heard about them. "There was a story in the *Daily Courant* the other day. Lord Salisbury has been the object of unscrupulous scheming."

"Capital. Of what kind?" asked Tom with a smile.

"He has been buying slaves from a trader whom Edward Fairfax knows," Harry began.

"Oh yes," Tom replied. "I remember him showing off about it."

"Well, it turned out that Fairfax's trader was charging them for the full boatload that he brought from Africa, but he was in fact stealing fifty slaves or so to sell to another man. He told Fairfax and Salisbury that the slaves had died on the voyage."

"To judge from Salisbury's description of the boat, I should have expected the slaves to be dying in vast numbers. It sounded infernal."

"Some of them were dying, of course," Harry replied. "But not nearly so many as the trader pretended. He was selling them off to a second dealer, who took them off the slave ship before it docked. So Lord Salisbury has been paying for somebody else to have cheap slaves. He is wild about it, as you might imagine."

"I am glad to hear it. But how did Salisbury discover the fraud? God knows he is never in Barbados."

"Oh, the second dealer, the man who bought the 'dead' slaves, was running quite a regular racket out there. His name was Dupont, a Frenchman. Apparently he was once the manager on one of the plantations, until he was dismissed for stealing the sugar."

"A Frenchman," said Tom. "Lord Salisbury should have known there would be trouble."

"Dupont's scheme was rather clever," said Harry after a short pause. "He had a partner in London who made all the arrangements, raised the capital for him to use, and found plantation owners who wanted to buy the slaves in the West Indies. But somebody got wind of the scheme and told Fairfax."

"I wondered how it had come to light," said Tom. "It's far too clever for Lord Salisbury to have worked it out."

"This Dupont is obviously a man of talent," Harry agreed with a smile. "Or at least his partner in London is. I've half a mind to get in touch with Dupont myself to offer my services. A shame that I have no energy for work, or I might become rich."

"It is a pity that James Douglass is not present to hear your story," Jervas piped up. "It would divert him."

"Divert him!" Harry rejoined. "He would rant and storm that he did not think of it himself. It is just his sort of affair. Was he not in Africa himself once?"

"Perhaps Douglass *is* Dupont's man in London!" Tom said with glee. "After all, he has just gone to ground himself!"

"Douglass is always disappearing and reappearing—never the worse for wear, and always filled with cheerful optimism that his next scheme will make his fortune. A rum fellow, but capital."

"Yes," Jervas agreed. "The town is dull without him."

The months went by. Summer became autumn; autumn, winter. At long last, it turned to spring again, and *The Rape of the Lock* was published. Alexander went to Whiteknights to give Martha a copy of the poem. He knew that she was there alone; she had told him in a letter that Teresa had gone to join Arabella in Bath for the new season. It had surprised Alexander to learn that the cousins' friendship had continued, but he concluded that Arabella must now depend upon Teresa for a companionship that she had not needed in the past, and that a winter spent in the country had provided Teresa with the perspective required to overlook Arabella's offences during the last season.

"I should hardly be making you, of all people, a present of *The Rape of the Lock*," Alexander said to Martha as he gave it to her while they walked in the garden, "for you know all too much about the tale of Miss Fermor and her stolen hair. But I promised it to you last year, and I feared that you would think me negligent were I not to present it now." He smiled, and then said, "The volume has been so long in coming out that Miss Fermor's charms will have half decayed while the poet was celebrating them, and the printer has been publishing them. Perhaps you had better not pass that last observation on to Miss Fermor," he added.

"I am very pleased that you have brought the book to give to me today," she answered. "But your visit to Whiteknights is almost as precious to me as the verses themselves."

"It should be more so, Patty," he said. "The postage would have cost me twice as much as the book. If Lintot is making his fortune from this venture, he will most certainly not make mine. But even if the *Rape of the Lock* is wearisome to you, you will enjoy the other poems in the *Miscellany*, which are said to contain passages that a lady may not look upon without being in danger of blushing."

"Well, I blush rather easily, Alexander, as you know," Martha replied, suiting the action to the word as she spoke.

He replied in a grave voice, but with a smile that would show he was speaking lightly. "Since blushing becomes you better than any lady in England," he said, "I shall be the party in much more serious danger, merely from looking at you. There: now I have made you blush still further, and our troubles begin again."

She laughed. "Alexander!" she exclaimed. "I shall have to forbid your visits here if you come only to flatter and flirt with me. If it is so pleasant to be at home, I shall never have a reason to go out—and then what will become of my prospects?"

Alexander liked this new Martha altogether, as much improved in spirits as in looks, and he gazed at her affectionately. "What will become of your prospects indeed?" he echoed. "Very well! In the future I shall make myself so disagreeable when I visit that you will want to leave the house immediately. And I shall visit so often that you will always be out to me when I call. The arrangement will work admirably." He hesitated ever so slightly before going on. But then he smiled and said, "Indeed, people will think us just like a married couple."

Martha looked down.

His face became serious and he said, "I shall come to visit you again very soon, dear Patty. And will you give my affectionate regards to your sister? I hope that she is well."

Martha heard the earnestness in Alexander's tone, and she came to a halt, motioning for them to sit down on a nearby bench. She had expected Alexander to ask about Teresa long before now, though she had been pleased when he did not. But she had privately determined that she would answer any questions about her sister without sounding awkward or disappointed.

"I have seldom seen her better," she said. And then, with a wry inflection, she added, "For the first time in her life, she has the advantage over Arabella. Indeed I believe that Teresa is now pleased to have been so much overlooked by Lord Petre. She can claim to have seen through him from the very beginning, and to have understood exactly the kind of man he was." Martha paused, and then gave a little laugh. "Which I suppose, after a fashion, she did," she added.

They were silent for a moment, and then Alexander said, "I hope that you will give Teresa my love when next you write to her, and that she will receive it without disgust."

Martha looked down at her lap again, and said nothing. Alexander noticed her confused expression, and got up from the bench to stand before her.

"Patty, I want you to know that you have at last gained the conquest over your fair sister," he said with a smile. "It is true: you may not be considered as handsome," he continued, "but only because you are a woman so you *think* that you are not. Your good humour and understanding have for me a charm that cannot be resisted. Now! You have gone quite scarlet again, and I am in the gravest danger of blushing myself!"

He held out his hand to her, and she stood up to take his arm. They turned towards the house once again, and each lifted a hand to wave to Sir Anthony, who stood on the yew terrace, watching as they approached.

Epilogue

Alexander's poem was a huge success. In coffee-houses and salons and at balls across London, everybody talked about *The Rape of the Lock* and its brilliant author. But he was not satisfied. The more he thought about the poem and its subject, the more he wished that he had written a longer piece, reaching beyond the facts of the story to satisfy the full scope of his ambitions. The first edition was so popular that he thought Lintot would print a second, and he decided that it ought to be twice as long, published separately in a volume of its own. He began work on it, but the new verses took him a long time to write, and it was nearly two years after the day at Hampton Palace that Alexander arrived in Button's coffee-house in London to read them aloud. Button's was owned by Steele's collaborator Joseph Addison, and Alexander hoped that a good audience at the reading would remind Addison of his promise to advertise his new poem in the pages of the *Spectator*.

When he reached the coffee-house on the afternoon of the reading, a large crowd had already gathered. Among them he saw Richard Steele sitting with John Gay and Jonathan Swift. He found that he recognized nearly all the other men in the room, too, and he was aware of being spoken about in lowered tones. With feelings of pride, and a self-consciousness that he could not quite keep in check, he walked directly up to his group of friends.

John Gay saluted him loudly. "He is come! Pope is here!"

Richard Steele likewise sprang to his feet, crying, "My dear fellow, you are in excellent health, I see. I am in the gout once again and suffer mightily, but it will pass soon enough!"

Swift was on his feet too, shaking him by the hand and pulling him on to a chair; Addison was rushing up to offer him refreshment. He could see the poets Ambrose Philips and Thomas Tickell on the other side of the coffee-house, sitting with his former mentor William Wycherley. He crossed the room to greet them, and noticed that Wycherley looked dour, but Philips and Tickell jumped up to wring Alexander's hand.

"You are being named as the genius of our age," Philips said with unstinting warmth. "The idea for your poem was brilliant, and every day I wish that I had thought of it—but then I wager that there isn't a man in this room who hasn't had the same wish cross his mind."

Alexander turned to Wycherley, and shook him by the hand. "A very lively satire, sir," Wycherley said to him. "And just the thing for the modern age. Twenty years ago it would not have been understood, but we have paved the way for you." Alexander was not particularly surprised by the mean-spiritedness of Wycherley's response, but he saw that the other two fellows looked embarrassed. He was about to extricate himself from the group when a new gentleman, about the same age as himself, came up with a friendly smile. Alexander recognized him as Edward Young, a good-hearted fellow, though of a nervous disposition. Alexander had heard that Young was given to bouts of frenzied high spirits, followed by interludes of impenetrable gloom. He knew that Young longed to be a poet. Alexander shook him by the hand.

"You have written such a lively, spirited piece," Young exclaimed. "So easy; so full of wit and merit. I admire you and I envy you, sir—in equal parts." He laughed so generously that Alexander could not be in the least affronted.

"I do thank you, sir," he replied. "Your own poems progress well, I hope."

"I have lately written a piece on the death of Lady Jane Grey," he replied. "It is very grand and melancholy, but I fear that it will not please. Something with more humour in it would serve me better. Perhaps I shall try a satire. Yet I seem to be more suited to sombre strains."

"People love to be made sad as much as they like to laugh," Pope replied. "If they are smiling this week, they will want to weep the next. Keep your melancholy thoughts, Young. Their time will come."

When Alexander returned to his own table, Swift beckoned him to sit down at his side. "The new version is a masterpiece," he said, making Alexander's heart swell as he continued, "You will doubtless know that I have a reputation for disliking all of mankind. But in your case my renown will serve a purpose: when I tell you that you are a man of genius, you are more likely to believe me." He paused as Alexander laughed at his praise, and then asked, "Why did you call Miss Fermor by the name of Belinda in the poem?"

"I thought that I should conceal her identity," Alexander answered, "though I have not done so very strenuously, since Miss Fermor's friends all call her 'Bell'. The name is my own invention, but I hope that it may catch on," he said with a self-deprecating gesture.

"I have seen the real Miss Fermor but once, and I do not recall whether she enjoyed as great a share of beauty as your Belinda."

"She is exceptionally handsome," Alexander replied. "And yet I did always feel that her hair, for which she has been envied, was rather too luxuriant."

"Then posterity will credit you with correcting the only fault Miss Fermor ever had, by giving her a haircut," Swift answered. "Who would have thought a lock of hair could have so much satire in it?

"There is but one objection that I would expect to be raised to your new verses. People will want to know how you came by the details of the story. You hint at an affair between your hero and heroine; you give the suggestion that Jacobite strife was involved in the intrigue—readers will ask how you can be sure of your facts. I have always found that it is a dangerous thing for a writer to dabble in the truth; it supplies people with an excuse to say that you are in error."

Alexander had given a good deal of thought to this, and he had an answer ready to give his friend. "Oh! I hope that nobody should think my poem true *in point of fact*," he said lightly. "Truth is but a frail and sickly creature, and soon forgotten. After all, Arabella Fermor's beauty will fade, and the present Lord Petre shall be the baron only for a little while. The Jacobites will carry on with their plans for rebellion, and who knows who will succeed the present queen? Although my poem may not be strictly true, I hope that it might prove a more—how shall I say it—a more *enduring* record. After all, nobody really cares for the truth, do they, Dr. Swift?"

"Do you know, Pope, I believe that you are right," Swift said, shaking his head. "The trouble with the truth is that it always brings such bitter disappointments."

As Alexander and Swift came to the end of this exchange, a gentleman sitting close to them could be overheard reciting the closing couplet of *The Rape of the Lock*, followed by a loud hurrah from himself and his friends.

"This Lock, the Muse shall consecrate to Fame, / And mid'st the Stars inscribe Belinda's Name!"

This caused another group of fellows to propose a toast to "Belinda and the baron—the romantic heroes of the modern age."

Alexander watched as Richard Steele leaned confidentially across to one of them, and said, "You should more properly be toasting Miss Arabella Fermor than Belinda."

Though Alexander attempted to silence Steele's indiscretion, the youth turned to his friend. "Arabella Fermor?" he repeated. "Who is she?"

"How should I know?" the friend said. "Another lady, I suppose."

Then he too turned to address his companion. "Who is Arabella Fermor?" he asked.

"Never heard of her," the young man replied callously, drinking from his mug of ale. "Do you know of a lady called Arabella Fermor?" he asked another man in the party.

"Farmer?" the friend echoed. "No—is she a real person?"

"Who knows?" he replied with a laugh. "In any case, a toast to Belinda—the most beautiful girl in London—and the poet who created her."

Steele was about to cut in and correct them, but Alexander motioned to him to be quiet.

"Arabella could not be London's reigning belle for ever," he said merrily, with a chuckle. "Let Belinda have her day."

As Alexander stood up to begin reading he felt a wave of anticipation sweep through the room. Everybody was watching him: some of them admiringly, others enviously; some affectionately, others coldly. What a great variety of men were to be met with here, he reflected. What a cruel world this was, and how brief was each man's moment of celebrity. Who, from this motley band, would be remembered?

But suddenly he felt a surge of excitement. As much as he disdained Grub Street, he saw that it was a new world, yet to be explored. The people who inhabited it—the publishers, the editors, the printers—were new men, and the activities in which they engaged were new, too: the buying and selling of books, the printing of newspapers, the raising up and dragging down of writers and critics and essayists. It would call for a steady head and nerves of iron to succeed, but the prospect was bracing.

All around him the room fell silent and attentive as they quieted their babble. He began to read the opening lines of his poem:

> *"What dire Offence from am'rous Causes springs,*
> *What mighty Contests rise from Trivial things,*
> *I sing."*

He glanced up, and saw that they were watching him, entranced. Not a breath could be heard besides his own voice. Everybody was spellbound, and a wild rush of exhilaration overcame him. He had done it, he thought—he had written a poem that would make him the most famous poet in England.

Afterword

Alexander Pope did indeed become the most famous poet in England. The 1714 version of *The Rape of the Lock* sold 3,000 copies in the first week after it was printed, and is a standard text on every undergraduate English syllabus today. He is the first writer in English history to become independently wealthy from the sales of his own books. In 1719 he built a large villa on the banks of the Thames in Twickenham, just outside London, for which he designed one of the most fashionable gardens in England.

Arabella Fermor's fame as a beauty was largely eclipsed by the much greater fame of her fictionalized character, Belinda. She was twenty-five years old by the time she married Francis Perkins, the owner of Ufton Court, a moderate estate in Berkshire—practically an old maid by eighteenth-century standards.

Robert, Lord Petre married Catherine Walmesley in 1712, but died of smallpox less than two years later, just before the second version of *The Rape of the Lock* was published. Ten weeks after the baron's death, Catherine Walmesley gave birth to the Petre heir. In later life she remarried, and became celebrated as an educational philanthropist.

Martha Blount remained Pope's closest friend and companion. Rumours always abounded that they had secretly married, but nobody knows for sure. In 1743 Pope, who had long wanted Martha to establish a house of her own, bought the lease on a house in Berkeley Street in London. When he died he left Martha all his goods and chattels and the income on his estate for the rest of her life.

Teresa Blount fell in and out with Pope, as well as with the members of her family, for the greater part of her adult life. Pope always took care of her financially, settling on her in 1718 an annuity that was to be paid until her death. Her relationship with Martha was fraught, but they remained close to each other. Teresa never married, but when she was in her forties she conducted a long-running affair with a married man named Captain Bagnall. Martha and Alexander strenuously disapproved.

John Caryll finally managed to relieve himself of responsibility for his large brood of children by arranging for them to enter into well-appointed nunneries and monasteries in France. His eldest son, the only one of his children to marry, became a man of considerable prosperity. Caryll successfully dissociated himself from further suspicion of Jacobitism, and lived out his days happily and peacefully in Berkshire, in company with his much-loved wife.

Charles Jervas remained the most fashionable portrait painter of his day, winning the patronage of the Prime Minister, Sir Robert Walpole, and eventually becoming the official portraitist to King George I in 1723. In 1726 he married a wealthy heiress, whose money enabled him to maintain a house in the country, but he always kept the house in town where Pope had stayed in his youth.

Mary Pierrepont eloped with Edward Wortley Montagu in 1714, thereby relinquishing the fortune she would have inherited. In 1716 she travelled to Turkey, where Wortley was posted as ambassador, and published a record of this trip in her famous collection, *The Turkish Embassy Letters.* As a result of her observations and experiences in Turkey she introduced the smallpox inoculation to England in 1721. She and Pope became close friends, but eventually had a bitter falling-out and remained implacable enemies. In the 1730s, Lady Mary abandoned her husband and went to live in Italy and France, becoming an eccentric, unconventional, celebrated woman of letters.

Jonathan Swift went on to write *Gulliver's Travels,* one of the most famous books, and probably the most famous satire, ever written. He worked as a political writer and adviser to the Tory government in London until 1714, hoping that his work would secure him a high-ranking clerical position in the Church of England. But when Queen Anne died and the Tories were superseded by a powerful Whig government, Swift was forced to return to Ireland, where he became Dean of St. Patrick's Church in Dublin. He lived there for the rest of his life, becoming celebrated as a great champion and defender of Ireland, a role about which he always felt a great deal of ambivalence. He and Pope remained close friends.

Richard Steele is remembered as the co-writer and editor (with Joseph Addison) of the *Tatler* and the *Spectator*, groundbreaking periodicals, and the forerunners of the *New Yorker*, *Harper's Magazine*, *The New Statesman*, and *The Spectator* (descended from Steele's own journal).

John Gay later wrote *The Beggar's Opera*, another of the most important and inventive works of English literature. The play was a runaway success; it ran for longer than any drama previously, inspired a deluge of play-related "merchandise" and made Gay's fortune.

Acknowledgements

I have been extremely fortunate to have Toby Eady as my agent in London, and Jennifer Joel as my agent in New York. Without Toby, I would never have had the confidence to begin writing this book; without Jenn, I would not have had the confidence to finish it. My sincere thanks, also, to Laetitia Rutherford, Samar Hammam, and Jamie Coleman at Toby Eady Associates, and Katie Sigelman at ICM New York for all that they did along the way.

With gratitude and admiration I acknowledge the advice, judgement and experience of my editor at Scribner, Nan Graham, and my editor at Chatto & Windus, Alison Samuel. I have been lucky to have them. I also acknowledge, with deep appreciation, the work done by Samantha Martin, editorial associate at Scribner. I thank Rachel Cugnoni at Vintage for her encouragement and guidance, and David Parrish at Random House UK for his support. Particular thanks, also, to Suzanne Dean. I gratefully acknowledge the assistance of Suzanne Balaban, Susan Moldow and Katherine Monaghan at Scribner.

At Random House Australia, I thank Margie Seale, Carol Davidson, Karen Reid, Jessica Dettman, and Ally Cohilj for invaluable assistance. Also in Sydney, I thank Jane Palfreyman and Benython Oldfield for their help and encouragement.

My teachers at Harvard and my colleagues at Princeton taught me how to think about English literature, about history, and the world that I have written about here. I particularly acknowledge the influence of Barbara Lewalski, James Engell, Marjorie Garber, Stephen Greenblatt, Philip Fisher, Claudia Johnson, Nigel Smith, Michael Wood, Diana Fuss, James Richardson, Oliver Arnold, and Jeff Nunokawa.

Several academic studies have been indispensable in the writing of this novel. I have relied for both information and historical understanding on Maynard Mack's biography *Alexander Pope: A*

Life, Valerie Rumbold's *Women's Place in Pope's World*, Howard Erskine-Hill's *The Social Milieu of Alexander Pope* and Isobel Grundy's *Lady Mary Wortley Montagu: Comet of the Enlightenment.* I have also made extensive use of the definitive Twickenham edition of Pope's poems and the Clarendon edition of his correspondence.

Finally, I would like to acknowledge the loving support and help that I have received from my mother and sister, Liz and Harriet Gee.